ZANE PRESENTS

Candace
REIGN

Dear Reader:

Sharai Robbin's debut novel, *Candace Reign*, is a contemporary urban fiction title surrounding a twenty-something single mother who strives for a better lifestyle out of the hood. It's a tale of seeking career advancement and achieving a certain status mixed with the challenges of the streets.

Set in Philadelphia, readers learn that the street-savvy Candace keeps connected with her ten-year-old baby's daddy, Prince, who's locked up, and eventually, her world rocks when suitors, Bam, a sugar daddy; and Chris, a handsome thug who's much younger, emerge on the scene. She works her magic and manages to become entangled with both men who sweat her endlessly. Meanwhile, she deals with office drama when a coworker is determined to block her from moving up the corporate ladder.

The author deals with these issues of family, career, parenting and dating and focuses on how to balance temptation and keeping a level head while working toward your dreams.

As always, thanks for supporting myself and the Strebor Books family. We strive to bring you the most cutting-edge, out-of-the-box material on the market. You can find me on Facebook @AuthorZane or you can email me at zane@eroticanoir.com
Blessings,

Zane

Publisher
Strebor Books
www.simonandschuster.com

ZANE PRESENTS

Candace
REIGN

WITHDRAWN

SHARAI ROBBIN

SBI

STREBOR BOOKS

NEW YORK LONDON TORONTO SYDNEY

SBI

Strebor Books
P.O. Box 6505
Largo, MD 20792
http://www.streborbooks.com

ISBN 978-1-59309-657-1
ISBN 978-1-4767-9893-6 (ebook)
LCCN 2015934633

First Strebor Books trade paperback edition September 2015

Cover design: www.mariondesigns.com
Cover photograph: © Keith Saunders/Keith Saunders Photos

10 9 8 7 6 5 4 3 2

Manufactured in the United States of America

For information regarding special discounts for bulk purchases,
please contact Simon & Schuster Special Sales at 1-866-506-1949
or business@simonandschuster.com

The Simon & Schuster Speakers Bureau can bring authors to your live event.
For more information or to book an event, contact the Simon & Schuster Speakers
Bureau at 1-866-248-3049 or visit our website at www.simonspeakers.com.

For Alana & Lyric, the reasons why quitting is never an option

ACKNOWLEDGMENTS

I would like to thank God above all. Without his grace and unending mercy, I would have never been able to see this thing to the end or believe this was the beginning of something greater.

Thank you to my mother, DeAnna, who has always been my biggest fan and supporter. To my brothers, Kory and Donta (the best uncles ever), who kept an eye and elbow on my girls during many late hours of writing. You guys are amazing and for you, I am eternally thankful.

Thanks to my sister, Briahna, for being my first friend and reading my poetry in the seventh grade. I love you for loving me.

To my best friend, Cashmere, for always having my back and believing in me even when I didn't believe in myself.

Thanks to Karen E. Quinones Miller who saw the writer in me from the start and never stopped pushing me to achieve. I love you so much.

Thanks to Ernst for inspiring me to write again. You are always my friend.

Thanks beyond measure to Eveningstar Writer's Group, for late nights, critical thinking, honest opinions and the genuine opportunity to sharpen my craft. Akanke and Fiona, you ladies are amazing and I am so grateful.

To all my friends and family, who have always accepted me for the bookworm I am and have never tried to change who God called me to be, I am blessed to have the opportunity to grow up with such strong roots. Thank you.

he house should have been still. There should have been no other sounds save the sleeping murmurs of her infant son in the two-story row home, but Candace was certain she heard a sound coming from the basement. She hit the mute button on the remote, silencing the big-screen TV. And there it was, loud and clear, a rustling sound, a rush of whispers. Candace was silent. Her chest tightened as she listened. The sound was steady. The shuffle of feet across the floor escalated, followed by quicker, louder whispers and creaking stairs. *What the fuck?* Candace's chest grew full and tight with captured breath. She stood up, back straight as a board. Her eyes darted to her son, inches away in his blue-and-gray Pack 'n Play, her breasts heaving under the heavy pressure of her thudding heart. She struggled only seconds to collect the jumble of thoughts running through her head before the basement door to her right burst open and three goons in black bandanas flooded the room, their guns drawn.

"Omigod!" Candace screamed, jumping back on the sofa. "Omigod!" *Oh shit, my son! My fuckin' son!* she thought but dare not speak.

The masked bandits moved in past Emmanuel's sleeping den and directly in front of Candace on the couch. One boy, broader in the shoulders than the rest, stepped in closer to her and pointed the business end of his nine-millimeter in her face.

"Where the fuck is it?" he asked.

Candace shriveled back. She felt faint, her body weak. She forced her knees to steady, and trembling, she faced the brazen men in her living room. The broad-shouldered boy, appearing to be the leader of the trio, gave a head nod and the two other goons moved toward her. The heavy, burly one grabbed Candace by the back of the neck and slammed her down to the wooden floor. Candace's face slapped the hard wood only footsteps away from her sleeping son. The third thug, smelling like warm Heineken and cigarettes, quickly knelt down beside her, pressing his knee into her back while tying her hands.

Ohmigod, her thoughts echoed in her head. *Breathe, Candace, breathe. They're here for this shit...You knew this shit was coming...Ohmigod, my son! Bitch, breathe.*

She struggled convincing herself to remain calm. Nausea swept over her body as she swayed helpless in the goons' arms. Candace closed her eyes hard, hoping that if she sealed them tight enough, the reality playing out before her would all become a short sequence in a bad dream. With lids pinched shut, she could feel the sweat from between the big one's fingers running down her arm. She clenched her teeth.

"Where the fuck's the money, Shawty?" Shoulders asked. She opened her eyes.

Oh, God! What the fuck am I supposed to say? What am I supposed to say? Just tell 'em? Shit!

The thoughts swarmed through her mind. Maybe she wanted to hold her ground. Maybe she didn't want them to get what they were after, but with her son sleeping inches away from these gunslinging goons, Candace could only focus on his safety and her duty to protect it.

Smack.

Shoulders brought the gun down across the side of her face. The contact of the cold metal against her bony cheek hit like a ton of bricks. She dropped to her knees and pain surged through her face. She could not move her mouth. Her head spun and her eyes grew heavy. She could not see them, but she felt the hands supporting her, cupping and fondling her right breast.

Candace wanted to scream but the muscles in her face burned and the throbbing of her jaw rendered both her body and mouth motionless. The tears began running down the side of her face.

Oh God. Just go, please just go, she thought. *Don't touch my baby. Please don't see my son.*

"Bitch, I'm not goin' keep asking you. This shit can get real fuckin' ugly. Feel me?" Shoulders barked, pressing the barrel of the gun to her forehead. "Where the fuck is the money? We know that nigga Prince holdin', Shawty. Now tell me where da' stash at."

Candace couldn't move her mouth, the pain tearing through her from head to toe. *Upstairs*, she heard the words in her head but could not get them from her lips.

Shoulders leaned further into her face with the gun.

Her eyes closed. The pressure of the metal against her brow sent chills down her spine as her face continued to throb from its initial introduction.

"Imma ask you one more time, Shawty," Shoulders said, stepping away from Candace and closer to the Pack 'n Play.

Fuck no! Candace's body perked like a hunter's ear. She struggled to stand, pulling herself away from the foul one's grasp. Shoulders pointed the gun directly into the bedding. Candace leapt toward him.

"No! No!" she forcibly voiced, her mouth running wet with blood. She spat the words at Shoulders lunging toward him. "Get the fuck away from my son!" she screamed.

Emmanuel stirred beneath the blue covers.

"Get the fuck away from my son." Candace's voice fell to a whisper. "In the closet floorboard in the back bedroom."

"Now, see. Wasn't that simple," he said, laughing behind his bandana. Turning to his partner, he spoke firmly, "Don't let this bitch move." He tucked his gun in his pants pulling another bandana from his back pocket. He tossed it to the goon beside Candace who bound her mouth as Shoulders headed for the stairs. Candace's lips closed around the stiff, dark fabric. It was a new bandana, never worn with crisp edges. Candace eyed the covering over the putrid one's face—his, too, revealed newly unfolded creases. She knew they had been purchased for tonight's special occasion.

Just for me, to kill me and my son. She felt so weak, defenseless. *What kind of mother am I?* she wondered. *They're goin' kill me and my son over some fuckin money. What the fuck! Oh God, my face.*

As she tasted the starched material, Candace tried to convince herself the rough part was over. *They gettin' what they came for, right? They should finish up with their heist and be on their way.* There was no need to kill her or her son. She'd given them what they wanted. *And stickup boys aren't killers, right?* They had what they were looking for and now all she had to do was keep breathing and they would go away.

It's almost over. Candace stood quietly concentrating on breathing when suddenly, the smelly one pushed her back down to the couch. His eyes scanned over her. She knew it was his hands she'd felt before. His breath was quick and dry like train smoke and stale urine permeating through the dark material over his face. She wanted to cough him away, but the bandana in her mouth wouldn't permit her to catch her breath. She could only breathe through her nose and the scent of him intensified, making her sick to her stomach. He leaned in just short of her face with the gun aimed at the top of her head.

"You a pretty bitch," he mumbled.

Candace snarled, looking up and away from him. Suddenly, she felt his hand on her breast again. *Ohmigod!!!* He squeezed and grunted a satisfied sound. Candace squirmed. *Get the fuck off me. God, no.* The boy cocked his gun.

The sound sent chills through her like shards of glass and Candace froze. She shut her eyes. His hand steady massaged her full bosom, and his fingers traced the imprint of her nipple and pulled hard. Candace winced. She could feel the weight of him leaning down on top of her. He moved his hand from her breast down to her thigh; she trembled trying to be still.

No. God, no.

Candace struggled swallowing as he stood up in front of her, massaging himself. He took a step back reaching for his zipper and backed right into the Pack 'n Play. Emmanuel stirred in his sleep and awoke with a startled cry. The gunman jerked, spinning his body and his gun toward the sound. Candace stood up; her balance strained by the weight of her bound wrists behind her. *No. No. No.* Her eyes pleaded behind fear and horror. The fumbling goon's eyes, full of startle and surprise, darted back and forth in rapid succession. He drew back his firearm from the infant, turning to Candace and raising his weapon to her face. She shuddered at the relief she felt in having the pistol pointed back at her.

"Shut the baby up," the goon commanded, reaching for her. Suddenly, the two men from upstairs came bounding down with stuffed pillowcases in hand.

"Come on, nigga, let's go," Shoulders shouted to the one clutching Candace.

"The baby crying," he responded.

"Man, fuck that bitch and that baby! We out!"

CHAPTER 1

andace stood naked in her bedroom window overlooking the cobblestone walkway in front of her apartment. She peered through the sheer gold curtains, patting the itch under her leopard-print headscarf. Candace was certain that any neighbors, regardless of how few there were on the tiny block, could see right up to her bare breasts, but she didn't care. She enjoyed the way the sun broke through the trees, stretching a warm glow across the length of her statuesque brown body and along the spacious hardwood floor in the bedroom of her Chestnut Hill apartment. She breathed in and out slowly, taking a few moments to embrace the day.

It was 7 a.m. and her morning had just begun. There was a deep exhale to steady her calm, then a quick turn from the window. Grabbing her pink silk robe from her bedside, she covered herself as she made her way out of the room and down the hall, stopping at the second door to her right. Candace entered the room and flicked on the light.

"Good morning, Man."

A muffled groan came from the black bed on the far side of the room followed by a tussle from under the sheets. Candace stepped further into the room.

"Emmanuel. C'mon, son, it's time to get up."

There was another tussle beneath the covers, but by this time, Candace was at the bedside pulling the covers back off the sleepy, ten-year-old boy in the bed.

"Mom," he whined, face in the pillow.

"What?" Candace asked, pinching his side.

Emmanuel yelped, turning over on the bed facing his mother. Candace stared down at her handsome chocolate boy. His large, dark oval eyes, exactly like his father's, were unmistakable. His beautiful full lips were like hers and smooth dark skin, another one of Prince's traits. Emmanuel smiled turning over and his smile warmed her heart more than the brilliant rays of the summer sun. He yawned, his warm breath smacking her in the face. Her eyes watered.

"You're disgusting," she cooed, patting him on the nose. "Go brush your teeth. It's time to get ready for school."

The bright-eyed boy stretched, extending his budding body across the mattress. Candace patted him again. Her soft tap landed on his nose and again the boy smiled. Candace brushed the dry coal from his eyes and kissed the top of his head.

"C'mon," she instructed, standing to lead the way. As she moved to exit the room, Emmanuel stretched again and swung his legs, long like his mother's, over the edge of the bed. He stared blankly at the floor for a moment before standing to follow her.

"Ma," he called. Candace stopped at the door and turned her attention to him. "It be the morning too soon, Mom."

She chuckled. "Tell me about it, son."

Candace was already in play mode of her morning routine, up by seven, out by eight fifteen. This gave her enough time to enjoy breakfast with her son.

Emmanuel liked waffles and apples. He ate almost any fruit, strawberries and peaches, oranges and grapes. Candace kept her refrigerator stocked with fresh fruits for their morning meal. Some mornings Emmanuel would walk the few blocks to school with his friends or Candace would drop him around the corner at Henry

H. Houston Elementary School. She laid both their clothes out the night before so there would be ample time in the mornings—before she rushed off to her job as an accounting manager at a nursing home—to enjoy the company of her son. Each night she selected her version of professional attire from her closet full of tailored suits, slacks, pencil skirts, dresses and blouses. And she had shoes beyond measure, a pair for every occasion. Candace bore a selfless motto, "You can buy shoes from anywhere and you must buy them from everywhere."

Emmanuel was his own stylist and he liked his faded jeans and colored polo shirts. He convinced his mother to buy them in every color. At ten years old, he collected a rainbow assortment of shirts that ranged from royal blue to pastel green, salmon to gray; each shade complemented the hues of his chocolate skin. Emmanuel especially preferred his white ones; of those, he had at least a dozen and he liked them clean and crisp. He stood by Candace's side as she pressed his collars down under the hot iron making sure the heat didn't fringe the alligator of his Lacoste or the pony on his Polo. He was quite the particular child. Occasionally, Emmanuel threw on a character tee over his jeans. He chose his sneakers with the same precision and quest for originality as his mother in her selection for shoes. His closet was full of Nikes, Vans and Adidas boxes; he wasn't partial. He liked what he liked, just like Prince, and that alone between Emmanuel and his mother, forged a mutual bond of respect and admiration.

Fully dressed, Candace stood in the kitchen over the counter. She waited for Emmanuel to put on his clothing, knowing he'd take his time and be down to eat whatever breakfast she prepared. This mid-May morning, Candace had covered her full five-eleven frame in a blush-pink, silk chiffon, sheath dress and a pair of mauve peep-toe pumps. She was slicing into a fresh cantaloupe when a fully dressed Emmanuel emerged from the hallway into the kitchen, wearing a white Lacoste polo shirt and faded gray jeans. His black-and-gray hi-top Nikes were tied neatly on his feet. It was the end of the school year and all the kids had stopped wearing their uniforms. Candace checked the time: 7:32.

"You walking or you want me to take you?"

"I'll walk today, Mom. Isaiah said he's gotta tell me something that can't wait."

"Oh yeah." Candace leaned into her son across the table. "About what?"

"Awww, come on, Mom."

"You not goin' share your little secrets with your mother?"

Emmanuel pouted his pink lips. Candace mocked him and shrugged.

"Fine, have your secrets." She continued slicing. Candace made Emmanuel a plate of melons and fresh toaster waffles and sat down across from him in the bright eat-in kitchen of their two-bedroom apartment.

Emmanuel drowned his waffles in syrup and bit right into them whole. Candace shook her head. He smiled, setting his fork into a big juicy piece of melon and taking it down with one bite.

"Slow down, boy," she instructed with a smile, still sipping her coffee between bites of her cantaloupe.

Emmanuel eyed his mother. He stared into her slender, soft brown face and almond-shaped brown eyes. Candace stared back. Emmanuel did not look away or avoid her gaze; instead, he dropped his head to one side and spoke.

"Mom..." he began, pausing for confirmation of her attention.

"Yes, Manny."

"You're cute, Mom," he said matter-of-factly.

Candace smiled. "Awww. Thank you, son. You are a very handome young man yourself. Now, what do you want?"

Emmanuel chuckled. "I 'on't want nuffin'. I'm just sayin'."

"Well, thank you."

"You're welcome," Emmanuel said with a shrug, diving back into his plate.

After they'd finished breakfast, Emmanuel opened the door with a small book bag slung over his shoulder. His comrades were waiting on the curb and greeted him in the warm morning light.

"Wassup, E."

"Hey, E-Man," the young boys chimed salutations to the other member of their pack.

Emmanuel coolly and confidently pulled the door closed behind him. "See you later, Mom."

Candace was waving to the fresh coat of white paint on the back of her kitchen door. She slipped the plates into the soapy water and was drying her hands on the blue-and-white dishcloth when her house phone rang.

"You have a collect call from Gratersford Prison." There was a static-filled pause and a rough voice over the receiver. "Prince," the voice grumbled.

"Will you accept the charges?"

She spoke calmly into the phone after she'd pressed one. "You just missed him."

"Hello." The voice sounded confused. "Candy?"

"Yeah, Prince."

"Hey, baby girl." His deep voice was a groggy muffle. "Where my boy?"

"He's gone already."

"Damn. It's too damn early to be sending my son off to school. Why you rushing him out the house like that?"

"Prince, please, he was out the door before I finished my breakfast. That boy got a mind of his own, and ain't no stopping him when he wants to do something."

"Yeah? That's my boy." Prince yawned with pride at the other end of the phone. "But I ain't talk to him all weekend. I was trying to catch him this morning."

"Try back tonight. We should be home by six."

"Yeah? How you doin', Candy? Work good?"

"Shit is cool, you know? I be working hard as hell; I damn near run that office. I like it, but the money could be better," she replied.

"What?!? You bougie bitch." He laughed. "You just can't get enough, huh?"

"Nigga, please, it costs money to live out here. But I guess it's been a while for ya. Speaking of which," she crossed her arms atop her chest leaning back against the Kenmore refrigerator, "Where my money at, Prince?"

"What?" Prince asked in surprise. "You ain't see Brother this month yet?"

"Yeah, I seen 'em."

"Did he give you some money?"

"Yeah."

"How much?"

"Not enough."

"What?!? I swear you really are a bougie bitch! You makin' nice money out there. My boy is doing good and what, you still want more?"

"I learn from the best." She grinned, biting into a juicy piece of cantaloupe. "How ya girls doing?"

"Dey good. Aisha brought them up to see me last week. When you goin' come up here with my son?"

"You know I am not coming up to nobody's prison, Prince. Ya mom can keep bringing Man when she comes up there, but don't be expecting me."

"You's a punk. You used to be a rider, Candy. What happened to you? You must be getting old."

"Old? Listen here, Mr. Nigga, I am in the prime of my life and that's just one reason why I ain't visiting no no-good nigga on lockdown, especially when he ain't my nigga."

"Umm, I know what that sounds like," Prince said.

"What?"

"Sound like you need some dick!"

"Ohimigod." She laughed.

"I know I'm right. Ain't no nigga out there breaking ya long ass off right. You need some good dick; maybe then you wouldn't be so tight about ya ass...and ya cash."

"Money is tight 'cause life is hard, Prince."

"So's this dick. You need some."

"Now here you go. That's why I'm single now. Caus'a shit like that. You locked up, you know you got ya other baby mom on ya pipe, and you still talking about giving me some dick. Dudes is trifling and I'm not for it."

"Whateva. You need somebody to loosen up them panties. You be aight! Tell my son, I love em. I'll call ya'll back tonight."

Click.

Candace could only shake her head at her son's father. He was such a uniquely perceptive and clever man, it amazed Candace how he'd managed to go to jail for involuntary manslaughter. She thought Prince would have known better, but he didn't and had spent the last six years of his life behind bars, because he couldn't control his temper.

Damn dummy, she thought, wiping away the images of cleaning blood splatter off their apartment wall. Prince's temper was the major reason Candace had left him shortly before he'd gone to jail, that and his uncontrollable and insatiable desire for street life.

Prince had a reputation for getting to a dollar. He and his identical twin—who their mother named Brother after his surprising and unexpected arrival twenty-seven seconds after Prince pushed through the birthing canal—were both notorious in their neighborhood for their street activity.

Candace knew Prince was hood and she loved everything about him from the moment she saw him. She was sixteen when they met, a year after her father, Derrin, died from a heart attack on his bus ride home from work at Hatfield Meat Packaging Company. It left her mother, Karla, a poor widow and forced them to move with her Aunt Patty in North Philadelphia. Prince lived four blocks away.

"He's sooo cute," young Candace told her even younger half-sister, Marcine, one afternoon when she'd seen Prince coming from the corner store.

Marcine giggled on the other end of the phone. She was only eleven but was already Candace's closet ally. The two shared a father and though Derrin's indiscretions deeply hurt Candace's mother, the pretty, brown-skinned baby was welcomed with open arms and spent summers between her home and Candace's.

After their father's death, the girls grew closer even though Marcine lived with her mother and her mother's well-to-do husband, Richard, in Southwest Philadelphia.

"Did you talk to him?" Marcine whispered.

"No, he ain't even see me," Candace whispered back.

"You gotta make sure he see you," Marcine advised.

"Okay. Okay, I gotta plan…"

"Mom." Candace's strong teenage legs galloped down the stairs. "I'll be back," she shouted to her mother and aunt sitting on the couch while she held the doorknob.

Karla took another sip of Slo Gin and milk, looking up at the long legs almost bare before her.

"Where you think you going?" she asked, scanning her daughter's stretching body. Candace's young bosom was pushed up to a full cleavage spread in her white tank top, and her tight strong thighs glistened under denim shorts.

"Mom," Candace huffed, "I be back."

She was out the door, taking the front steps two at a time until she hit the pavement. Long strides carried her down Woodstock Street toward Susquehanna, her heart an eager race with each step. She turned the corner with bright-eyed anticipation and there he was, Prince Reynolds—big, black, beautiful Prince Reynolds. The chocolate young man stood beside his twin, Brother Reynolds, across from a group of corner hustlers. Candace pushed down the lump in her throat and made her way toward the crowd of young men. She crossed in front of Prince's blue Acura double-parked in front of the Chinese store. She knew some of the guys hanging out on the corner from visiting her aunt for years. Some faces were new, but all seemed glad to see the sexy young girl move into their neighborhood.

Candace smiled as she passed Prince. He smiled back, his eyes seeming to follow the length of her body as she moved.

"Damn, Candace," one of the young men began. "Ya mama know you got them lil'-ass shorts on?"

Candace ignored him, praying only for Prince's attention. The brothers stood out in the crowd of black men. With the striking exactness of their facial features, huge dark eyes, thick brows and strong chins under full beards, it would have been hard to tell Prince and Brother apart had they not been so undeniably different. Brother's stance was of a grimacing beast, round about the shoulders, bulging tattooed biceps and a thick beard. He was more muscular than Prince who was cut but lean. Both kept their fades close cut, but Prince kept a trim, neat beard under his plump pink lips, big dark eyes and thick full lashes. Candace had fallen for him the very first time she laid eyes on him, on that same corner in the beginning of the summer chatting it up with the neighborhood dope boys, Rick and Juan. She didn't paid much attention to the corner boys. She never found the young hustlers appealing, but Prince was different. His shoulders were always raised, his head always high. He walked like he shit gold. He was confident and fly.

When she came out of the store, Prince stepped beside her and began to walk with her.

"Wassup, legs?"

Candace smiled. Prince stepped into the street with her, looking her up and down her long body.

"What's your name, pretty girl?" he asked. He stopped walking and settled his backside against the hood of his freshly polished car.

She stopped and turned to face him, her butterflies in romantic jubilee. She licked her full juicy lips. "Candace."

He reached for her hand. She gave hers. "Candace what?"

"Candace Reign Brinton," she replied.

"Oooh, Candy Reign." He laughed—a grin easing across his perfectly sculpted face.

Candace trembled.

"Myyy love," he sang, nodding his head. "Tell me what you want and I will give it to yoouuuu. Cuz you aaaarrrre myyyyyyy love, my love. Do you ever dream of candy rain? Yeeeaaah."

Candace burst out laughing.

Prince smiled at her. "I like that, Miss Candy Reign. My name is Prince." He bowed.

She blushed at his gesture, then asked, "That's ya real name?"

"Yup." He nodded. "And that's my twin brother, Brother." He glanced in his twin's direction.

Brother tossed Candace two fingers, continuing his conversation.

Candace stared hard at Prince's succulent lips.

"How old are you?" he continued, shaking her from her daydream.

"Sixteen. I...I'll be seventeen in September," she stammered.

Prince chuckled, his bright whites almost blinding her. "Almost seventeen?" he teased.

She pouted her full pink lips. "Yeah."

"You long as hell, baby girl. How tall are you?"

"Five-eleven."

"Cool, cool. You all legs, though," he said with a smile that made the muscles in the pit of Candace's stomach tighten.

"How tall are you?" she asked.

"Six-four. Is that good for you?"

Candace nodded.

"You live round here with ya people?"

"My aunt. We staying with my aunt, me and my mom."

"You got a man, Candy Reign?"

She giggled at the sound of her new pet name. "I got a boyfriend."

He laughed again. "Yeah. How old's your man, baby girl?"

"Seventeen."

More laughter. "I guess so."

Candace rolled her eyes. "You guess what?"

"I guess that's cute. I mean you a young buck ya self."

"How old are you?" Candace asked with a neck roll.

"Twenty-one. I'll be twenty-two in November," he mocked.

"You ain't that old."

"It's not the number, baby; it's the life experience."

Candace poked out her lips again.

A thin, slick grin slid across Prince's handsome face. "So you love ya lil' boyfriend, Candy?"

"He okay."

"Where you meet him at?"

"We go to school together."

"Yeah. You still in school? You see him during the summer a lot?"

"Sometimes."

"Not enough, huh?" he said, reaching for her arm. Candace blushed. "You are gorgeous, Candy."

"Thank you."

"Ya lil' boyfriend goin' be mad if you take my number?"

Candace shrugged; she didn't care much about Reginald Bailey at the moment. Prince opened his car door, sinking in behind the wheel. On a small piece of paper, he scribbled down his number. He nodded for Candace to come closer to the car and slid the paper into her hand.

"Make sure you call me."

She clasped her palm tight. Candace could barely keep a calm pace as she headed back toward her aunt's. He was in her dreams that night. She was too nervous to call him; she didn't even know what to say. A few days later, there was a basketball game in the neighborhood and Candace and Marcine galloped around the corner.

A giggly group of teenaged girls stood on the far side of the basketball court watching the summer leagues play. Prince was there, as she expected, and Candace could hardly breathe when she saw him. Her heart thudded as Marci nudged her excitedly. *He's coming this way*, she thought. *He's coming over to me.*

"Take this ride with me, Candy Reign."

It wasn't a question and she dutifully obeyed, following him out of the playground. He opened the car door for her and the smooth leather sucked her in.

"Where we going?" she asked.

"For a ride."

He rolled down the windows of his Acura and the cool air smacked her tenderly in the face. Warm strings of her hair stung her cheeks.

She smiled. Prince made a few runs around the city, but he kept his eye and conversation focused on Candace.

"You all right?" he asked.

"I'm fine. You cool?"

He smiled and nodded, long clean teeth, pushing his cheeks back and forming high triangle dimples above the corners of his beard. Candace grinned again. He was beautiful to her and she felt comfortable in his presence.

"You really are gorgeous," he said coolly. "I see I'm goin' have to keep you next to me."

"Yeah?"

"You too sweet, Candy. I can't let you out of my sight." She nodded, the wind and his words taking her breath away. "I like you," he continued. "You goin' let me take care of you?"

"I don't need nobody to take care of me."

Prince playfully tapped her thigh. "Oh…is that so?"

"That's so."

"So tell me this, lil' mama, what kind of stuff are you into? Like what do almost seventeen-year-olds like to do? You chill at the mall with your girlfriends?"

"I…I do a lot. I hang out with my friends. I chill with my mom a lot since my dad died and… I don't know. I'm good at school. Math is my strongest subject."

"Is that right?"

"That's right."

"So you like a nerd and what not?" The car was slowing down.

"No, hell no! I ain't a nerd. I'm just good at math. I mean, it makes sense. Two plus two is goin' always be four. Like that, you know?"

"I guess." Prince shrugged. "I'm pretty good with numbers too, boo."

"Yeah?"

"Yeah, like multiplying my money." His laugh was loud and proud and Candace couldn't help but to join in. Her genuine chuckle forced him to laugh harder, and he grinned her way as he pulled into a parking space in the open lot next to the Art Museum by the side of the Schuylkill River.

"Come here, baby," he instructed, pushing up the armrest between them. Candace slid closer, scooting her body under his awaiting arm. She was so close to him now that she could smell his cologne with every breath, his mouth only inches from her own. Candace squirmed in her seat. *He's gonna kiss me. Ohmigod, he's gonna kiss me.*

Prince coolly placed his hand under her chin, leading her mouth into his until their lips met. He pulled passionately at her eager lips with his, sucking and sliding his tongue into her mouth. Candace melted into him. Prince held her up, pulling her closer in the embrace. When Candace was finally able to open her eyes, there was no doubt about it, she was in love.

That summer was one of the best of her life. Candace spent most of her time riding shotgun beside Prince who took all the pleasure in showing her off and kissing her plump lips. He spoiled her rotten, giving her whatever her heart desired. Candace couldn't get enough of him.

He'd taken her out shopping for her seventeenth birthday and was stroking her long locks on his couch after dinner. She had been to his apartment a dozen times and he'd been kissing her for months, all over her neck and breasts. She liked when he licked on her nipples. Prince had even gotten as far as pressing his fingers into her wet panties and massaging her swollen clit. She groaned and squirmed all over his bed. But, Prince never pressed the issue of penetration, not until he thought she was ready.

This night after celebrating with her and taking her shopping, Prince spread her legs on the bed and began to lick and suck on her young womanhood. Candace thought she was going to die. The wet tingling sensation surged through her body and Prince pulled back on her clit with his pursed lips. She screamed. Then he twirled it, kissed it and sucked some more. He put his long fingers inside of her; first one, turning it and sliding it to let her feel every inch and muscular movement. Then another finger slid in. Candace pulled at the sheets. Prince turned and twisted the two together, then snapped his fingers inside of her. The tremors rolled through Candace like waves in the ocean. She started to shake. Prince snapped his fingers again. He then took her hand and placed it on his lap so she could feel him. Candace jumped up. Prince's dick was just like him—big, black and meaty.

"Prince, that's gonna hurt," Candace whined, the innocence oozing from her eyes.

"I'm taking claim to the pussy. You hear me, baby?"

Candace nodded.

"I'mma be gentle," he assured her as he laid her back and climbed on top of her. He pushed the tip of his manhood into her moist opening.

Candace damn near fainted. "Oh, no, baby!" She jumped back off him, crawling to the back of the bed.

Prince scooped her long body up in one arm and held her in place. "Now, don't run, baby," he instructed. "That's goin' make it worse. You gotta let me get inside of you, okay?"

Candace nodded as tears began forming in her eyes.

"Do you want me inside of you?"

Again, she nodded.

"Say it, Candy. Tell me what you want."

"I want you inside of me."

"I'm goin' give you everything that you want. You hear me?"

He was moving his manhood toward the lips of her womanly

opening. The pressure felt like fire trying to force its way in her. But Prince took his time. He pushed gently and slowly, making sure not to move too hard or too fast.

He kissed her mouth greedily as he grinded his waist on top of her, inching himself in. She struggled to keep still, but he held her firm in his strong grasp. Slowly, Candace began to feel the penetrating pleasure deep inside. Prince kept at his slow pace seeming to fight the urge to explode in her tight wetness. Candace nearly lost her mind as he stroked steady, filling her insides, and the convulsions came over her body suddenly. Prince's orgasms quickly followed, damn near sucked out of him by Candace's contracting muscles. He fell to her side.

"Did you like that, Candy?" he asked, kissing at her ear.

Candace trembled—partly from aftershock, partly from the sensation of Prince caressing her bare breast. She could only nod.

"Do you want to do it again? It gets better." He smiled at her. "Come here; let me show you."

He started to straddle her again. Candace's young vagina was dripping wet and Prince found his way a little easier. This time he stood his ground and stroked on top of her for what seemed like hours. The orgasms came to her in waves, taking over her body leaving her wet and trembling. Candace's long body oozed sweet juices. Prince kept at it until he finally could not take the tension building in his loins, and he came hard and long. Candace studied his face on top of her. She stared into the creases of his cheeks, the dimples and close-cut fade. She memorized the wrinkles of his nose while he was sleeping. She knew then merely by the way that he breathed, she would love Prince Reynolds for the rest of her life.

By the time she was nineteen, she was a mother and living with twenty-four-year-old Prince. She couldn't deny that she liked the money he brought in and the freedom she had in shopping and always rocking the newest bags to her business classes at community college. She never had to take the subway. Prince would drop her off every morning in his big black rimmed-up Cadillac, and with her feathered hair and Louis Vuitton sneakers, Candace was the envy of all her classmates.

Candace counted thousands of dollars for Prince on any given night and he was always generous. He made sure his woman and son had the best his money could afford, even if that meant he had to disappear for days. He took care of business in the streets and Candace learned to ask few questions. There were some things she simply did not want to know. When Prince returned home one evening with a cut above his eye, Candace iced his face and bandaged his wounds. When Candace would wake in the middle of the night to see Prince's large body squatting down tucking something in the back of their closet, she simply smiled and said, "Good morning." When Prince and Brother drove ten kilos to Virginia, she packed them lunch.

Candace adored Prince despite his heavy hood stomping and guiltless obsession for the newest and shiniest of things. Yet, as everyone has their vices, Prince's predicament, alongside his some-times ravenous temper, was his boastful and showboat nature. He always had to have the biggest, the baddest and the best. Ever the perfectionist, he hated when things didn't go his way and took it out on anyone in his path. Candace recalled seeing Prince hop out of the car while they were driving down Germantown Avenue and punch some man right in the face. The guy hit the thick glass of the barbershop window behind him and fell to the ground. Prince calmly climbed back in the car and pulled off. The scariest incident Candace could remember was when one of the young guys Prince kept around, smashed up his new Infiniti. Prince and Brother called him over and stomped size-eleven Timberland boots into the kid's head. Candace was left to clean up the blood spatter on the walls and ceiling. She tolerated Prince's tactics because she loved him—not because she approved.

As Prince grew, his reputation scowled its way through the Philadelphia streets and more money started coming his way. His ego boosted and arrogance swelled. Prince, in turn, became controlling and more possessive, especially of Candace. The leash was tight and he always needed to know her every move. Dollars were steady in her pocket, but the strict allowance never permitted more than he felt she needed. Candace didn't maintain consistent friendships because Prince didn't like her wasting time going out with a bunch of cackling girls.

One Friday night, while Prince was out of town on business and Candace had gotten paid from her new job as a receptionist, she decided to hang out a little late at an after-hour spot in University City with some coworkers. The after-hour was progressively transfiguring into a club scene while Candace was cracking jokes and throwing back drinks with her new friends. Before she knew it, she was drunk and had six missed calls on her phone. She stumbled into the bathroom to call Prince back. It was after ten. Prince was calm. He'd gotten back early and wanted to make sure she was okay.

"You sound drunk. Do you need me to come get you?" he asked.

Candace declined.

When she walked through the door, she was met with a brutal backhand across her face. She hit the floor instantly, Prince standing over her growling.

"So, you on some sneaky shit!" he barked. "I been calling you all fuckin' night!"

Candace was in shock on the floor. She crawled into a corner in the room holding her face. No one had ever hit her before and she was not prepared to handle it. Five years she'd been with Prince and she'd taken a few stern grabs and some choking during rough sex, but never a hand to hurt her. How could he? Prince turned and walked out of their large apartment. Tears ushered her to sleep, and when she woke up, she was still on the floor and Prince still wasn't home. When he finally showed up, his eyes were puffy and swollen like he'd been crying. He begged for forgiveness.

"I never meant to hurt you," he pleaded. "You know I love you. You're my wife."

Candace didn't speak. Prince cried into her arms; she could smell the alcohol and marijuana oozing off of him. He forced her arms open and pressed his body into her. She did not resist and cradled him in her arms. He slept while she held him. She eventually fell asleep as well. She awoke in the middle of the night, Prince still in her arms. He did not look the same to her.

On Monday morning when it was time for work, she did not look the same to herself either. The bruise on her face was apparent and she was worried about what the other women in the office and her boss would think.

After the slapping incident, Candace was offered a promotion at work. She took it eagerly, wanting to learn all that she could. The fact that Prince controlled her whole life grew more and more terrifying. She worked harder and decided to go back to school. The more she worked, the more Prince stayed out. He would get more calls in the middle of night and come back with bloody knuckles or not come back at all until the next day or two, maybe. He never offered any excuses, but Candace knew her man was different and nothing changed a man's actions more than another woman.

"I don't know who the fuck you think you talking to, Candace Reign Brinton!"

"You, Prince Devante Reynolds, you sneaky mothafucka! I don't know what's up with you, Prince, but you actin' real different. It's something funny about you."

"Funny? 'Cause I'm chasin' this money?"

"You been chasin' money, Prince. I'm talkin' 'bout a bitch. You out here chasin' some bitch and I can smell it!"

"What the fuck is you talkin' about?"

"You out all the time chasin' this bread, so you say; you just gotta have it. Okay, we got nice shit; we living good. Now what?"

"What? More nice shit, better living. Candy, is you stupid?"

"More shooting and robbing or more drugs? Which one is it, Prince, to get more of what the next man got? This shit is corny. You always out in the fuckin' streets! Doin' God knows what with God knows who."

"This shit corny! Bitch, is you crazy?!?" Prince grabbed her by the shoulders and lifted her off her feet. "This shit corny! You know what the fuck I've done for this corny shit!" He tossed her onto the couch.

"You selfish bitch!" He lunged, punching her twice in the face. "You got a little associates degree and a fuckin' paycheck and you think you big shit. I been fucking take care of you off this street shit! Ain't nothing goin' change! I make the bread in this bitch. This my shit and I'm only getting started!"

Candace cowered on the couch, her face throbbing. Shock rendered her motionless and she stifled the tears until she heard the front door of their Overbrook home slam shut.

She drove herself to the hospital where she was treated for swelling and pain; no broken bones even though her face felt like it had been shattered into pieces. When the officers in the ER asked her what had happened, she told them she'd fallen. One bald older officer returned to her side several times that night. His smile was genuine; she could tell he wanted to help. But she did not say a negative word against her son's father. Prince didn't come home that night and the next day, she packed her and her son's things and moved out to her mother's. Prince was gone for days without a word. He didn't come looking for her. He didn't call. She asked around. The whole neighborhood knew her baby's father and she hadn't gotten word that he'd been hurt or locked up. So where was he? Why didn't he come after her?

The news she'd anticipated came back a few days later. Prince was crashing with Aisha, a young girl from around the way he'd been dealing with. There was a shootout the night he left Candace, and Prince was laying low with his jump-off. Candace wasn't surprised. The real shock came less than a month later when Prince was booked on homicide charges. One of the guys he was fighting before the shootout died in the ER. Prince got twelve years. Aisha had twin girls five months later.

Candace still had the phone in her hand when the fast busy signal started to blast through the slim grey device. She was leaning against the refrigerator in her kitchen. Quickly dropping the phone down on its base, she checked the time on the microwave. Ten after eight. Candace pulled the silk scarf off her head. Her cinnamon curls fell down to her shoulders. A snatch of her keys from the hook on the wall and she was out the door.

CHAPTER 2

here the hell is everybody? Candace wondered, entering the empty business office suite of Wyncote Medical Rehabilitation Center. It was 8:29 a.m.; both Danielle and Allyson should have been at their desks, but no one greeted her as she pulled her keys from her black Michael Kors bag and unlocked her office door.

"Good morning," she said to herself before looking up to see a bright yellow post-it note in front of her on the door. It read in almost illegible scribble, "Danielle called out sick. 7:15 am. Allyson out sick 7:30."

"Oh, great, both these bitches sick," Candace said with a sigh, "they don't pay me enough for this shit."

Candace hung her chunky leather bag on the back of her office door. The small room was tidy and adorned strategically with pictures of her and Emmanuel on the desk and window ledge she faced almost eight hours a day. She was alone in her office most of the time, dealing primarily with dollars and figures, a position she much preferred over interactions with people. Candace liked numbers and because of her affection for mathematics, she was damn good at her job. Candace was skillful in tracking residents' personal accounts and finances. She billed Medicare, insurance companies and private pay families with precise calculations. She guaranteed accurate billing and professional customer service. She was always courteous, always on time, and always fly.

As business office manager, Candace supervised the receptionist and payroll clerk, who both called out. This didn't look good for Candace or her department. She ran her fingers through her cinnamon locks, trying to push away the growing irritation. Though she had been with the company for seven years, she still worried about how this type of slack in her department would reflect on her management skills. The day was busy and with both her staff out, Candace was stuck answering the phone.

"Good morning, Wyncote Medical."

"Bitch, whatchu doing answering the phone?" Her little sister's voice caught her by surprise.

"Hey, Marci, what's going on?"

"On my way to my new gig."

"Oh yeah, that's right. What salon are you starting at?" Candace asked her sister.

"D's Design in Darby."

Candace chuckled. "Damn."

"I know, right." Marci giggled. "But it's cool. It's a job, first gig since I got my certification, plus the location is good. It's right on Sixty-ninth Street."

"That's what's up. You excited?" Candace asked.

"I guess so. I mean, I'm anxious to get in there and show these bitches what I do," Marci replied coolly.

Candace chuckled. "I know that's right, sis. You better do the damn thing."

"Don't I always?"

Candace smiled. "Yeah, well. I gotta go, these damn lines are ringing. Good luck, lil' sis. Love you."

"You too."

Candace glanced at the clock on the car dashboard: 6 p.m. Stopping at a red light, she closed her eyes, imagining a warm bath, a chilled glass and a plush bathrobe waiting for her at home. And Emmanuel. No stress, no phones, no…the blaring of the horn behind her startled her from her reverie.

Once she arrived, Candace slipped her shoes off at the door, tossing her bag onto the table as she entered her tidy apartment. Her keys hit the kitchen counter and her bottom hit the couch, before the door closed behind her. Emmanuel burst in a moment later.

"Hey, Mom. I need seventy dollars for camp," he hollered, walking into the living room.

"Oh, God," she moaned lowly. "There's always something." It was nearing the end of May, school would be over soon and Emmanuel needed somewhere constructive to spend the day. She didn't like the idea of her son hanging around in the streets all summer.

"Mom, did you hear me?" Emmanuel asked, leaning over Candace on the couch.

"I heard you," she replied, reaching for her pocketbook. "When is school over?"

"Two weeks."

Candace shrugged. She had time to work the weekly expense into her budget, but the registration fee was needed up front. "Okay, I'll write them a check tomorrow."

"Cool. What's for dinner? I'm hungry."

Candace stood and walked into the kitchen to make her son something to eat. She pulled some leftover ribs and macaroni and cheese out of the refrigerator, made a plate and stuck it in the microwave.

"Make sure you do the dishes after you eat," she instructed.

Emmanuel nodded.

After his meal, Emmanuel wrung out the excess moisture from

the cream and red dishtowel he was holding into the empty sink.

"Dishes are done, Mom," he said.

Candace looked up from the kitchen table she was wiping clean and nodded.

"Anything else?" he asked.

"No, I'm good, boopie. You need to get ready for tomorrow."

Emmanuel bounded down the hall but stopped instantly hearing the phone ring. Eyes wide, he leapt for it and was silent a second after answering.

Candace recognized the pause. After a moment, she heard her son speak.

"Sup, Dad." Another long pause. "Nah, I'm good…" Without another word to Candace, Emmanuel walked off down the hall with the phone cradled on his shoulder.

Candace yelled after him, "Let me talk to ya dad before you hang up!"

She sat back at the kitchen table while Emmanuel chatted with his father and pulled out her checkbook. Money was tight and her take-home was just under $2,500 a month. Her rent was $850. Bills; cable, Internet, cell phone and the credit card payments for mistakes she'd made in the past came to around $400 a month. Car note and insurance on her 2012 Honda Accord was $410, food was about $300 a month for her and Emmanuel. She cooked a lot and was an advocate of leftovers and bulk shopping. Her cosmetics—hair and nails—were around $100. Marci styled her for cheap and Brother took Emmanuel for weekly cuts. With gas prices more than skyrocketing she averaged no less than $250 a month just to get around. There were a few dollars left at the end of the month, but the $500 or $600 Brother passed her way was always needed. Emmanuel's camp was going to be $90 a week.

Candace worked the numbers over and over in her head. There was always just enough to cover the spread.

Never enough to quit this paycheck-to-paycheck shit, Candace thought. *Gotta rob Peter and shoot Paul.* However annoyed with her financial disposition, Candace did take pride in her ability to provide. Her son was well taken care of and they both wore the best of things. It wasn't Gucci, but Candace was proud of her Macy's and J. Crew attire, her clean ride and spacious Chestnut Hill apartment. But still she wanted more.

Never enough to have my own shit. Pay off my car. Put some money down on a house. Take a fuckin' vacation. No, 'cause shit is always due.

Candace was curled up on the couch when Emmanuel strolled out of his room and down the hall, the phone pressed to his chocolate cheek.

"Aright, Dad. Love you, too," he said before handing Candace the phone.

She nestled into the light, puffy fabric of her sofa and spoke into the receiver wiggling her long body, attempting to find the perfect spot. "Hey, Prince."

"What up, Candy? How you feeling?"

"I'm feelin' all right, Prince. How you?"

"As good as I'm goin' be for right now, baby girl. Wassup witchu?"

"Nothing, Prince. I'm just going over these bills and it's not okay." She rolled her neck as she spoke.

"What's not okay, Candace?"

"I don't have enough."

"Enough what?"

"Enough money, Prince."

"Get the fuck outta here, Candace. Here you go with that shit again."

"What shit, Prince? All I'm saying is I want a better lifestyle for me and my son."

"My son!" Prince snapped.

A smooth shudder swept through Candace as she pulled in her

breath to speak, "Whateva. Our son. I still need shit for him, for us."

"Like what, Candace?" The agitation surged through his words.

"Like a house. A better school district. Manny will be going to high school soon. Um…let's see, money for college."

"So whatchu sayin', C?"

"I'm sayin', I need some more fuckin' money, Prince. Whatchu think I'm sayin'?"

"What the fuck you want me to do from where I'm at, C? Stop bitchin', like you don't have everything you need."

"Bitchin'? Damn right, I'm bitchin'. I got the basics. I want more… better shit. Ain't that what you say? Am I wrong for wanting more for me and my…*our* son?"

"You can want what the fuck you want. You need to get ya grind on and stop thinking ya lazy spoiled ass just goin' be handed shit."

"Lazy!?! Fuck you! I bust my ass all day to take care of this boy!"

"And I put my fuckin' bid in from behind bars!" Prince barked back.

Candace could not argue.

Prince was right. He did what he could from where he was and his mother, Miss P, and Brother had Emmanuel almost every other weekend. He was always invited to hang out with his cousins. Brother had five kids and three baby mamas, but never left Emmanuel out of the family fun. They were a close-knit bunch and for that, Candace was grateful.

"I take care of my fuckin' son, too, Candy!" Prince boomed.

Candace groaned her response, "I know and that couple hundred is helpful, but I still don't have much left at the end of the month to put away. Things cost money—clothes and camp."

"What else you want me to do while I'm locked the fuck up, C?"

"Nothing at all, Prince." She paused. "I'm going to bed."

Click.

The next day Candace stepped back into her office after a long, boring morning meeting when Allyson, the receptionist, informed her she had a call on line two.

"I think it's your sister," the pudgy face, cream-skinned girl said.

She closed her door and eagerly picked up the phone.

"Yo, we're goin' out tonight!" Marci declared.

Candace barely had time to process a response.

"And bring Man up here. Mommy wants to see him."

"That's crazy, you callin' me all hype," Candace said, laughing lightly.

"Why?"

"'Cause you're hype as hell. What are you talking about?"

"Girl, I said we goin' out tonight! My homie just came home from Iraq and his b-day is Tuesday. We ballin' tonight, bitch. I'm talkin' limos, poppin' bottles, all that shit."

Candace groaned. "Marci, you know I am trying to save my money up right now. I can't go wildin' out with you all crazy. I don't have a lot of partying money in the budget."

"Bitch, please, ain't nobody spending nothing. Trust me, you don't need a dime."

"I on't know…"

"Whateva," Marci interjected, "just be at my house by eight. Oh, and C…"

"Yeah?"

"Stop playin' that broke shit; it ain't cute."

CHAPTER 3

*M*arci and Candace were extremely close and Candace loved having a little sister around. Growing up, they swapped stories about boys and Marci had someone to tell all of her secrets. She would hold her lips tight until she could get to her big sister to spill the beans. When Candace lost her virginity, Marci was the first to know, and when Marci needed a hideout from her mother, she ran to Candace. At sixteen, when her twenty-year-old boyfriend needed somewhere to meet her, it was at Candace's house. And Marci was right there when Candace met Prince. She was by her sister's side when Prince brought her home, sore and proud. Even though Marci lived with her mother, they stayed tight. In and out of Marci's relationships and fashion trends and even after their father's death, they remained closely bound.

Candace supported her sister at every turn but never hesitated to put her in check. At twenty-three, Marci had just graduated from Empire Beauty School and landed a job at a nice salon. With a steady clientele of her friends and family, she brought a lot to the table at her new place of business.

Marci stepped out of the shower when her cell phone rang.

"What you doin' tonight, baby?" a smooth voice cooed through the phone.

"Hi, baby." Marci was beaming. "I'm going out with my sister and some friends."

"You not goin' have time for me, huh?" Tommy asked.

"You told me you was busy tonight."

"Yeah, but you know I get jealous when you go out and have all my sexy body on display for them lame niggas out there."

"You can't be jealous; it's not cute."

"Nah, I'm only teasin'. You know I'm not even that kind of dude."

"I know, baby. That's why I love you."

"Good. Now make sure you be good tonight and send me some sexy pics. I need that, okay?"

"I gotchu, love."

"What you got on now?"

Marci grinned proudly. "Nothing. I just got out the shower."

"Yeah," Tommy's voice deepened. "You want me to come hit that before you start your day?"

Marci giggled. "Only if you want to, baby. You know you can get this whenever you want it." Marci sat back on her bed, cooing into the phone naked with her legs spread, massaging herself.

She was in cutoff shorts and a tee when Candace arrived a few hours later. Marci jumped up from her messy bed to let her sister and Emmanuel in, then returned to rummaging through her massive clutter of a closet, pulling clothes from overflowing hampers and poorly hung hangers. From BCBG minis to Gucci pumps to skimpy Bebe dresses, Marci's closet was an extensive and expensive mess. She finally tossed her dress for the evening on her cluttered bed. Emmanuel came in behind Candace, kissed his aunt and headed straight for the basement, the game room, where he found Marci's youngest brother, Marcus, deep into his PS2.

Marci twirled Candace's long cinnamon locks into voluminous curls, graciously framing the soft angles of her face.

"Sit still, let me do your makeup," Marci instructed with one hand on her sister's shoulder.

Candace's long seductive frame gave complement to a smooth, form-fitting, light-gold dress. Stopping just above her knee, it accented her strong thighs, and thin roping straps hung tight across her bare shoulders. She comfortably slid on her strappy, gold-accented BCBG heels and stood up over six feet tall. A perfect size ten, Candace's long athletic legs provided ample support for her firm body.

Marci had not inherited all their father's height. At five feet seven inches, Marci had a more thin and petite body frame, still, with great legs like her sister, both developed from years of track meets and high-heels.

Candace stood in the mirror, admiring the work her sister had done on her face. "Mars, I can't believe you got all this dark shit on my eyes, and it still really looks good."

"Chill, chick. I know what I'm doing," Marci shouted from inside her closet.

"Well, I wish you figure out what the hell you're wearing. It's hot as hell in this room."

Marci stepped from behind her closet door wearing a black halter dress with a cinching waist that pinched her tiny size-four frame. She strapped on a pair of black and silver stilettos elevating her another five inches.

As the sisters were primping, pampering and preparing for the night, one of Marci's girlfriends, Tasha, showed up with her shy cousin, Angela. Tasha, in her high black heels, tiny red top and black shiny leggings was almost as tall Candace. Her strapless bra was tight and pushed her breasts up and out. She jumped right into the makeup mix and shortly, the group of stunning ladies headed out the door. They piled up into one car and headed toward Marci's friend Warren's house.

Halfway down the road, Marci's phone rang. "Hey baby. How's the cookout?" Marci asked Warren, the birthday boy.

"Happy Birthday, Warren!" Tasha shouted into the phone.

The girls all shouted, "Happy birthday! Happy birthday! Happy birthday!"

Marci listened with a wide smile. "He said thank you. And the limo bus is there."

"Yeah!!!" Tasha squealed.

"But they don't have no liquor, so we gotta make a stop," Marci said.

Tasha was behind the wheel and swung a sharp right. "Not a problem."

They pulled into the parking lot in front of a Wine and Spirit Shoppe.

"C, what you drinking tonight?" Marci asked.

"Oh, girl. I don't know. Whateva at this point."

"You know I'm Patrón all day!" Marci giggled, making her way through the store. "I'm gon' make sure you have a good time tonight."

"Bitch, we goin' get fucked up!" Tasha chimed in, holding a bottle of Patrón in the air.

They spent close to $300 at the liquor store buying two bottles of Patrón, some Cîroc, Hennessy, Bacardi Pineapple Fusion, Pink Moscato and sodas.

Tasha pulled up in front a tall home in Overbrook, the music from the speakers in the yard rocking the neighborhood and vibrating their car. Warren jogged up to meet them, kissing Marci directly on the lips.

"Hey! Hey! Hey, ladies. Y'all all lookin' gooder than a mug. Um," he said, squeezing Marci's backside. "Women like this make a nigga not wanna go back overseas."

The girls laughed and shortly after, Warren, his brother, Woody;

his homies, Terrence, Ja'quan, and Shawn, were all out back, behind the house enjoying the cookout that had been thrown in honor of the returning soldier.

Candace and Marci shared a burger.

"You betta eat something, girl," Marci warned. "We finna get fucked up."

Candace smiled. "I'm wit' it. And ya' soldier boy is cute."

"Ain't he though," Marci replied, beaming.

Warren stood a few feet from them, brown-skinned, tattooed and muscular. Candace watched him down the drink he was holding, then throw his hands up into the air.

"Aight!" he hollered. "Let's get this show on the road!" And with that, Candace and her squad, followed by Warren and his crew, began boarding the limo bus.

Once on board, Marci moved to the rear of the bus, pulling out the liquor she was carrying and setting it up on the small illuminated bar to her right. Warren moved in next to her, surveying the drink selections and smiling.

"Good job, slim," he said, nodding at Marci and grabbing a bottle of tequila before taking a seat beside her. Once in the soft leather seating, he popped out the stiff cork and threw back a strong shot. He passed the bottle to Marci and she did the same.

Terrence, a golden-brown brother with long golden-brown dreadlocks, stood, holding and waving a bottle of Hennessy in his right hand as he spoke. "It's good to be home, ya dig!"

"You were in Iraq, too?" Candace asked immediately.

"Sure was, ma. I served the last year with the birthday boy and just making it home with this nigga is reason enough to celebrate."

"I know that's right," Candace said, holding her glass high in the air.

Marci and Tasha grabbed bottles and began filling glasses with

Patrón. Once everyone had been served, Warren counted it off.

"Man, it's my birthday and I'm here with my niggas, some bad bitches; my night lookin' good already! Throw it up!"

They all took the shot.

"Can we blaze on this bitch?" Ja'Quan, a heavy-set, light-skinned brother, asked.

Warren threw back the bottle again. "This my limo! I do what the fuck I want! Roll that shit up!"

Ja'Quan did not hesitate and pulled a large sandwich bag from his back pocket.

Candace watched the bag of marijuana unfold.

"That's what the fuck I'm talking 'bout, Quan! That's why you my fam," Woody, Warren's darker and less attractive older brother with big teeth, cheered. He reached into his back pocket and pulled out a box of dutches.

"That's why you my nigga," Quan agreed, catching the box of dutches Woody tossed him.

Weed was puffed hard and plenty shots taken, and before they made it into Center City, Candace was feeling good. The timid and short Angela whipped out her phone to take pictures, and Candace grinned and poked out her booty as the lights flicked. She could see the men on the bus eyeing her as she posed for photos with her sister.

"I wanna picture with you," Shawn, a brown-skinned brother with short, kinky twisted hair, stated. He stood from his seat with a glass in his hand.

Candace looked him over. He was not her type at all, but the night was for fun and she obliged, propping herself on his knee. Shawn wrapped his arms around her waist and put on his toughest face while Angela snapped the photo. Before long, everyone was taking pictures. Marci beamed into the camera with her arms wrapped around Candace; they both squeezed.

Aura was their first stop. They were ushered into the VIP section through the side door and up the second level of the club. Every reserved table was set with a bucket of ice, and two bottles of juice: orange and cranberry.

The party was already live and their five male escorts kept their drinks flowing all night. Angela and Candace were dancing when Terrence came up behind them and noticed their glasses were low.

He shouted to the cocktail waitress walking past, "Aww, hell, nah! I got these lovely ladies here and they need some drinks. Ya dig? I got to keep my ladies happy." He leaned into Candace's ear. "You having a good time, sexy?"

"I am. You are, too, huh?"

"Yeah, ma'am. How can you tell?"

Candace pressed her back into him. "'Cause you got your hands all ova me."

Terrence did not release his grip. "I can't help it, baby." He held her tighter. "You look damn edible in that dress. Ya dig?"

Candace couldn't help but laugh.

The club was packed; even the VIP section was full of well-dressed, clean-cut men and sexy women. After her glass was full, Candace stepped back to the dance floor with her sister. Marci was swaying her hips rhythmically like a seductive snake charmer as Warren stared, entranced, yet holding on.

"You good?" Marci screamed to her sister over the music.

Candace nodded with a smirk.

"You fucked up?"

Candace nodded again with a smirk. They both giggled.

Suddenly, Angela, looking less able to hold her liquor than the rest, came stumbling toward the sisters.

"I gotta pee," she announced.

"Come on." Candace grabbed her arm. "I gotta go, too. I'll go with you."

Tasha was busy on the dance floor and Marci turned her attention back to Warren who was holding her waist and grinding his body toward her.

Candace and Angela stepped past the velvet rope to get to the bathroom. The bouncer at the VIP entrance looked Candace up and down.

"Don't forget me," Candace said, "I'm coming right back and you betta let me back in."

"I ain't goin' forget you, gorgeous," the husky man replied.

Candace smiled and as she turned to take the steps that led to the lower level, a light-skinned brother with green eyes and sandy brown hair, bumped chest to chest with her. Candace stumbled, pushing back on Angela. The well-trimmed brother with a sexy cinnamon beard that connected to his sexy cinnamon sideburns, caught her by the arms under her elbows. Angela was not as lucky as Candace and the drunken stumble caused her to lose her balance and hit the ground. Candace bent to help her, but the alcohol infused with her laughter, and she was immobilized in helpless hysterics. The six-foot-five brother with an athletic build and full moist pink lips bent and effortlessly lifted Angela from the ground. She was not fazed by her fall and recovered quickly.

"I'm good. I'm good," she said, brushing off her shoulders.

"Ya'll all right?" he asked, his question directed to Candace.

"I gotta pee," Angela responded.

"We're fine," Candace replied, grabbing Angela's arm and moving her quickly down the stairs. She checked behind her and caught the handsome brother's eyes tracing the arch of her legs. He looked into her eyes unashamed at being caught staring, and smiled. Candace pushed Angela into the bathroom as the velvet rope was lifted and the brother strolled into the VIP section.

Candace hiked up her skirt, squatting over the toilet and holding on to her knees for balance. She was washing her hands when

Angela emerged from another stall, with the red pumps she'd been wearing in her hand.

Candace's face twisted in disgust. "Really?" she asked the drunken girl. "Bare feet on the club bathroom floor! That's just fuckin' nasty."

Angela was too drunk to comprehend and simply shrugged.

Candace could never imagine being so gross. Her motto was, *"Strut like it's nothing. Your feet could be bleeding and split in pain, but no one should ever be able to tell."*

When they made it back to the VIP, Candace pushed Angela into an empty seat next to Tasha, who took one look at her friend and returned to her drink and her conversation.

The handsome brother Candace had seen on her way to the bathroom had on a white button-down shirt and she was checking for him hard. Her prey was spotted across the room with his back to her at the bar. The tall, cream-skinned brother spun around with a bottle in hand and headed toward the birthday boy, Warren. The men slapped hands and hugged briefly. Candace could see their lips moving but could not make out the words as Warren accepted the bottle and moved over for the brother to sit beside him. Brother in the white spoke to all the men she'd come with. She couldn't tell if he knew them all, but he was comfortable and confident in his approach. Candace didn't realize she was staring until Marci pinched her.

"Who dat?" Marci asked over her right shoulder.

Candace shrugged.

"He fine as fuck," Tasha added, appearing over her left. The brother must have felt the eyes peering his way and looked up at the ladies. He smiled.

Candace looked away. Marci and Tasha waved. He raised his glass toward them. Tasha blew him a kiss. He grinned, revealing a small dimple on his left cheek.

"Damn," was all Tasha could manage.

Candace shook her head. *Too damn fine*, she thought.

Marci huffed. "I be back." And with that, she marched over toward Warren and the handsome stranger.

Candace moved back to the dance floor, attempting to avert her eyes from her sister and the inevitable. But as she suspected, after a few moments passed, Marci returned with the handsome stranger in her arm.

"Chris, this is my sister, Candace. Candace, this is Chris."

He was even more appealing at a second inspection—fair skin, strong jawline and light eyes—but Candace could tell he was young; younger than she preferred.

"How you doin'?" She extended her hand for a formal shake.

He kissed it.

Marci bounced away.

"You are tall and sexy as hell, Candace."

"You're not bad to look at either," she replied, shouting over the music.

"I been watching you dance. Can a brother getta chance to show you some moves?" He raised his hands to his chest and started pumping the air.

Candace smiled. *He's funny.*

Before she could respond, he pulled her close and began leading her deeper into the crowd. The music was thumping and Candace couldn't resist the urge to move her hips. Chris seemed as if he couldn't resist the way she moved and was soon behind her with his hands roaming the grooves of her waist. He caught it while she threw it back and after a few songs, Candace was out of breath.

"I need a drink," she said, stopping to wipe her brow. She began to head back to the table where her friends were gathered.

"I gotchu," Chris said, pulling her back into him. He reached into his pocket and pulled out a knot of money.

Candace rolled her eyes. *Yeah, he's a young bul*, she thought.

"Don't move," Chris instructed as he moved quickly into the crowd. *But damn, he is fine.*

Candace was alone on the dance floor when Tasha danced over to her.

"We 'bout to head to the other club. You ready?"

Candace searched the crowd for her good-looking dance partner, but he was out of sight, so, opting to leave the showboating little boy, she followed Tasha to the door.

"Where's Marci?" Candace asked.

"Already on the bus; they walked Angela out," Tasha replied. "She was feelin' sick."

Candace and Tasha joined into a bustling throng of people who all seemed to be leaving the club at the same time. The crowd emptied from the club into the street. Candace hadn't noticed where the party was heading and was shocked when she boarded the private limo bus to find it completely packed. More than thirty people had crammed on board. Candace made it as far to the rear as she could, clutching tight to Tasha's hand. She could see her sister and Warren seated in the far rear. With no room to move, Candace found a seat on Shawn's lap down from Marci and Warren who were locked in a passionate embrace. Shawn secured a steady grip of her waist for the short ride. Before the doors closed and the bus took off for another destination, Candace saw Chris jump on. He was pinched tight in the front between two giggly girls who didn't seem to mind him squeezing them too much.

They traveled a few blocks to Rumor and everyone piled off, flooding the sidewalks and streets. Shawn kept his grasp when Candace tried to move. He held her tight and Candace let the flow of traffic pass.

"Chill here and smoke this killa with me," he whispered in her ear. Before everyone could get off the bus, he lit it.

She took a long pull. "My sista is goin' be looking for me."

"You good, ma. Just relax."

Candace giggled. He didn't know her baby sister.

Outside the club, Marci realized that Candace was not behind her in the crowd of people waiting to get in the line. A drunken Marci started screaming. "C-C!" she screeched loudly. "C-C!" she screamed again, standing in the middle of Sansom Street.

Candace laughed aloud, passing the blunt back to Shawn and hurrying off the bus. "Why the fuck are you screaming?" she asked her frantic sister, stepping down into the street.

"Bitch," Marci began but paused when she saw a staggering Shawn following off the limo. Marci was standing in the middle of the crowded street still hollering. "Ooohhh." A long drunken slur. "What the fuck was ya'll doin'?"

"Not a goddamn thing." Candace grabbed Marci's arm, quickly moving into the crowd. Warren was at the club door and took Marci's arm, helping her navigate through the dense mob. They finally made it in. The walls inside the club were lined with drunken men, gawking at the women as they squeezed by. As Candace passed, one of the partyers against the wall leaned into her.

He whispered, "Shawty, you my favorite."

Candace couldn't help but laugh. *That's new.*

The group—Candace, Tasha, Angela, Marci and Warren and his crew—made it to the third floor and motioned for the waitress to get their party's drink order. Candace looked up to see Chris moving elegantly through the crowd with a bottle of Cîroc and two glasses in hand. He eased down on the arm of the red velvet sofa she sat in.

"You left me," Chris declared, handing her a glass.

Candace accepted. Her confidence bolstered by alcohol, she responded, "I know."

"You was working that shit back at the other club, though, ma."

"I know."

"You wearing the shit out that dress, too, baby girl."

"I know."

Chris smiled. "You got a smart mouth. I like that. Where ya man at?"

"I'm allergic."

He sipped his drink and laughed. His eyes were a brilliant shade of green, almost eerie in the dim club light, above a subtle spatter of freckles.

"How old are you?" he asked.

"Twenty-eight. You?" she replied.

"Twenty-one."

Candace stood to walk away, but he grabbed her arm.

"Hold up. Hold up! Where you goin'?" the young man inquired.

"You just a baby, baby. I don't date kids."

He stepped into her face. "Who the fuck is talkin' 'bout datin'? I just wanna get you a couple drinks, maybe dance a little. Feel me?"

Candace rolled her eyes.

"Damn, shawty. It's like that? You put a good brother down just because he ain't got as many years as you? You was backing that ass up on me 'til you found out how old I was."

"I'm just saying..."

"Sayin' what," he interrupted, leaning directly into her ear, his voice smooth over the music. "Maybe you need a young fresh outlook on life."

He refilled the glass in her hand and motioned for her to sit back down.

Candace hesitated a moment but accepted the drink and the seat.

"Where you from, Ma?" he shouted into her ear over the music.

"I live in Chestnut Hill," she hollered back.

"You got kids?"

"One."

"Baby daddy?"

"He locked up."

"Word. You ridin' for him?"

"We're friends, but I'm not his bitch."

"Whose bitch are you?" His words were slurred as he stared hard into her pretty face.

"Yours," she slurred back after taking another swig from her cup. Candace stood and began swaying seductively toward the dance floor. Chris followed with bottle in hand. He danced behind her, guiding her movements into a dark corner. He pushed against her until her back met the wall. As he raised the bottle to her mouth, he tried to slip his fingers up under her dress. Candace swatted his hand, then wiggled away from his grasp, switching her hips as she made her way across the dance floor toward Marci. She found her sister and her crowd gathered on a set of sofas to the far right of the spacious room. Tasha flailed her arms around Candace as she walked up and Terrence two-stepped in front of them. They threw back their drinks and Terrence refilled their glasses. Candace could feel the boy's eyes steady on her bronze legs as she danced with Tasha and Terrence.

When the lights clicked on in the club at two a.m., the stumbling crowd started to make its way up the stairs and outside. Chris pressed into Candace in the procession.

"Where are ya'll headed? Can I come, too?"

"Yeah? You wanna come with me?"

"Yeah, ma. I tryin' to be where you at."

"Is that right?"

"All night long."

She shook her head. When they made it out into the cool night air, he didn't leave her side, his persistence resounding.

"You goin' let me see you or what?"

"I'm going home, boo."

"I'm sayin, I'm cool with that. Let's go home then."

Candace pursed her lips. "I don't think so."

"Ight, Ma. I feel you. At least put my number in your phone."

Candace pulled out her phone. She stored the numbers he gave quickly before turning to walk away.

Chris stepped in her way. "So you just goin' leave a brotha thirsty? No hug or nothing?"

Candace extended her arms around his neck. Chris was tall enough for her to slightly lift her toes. He opened his chest wide eagerly welcoming the embrace and pressed into her. His chest felt good against her. He clutched her tight, seemingly reluctant to let go, but Candace pulled away and jumped onto the bus.

The bus emptied at its original location and the girls climbed into Tasha's car in front of Warren's house. Candace didn't remember much else after Marci rolled her into bed and tucked her in before dipping back out the door to meet up with Warren.

When Candace climbed out of her sister's bed the next morning, Marci was already in the kitchen. The clock over the stove blinked 10:53.

"Girl, you should have given that boy some pussy. He was cute as shit and God knows you need some dick," Marci started in, pouring her orange juice.

"Shut up."

"He was on you all night."

"He was on my top." Candace took a cool sip. "And he was cute as shit."

"That he was," Marci said, grinning. "I saw ya'll chatting it up outside Rumor."

"He wanted to tag along."

"You should have let him; he'd a tapped that ass for ya."

"Everybody ain't as stank as you, Marcine."

Marci shrugged. "You only live once."

"I guess you would say that at twenty-three. He's ya age. Fuckin' kids. That's all ya'll think about. I got better things to do than broke-ass lil' boys."

"You's a tight ass. I got my back blown out last night. Sent his ass back to Iraq happy than a mothafucka."

Candace burst out laughing.

When it was time to go, Candace nudged a sleeping Manny from his curled-up position beside Marcus on the basement couch. Her phone sounded with a text message from Chris on her ride home.

I can't get you and that gold dress out of my mind. When can I see you? She texted back, in the mood to flirt, *Soon I hope.*

Candace awaited a savvy rebuttal, but there was none. She resisted the urge to dial back the number. She hadn't been out in a while and wasn't sure how the rules of dating worked anymore, but she was not eager to be chasing after some young kid.

She busied herself with cleaning and cooking most of that day. Emmanuel had gone out to play basketball down the street. Candace was home alone on a beautiful Saturday. She cracked her books and tried to get some studying done, but that tall, light-skinned boy was definitely on her mind. All day she was tormented by the image of his thick lips; still she refused to call him. The evening darkness gave way to different emotions and she could no longer resist picking up the phone while reflecting on his charming eyes. She caved and called, but he didn't answer and she didn't leave a message.

That evening Candace touched herself in her warm place until she erupted on her own fingertips before falling asleep. She dreamt of the young boy's mouth on the trim of her panties. She trudged through Sunday without a return call.

CHAPTER 4

"**C**andace, do you have the 401 book for the UMR review tomorrow?" Jennifer, the facility's admissions coordinator, asked, walking into Candace's small office Monday morning.

This bitch. Immediate agitation rose up Candace's spine like prickly vines. Without a word, she reached behind her, pulling a blue binder from one of the shelves. She handed it to Jennifer and returned to her desk.

The thin, late thirty-something woman's pale face stretched as she continued to prod. "Did you get those admissions I put in your box?"

"Not yet."

"Oh." Jennifer hesitated for a moment, then spoke again. "Well, make sure you get them. We need to have everything on point for tomorrow's big review. You are ready, right? You know it's going to be huge."

"Yup." Candace didn't look up, turning on her computer monitor and waiting for her machine to load.

"You've got all the files since October?" Jennifer continued with her inquisition.

"Yes."

"You know that they're going to look at all your billing and the patient accounts for all our medical assistance patients."

"I know what they are looking for, Jennifer." Candace's annoyance was almost boiling over. Jennifer enjoyed pushing at her nerves, but this morning was not the morning for foolishness.

Candace recognized Jennifer's disdain for her. She could tell from the way Jennifer grimaced when she addressed her, or how she always seemed to forget to speak in the mornings, how Jennifer never invited her to lunch like she did the other department heads or included her in any after-work social events. Candace thought Jennifer looked down on her because she had her associate's degree from community college and Jennifer always went on and on about her grand experiences at Penn State. Jennifer didn't know Candace was enrolled part time at Temple University taking courses toward her business management degree and Candace didn't care to share that information with her. It was none of her concern. Still, it could be Jennifer hated her because she was young, black and successful. Maybe it was both. Candace didn't know why the scrawny, pencil-necked white woman gave her so much grief and she didn't care much either. All she knew was Jennifer had better stay out of her way or things were going to get ugly.

Jennifer didn't seem to sense the tension building around Candace's temples. "Oh, by the way," she continued, "you know the company didn't do well last quarter, and I hear there are whispers of them starting up the AIT program again this year."

Candace's pupils widened. She remembered hearing about the Administrator in Training Program about three years ago. It was a fast-track program her company offered to become an administrator of a skilled nursing facility.

Oh wow, she thought. *I remember this.* Candace squinted her eyes, thinking hard about the opportunity. *When the company's short on leaders, they promote from within. This is the program for a qualified applicant to become an administrator ASAP. Need that!*

Candace knew she wasn't qualified when she'd first heard about the AIT program, but this time around, things were different. *I'm close as hell to getting my degree. I could really get this shit.* Candace sat up, intrigued. She knew department head managers were either nominated or applied to the program. *I need to figure out how.* Candace finally looked up at Jennifer. "I hadn't heard that."

Jennifer smiled. "Yes, you know regional staff makes their selection based upon openings, seniority, and performance. Especially performance in the state reviews like the one tomorrow."

Candace rolled her eyes.

Jennifer continued, "But I do believe you have to have a four-year degree. If I'm not mistaken."

Candace's French manicured nails made loud clacking sounds as she tapped her fingers against her desk. It never failed.

"You've been with the company a long time, right, Candace?"

Candace turned to face her; with twisted lips, she stared daringly into the pale woman's face.

Jennifer must not have noticed the disgusted look on Candace's face as she continued, "And you *only* have an associate's, right?"

"What's your point, Jennifer?" Candace swallowed the expletives trying to force their way out of her mouth. This is the workplace, she reminded herself.

"Well, I have my business administration degree from Penn State and I've been in this business a long time, but I wouldn't sign up for that if they handed it to me, even though I am more than qualified. It's so much work and I hear the exams are really difficult for some people. You know, being an administrator is sooo time-consuming. I mean it's an around-the-clock position. You practically have no life. You know, I could probably do it with my eyes closed, but I just wouldn't want to."

"What's your point, Jennifer?" Candace repeated, a slight growl behind her words.

"Nothing, nothing," the woman answered, backing out of the office. "I think you have to have all your ducks in a row before you get into a program like that. They review everything."

Candace stood up as Jennifer moved away. "I know," Candace said, placing one hand on the office door.

Jennifer opened her mouth to speak, but Candace closed the door in her face.

As soon as Candace sat back at her desk, she sent an email to one of her connections in Human Resources; she had to check the facts, searching for any truth to Jennifer's gossip.

Her fingers moved quickly across the keyboard.

Hey Sue,
How's it going? I heard the AIT program was opening up. Is there any truth to that?

The response came less than an hour later as Candace was returning to her office from the morning department head meeting. She read the email anxiously, her eyes scanning every word.

Hey Candace,
Fine. Thanks. How are things with you? And yes, from what I hear the AIT program is, in fact, in motion. There are a lot of administrator openings in the central and eastern regions so the big-wigs are looking to promote and fast. You'd have to have your bachelor's degree or have at least 80 credits in a degree program. Once you get in the program, you have to sit under a current administrator for mentoring and training. There are two courses you have to take. Then you have to sit for your state exam to get a nursing home license. Once you start the on the job

training the pay is $55K. But they're starting licensed Nursing Home Administrators at a minimum of $79K a year. The trick, though, is getting in. You've got to get nominated by your administrator and the word is there are only four seats in this region and two are already filled.

Are you going for it? I heard it's tough, but worth it. If you are, good luck, girl. ☺

This is it, Candace thought. She swallowed hard thinking of all the things she could do with that kind of money.

Umm. Her eyes rolled back softly and closed. *Almost $80 K a year. I could pay off my car, buy me some new fly shit. Like a Range Rover, umm. I could finally put a down payment on a house, send Manny to a good school, stack change for college. Umm...and a vacation. Yes. Lawd knows I need a vacation. Umm, you wouldn't be able to tell me nothin' with that kinda bread...*

Candace knew she was qualified for the job and opted not to let Jennifer get to her. She had bigger fish to fry. The upcoming review was no big deal, her figures were tight, but Candace had a paper due for her Applied Administration Theory course and her Medicare claims needed to be released. Her rent needed to be paid, Manny needed money for his trip, and she needed a break.

Candace sat back in her chair, eyes still closed. She inhaled deeply and released a heavy sigh. *This shit is crazy. Maybe Prince and Marci were right*, she thought. *I could use some good dick.*

CHAPTER 5

arci spun the deep-blue salon chair around and the seated older woman stopped directly in front of the round mirror at Marci's station; her sharp bob swaying to a perfect halt, causing her to smile. Marci smiled in return, contemplating the tip she knew she'd earned.

Old school classics from Teena Marie and Al Green settled as background noise in the bustling salon. Several ladies seated in the waiting area in the far-right corner chatted on over folded magazines and cell phones. The hooded hair dryers hummed. Blow-dryers buzzed. The smell of coconut oil and relaxer filled the air. Anxious customers filled every stylist's seat, ready for their hair to be parted and pulled. Beauticians leaned in to confirm cut, color and style. The washing station in the rear of the spacious salon held four full seats. Conditioner rinsed through the crimson basins. The phone rang, the front door opened and the young, petite receptionist with big brown eyes responded to both with warm salutations. It was an average Saturday morning at D's Designs. Marci's neighbor had brought her two teenage girls in to get their hair styled. Tyisha and Tasia took up two seats at the washing station talking and texting.

Cherise, the receptionist, stood from her seat at the front desk after she scribbled down a message and headed past Marci to the washing bowls.

"Who you want first?" she asked Marci, gesturing toward the teenage sisters.

"Tyisha, what you want?" Marci called to the oldest girl.

"I want a wash, blow-dry and curl," the bright-faced girl said. "She wants some tracks." She nodded toward her sister. The girl beside her held up a short pack of curly black hair.

"Wash Tyisha first," Marci instructed Cherise, "then do Tasia and set her under the dryer."

"You movin' 'em, huh, girl?" Quinita, the red-haired, high-yellow stylist to Marci's left, asked with a smile.

Marci smiled back. "You know it, boo. I got things to do."

"I know that's right." Quinita tapped the shoulder of the woman still seated in front of Marci. "And you look good, miss lady. That cut is sharp on you. Oh, I see Imma enjoy havin' you around, Marci. You do the damn thing with some scissors, girl."

Marci beamed. "Don't I?" She turned back to the woman in the chair. "Come on, Miss Charmaine. I'll ring you out."

"I think you should let me do that," a scratchy voice called out from the corner of the salon. Marci rolled her eyes as Lateesh moved nearer. "You know Donna ain't goin' want your new hands all over her register," the girl snapped at Marci but her voice softened, extending a hand to Miss Charmaine who was silent. "I'll take you up front."

The woman did not move. Marci tapped her client, an old friend of her mother, gently on the shoulder. "Go 'head, Miss Charmaine, it's fine."

The older woman rose to her feet and dug her hand into the front of her cream-colored blouse, pulling a neatly folded ten-dollar bill from her bosom. She stuffed the bill in Marci's hand.

"Here you go, baby," Miss Charmaine said with a soft neck roll before she turned to follow the short, brown-skinned girl with the asymmetrical cut to the front.

"Thanks," Marci said. Her eyes steady on Lateesh, Marci shook her head and released a hefty sigh.

"Don't sweat that chick," Jerel, the stylist to her right, spoke up, sucking her teeth. "She don't have nuffin else to do than ride Donna dick. Even when she ain't here."

Marci laughed. She liked Jerel who was short and sassy and rocked a fierce Mohawk with shaved sides and had the widest hips and biggest ass Marci had ever seen. She teased Jerel often, telling her "a booty like that didn't belong on someone so short."

Jerel responded by turning around and twerking her round cheeks. "I know how to work this thang, though."

Marci was fond of all of her new colleagues, with the exception of Lateesh, who was the shop owner Donna's puppet. Come to think of it, she didn't like Donna much either. Donna was a tyrant of a boss. She gossiped uncontrollably, flaunted her gaudy jewelry and expensive bags around the shop, and seldom had a nice thing to say to anyone other than the customers and Lateesh ever so often.

"She don't want it wit' me," Marci responded to Jerel as they both stared with twisted lips in Lateesh's direction.

Marci was sewing the track into Tasia's braided scalp when the salon door opened and her girlfriend Tasha walked in.

"What's up, girl?" Tasha spoke to Marci from under a hunter green army hat. She surveyed the well-decorated, blue and green salon. "This where you at now, girl? This cute."

They hugged before Tasha took a seat across from Marci's station. She continued her conversation loud enough for her words to be heard across the room. "Bitch, I am tired as hell."

Marci looked up from the girl's scalp. "You still seeing Terrence?"

"Girl, he just left this morning. He on his way to New York, then he gets deployed back to Iraq tomorrow. I'm sad."

"Awww. You stupid."

"I love him. Whenever he come home, we have a fuckin' ball."

Donna, who had returned to the salon and was seated behind the register, nosily turned her head in Tasha's direction, "Watch ya mouth in the salon, ladies. We ain't in no bar."

Tasha turned to Marci. "Who she talking to?"

"Shut up, Tash."

"What?" Tasha rolled her eyes and crossed her legs. "I'm grown. Shit."

Either Donna didn't hear her or she pretended not to, because she didn't say a word.

"You talked to Warren?" Tasha asked Marci while scratching at her hat.

"Nope, he been left. I should be getting a letter soon. You know he gave me back five hundred dollars for all the liquor we bought that night."

"Awww, that was sweet. It was his birthday."

"I know, right? I told him he didn't have to, but he insisted. So you know I took that shit."

Marci clenched as soon as she finished the last of her sentence and looked in Donna's direction. She had heard that one.

"All right, little Miss Marci, I'm not goin' warn you again about your language. Next time I'm gonna fine you. Clear?"

Marci nodded.

"And that goes for everyone else, this is a family-friendly salon. We don't have that nonsense going on in here."

Tasha rolled her eyes. "Bitch," she mouthed to Marci who struggled to keep in the chuckle. Tasha scratched her hat again.

Marci's eyes tilted inward. "What's under there?" she asked.

"Girl, you don't wanna know."

Marci laughed. She picked up the curling iron and began to press out the weave she'd put in. "Take off ya hat. Lemme see," she instructed.

Tasha pulled the army cap off her head and a matted mess of curly weave fell to her shoulders. Marci, Jerel and Quinita gasped, then all burst into laughter. Tasha joined in.

"Y'all ain't gotta do me like that." She chuckled. "I had a rough weekend."

"We see that," Jerel joked.

By the time Tasha made it to Marci's chair for her style, Donna had stepped outside.

"That's your boss?" Tasha asked while Marci draped the cloth over her shoulders.

"Yeah."

"Y'all cool?"

"Not really, she's fuckin' annoying. The loud hype type."

"Oh, I know what you mean. She need a fuckin' girdle, fat-ass belly." They both laughed. "So you still seeing the bul Tommy?"

"Of course," Marci squealed. "That's my boo. I seen him last night."

She hung her wrist over Tasha's shoulder and a shiny silver bracelet dangled down her slender hand.

"That's from him?" Tasha asked, admiring the charms.

"Yup, I get a new charm every time I be a good girl."

Marci began to clip out the sewn-in weave she'd given Tasha a few weeks earlier. She was in a groove when the salon door swung open and Donna stepped in carrying several hair care bags.

"Cherise," Donna shouted at the receptionist. "Come help my husband get these boxes of conditioner."

Cherise jumped, as if catapulted from her seat and scurried out the door behind Donna.

"That bitch got a husband?" Tasha gasped. "Oh, I must be doing something wrong."

Marci, trying to hold back her laughter, chimed in, "Yeah, but I ain't never seen him. She always be like 'my husband this' or 'my husband that.' I bet he a funny-lookin' dude and prolly be fuckin' around on her ass all the time."

"Could you blame him?"

Marci had Tasha's hair in thin parts holding the left quarter of her locks in her palm. The front door swung open again. Donna wobbled in with more bags only this time a handsome Dominican-looking dude strolled in behind her carrying several boxes.

"Tomas, come on, baby. Take them down to the basement," Donna instructed.

Marci's throat clamped tight as the man entered. She damn near screamed clutching Tasha's hair in a tight fist.

Tasha let out a high-pitched yelp and everyone in the salon turned to face them, including Tomas. Marci could not stop staring, but Tasha's lashing against her arm quickly brought her back around.

"Awwww. Gotdamn! Marci, what the hell was that?"

"I…I…uh…"

"Damn, girl," Tasha whined, rubbing her sore scalp. She looked up at Marci who was still staring in the direction of the handsome man, descending the basement stairs behind Donna. Tasha nudged her. "Girl, that's her husband? He fine as hell."

Marci leaned forward into Tasha's ear, her lips quivering through the whisper. "That's Tommy."

"What?!"

Tomas came out of the basement alone. He paused in front of Marci's station, smiling. "Looking good, ladies," he said, winking at Marci.

CHAPTER 6

"How can I help you, Candace?" Denise, the dark-eyed Italian administrator, asked, looking up at her from a clutter of files on her desk.

"Denise, I'd like to talk to you about the Administrator in Training program."

"What about it?" Denise replied, sitting back in her large black leather chair.

"I would like to formally submit my application for consideration to the program." Candace rushed the words out of her mouth. Her heart was beating faster than she'd anticipated. She took a deep breath and continued. "I believe my experience within the company would prove a viable asset and I am currently working toward my B.S. in business management. I am confident that I will exceed all expectations of what is required of the position."

Denise leaned back in her chair and crossed her arms atop her small breasts. She smirked, raising her head in a nod of acceptance.

"Well, thank you, Candace. I will take that into consideration."

Candace suppressed the rumbling growl that was growing in her. *Into consideration? Bitch! Is she serious?* Candace forced a smile. "Thank you," she said, turning to exit the office. As she pulled the office door open, Candace found Jennifer standing directly behind it. Candace grimaced as Jennifer passed her.

"I have to talk to you about this afternoon's admission," Candace heard Jennifer say to Denise, as she closed the office door behind her.

Bigger fish, Candace reminded herself. She toyed with the notion of snatching Jennifer up into a closet. *Nobody would miss that bitch.* But Candace decided against it. It wouldn't do much good for her career to have a skinny white woman's body fall out of her office closet in the middle of a meeting.

After work, Candace pressed the button behind her steering wheel that changed the radio station. Mary J. Blige's "Real Love" came bursting through her speakers. Candace turned it up and sang along as she headed home.

"Doc B be jammin'," she said to herself, singing aloud to the local DJ's five o'clock spin. She whipped her car coolly along Stenton Avenue and before long, she was pulling in front of her apartment. Candace pushed her key in the door and exhaled loudly.

It's good to be home, she thought. Emmanuel would be home any minute from his after-school program. She changed her clothes quickly and began preparing dinner.

Candace was sitting cross-legged in pink-and-gray Victoria's Secret sweats on her sage sofa when she called down the hall to her son. "Manny!"

"Yea, Ma?" he called back.

"What are you doing?"

"Playin' my game!"

Candace sat up on the sofa in her small living room, eyes fixed on her favorite show, *Law & Order SVU*. She waited for a commercial before she headed into the kitchen to check on dinner.

Baked chicken crisping in the oven, and rice and peas simmering on the stove, both left the room aromatic. She pulled the golden chicken out, checking over to the living room television to make sure she didn't miss any of her show. The large TV sat on a black storage unit that housed her DVD collection on the far side of the room. Her coffee table and comfy sofa sat directly across from it. Her bookshelf with her books from school and her leisurely readings were in the right corner of the room, and pictures of herself and her handsome son, photos of her mother and Marci were strewn over the off-white walls. She rested on the edge of the sofa, allowing dinner to cool. The credits rolled and Candace prepared her son a plate.

"Come eat, Manny!"

The hip-hop soundtrack resonating from his PlayStation 2 came to a quick pause. He moved down the hall in smooth bounds.

"Go wash your hands!"

Emmanuel stopped the bound, hung a U-turn and headed back down the hall toward the bathroom. When he made it to the kitchen, his brown hands were dripping wet. Emmanuel reached to pet the moisture off on his pants, but Candace shoved a dry towel at him. He accepted, patted his hands dry and slam-dunked the crumpled ball into the trash can before he plopped down at the chrome and white dining table.

"Mom, Isaiah said his daddy is going to jail."

"Omigod, Manny. Why? What happened?"

"He said his dad was fighting his mom's boyfriend and she called the police and now his dad going to jail."

"Oh my," was all Candace could manage.

Emmanuel bit into his chicken. "Yup, and Isaiah is mad with his mom."

Candace winced.

"Isaiah said he hated her 'cause now he can't see his dad and he don't like her boyfriend no way."

"Poor Isaiah."

"I woulda beat him up, huh," Emmanuel declared.

"Beat up who?"

"Her boyfriend."

"Why?"

"'Cause Isaiah said he's always mean and loud and he don't share the TV."

"That's no reason to be violent, Manny."

"Yes, it is, Ma. Nobody better not be mean to you, else I will beat them up."

"And you will go to jail, son."

"So! Nobody betta not be mean to my mom. If my dad was home, he wouldn't let nobody be mean to us. He would beat 'em up."

"And that's why your dad is in jail now."

Emmanuel pouted and turned his gaze. Candace noticed the offense run through his dark eyes. She winced again. The subject of Emmanuel's father was one she always approached with caution. To Emmanuel, Prince could do no wrong, and she struggled to maintain the image of a loving man her son adored though she knew Prince could be a monster. But that savage beast never existed to Emmanuel, and, as far as Candace was concerned, the longer she could keep it that way, the better. Still, never wanting Emmanuel to follow in Prince's footsteps, she weaved the truth with subtle omissions.

"Do you want to be like that? Like your dad?"

Emmanuel lowered his dark eyes, his full thick lashes fluttering. He didn't respond.

"You have to want better to do better. You goin' follow the pack and do dumb stuff like your dad? He chose to do things that he ain't have to do."

"You gotta do what you gotta do; that's what my dad says."

"Well, Man, you still have choices."

"What if you don't have a choice? What if there is only one thing that you can do?"

"You always have options, Emmanuel. Sometimes they ain't easy choices and it may be hard, but you have to choose to work hard and try hard or you goin' just be average or get caught up in dumbness, just like your father."

Candace stared into her son's beautiful eyes. She didn't like to direct such harsh criticism toward Prince, but how else could she reaffirm how important it was for her son to make the right decisions in life?

"You can choose what you want to do with your life, Man. You don't have to be like anybody else. You can do whatever you want. You hear me? All you have to do is work hard. Life is not easy and it's not gonna always be fair. But the choices you make when things are hard separate you from the men who got big houses and fancy cars from the knuckleheads behind bars."

Emmanuel nodded.

"Do you follow me, Son?"

"Yea, Mom."

She laughed to herself when Emmanuel leapt from the table. *There's something new to parenting every day*, she thought. There would be many more talks to come.

The following week after her usual morning meeting with the department head team, Candace heard Denise Valinoti's voice blasting through the loudspeaker summoning her to the office.

Candace was quickly on her feet scurrying down the hall.

"I know that you are interested in the AIT program and think that you are very capable, Candace," Denise began once Candace was in the room. Candace held her breath anticipating the words coming from her administrator's mouth. "It is a rigorous program; you do understand that?"

"I do."

"You have been in this building for several years now and have managed well in every task," Denise spoke calmly and slowly.

Candace was nodding her head and trying to keep calm when she heard a knock on the door behind her.

"It's me," Jennifer called, pushing the door open. Candace's shoulders sank, *Not this bitch. Not right now.*

"You wanted to see me?" Jennifer asked Denise.

See her? For what? Doesn't matter. Not now, bitch. Bye. I'm 'bout to get this AIT position and I'm outta here.

"Yes," Denise replied. "Come in and close the door."

Jennifer complied, stepping in and standing beside Candace.

What the fuck?

"Jennifer, I was just explaining to Candace how well she has done since she has been with us. Wouldn't you agree?"

"Of course. Of course," Jennifer raved.

"Well," Denise continued. "I can say the same for you, Jennifer. Wouldn't you agree, Candace?"

Candace nodded, speechless. *What the hell is she getting at?*

"Good, ladies. Then you can see my dilemma. I have an opportunity to catapult one of you into a great program that will move you forward not only in this company but in your careers entirely."

One of us? The words did somersaults in her head as Candace fought to keep her eyes focused on Denise.

"As you know the company is promoting the Administrator in Training Program again this year and the slots in this region are few. Three seats have already been filled. I have a few connections,"

Denise said with a smile, "and this final seating belongs to the building."

Jennifer wriggled her shoulders. Candace dug her heels into the floor. Her chest heaved anticipating the words from Denise's mouth.

"The seat belongs to one of you."

Jennifer giggled clapping her hands.

No. No. No. No. No. Nooo! Candace wanted to scream. *This bitch is serious. Ohmigod, Denise, you're trippin'. You and this conniving bitch.*

"This is so exciting," Jennifer spoke up.

"It is indeed, Jennifer," Denise added. "With two overly qualified candidates in front of me, it is impossible for me to make a quick decision. So, from this point on, consider yourselves in the running. The two of you will be competing for the last AIT slot. There will be opportunities provided to you to prove yourself through a series of tests or challenges set up by myself as well as Dick Burny, the regional director. He will be visiting the building frequently and will be assisting me in monitoring your work, your progress, consumer interaction, conflict resolution and problem-solving skills amongst many other key factors deemed necessary in facility administration. This is no small feat, ladies. Whichever one of you secures this slot is looking at a large salary increase and immediate transfer to begin the mentorship portion of the program."

These bitches got it out for me. I have to get out of this building. Candace was silent, her face a stone.

Jennifer bounced with delight.

"Candace, are you okay?" Denise asked.

Like you give a fuck? I'mma get this job, get my own building and both y'all can kiss my black ass.

Candace nodded. "I am fine...more than fine."

"Yes," Jennifer interjected. "This will be fun. I am looking forward to this. Aren't you, Candace?"

Candace's lips burned as they thinned across the bottom of her face into a tight smile. "I sure am."

"Great," Denise said with finality. "Well, ladies, all I can advise you at this point is to be on the top of your game because we are watching." And with that, Denise dismissed both Candace and Jennifer from her office.

Jennifer stepped out into the lobby first and turned to Candace as she spoke, "You know, this *really* will be enjoyable."

Candace's eyes narrowed; she could feel the heat rising up the front of her chest but could not speak the words that spun circles behind her folded lips.

You muthafuckin', stupid-ass, lyin'-ass, dipsy fuckin' bitch...I swear to...oooohhhh...this BITCH...

CHAPTER 7

*T*his is unbelievable, Candace thought, massaging her temples and waiting for the light to change on Flourtown Road. Candace's shoulders slumped heavy with the weight of the day's frustrations. Her eyebrows furrowed thinking of Jennifer's shrewd grin and trying to shake the image away before she made it home. Her phone rang before she could clear her thoughts.

"Hey, ma," Emmanuel spoke excitedly.

"Hey, babe."

"Uncle B called. He havin' a cookout and Grandma P said bring our asses."

"Boy," Candace hissed into the phone.

"Bye, Mom. See when you get here," Emmanuel said, hanging up the phone as Candace shook her head again.

Just like Brother, Candace thought. *The first day of warm weather in the city of Philadelphia and this nigga havin' a cookout.*

Emmanuel was outside sitting on the step with his blue book bag between his legs when Candace turned the corner. He stood up rushing toward the street as she approached.

"Ma, can I stay the weekend at Uncle B's?" he asked through the window before Candace parked.

"Well, hello to you, too," she said, coolly lifting her shades.

"Hi, Mom. How was your day?"

Candace winced. "Don't ask."

Emmanuel looked puzzled, his eyes lowered and lips protruding.

"Why? What happened?" he asked, leaning into the clean black Accord.

"They out to get me, Son," Candace said with an exaggerated sigh.

"Who? Who out to get you?"

"Get in," Candace instructed.

Emmanuel complied, bouncing around the car so he could hop in the passenger side.

"You not gonna change your clothes?" he asked, sliding into the seat. Emmanuel snapped his seatbelt and looked over at his mother.

She looked down at herself: gray slacks, peep-toe black pumps and a soft white blouse that wrapped around her waist and tied in the back. "Nah, I don't even feel like it, babe."

"Why, Ma? What's wrong? And who out to get you?"

His inquisition made her smile. "These crazy-ass women at my job, Man."

Emmanuel nodded with full attention.

"I'm going out for a big promotion, baby. And these wenches are trying to stop me."

"Yeah?" he asked with concern.

"Yeah, but don't worry about it. Your mama got this. I'mma show these broads what I can do."

"Okay, Ma," Emmanuel cheered. "That's what's up. Whatchu going be doin'?"

"Imma be doin' the damn thing," Candace boasted.

Emmanuel laughed. "No, Mom. I mean the job. Like, what's the promotion?"

"Oh." Candace chuckled at herself. "It's to be a nursing home administrator."

"That's what's up, Ma. Yeah!" he shouted. "You goin' be the boss, of like, the whole building?"

"Not that building, but one of my own, Son. Yes. That's the plan."

"That's what's up," he repeated, smiling.

"Well, don't cheer yet. I have to get the job first."

"Aw, Mom. You got it. Don't even sweat it."

"Thank you for the encouragement, baby. But it's a choice between me and someone else, and I think my boss might like her better," Candace responded, navigating down Cheltenham Avenue.

"That ain't cool."

"I know."

Emmanuel was silent for a moment. "Well, don't matter who they *like*. If they want the best person who goin' keep everybody in check and make sure stuff gets done, then they goin' pick you," he said matter-of-factly.

"Aww, thank you, Son." She reached over and patted his leg. "You really think so, huh?"

"I know so."

"You're the best, kid." She smiled.

"No, you're the best, Mom. And you got this job hands down."

Candace was still smiling when she pulled into the parking lot in the rear of Lynnewood Gardens, the luxury apartment complex on Cheltenham Avenue directly across from the Cheltenham Mall.

As she parked and noticed the crowd gathered on the lawn, Candace laughed at how right she was; the weather was welcoming and only Brother would have an impromptu cookout on a Friday afternoon and get the whole apartment complex rocking.

Brother was good fun; his whole family was, even his mother, Emmanuel's grandmother, Miss P, who always wore a huge smile on her tiny dark face. She was a short and petite, dark-skinned woman with gray hair so short Brother kept it faded for her.

There had never been any bad blood between Prince's kin and Candace. They'd always welcomed her with open arms and showered Emmanuel with all their love, as well. Hanging out with this side of Emmanuel's family always provided her a good laugh, a stiff drink and some reminiscing.

Candace and Emmanuel moved into the crowd in the wide grassy area in the rear of the apartment where Brother lived with his girlfriend, Charlie. Charlie bounced up to Candace when she saw her crossing the lawn. She beamed with bright salutations. "Hey, Candace!" the young, curvy girl shouted, throwing her arms around Candace's shoulders.

Candace tightened up, patting her back quickly and stepping out of the hold. *This dippy broad is always extra excited*, Candace thought, giving the young girl, who was bent over beside her squeezing Emmanuel, the once-over.

"C'mon, everybody's here," Charlie announced, standing up straight. She was much shorter than Candace but far more full in hips and breasts.

Candace and Emmanuel followed Charlie toward the grill. Brother was sipping a Corona and smoking a cigarette with one hand while flipping burgers with the other.

"What up, C? Hey, Man," he said, raising his drink in the air. Candace hugged Brother, seeing her own son in his eyes. Emmanuel darted across the grass toward his cousins as Candace propped up her feet on a lawn chair next to Miss P.

Charlie brought her a red plastic cup to help ease her load and Candace took strong swallows of Bacardi and cranberry. The music from the speakers boomed across the yard as people mixed and mingled with full plastic plates and cups and Candace nodded her head to the beat. She was having a good time grooving to the tunes and shooting the breeze with Miss P, until she glanced up from her cup to see Aisha sashaying across the grass. Aisha smirked as she spotted Candace. Candace's stomach knotted while her eyes rolled. *Here we go.*

Aisha was small in stature, like Miss P, but not as dark in complexion. She was a pretty brown color with a little waist and skinny neck that jutted out between her pointy shoulders. Two pretty chocolate girls lagged behind her, Prince's girls. They climbed the green hill, pushing each other side to side as they went. They were the same color brown as Emmanuel and beautiful beyond a shadow of a doubt.

Candace stared at their swinging pigtails. *What are they? Like seven, now?*

She paid no mind to Aisha, who stepped in close to speak to Brother and Miss P. The skinny girl kissed her kids' grandmother, the grandmother they shared with Emmanuel, on the cheek and retreated toward the coolers without a word in Candace's direction.

Candace knew Aisha didn't care for her. For whatever reason, Aisha never spoke directly to Candace. She always scowled when she saw her and the most disappointing of all, she never allowed her daughters to see Emmanuel except for when they were with their grandmother. Miss P didn't play like that and she made sure her grandkids knew each other.

"Second Baby Mama Syndrome," Candace called it. She assumed Aisha was angry Prince still kept in touch and would do anything for her and Emmanuel. Candace needed a lot less help than Aisha, who didn't work and collected checks from the government.

If she want better, she need to do better, Candace thought.

Aisha hadn't been at the party twenty minutes before Candace could feel the chill of her icy gaze. Aisha stood nearby chatting off some girl's ear, and with her neck extended and eyes rolling, she stared at Candace.

"Here this bitch go," Candace mumbled to herself. She could overhear Aisha and the other chick laughing loud and hard as she poured herself another drink.

"Girl, she think she cute! It's a fucking cookout; like come on with the fuckin' bitness attire."

Candace cringed. She'd already had enough of the bullshit at work and decided it was time to go. She looked for her son, who of course, wanted to stay; his overnight bag was already in his uncle's apartment. Candace knew he would be fine. She tapped Brother on the shoulder before she left. "You got something for me?" she asked in his ear.

"Whatchu want, C?" His voice was like Prince's.

"Some tree," she whispered.

Brother slid his hand into his front pocket under his apron that read *Bros. B-B-Que!* He retrieved a small plastic baggie and slipped it into Candace's palm.

"Smoke it slow," he advised. "It's some killa."

Candace looked down at the thick marijuana-stuffed bag in her hand. She tossed it in her purse, and still clutching her red cup, headed toward Emmanuel in the grass.

He looked up as she approached and ran to her.

"Be good, Son," she warned, squeezing him while staring over at Prince's twin girls.

Emmanuel nodded and darted off.

So she pulled off, on a beautiful Friday evening without her son and with nowhere to go. The tall, light-skinned boy from the club crossed her mind.

Maybe I could have a little fun, she thought. Candace tossed back more of her drink before setting it in the cup holder and picking up her phone to call his number. The phone rang and went to voicemail. She didn't leave a message.

After a frustrating day at work and unnecessary heat and attitude from Aisha, Candace decided she was ready to go home for some well-deserved rest.

She needed to grab some dutches for the dime bag Brother had stuffed into her palm. Candace rode with all the windows rolled down letting the air smack her in the face as she tried to focus on the road. She pulled into a gas station off Stenton Avenue and began digging in her wallet for some loose bills. Her head was down when a blue 745i pulled up directly beside her causing her to squint at the bright lights. She rolled her eyes, then stepped out of the car and bounced into the store. Candace retrieved what she needed and was about to step back into her black Accord when she heard a husky voice behind her.

"You good, honey?" He was outside leaning on his car.

"Yes, thank you," she replied quickly to the large man with the thick mustache standing beside the shiny BMW.

"You are a beautiful young lady. Your old man let you out by yourself?"

"I don't have an old man."

"Then maybe you need one." He grinned moving in closer. He handed her his business card: *Ty Jefferies*, gas station and tow truck company owner. Candace looked over at the tow trucks on the side of the parking lot that read: *Jeff's Tow*.

"Only God knows what I need right now," she said, slightly under her breath.

"Maybe I can help," he continued. "See, I'm a businessman, baby. I know how to take advantage of a situation, how to get things done. You know what I mean?" His smile widened and thin lines crept under his eyes.

Candace looked down at the card, then back up at the large man standing in front of her. *He's a big old head*, she thought, checking out his round belly. *But he's kinda fly.*

"I think I get it, Ty," she said.

"Bam, baby. Call me Bam," he said, smiling and looking Candace up and down. "You look like you had a good night."

"Bam, huh?" Candace confirmed. "It was all right."

Her eyes were glassy as she leaned back against her car still hold-ing the wrapped cigar in her hand.

"You smoke that stuff?" Bam asked, eyeing the cigar.

"That's none of your concern."

"Pick your poison, brown sugar." He shrugged. "I'm a Southern Comfort man, myself." He paused and looked her up and down again. "And pretty women, um, yes. I gets myself in trouble every time."

Candace stared, taking all of him in. He was big, tall, at least six feet three inches and well over 260 pounds: round in the shoulders, round in the face and round in the belly.

"I would love to take you to get something to eat in the morning," Bam said. "It's only a couple hours 'til the sun rises."

Candace smirked. His smile and pockets were wide enough to forgive his size, but she still felt a little uneasy about the gray streaks in his hair and on his face.

"We'll see," she replied, opening her car door.

Bam stepped aside as Candace slipped into her car, then he leaned into her window once she settled down in her seat. "Well, make sure you give me a call, gorgeous. It'd be my pleasure to take you out to breakfast."

Candace smiled and pulled away into the night. When she reached her empty apartment, Candace settled in for another lonely night. At home, she rolled the weed in the dutch, took a few puffs and masturbated before she fell asleep.

It was loneliness that prompted Candace to reach for the busi-ness card in her wallet and call Bam by ten the next morning. He answered on the third ring.

"Baby girl, you feeling the effects of last night? Would you like to get some breakfast?"

"Yea, I think I'd like that."

"I can come pick you up. Or would you like to meet me some-where?" he asked coolly.

"You can meet me on my block in a half hour," Candace said, still under the covers. She gave Bam directions, making sure to leave out her exact address. And he arrived promptly in thirty minutes, clean-shaven and smiling hard from ear to ear. He must have enjoyed the sight of Candace in her fitted jeans and tight gray tee; he grinned from the moment she saw him turn the corner and set his eyes on her. He slowed his car to where she stood on the curb and Candace heard the power locks pop inside the BMW. Bam rolled down his window and stuck his head out, still smiling. "Good morning, gorgeous," he said cheerfully.

Candace hesitated at the hood of the car. *This fat mothfucka is really not goin' open my door?* Bam was still seated and smiling. Candace shook her head and continued walking toward the passenger side. *Chivalry really is dead.*

Bam started in as soon as she slid into the seat. "You are a beautiful woman," he stated. "Why are you single, again?"

"By choice," she responded, staring straight ahead.

"Good choice."

Candace glanced over at her companion, unsure of what to say. But she didn't have to worry; in a few seconds, Bam was into a story of his own, chatting on about how he dropped out of college and worked at a gas station and now he owned his own gas station, and his towing business was doing very well. He spoke the entire ride about his accomplishments, his money, his guilty pleasures. Candace feigned interest, smiling and nodding as he spoke. Her opportunity to interject finally presented itself once they were seated at a small table at the Cracker Barrel restaurant in Conshohocken.

"How old are you?" she blurted out as soon as Bam closed his mouth and picked up his menu.

"How old do I look?

"I don't know, fifty."

Bam smirked. "Forty-nine. And you?"

"Twenty-eight."

"I have a daughter your age. My baby girl is twenty-five."

"You date a lot of women your daughter's age?"

"I date beautiful women, Miss Candace. I'm not preferential to age. I like to enjoy my life and I enjoy having nice things and beautiful women around me. You know what I mean?"

Candace nodded.

"I don't want you to be shy with me." He placed his hand on her thigh under the table.

Candace abruptly pushed it aside. "I'm not shy at all. I've just never dated a man your age before."

"Does my age bother you?"

"Honestly? A little."

"Why?"

"You're old as my mother."

Bam laughed nervously. "Is your mother as fine as you?"

Candace laughed aloud. "Yes, I get it honest. Why? You want her number?"

"Nah, I think I'll keep what I got."

"You ain't got nothing yet, Mr. Bam."

Bam smiled. "I got a pretty lil' thing on my hands and I just want to be your friend. Is that all right with you?"

Candace shrugged. "I can't argue with that."

"Good, Candace. I'm trying to show you a good time. Take you some nice places, introduce you to some nice people. You not too busy to have a little fun, are you?"

Candace peered into the slanted eyes above his sheepish, chubby grin. There was something there she couldn't put her finger on.

"It depends on what kind of fun you talking about."

"I'm into all kinds of things." He patted her knee. "You'll see. Bam goin' take good care of you."

Candace looked over her menu and placed her order once the waitress returned. Bam stared over at Candace who brushed away the thin wisps of hair that fell into her face.

"Your hair is beautiful," he remarked. "Do you ever wear it up?"

Candace peered up from her glass of orange juice. "Sometimes."

"How much does it cost?" he asked.

"How much does what cost?"

"Your hair. If I offered to pay for you to get your hair done up, would you be offended? Would you do it?"

"I might."

A wide smile eased across Bam's even wider face. "Good."

The waitress appeared setting full plates in front of them on the table. Candace dug into her omelet. Bam chomped on a Southern-style smothered steak with scrambled cheese eggs. He stopped chewing to ask a question.

"So how much is it?"

"How much is…oh, my hair? About fifty bucks for an up-do."

Bam reached for his wallet in his back pocket. He pulled out a hundred-dollar bill, placing it on the table.

Candace was still for a moment, not sure of his intentions.

He pushed the bill toward her.

She stared at him, eyes narrowed.

"That's for you, sweet lady," Bam insisted, pushing the bill closer to her.

Candace reached slowly, taking the money in her palm. "Thank you."

Bam smiled. "My pleasure, babe. You will learn being friends with Bam has its benefits. I think we will be good friends. You are so sweet, so compromising."

Candace winced. *Compromising.* She didn't like that word.

But Bam continued his boasting. "I want you to wear your hair up when I take you out. I know you like to shop; what woman doesn't? Maybe we can take a trip to New York. Would you like that?"

"I might."

"We'll see how that goes, huh? If you enjoy my company, then maybe I could take you on a big getaway to Vegas."

"Vegas?" Candace's eyes widened.

"Yeah, some of my old boys are getting together for some gambling and drinking. Couple of good fellas, like me. I been looking for the right young lady to be my escort for the weekend. Limousines, powerful business men, play a couple games, catch a couple shows. Does that sound like something you might like?"

"Maybe." *I haven't been on a vacation in a long time,* Candace thought. *Maybe I should keep this big nigga close. He may be good for something.*

"I've got plenty time to help make up your mind," Bam gabbed on. "I'm goin' make sure I see you as much as I can until then."

As Bam drove her home, Candace's mind wandered to thoughts of being spoiled and taking trips she didn't have to pay for. Still there was something about Bam that left her unsettled. *What are his intentions? He just wants to spoil me and fuck me,* she thought as Bam leaned in for a kiss when they pulled back in front of her apartment. She pecked him lightly on the cheek before hopping out of the car.

Once inside her apartment, she tossed the money Bam had given her onto the dresser after stripping out of her jeans. Though she was thankful for the cash, there was something off about this guy who was willing to push a hundred-dollar bill in her hand their first time out. Something wasn't right. Candace remembered what her mother used to tell her and the old adage resounded in her head: nothing in life is free.

CHAPTER 8

The blue Charger pulled into Marci's driveway, causing her to bolt toward the front door. She flung it open to see Tommy step onto the path in front of her house; her heart thudded watching him approach.

"You ain't shit, Tommy! Why you ain't tell me you had a fuckin' wife?" she screamed from the foyer.

"I told you I had a situation, baby," he said in a low whine, approaching her.

"You said *your girl* was just helping you get your feet off the ground, not your fucking wife. You're married to that bitch, like really fucking down-the-aisle-wedding-ceremony married to Donna! My boss!" Her arms flailed wildly.

"Baby, calm down," Tommy responded, moving closer.

Marci propped a hand on her exaggerated hip, swinging her finger rhythmically in Tommy's face.

"Don't mothafuckin' baby me, you lyin' son of a bitch! And you knew what salon I was at. I been told you when I first started working there and you ain't say shit!"

"I know, baby, I..."

Marci rolled her eyes. "What the fuck if I'd a made nice with Donna and yesterday I just so happened to have been talkin' about my man, and she woulda been talking about her husband. And oh, turns out we talkin' 'bout the same sneaky mothafucka!"

"Marci, baby," he begged, stepping close to her with arms extended.

"You gotta hear me out. I don't love that girl. All she about is flaunting and her money and showing off for her funky-ass friends. I married her when I was dumb and broke and she took care of me. But there's no way she could have my heart; it was too easy to give it to you."

Marci stepped out of his reach, turning her back and heading in the house, then down the long hall to her room.

Tommy quickly followed, continuing his plea. "I didn't want to scare you off. When you told me where you was working, I was already feeling you. I was like, fuck, you know? I'm not trying to put you in a situation like that. I'm not trying to see you hurt."

In her bedroom, Marci leaned back against her cluttered dresser and stared at Tommy.

He moved slowly in to her again.

She raised her hand to his chest. "Tommy, I don't…"

"I know you can't fuck with me no more." He grabbed her hand, staring into her with deep pleading eyes.

She pushed his hand off. "I do what I want!"

"Then what's the problem, baby? I want to be with you, you know that. I love looking at that beautiful body."

Marci folded her arms across her chest, poking out her lips.

Tommy grinned, sliding his hand around her waist. "I love kissing your sweet lips." He pressed his mouth into hers. "I love touching you."

Marci pinched her pelvic muscles.

"You want me to stop?"

Marci did not respond. Eyes closed, she swallowed his wet kisses.

"Baby, do you want me to stop?" He persisted with his hands squeezing her firmly.

Marci pushed away and stepped toward her bed. She sat down tucking one leg beneath her, extending the other to the floor and pulling a pillow onto her lap.

"This shit ain't cool, Tommy. What am I supposed to do every day lookin' at that bitch?"

"Aye, I know, baby," he pleaded, dropping to his knees in front of the bed and reaching for her hand. "I know I am asking a lot from you, but I need you to be patient with me."

"Why the fuck did you lie to me, Tommy?" Marci placed both feet on the ground and turned her body toward him.

"I didn't want to lose you."

A slight smile rose on Marci's lips.

Tommy leaned in to kiss her strongly, deeply and with passion resonating from his hips to Marci's heart.

Her shoulders fell as she indulged in his embrace.

"You want me to go?" Tommy asked between kisses.

"No, baby," Marci moaned.

"No?"

"No." She raised her chin allowing his wet lips to move down her neck.

His hands moved the pillow aside and he quickly found her waist and pulled her forward on the bed into him. "Do you want me to stop?"

Marci was silent, eyes closed contemplating the pulsation between her thighs.

"Do you want me to stop?" he repeated.

"No," she stammered, spreading her arms open around his neck.

Tommy grabbed her from under her backside and stood lifting her up. She wrapped her legs around his waist, still kissing his full lips. Tommy laid her backward on the bed and began to slowly undress her kissing at her bare skin along the way. His lips massaged her nipples as he pulled her pink tank over her head. They twirled at the ring on her little brown belly button before they moved down to her cotton black shorts and kissed down her thigh. Marci arched her back as Tommy slid her shorts down. He pressed his face between her coffee-colored legs, his lips finding and caressing all the soft places she desired.

Marci moaned, clasping her hands onto the top of his head. "You love me, Tommy?" she asked, lifting his wet face.

"Yes, baby. I love you."

"Oh, yes, Tommy," she screamed as he slid inside of her. "I love you, Tommy. I fuckin' love you!"

CHAPTER 9

C andace was on the phone with a caseworker at the County Assistance Office when Denise walked into her office Monday morning.

"No, sir. I do appreciate that, but I was able to get in touch with the family and I have the documents. I'll fax them to you now if you need."

Candace nodded, acknowledging her boss's presence while Denise slid into one of the two blue fabric chairs in front of Candace's desk. She looked around the room in silence while Candace continued speaking into the phone.

"Your direct extension?" Candace scribbled some numbers down on a Post-it. "Thank you. I'll send it over in a few. All right, good-bye."

"Candace," Denise began when Candace hung up the phone.

Candace's eyebrows rose.

"What's on your agenda for today?" Denise asked.

"Billing, adding in client charges. Why? You need me?"

"Social Service does."

Candace's eyebrows furrowed.

Denise continued, "Chrissy is swamped with discharges and placements. I believe you have a good handle on your department and could assist for some time. Plus, it would be good for you to get to know the ins and outs of the departments an administrator oversees."

"Sure," Candace said optimistically.

"Great." Denise stood. "She's upstairs in her office. Head up as soon as you can."

"Sure thing," Candace said with a nod as Denise exited the room.

Candace cleared her desk, grabbed a notepad from her drawer and headed to the elevator.

This shouldn't be too bad, should be interesting. I should be all right. Knock this shit out, show Denise how I do things. Plus, I always liked Chrissy; she's a goofy ass girl, always smiling and chipper. Candace laughed aloud exiting the elevator.

She turned and walked to her right, stepping into the middle of a tiny cluttered office. In it was a small gray desk, covered with small piles of paper and facing a painted white concrete wall and to the left of that, a long tan folding table piled high with over-stuffed manila folders, some with rubber bands around them to secure the overflow of paper inside. Short stacks of folders also teetered alongside the steel desk. Candace inwardly gasped. *There's shit everywhere.*

Chrissy waved her heavy arm—the fat beneath it wobbling and wiggling—to welcome Candace into the dense mounds of organized clutter.

Candace surveyed the perimeter. It was nothing like her own neat and tidy office space. This room was smaller and tighter with one window that opened out into the stuffy physical therapy gym. Candace sighed.

Chrissy was smiling, as usual, and her hot-pink lipstick spread across her thin mouth. She always had on some intense, off-the-wall makeup: bright blushes and bold colorful eye shadows. Her blond hair was stringy and teased about her shoulders.

"Hey, Chrissy," Candace spoke.

"Hey, Miss Candace. I heard you're here to help me out," Chrissy said, grinning and moving a pile of folders from a chair to the floor.

Still staring at the mess, Candace replied, "I am, but what the hell is all this?"

Chrissy's smile widened. "This is my life, darling. This is Social Service, me all by myself. Documenting, tracking all the developmental needs of everybody who comes through the door. Creating charts for each new admission, handling the discharges for every patient. You name it, Social Service, which is me, does it."

"Oh, wow."

"Yup." Chrissy beamed. "I do my best. I get most of it done but Admissions keeps bringing in these medical assistance patients that don't pay any money and have no real skilled need and we can't do nothing with 'em. Then it's my job to find them placement."

"Why admit the patients then?" Candace asked.

Chrissy laughed. "For the numbers, darling. At the close of the day, all the big-wigs wanna know is if the beds are full. They don't care nothing 'bout quality clients. That's why we got drunks recovering from getting beat up in bar fights on the first floor. They don't have anywhere to go; we give 'em PT, then we have to discharge them somewhere. Can't put them out on the street."

Candace's eyes widened. "So what you're saying is Jennifer brings in the trash and you have to take it out?"

"Sounds about right."

Candace shook her head. "I can't stand that woman."

"Well, I don't think she's anybody's favorite," Chrissy said.

"Definitely not mine."

"Yeah, she can certainly be a pain."

"Her and Denise all buddy buddy," Candace said, neck rolling.

"That's because Jennifer is what is referred to as a brown-noser..."

"She's a kiss-ass," Candace interjected.

Chrissy erupted with laughter, her round belly jiggling and shaking.

Candace chuckled lightly. "She is. I promise you, Chrissy, I can't stand her and she can't stand me, and at this point, the gloves are off."

Chrissy's soft blue eyes grew large under bright-green eye shadow. "Oh my. What on earth is the friction between you two?"

Candace relaxed her shoulders. "She's always had it out for me, Chrissy. Always been nasty and rude. I never bothered that woman; don't care nothing 'bout her or whatever her issue is. But she is so condescending."

Chrissy nodded.

Candace continued, "She's always boasting and showing off like she's all this and that."

Chrissy chuckled. "I know what you mean. She is very snooty."

Candace continued, "Like she knows every damn thing."

Chrissy slapped her round knee with her jeweled hand. "She doesn't know what she's doing. She just does what she's told. Poor skinny thing is a puppet."

Candace laughed.

"She looks like a puppet, too," Chrissy continued. "Long gangly arms and scrawny neck, can barely hold up that bobble head of hers; thing swinging around like a rattle when she walk."

Candace burst into laughter, covering her face with her hands. "Chrissy, you're a mess!"

Chrissy smiled shrugging her round shoulders. "I'm not going to lie to you, darling. It's as plain as I can see. There's no other reason an educated woman as herself would continue to scrape the bottom of hospital barrels to fill vacancies in a rehab center. It doesn't make sense to me."

Candace shook her head. "Me either."

Chrissy turned her short round body to her desk, chuckling slightly, and pulled a folder from the top of one of the small piles. "Well, Miss Candace, let's get started."

Chrissy handed Candace the folder and began showing her the paperwork needed to develop a chart for new patients and the documents necessary to discharge them. She also showed her the goal assessment sheets that needed tracking as well as long-term analysis forms, social development documentation and discharge planning sections.

Candace found herself face-down in piles of paper, sorting through nursing notes and summarizing assessments for every client in the building. The facility had over one hundred beds and almost all of them were full. Some clients were long-timers, requiring serious care, twenty-four-hour nursing supervision and assistance with all daily living activities. Most of the long-timers stayed on the second floor with very routine schedules. Some paid privately for all of the amenities of Wyncote Medical Rehabilitation Center.

The first floor, however, was a revolving door of clients recovering from various surgeries and hospital discharges. Some stayed weeks, even months, receiving therapy treatment, wound care, dialysis, nursing assistance, transportation to doctor's appointments, meals, and activities for as long as their insurance afforded. Some had little to no insurance and state aid barely covered what it deemed necessary. And at the completion of their stay, Chrissy was responsible for their discharge. Most of Candace's training focused on how to call other facilities, verify patient needs and abilities, and confirm open beds.

By Wednesday, Candace was frantically rummaging through the bottom of Chrissy's cluttered desk drawer.

"Where did you say they were?" she hollered to Chrissy who was coming down the hall.

"Bottom left," Chrissy hollered back.

Candace kept digging. Her hand finally landed on a small green plastic bottle. She pulled it out, popped it open and shoved two Excedrin into her mouth. Her water bottle was within arm's reach and Candace swallowed hard. So hard she almost choked.

Chrissy caught her red-faced and gagging when she entered the tiny office space. "What on earth?"

Candace patted at her own chest.

"Candace, you can't O.D. on Excedrin. It's only headache medicine, darling."

"Chrissy, this is crazy," Candace began, sipping her water, slowly composing herself. "What the hell am I supposed to do with this man who has no insurance coverage, no money and no family? His referral's been rejected by six different facilities; no one wants him."

"Keep trying, Miss Candace," Chrissy said, giving a smile and light chuckle.

Candace rolled her eyes and stepped out of the small office. *Don't nobody have time for this bullshit.* She checked the time on the large wall clock over the nurse's station. *Quarter after four.* She shook her head. *And I got class tonight. Shit. This is a setup. Denise is tryna sabotage me. That bitch wants to see me fail. Well, huh, I won't give her the satisfaction.*

Candace hurried toward the business office to check her messages. Mondays and Wednesdays Candace left work at 4:30 p.m. on the nose, and Miss P picked Emmanuel up from camp while she headed to class down Broad Street at Temple University.

"Here you go." Allyson handed Candace a half-dozen message slips. Candace walked, head down into her office, scanning through the thin slips of paper for any glimmer of hope in placing her difficult patient. One slip was from a Brenda Greiner of Pathways Shelter in Pottstown. Candace quickly dialed the number.

"Oh, yes," she said after a few minutes. "We can arrange for the transportation. I'll make sure to get him there by one o'clock tomorrow afternoon. Thank you so much."

She hung up and hurriedly began scribbling out the discharge notice, then handed the paper to Allyson.

"Make fifteen copies," she instructed. "And put one in every department head's box. Thanks."

Candace could not contain the smile spread out across her face. Her pretty teeth gleamed as she locked up her office and headed toward Denise's.

Knocking softly, Candace peeked inside to find Denise reading a thick booklet from the Department of Public Welfare. Candace shuddered at the dense reading material. *Not looking forward to that.*

"Hey, Denise," she spoke from the office threshold. "I'm headed to class. Mr. Magdule has placement."

Denise raised her eyes. "Really?"

"Yes," Candace answered. "He'll be leaving for a shelter in Pottstown tomorrow around lunchtime."

Denise smiled, slightly nodding. "Pottstown, you say?"

Candace nodded.

"Good. Good stuff," Denise said, glancing up at Candace momentarily before her eyes fell back to the booklet at her desk.

"Thanks. Have a nice night," Candace said quickly.

"You, too. Thank you," Denise replied without lifting her gaze.

Candace turned from the office to see Jennifer walking toward her down the hall. Candace threw her big bag over her shoulder and raised her head high. She continued to saunter toward the front door.

"Leaving so early?" Jennifer asked, stopping in front of Candace.

"None of your business, Jennifer."

"Perhaps it is none of my business, but it is my concern. Especially if you are going to make a habit out of leaving work early every day. How is an administrator supposed to run a building if she always has somewhere else to go?"

Candace rubbed the irritation in her eye. Breathing slowly, deeply, she waited several seconds before she spoke. "It's not every day, Jennifer." Candace struggled suppressing her growl. "And what I do with my time when I'm off the clock is none of your *damn* business."

Jennifer pulled her hand to her breast. "Oh my," she gasped.

Candace was out of the door. *Simple bitch. It's none of her goddamn business where the fuck I'm goin', when I'm goin'.. Where the hell you been at while I'm getting dogged out in Social Service? Huh?*

Her Accord started with a subtle engine roar followed by steady acceleration that quickly propelled Candace through Flourtown, down Stenton Avenue, and to Broad Street. Her sleek black ride slipped through the ebb and flow of traffic on the major thruway in Philadelphia.

"Why does this bitch always try to take me there?" Candace asked herself, smoothly working her hands along the leather steering wheel. "It is my concern if you're leaving early every day," Candace said, mocking the squeak in Jennifer's voice. "Shut the fuck up."

She laughed, shaking Jennifer from her brain. She giggled lightly and thoughts of the tall, light-skinned guy from the club came rushing back to her. Candace tried to shake them away, too, but the images of him and his full lips and strong shoulders lingered with her until she could no longer fight the urge. She whipped out her cell phone to make a call.

She tried Chris's number again, still no answer. *Fuck this*, she thought, pulling up the contact in her phone. Candace's eyes darted from the phone to the road, then back to the phone again. Menu button, delete. *I'm not goin' keep blowing up this kid. I ain't no damn stalker.* She pressed the button, erasing the contact name and number from her list and tossed the phone back into her bag before parking on Berks Street behind Temple. She hurried to class.

Candace heard her phone ringing in the bottom of her purse on her way home. Bam's voice came in heavy and smooth over the line.

"You turn me on, Candace. I got some special things in mind for your sexy self. I'm really looking forward to seeing you again."

"Well, hello to you, too, Bam."

Bam chuckled. "My apologies, pretty lady. You see what you do to me? Got my manners all out the window."

"Um, I don't know, Bam."

"Don't know what, Candace?"

"If you can handle all this," she teased.

A deep laugh erupted from over the receiver. "Baby girl, you got the right one. I don't know how these clowns out here treat you, but you dealing with a grown man. Get ready for the ride, baby."

"Is that so? I don't know, Bam. I'm a grown woman, too, and I think that you have a thing for my looks. You don't know about the rest of me. You just like what you see."

"Aw, baby girl. Don't say that. You are a sexy sight, ain't no lie. But I know you're grown. That's why I wanna show you how grown folks get down. I'm not about games, and I speak my mind—no matter what it is. You turn me on, Candace, and I want you, but I know how to treat you. You have to decide if you can handle a man like me."

Candace smirked. "I think so."

"I don't want you to think so, baby. I want you to be sure," he said seductively. "I am bringing a lot to the table. You need to know if I am the kind of guy you can fuck with. I want you to think about it, okay? Let me know when you ready for Big Daddy. I ain't goin' chase you; I just want to be your friend. If you scared, say you scared. If you want this, let me know. I'm here to show you some things."

Candace shook her head, pulling up in front of her door. "I ain't never scared, Bam. But I'ma have to call you later."

Candace hung up the phone, stretching outside of her car. She was two steps from her front door when Miss P pulled up with Emmanuel in the front seat.

"Hey, ma," he shouted.

Candace smiled, turning to face the curb. "Hey, babe. Hey, Miss P."

"How are you, baby?" the chocolate-colored woman called out.

"Good, good. Tired is all. Class was long."

"Um-huh," Miss P moaned from the window of her big black Cadillac. "Well, make sure you get some rest. And Emmanuel," she turned to her grandson, "make sure you help your mother out. You hear me? Boys are supposed to be a blessing to their mothers, never a burden. You got that?"

"Yes, ma'am." Emmanuel nodded, climbing out of the wide-body vehicle.

"Love y'all!" Miss P hollered, driving off.

Candace grinned, watching her son approach.

"Wassup, Mom?"

"Nothin' much. Wassup with you?"

Emmanuel shrugged.

"Did you eat?" Candace asked, unlocking the front door.

"Yeah. Did you?"

Candace paused. "No."

"You gotta eat something, Ma," Emmanuel stated, walking behind his mother.

"I know. I'll make something quick before I go to bed."

"You supposed to eat before school," Emmanuel informed her. "That way you can concentrate in class. Did you concentrate in class?" Emmanuel flung his backpack onto the sofa.

"Yes, I concentrated," she replied, walking to her bedroom and shaking her head.

Candace made it to her room and under the covers without eating. She was back up at seven the next day to do it again.

CHAPTER 10

The week dragged on and Candace was back in her own office by Friday with piles of new admissions on her desk. She shook her head, *Ain't this a bitch.* She jumped right in, sorting through the mess, making calls and checking insurance information with the facility's newest arrivals. On her way back from helping one resident, Candace noticed a text from a strange number on her phone.

How long you gone make me wait to see you again?

She stared at the message for a moment, unsure of whom the text was from. *Who the hell?* Candace thought it might be the cutie from the club, but it had been more than two weeks. She contemplated the right words and slowly typed her response: *Who is this?*

The reply was immediate.

Don't front on me, sexy. It's Chris. I'm still dreaming 'bout that gold dress.

I don't know what you're talking about.

Yea whatever. How long you gonna make me wait to see you again?

Candace blushed and typed, *depends on how long you're willing to wait.*

I want to see you tonight, he replied.

Rolling her eyes, Candace tossed her phone back into the drawer. She left her office heading to a meeting with a new admission's family. Candace returned after what seemed like hours to several missed calls. She was checking her call log when the phone rang in her hand.

"Why you duckin' me, ma?" the smooth voice cooed through the connection.

"I'm not ducking anything. I've been busy. You know how that is."

"You not goin' come outside to see me?"

"No, I'm not goin' be able to do it."

"I just want to set eyes on you."

"Yeah?"

Her name paged over the loud speaker.

"I gotta get back to work."

"Call me," Chris added quickly.

Candace hung up the phone, rushing back out on to the floor. *Thank God it's Friday.*

By the time Candace made it back to her office at the end of the day, Chris had called her two more times. She smirked but didn't return his calls.

I don't have time to play games with this little boy. She shut down her office. *Don't answer my calls, fine. Won't give you the satisfaction of thinking I give a shit, 'cause I don't.* Candace was exhausted, and ready to lie down to watch a movie with Emmanuel. *My son is home, work is done, no school. I can order a pizza and a movie and relax.*

Apparently, Emmanuel had other plans and greeted his mother with a huge smile and a plate of sliced mango when she walked through the door.

"Ma, can I go over Uncle B's? Please?" he whined with big pleading eyes and a hopeful grin.

Candace's body went limp on her fluffy sofa before she sighed with defeat. "Only if he comes to get you," she huffed.

"He already on his way."

Within twenty minutes, Emmanuel was gone and Candace was home alone.

She stripped down to nothing and admired her long, lean body in the tall bedroom mirror. She was solid, not slim but full in all the places that mattered; ample breasts, high firm behind and a little soft tummy she never cared too much about trying to tighten. Satisfied, Candace climbed under her covers. She reached for her phone from beneath the green sheets and dialed her sister's number.

"I can't fucking believe he's married, C," Marci started.

"Me either, boo. What you goin' do?"

"I don't know, C. I mean, why he have to lie to me?"

"You ain't talked to him?" Candace asked.

"Not since he came over to plead his case."

"Did you give him some?"

"No," Marci replied.

"Marcine?"

"Okay. Okay, yes, I gave him some."

Candace shook her head.

Marci whined, "He was just too good to be true."

"Girl, please. Niggas ain't shit no way. That youngin from the club a couple weeks ago, you know the one with the light eyes..."

"Yeah."

"He finally called. He tryin' to see me."

"So see him."

"I 'on't know. He seem like he play a lot of games."

"What, you rather go out with Grandpa than a cutie?"

"Shut up. I don't even know what it is to date anymore. It's been so long since Prince, and everything always ends up being just fuckin' and nothin' serious."

"You want something serious?" Marci inquired.

"I don't know."

"You need to get fucked; that's what you need. Ery'body ain't goin' be Prince, but you goin' need something reliable at some point. Shit, I love when Tommy beats this pussy up." She paused. "I miss him, C."

"Oh, girl, please. He be back, whining and begging and you goin' take him back."

"Why you say that?" Marci asked.

"'Cause you love hard, girl. You can't help it."

"I know, but at least I let myself love," Marci protested.

"You think I should call him?" Candace asked, changing the subject.

"You think I should call Tommy?"

"No!" Candace snapped.

"Yes!"

"Bye!"

Candace hung up the phone staring at the device for a moment and weighing the option of calling back the number she'd ignored. Chris answered on the second ring.

"Beautiful," he started right in. "You coming out tonight?"

"I'm kinda tired," she told him.

"Too tired to see me for a quick drink? I promise not to keep you out too long. We don't want your baby daddy gettin' jealous."

"Shut up." Candace curled her lips into a subtle smile. She fought against the relaxing feeling moving over her body. But after a few more sweet words, Chris convinced her to step out for a moment to enjoy the summer air. He promised to meet her at 7165 Lounge on Germantown Avenue.

Candace plucked a pair of pretty panties from her dresser and thought of Chris taking them off. She wriggled into a pair of dark denim high-waist shorts, tucked in a tight white tank, slipped on a pair of nude pumps and a beaded chain and headed out.

The security guard at the lounge door was an old friend from high school and Candace slipped in past the crowd. She settled into a seat at the bar and ordered vodka and pineapple juice before turning around to check out the scene. The DJ was mixing some hot reggae tracks and Candace grinded her hips in her seat. She swayed, sipped and waited. She checked her phone for the time. *Twenty minutes, though? Come on with this late shit.* Candace found herself checking for Chris hard, jumping at every tall, light-skinned brother who came through the door. *Calm down, girl.*

She surveyed the spot again. The crowd was a mix of young adults in their early twenties, some her age but quite a few noticably older.

"I still got this." She laughed into her glass, admiring her long legs in her skimpy shorts.

Candace was two drinks under and deep in her own meditative trance when Chris entered the bustling room. Candace looked up and he looked incredible; his smile wide and charming when he spotted her. His sultry swagger and proud brow borrowed the attention of most of the women around. The long, studded chain swung across his chest as he moved her way. She stood to meet him and he embraced her as if they were lost lovers—pulling her in tight, his hands all over her long strong back. The tips of his fingers slipped down under her bottom and squeezed.

"Girl, you make a nigga have wet dreams. I been thinking about them legs for a minute." He looked her over in her tight top and short shorts stopping well above her mid-thigh. "What you drinking?"

"Cîroc and pineapple."

"Cool." Chris leaned into the bar handing the bar maid several bills. After a moment, he turned back to Candace with two full glasses. He set one in front of her on the bar and settled into a seat next to her sipping the other. "You been here long?"

"Not too long."

"You wanna chill, or you ready to go?" he asked, swallowing a full glass.

Go? Candace thought, *is he serious? Where do he think he taking me already?*

"I'd like to chill for a minute. If that's cool with you."

"It's whatever, ma. It's all about you, ya mean? I been tryin' to get with you for a long time. I'm down for whatever tonight."

"Is that right?" She tried to resist staring into his handsome and well-sculpted face. The muscles in his jaw were sleek and strong. Chris's eyes glistened under a weed-induced haze, but his breath was cool and sweet. The desire to press her lips to his pulsated through her. Candace realized the throbbing sensation between her legs as she studied the parts his mouth made as he spoke. Suddenly, she wanted to feel the moisture from his lips seep onto her own. Candace felt the craving, the desire, the urge to feel skin-to-skin contact.

She quickly pulled her glass to her lips and took a long hard swallow. The vodka surged its way into her chest, smooth yet forceful. She looked back up at Chris. He hadn't turned away. He took the empty glass from her and handed her a fresh drink, smiling as she watched him. "Are you all right, ma?"

There was no response; no words escaped her lips. Candace took a strong gulp from her drink. When she set her glass down, Chris was still there and he was still fine. She watched his chest rise and fall succinctly with the diamond-linked chain around his neck. The certainty arose in her breasts as her breathing hastened. She wanted to fuck him.

The wet desire her sister had been howling about and the pounding sensation Prince had been edging her on to fulfill was suddenly rising in her groin. There was no Manny to be tended to tonight, no meeting in the morning, no suit to press. There was only animalistic desire escorted by alcohol to the forefront of her moist panties and Chris.

"I want to dance," was all she could muster, snatching Chris by the arm and leading him to the floor. She pulled him into her and Chris found the exact places on her body where Candace wanted to be touched. They drank and danced for most of the night until she was too tipsy to hold the beat on her own. She bopped her butt to the bass line while leaning her head into his broad shoulders.

Chris seemed more than obliged to assist her in keeping her balance. He was steady behind her, rocking her rhythmically to the beat. They grooved seductively together until the music slowed and the lights began to rise.

"You ready to get out of here?" Chris asked in her ear.

Though tipsy, Candace fumbled for her keys, certain she could drive. Chris was insistent that she not and he stayed close behind her, keeping his eyes and hands on her, supporting her weight.

"Let me take you home," he insisted, moving her toward the front door of the club, following the crowd exiting and filing out onto Germantown Avenue.

"I may be drunk, but I ain't dumb. You can't go to my crib; you might be a crazy stalker," she slurred.

"Where you want to go then, baby?" he asked with Candace anchored in his arms while walking her across the street toward his car in the cool summer night breeze.

When Candace looked up from her saunter, she was standing in front of Chris's black Impala. Chris opened the door and she melted into the seat. The leather reeked of marijuana; she cracked the window to release the scent and catch some fresh air. Chris pulled off quickly onto the clear and dark road, his hands rubbing up her thigh as he drove.

"You goin' let me part them thighs tonight?"

Candace let out a drunken chuckle at Chris's hand slipping through a small gap between her shorts and her thigh, finding the lace of her panties. She opened her legs at his pressing fingertips and his hand moved until his fingers felt the moisture where her thighs met. His fingers twirling slowly spread the wetness around her insides. After a moment, he pulled his sticky fingers out, bringing them close to his nostrils and inhaling deeply. He grinned and a look of enjoyment smoothed over his face. Chris drove away from the trolley track-lined streets of Germantown. With one hand at Candace's lap and the other clutching the steering wheel, he headed toward Northeast Philadelphia.

Candace was enjoying the cool wind whirling about her face and Chris's fingertips twirling inside of her.

Chris parked in the rear of the Roosevelt Inn on Roosevelt Boulevard and leaned in to kiss her. Candace was barely walking through the small blue lobby of the hotel before she realized, Chris was holding room keys and ushering her down the hall. Her shorts were unzipped and on the floor before the room door closed. Chris dropped to his knees burying his face in her lap and pushing her body upward against the wall. Her French manicured fingernails pulled at his freshly cropped head while he dug his face further into her moisture spot. She screamed out at the laps of his tongue smacking her swollen womanhood. He lifted her up, her body drunken and loose and the room spun, as quickly as Chris's tongue inside her thighs.

He brought her down onto the bed while tearing off the rest of their clothes. Licking his lips, he stared at Candace's long, toned body. She stretched out across the bed and he was back at her lap still devouring her. His body was like hers, long and well sculpted like a swimmer. He was lean with a subtle, yet defined, six-pack and broad shoulders, beautiful cream-colored skin and gray-green eyes that glistened in the light of the moon. His kisses were sloppy wet and full, his thick tongue moving into her mouth with ease.

Sucking back onto his tongue, Candace pulled his body closer and the passion pulsating between them sent electric currents through her, a feeling she had long been craving. She grabbed at his proud manhood. Chris leaned back, assisting her face into his lap. She attempted to slowly take him in her mouth with Chris resting his hand on the back of her neck. The alcohol seized control and Candace's wet mouth slobbered up and down on Chris eagerly. She held her breath moving his stiff rod to the far reaches of her throat without gagging. Chris growled as she took him down.

"You have condoms?" she asked from his lap.

His dark denims were on the floor so Chris stretched to pull the gold Magnum from his back pocket. Candace was on her back with her legs spread, the inside of her thighs winced with anticipation. She could feel the thickness of Chris's shaft when he held himself tapping his throbbing head on her swollen lips. He was rock-hard and the "pat pat" made her entire body vibrate. She attempted to lie still, thinking for a moment about how long it had been since she had been touched the way Chris was touching her. *Damn he's big.* She smiled off the fear of disappointment.

Chris moved well on the dance floor and Candace prayed he moved as well in bed and be all she needed and longed for. When he slid inside of her, Candace squealed; Chris was more. His size was overpowering and the motion behind his movement drove her backward on the bed. Her eyes opened wide with surprise. She couldn't believe that he felt so good so fast as Chris moved right to the places she needed him to.

"Oh God," she moaned.

Chris grunted pushing up into her deeper and deeper. Her breathing increased, as she felt him pressing against her insides.

She gasped at the intensity of the pleasure leaving her mouth hanging open, and Chris's tongue found its way back between her lips. The excitement caused the hair on her arms to stand. She kissed him passionately as he stroked away at her. Chris pulled his face back a little, staring down at her body beneath his, seemingly entranced by their entanglement. After a moment of intense grinding, he pulled her up on top of him. She came down slowly on his fullness, biting her lip and rolling her hips. Candace's round breasts bounced in his face. He licked at them as they met his mouth. The alcohol allowed for limber movement and she swayed effortlessly on her knees. Chris wrapped his arms around her body pulling her close. The sweat dripped between them, but neither stopped to dry their faces or catch a breath. When Chris flipped her over on all fours, Candace turned her neck around looking back at him. Her back stretching out before him, Chris extended his long ball-playing arms and gripped her around the neck.

"Oh, fuck," Candace howled. The tighter he squeezed, the harder it was to breathe, causing all of the muscles in her body to contract. Candace clenched her coochie walls around him and he choked her harder, quickening his pace.

"Ah! Shit! Fuck!" Candace yelped with excitement as his rhythm took her over. He slammed against her roughly and sternly, the length of him finding long-untouched places inside. Candace climaxed long and loud, drawing Chris's ejaculation out right behind hers.

After they'd finished, Candace hung halfway off the bed, breathing heavily and looking at Chris like he was insane.

"Really?" she asked in disbelief. "Did you really just do all that?" He smiled at her, standing and stretching beside the bed. Both of their bodies were bare and glistening with sweat. Chris stood over her, naked and unashamed, his dick wet and firm.

"Really," he said, leaning over to kiss her. Candace felt the pulsations between her thighs again and within moments, her legs were pushed back to the headboard as Chris swerved and pumped his body on top of hers.

They woke early the next morning and Chris took her back to her car.

"Am I goin' see you again? You know, you all select witchca time," he teased.

Candace smiled opening her car door and reaching for her Ferragamo shades. She slyly pulled them down over her red eyes and grinned. She turned toward him. "I'll pencil you in."

Chris leaned in, kissing her in the mouth deeply. "Try again."

Candace blushed behind her shades, trying to fight the growing tingle in her groin. "We'll see," she said coyly.

Chris took her in his arms, squeezing her backside and lifting her to the tips of her toes. He brought her down fast at the sound of his phone ringing.

"I gotta get outta here, ma," he said, pecking her quickly on the lips. "Make sure you call me."

Candace nodded, settling into her car, her body stiff from the night of wild love-making.

Chris pulled off in his Impala.

The next day, Candace rolled out of bed feeling the soreness of her body intensify. She smiled at the stiffness. Her phone chimed with a text message from Chris while she was reading over her notes for class.

You doin' alright ma?
I couldn't be better ☺.
Yea you could.
?
I need to see you again.

CHAPTER 11

"This is why I fuckin' hate working on Saturdays," Marci said aloud to herself while maneuvering her burgundy Altima through the heavy traffic on Sixty-Ninth Street. She was late for work—on a Saturday morning of all days.

Donna's shop was at the end of a busy, two-block strip of booming urban businesses. Several clothing stores, a few sneaker spots, a dollar store, a movie theater and the concert showcase, Tower Theater stood in the flow of heavy foot traffic and yielded the perfect shopping temperament.

Marci groaned as the light she was chasing turned red. It was 10:40 a.m. when she burst through the doors of D's Designs.

"Do you know what time it is?" Donna barked, without looking up from the press and curl she was doing.

"Donna, I'm really sorry. I..."

"Miss Marci, *my* clients deserve the utmost respect and consideration," Donna boomed, drawing the attention of the customers in the salon. "Now, if you can't provide them with that, or if you feel you too good to give *my* clients the common courtesies they deserve, then you don't need to be here."

Marci's jaws clenched. She pinched her lips together, folding her arms across her breasts and rolled her eyes. "I said I was sorry. It won't happen again," she hissed.

Donna smirked. "I bet it won't. I have a shop to run and I don't tolerate tardiness. Don't let me have to tell you again."

Marci turned away, walking toward her chair and assuming her position between Quinta, who was pinning up a ponytail and Jerel chopping at a blonde weave. There were several walk-ins already waiting, not unusual for a Saturday morning at Donna's salon.

Before Marci had a chance to hang her bag, the first girl was shampooed, dried and dropped in her chair. The young girl wanted a simple press and curl. *Quick and painless.* Marci parted the girl's hair. She primped and pressed silently. She was moving along effortlessly until the next lady in her seat wanted a full head weave. Marci sulked staring down at the beehive of braids. This was going to be some work only to chop all the hair down to a short, sleek cut. Marci liked cutting. She was sharp with the shears and enjoyed slicing the hair into intricate styles, but threading in a head full of weave bored the hell out of her. She silently dove into her work, drowning out everything else around. Halfway into the woman's head, Marci's phone rang in the back pocket of her tight distressed jeans. It was Tommy.

Marci's heart raced as she excitedly tapped the button on the Bluetooth headphones and accepted the call.

Tommy's voice smoothed over her through the connection. "Good mornin', baby."

"Good morning," Marci replied, beaming. Try as she may, Marci couldn't deny the charming and quick-witted man made her blush from ear to ear. She couldn't quite decide if it was his brown slanted eyes, or his sexy voice or maybe his thick sexy dick that made her panties so wet. But in any case, it didn't matter; she was hooked on the married man.

"Whatchu doin', baby? Workin' hard?"

"You can say that," Marci said, looking down at the length of track she still had to sew in. "I can't wait to get out of here today."

"Yeah? Whads the matta?" Tommy cooed.

"I was late today, causa you, and ya chick snapped at me."

"Aw, Marci. I got you in trouble?" he asked teasingly.

"That's not funny," she snapped back, staring at Donna who was across the salon talking to Lateesh. Quinita and Jerel were busy working on heads of their own.

"She there now?" he asked.

"Yeah. You don't know where ya woman be at?"

"Uh, fuck no. I don't keep tabs on her like that."

Marci shook her head. "That's jacked up."

"You looking at that fat cow now, ain't you?" he asked.

Marci chuckled.

"Look, she goin' tell me last night, she want us to do more stuff together this summer, like go down to the shore. I was like, what? Is she crazy? I ain't taking her big ass to no beach. She lazy as shit, babe. She not goin' do nothing but sit on her ass in the sand, like a fucking beach whale."

Marci bit down on her lip to stop from laughing long and loud. "Ohmigod, you stupid."

"You, on the other hand," she heard him lick his chops, "I'd kill to see you in a bikini. You own a couple, don't you?"

"Seven."

"Goddamn! See that's what I'm talking about. A young woman who takes care of herself. Keep her body tight and money right. Don't no grown-ass man want a fat-ass walrus on they heels all the time. A man wants a pretty bitch by his side."

"Is that what I am, a pretty bitch?" Marci whispered.

"Damn right. You know that's why I love you, girl." Tommy spilled the words like liquid into her ear.

Marci laughed again, feeling her heart swell. "I love you, too."

When she finished the sew-in in her chair, Marci's scheduled client was washed and waiting her turn. The salon was moving as expected. Whitney Houston poured over the hum of the hairdryers.

"What can I do for you today, Loni?" Marci asked the thirty-something brown-skinned woman in her chair.

"I want a long curly look. I bought the bundles."

Marci was parting into the fresh scalp when Jerel leaned in to her from the right.

"You awfully quiet today, youngin. You musta had a helluva time last night."

Marci chuckled. "I did."

"Well, girl, let me tell you 'bout my night." Jerel's juicy body moved with everything she said and her neck swayed as she ennunciated her words. Her arms waved, her ample hips swished from side to side, and her head rocked back and forth, whenever she got good into a story.

"So, I met this dude a couple weeks ago, right? He goin' chase me down at my sister cookout and hawk me for my number. You know the thirsty type, right. But he was kinda cute, so I gave him my number. He been calling me, trying to take me out and whatnot. So I finally says yes. I'm goin' let him take me to eat and get some drinks, right? 'Cause I was hungry anyway and I had this crazy craving for shrimp…"

"Ow, I had some good shrimp the otha day, girl?" Quinita chimed in from Marci's other side.

"From where?" Jerel asked.

"Snocky's down Washington Ave."

"Yeah, I had some crabs from there before. They was hittin'," Marci added.

"Oh, yeah. They good, but see, if dude was gonna take me on a date, I prefer Copa's. So, I told dude he can take me to there, you know? I was tryna look cute, you know what I'm sayin? Tryna take a stroll down South Street or somethin'. So anyways, I get all dressed and sexy and whatnot, take my time, get my makeup all fly and whatnot, and you know this negro ain't show."

"What?" Marci gasped.

"I hate that," Quinita chimed in again from the left. "Dudes be pressing you and then don't come through. That makes me sick."

"Girl, I was pissed." Jerel snaked her neck.

"Did you still go out?" Marci asked.

"You know I did. Right to the Crab House; I had to get my seafood fix. But the crowd be too much for me."

"Yeah, the Crab House do be packed, especially on a Friday," Marci said, nodding.

"Yeah, it do," Quinita added. "Where you was partying at last night, little Miss Marci?"

Marci smiled. "I was out with some friends down Olde City." It wasn't a complete lie. Tommy was her friend and they were in Olde City.

She bit her lip reflecting on how she'd orgasmed all over Tommy in the back of his Charger the night before. She wished they could go there again or be there even now. But instead, she was in the middle of two silly stylists in a busy-ass salon on a Saturday.

Marci looked to see Quinita, who, to her surprise, was still talking. Marci hadn't heard a word the girl said.

"Oh, yeah. I like Olde City. It's nice. A lot of white people, but it's cool. Where'd you go?"

"Some little hole in the wall," Marci replied.

"It's a lot of them," Quinita responded. "Tons of cute lil' spots all up and through Market Street.

"Girl, we got to go out sometime," Jerel spoke up. "I ain't been down Olde City in a minute. It's changed a lot."

Marci grinned. "You ain't missing much."

CHAPTER 12

"Mom, what is that?"

"What?"

"That," Candace said, pointing to the shiny object in her mother's hand.

"It's a miniature porcelain doll," Karla answered, dangling the thing in Candace's face for further inspection.

"Why do you have that, Mom?"

"Because it's pretty and I like it."

Candace shook her head. "What else you got in that bag?" she asked, reaching for the big red-and-white satchel on her mother's right arm.

Karla pulled back from her grasp and poked out her lips. "None of your concern," she replied, turning to the man behind the table where she'd selected her trinket. She handed the man a few one-dollar bills and tucked the doll into her bag.

Candace laughed. "Now, I know you bought a frilly toilet seat cover and the matching rug, and you bought picture frames, a mailbox cover, refrigerator magnets and a wind chime. Why on earth do you need a doll?"

"I'm redoin' my house, girl." Karla huffed, stepping beside Candace who dwarfed her mother in height, with Karla standing only five feet tall. But Karla's proud stroll matched Candace's and the two began walking down the long flea market aisle. "You know how much this stuff cost at these stores? You can't beat these prices out here."

Candace stopped at a sunglass stand. "You're right."

Karla reached for a pair of light-brown tinted shades. She slipped them on her face and turned to her daughter. "Whadya think?"

"Cute," Candace replied after looking up. She removed her designer shades and put a pair of big black rimmed glasses over her eyes. "How 'bout these?"

Karla frowned. "Um-unh, they too big."

Candace picked up the mirror resting on the stand and gave herself a quick inspection. "I like 'em like that. Big, black and all over my face."

"Nasty," Karla said, swatting at Candace who hopped out of reach laughing.

Candace was still laughing when she asked the small Korean girl, positioned behind the stand, smiling hard from ear to ear, how much the glasses were.

"Fye dolla," the girl replied, waving her arm over the table between them. She then turned to her right, over another full table of sunglasses and waved her arm again. "Theez eight dolla."

Candace and her mother moved simultaneously to the right to see the higher-priced selection. "Why are these eight dollars?" Candace asked.

Karla picked up a pair of aviator-styled shades from the table.

"Real glasses. More fancy, like you."

Candace's eyebrows furrowed. "Like me?"

"Like you sunglasses," the girl said, pointing to the leopard Kate Spade sunglasses Candace held in her hand.

"Oh no," Candace scoffed. "They are not like my two hundred-dollar sunglasses. They're knock-offs just like the five-dollar ones, boo."

"Candace," Karla called in a warning maternal tone.

"What?" Candace asked, looking down at her mother. "I mean they cute, but they're not like my glasses, at all."

"Glasses is glasses, child. You goin' buy some of these knock-offs just like you bought them two hundred-dollar ones."

Candace shrugged. "You're right."

"Ain't nobody too good for a cute pair of sunglasses."

"I'm not arguing wit' you, Mom."

"I'm just saying, everything you own don't have to be expensive," Karla continued.

Candace looked up to see Emmanuel glide by on wheels protruding from the heels of his sneakers.

"You're right, Mom," Candace repeated in defeat. "I'm not hating on the knock-offs. I need some cute shades to throw around, and besides, I'd much rather Man crush some cheap glasses with them Wheelies you bought him than my expensive ones."

Karla laughed. "He goin' kill his damn self."

"And it's goin' be all your fault for buying him those damn things."

"What was I 'posed to say? No? He wanted 'em. Besides, it's torture for him to be out shopping with his mom and grandmom all day."

Candace looked down the long row of booths and stands at her son skating back toward her. Emmanuel spun around her in circles. He'd been working on a turning spin, and the long aisles in the open market provided ample enough space for him to practice his new move.

"Be careful, Man," Candace instructed.

"I'm good, Mom, but I'm hungry."

"Me too," Karla added.

"Yeah, I could eat. What do y'all want?"

"We can do Applebee's," Karla answered, licking her lips. "I love their ribs."

"I like Applebee's," Emmanuel chimed in.

"Applebee's it is then," Candace said, handing the Korean girl a ten-dollar bill. "I'll take these; my mom wants the light-brown ones."

Candace always looked forward to the fun day she spent with her mother once a month. It was a ritual they both cherished and seldom broke. Emmanuel came along while they hit up the flea market in New Jersey and Sam's Club, then off to a late lunch.

After Candace's father had died from a heart attack, Karla struggled to take care of their small family. But after draining all her accounts to keep the roof over her and Candace's heads, she was penniless and unemployed and forced to move in with her sister, Pat. They stayed there for two years, long enough for Karla to find a job and for Candace to meet Prince. Karla eventually starting working as a receptionist at the welfare office on Broad and Lehigh, a position she'd held for the last ten years.

Karla held Emmanuel's hand as they crossed the large parking lot and headed to Candace's car. The restaurant was a few miles away and Candace pulled into another parking space in a matter of minutes.

"How's Prince?" her mother asked, sliding into a booth beside Emmanuel.

"As good as being on lockdown can get, I guess."

"Um-huh. I seen his mother at church on Sunday. She had all them grandkids with her."

"Did you speak?" Candace asked.

"I waved. She was all the way on the other side of the sanctuary. I wasn't 'bout to go all the way over there just to say hello."

"Ignorant." Candace chuckled.

"That's a lot of kids."

"She had the twins?" Candace asked.

"Yeah. They some cute little girls. I'll tell you that," Karla replied.

"I know. That's all Prince. 'Cause that hood rat Aisha…"

"Now look who's being ignorant," her mother interjected. "That girl ain't done nothing to you. You been done with Prince."

Candace shrugged.

"I'm just curious 'bout who you lettin' love on you now. Working so much and always chasing money isn't good for a young person. That promotion is goin' leave you single and lonely."

Emmanuel rolled his eyes. Candace winked his way.

"I'm not promoted yet, Mom. I'm still in the wringer. Once I finish all my training and sit for my license, then I will officially be promoted."

"Then the big bucks, huh?"

"Bigger bucks, Mom."

"Um." Karla jiggled her shoulders. "I know that's right, baby. Making money is good, but make sure you don't forget about letting somebody make you happy."

"Money makes me happy, Mom."

Karla chuckled, shaking her head. Candace wasn't lying; she always wanted to have the best of things. She wanted a big house with a huge backyard somewhere on the outskirts of Philadelphia. She wanted a nice new Lexus or Infiniti, something classy and fly. Candace liked Gucci, Chanel and Louis Vuitton and hated stressing about paying a bill or waiting on a few dollars to buy her son some sneakers.

Candace knew the position she was working toward would allow her to afford some of life's luxuries. She also was aware her mother didn't want her only child to miss out on love—a notion Candace didn't have much time to consider.

CHAPTER 13

Candace awoke early the next Sunday morning feeling refreshed. The time spent with her mother had done her good and she was in no rush to get back to work or school. When she headed down the long hall into the kitchen, Emmanuel was already there, greeting her with a toasted bagel and some orange juice.

"Morning, ma," he said, sporting the fitted baseball cap his grandmother had purchased the day before.

"Morning, Man," she replied, looking skeptically at the food in front of her before sitting down.

"I don't think I'ma go back to that camp," he said, half a question and the other half some sort of declaration.

Candace nodded knowingly. "There it go. Didn't even take long."

Emmanuel's eyebrows furrowed. "What? What didn't take long?"

"You and all this." She waved her hand over her plate. "I knew you wanted something. So, now, what is it?"

"Okay. Yeah, Mom. I'm not really feeling camp like that. It be hot in there and they started taking all the younger kids into the gym with my group, and it be way too many people in there, Mom, and no room to do nothing."

"And…"

"And I'm thinking that I can go to Uncle B's for the rest of the summer."

"What?" Candace near fell out of her chair. "For the summer?"

"Yeah, ma. Come on. It's so much better over there with Aunt Charlie."

"Who the hell is Aunt Charlie?"

"Uncle B's girlfriend."

"That ain't your damn aunt."

"She say she ain't going nowhere and to get used to her because she loves Uncle B."

"That's what they all say," Candace mumbled. She was shaking her head when Emmanuel interjected continuing with his petition.

"I can stay over there with BJ and PJ for the summer, Mom. Come on. It won't cost you nothing."

"Don't be worried about what costs me. I don't think you running the streets all summer is a good idea. You need some structure." She sipped her juice.

"No, Mom. What I need is a pool and people my own age. Aunt Cha…Uncle B's girlfriend, Charlie, don't work and she goin' be home to watch us."

"She watches BJ and PJ, too?"

"Yup, they always be over there."

BJ and PJ, Brother's oldest boys, were twelve-year-old twins. Their mother was a smoker with a bad habit she couldn't seem to shake, and Brother and his mother, Miss P, took good care of the boys. They were staying with Brother, who was living with his young love, Charlie, in Lynnewood Gardens.

"Well, I don't know."

"Please, Mom." The big dark eyes begged.

"I don't think so."

"Awww, come on." Emmanuel stood and reached into the refrigerator. He pulled out a bowl of sliced mango and slid it onto the table in front of his mother. "At least think about it."

On her way to work the next morning, Candace mulled over the idea of whether or not to send her son to his uncle's house. *I could use the break like a mofo. And Manny's right. Sometimes too right, like his damn father. I sure could use the extra money I'd be saving on camp.*

Money was in the forefront of Candace's thoughts as she entered the busy building. Money was the reason she kept coming back to this place every day, the reason she was $30,000 in debt paying for her college education to get a promotion and work for these crazy people.

Money is a mofo. She pushed open the front lobby door. *But I got to keep pushing. One way or another, something's going to give and I'ma come out on top.*

Candace was still warming herself up with a morale-boosting pep-talk when she turned the corner on the second floor heading toward the Social Service hole-in-the-wall.

There in the middle of the hallway was a portly senior citizen with wild wiry white hair sitting in her wheelchair and screaming to the top of her lungs. "I want to smoke! You can't tell me I can't smoke. I am sixty-eight-fuckin'-years old and I need a goddamn cigarette!"

"Miss Reed, you have to calm down," Nancy Cole, the facility's director of nursing, pleaded with the angry woman in the hall.

"I ain't gotta do shit. I want my damn smokes." The lopsided senior citizen had positioned herself in her wheelchair in a protest stance in the middle of the lobby and was barking at everyone in her view.

"You mothafuckas got some nerve, keepin' me locked up in this shithole and then takin' my goddamn smokes!"

"Miss Reed, please, your language is inappropriate," Nancy whined.

Candace watched Nancy try, with little effect, to calm the screaming woman. Candace curled her lips and approached the situation head-on. "Why are you screaming?" she asked, marching right up to Miss Reed.

"'Cause I want my goddamn cigarettes."

"So? Who do you think you talkin to?" Candace asked, propping her hands on her thick hips and staring directly into Miss Reed's wide-rimmed bifocals.

"Whoever! Everybody!" the woman continued to wail.

"Not in here, you're not." Candace grabbed the back of the woman's wheelchair, spun her around and began to push her quickly down the hall toward her room.

"Get the fuck off me! Help! Help! This crazy bitch is trying to kill me! Help!"

Once down the long corridor, Candace jerked the chair to a startling halt and spun Miss Reed back around to her. She pressed into the wrinkled woman's face.

"Knock it off!" Candace snapped. "You're goin' cut it out right now; you hear me!"

Miss Reed's eyes were full of surprise and alarm. She opened her mouth to speak, but Candace leaned in tighter and reduced her voice to a whisper.

"You goin' watch your mouth in these hallways. I know you want to fuckin' smoke. Just wait a damn minute. You ain't nobody's boss in here and you are not goin' just be screaming at whoever however you good and damn well please. Understood?"

The angry woman crossed her eyes and mumbled almost inaudibly, "Just gimme ma goddamn smokes."

Candace pushed the chair into her small room. "I'll be back at smoke break with your goddamn smokes."

"Bitch," Candace heard Miss Reed mumble as she walked away.

Candace shook her head, continuing down the hall to the tiny Social Service office. She turned inside to see Chrissy sitting at her cluttered desk holding a small box of sugar and pouring a large amount into her coffee cup. Their routine morning meeting hadn't even begun, but Candace knew by the lipstick rings around the porcelain rim that this wasn't Chrissy's first cup.

"Mornin', Chrissy."

"Well, good morning, darling," Chrissy said with a smile on her ever-cheerful face. "You working up here with me today?"

"Nope," Candace said, beaming. "Just came to grab my notebook I left in here on Friday and get as far away from Social Service and this office as possible."

Chrissy faked a frown. "Aww. I might be offended if I didn't know 'bout the boat load of paperwork built up in this department."

"I don't envy you. Besides, fooling with you all week, I now have a boat load of fiscal paperwork to process."

"Too bad, I could use your help today." Chrissy paused and sipped her coffee. "I could use the help any day."

"Not today," Candace said, retrieving her notebook from the top of a small cabinet. "Too much to do."

"Well, don't let me stop you, darling." Chrissy turned, reaching for something on her desk. "But do me this favor." She held out a discharge notice. "Can you make sure this gets in everyone's box for me, please? It's for Mr. Anderson."

"Oh, God." Candace rolled her eyes.

"I know. I've got to keep trying even though that old goat won't go."

"He's a whole mess."

"Don't I know it. Been here almost a year and won't get out," Chrissy said, shaking her head before taking another sip of her coffee.

Candace shrugged taking the paper out of Chrissy's plump hand.

"Don't know how folks stay where they ain't wanted. If you keep telling me I've got to get outta somewhere, I'll be darned if I'mma stick around for you to put me out."

"I know that's right," Candace said, turning up her top lip.

Chrissy shrugged and smiled. "So, how was your weekend, darling? Have fun?"

Candace's grin grew wide across her face. "Chile, I had a ball. Spent some time with my mother, bought some cheap sunglasses, got some good lovin'. I'm floating right now."

"Oh, my. I bet you are," Chrissy said with a chuckle. "That explains the smile you're wearing."

Candace blushed, the image of Chris's long limbs intertwined with hers spun through her mind. She closed her eyes, laughing lightly. When Candace looked up, Chrissy was grinning wide as a Cheshire cat.

"Um-huh. Look at you. Good lovin' got you all starry-eyed and daydreaming. I'm jealous."

Candace burst out laughing. "Bye, Chrissy. I'm not fooling with you today. I'll see you at the morning meeting."

After work, Candace sat in her business writing class twirling locks of her cinnamon hair. Professor Tadlock addressed the room in his usual dry and stoic voice, starting his lecture on the fundamental structure of business writing. Candace's shoulders drooped as he droned on and on. She hated this part of class and could barely keep her weary eyes open. It was the open floor discussion that she really enjoyed. So when Professor Tadlock finally took a seat at his desk and asked the room their thoughts on the week's reading, Candace sat up eagerly. She marveled at the way the room sparked to life when all the students chimed in with their thoughts and concerns on the text.

A skinny, red-haired girl with huge green eyes spoke up first, her voice small but confident. Another kid on the other side of the room disagreed with her and pushed the dark frames of his glasses up his nose while he spoke. His comment brought a response from an older white woman with a cute salt-and-pepper short cut. A young Muslim woman spoke up next. She had good points. Candace decided to chime in.

Candace enjoyed the interaction with her classmates, some her age, some younger, some older. She listened intently as they spoke, nodding her head in agreement, jotting notes in her book, or shaking her head firmly in disapproval. She felt good in class, like everyone, no matter their race, age, color or religion, was trying to achieve the same goal as her— graduation, a degree and big money. And Candace was close, only a few credits away from her bachelor's degree.

Candace was dragging by 8:40 p.m. when class dismissed. *What the hell?* She checked her phone while walking back down Twelfth Street. She had six missed calls: two from Bam, one from Manny and three from her job. She checked her voicemail. The first message was from Jennifer screaming about a late admission who'd come into the building but had no room to go into. Why? Candace had forgotten to inform her that Mr. Anderson, who was slated for discharge, had refused to leave. Candace cursed under her breath, then quickly called her job. A nurse on the second floor picked up.

"Yeah, girl. Jennifer was in here losing her mind," Robyn told

Candace over the phone. "She's gone now. We had to put the new admission up in Silverman's room til she get back from the hospital. Good thing the new admit rolled in here half dead any damn way. He ain't know what was going on."

"Jennifer was pissed, huh?"

"For nothing, though. We knew Mr. Anderson wasn't goin' leave and free up that room. That's why he been here so long, anyway. He get to the door and start screaming and falling down. He crazy. But Jennifer should have checked on that room before she rolled another person up in here. That's her fault."

"Yeah, I guess." Candace sighed, sliding behind the steering wheel. "Thanks, Robyn. I'll see you in the morning."

"Good night, girl, and don't worry about it. Jen is insane anyway. She's always too hype over nothing."

"I know. Good night."

This bitch is going to make this a big fuckin' deal in the morning.

Candace continued checking her messages as she drove. The next message was Bam breathing heavily. Something about her thighs and the New York skyline; she wasn't paying close enough attention to pick up any specific details. The last message was from Manny. Miss P picked him up from camp and he was okay. He only needed to let her know that Uncle B had gotten him the new Jordans, and PJ had broken BJ's iPod so BJ broke PJ's nose and they'd spent the last five hours in the ER. She could hear Miss P fussing in the background. Candace thought twice about letting him stay for the summer.

God, he's going to get into all kinds of shit with them twins.

A headache slowly formed in her temple and throbbed relentlessly as she maneuvered her car along Broad Street to the sanctity of her small quiet apartment. She called Chris but got his voicemail and hung up without leaving a message. She thought about calling again or sending him a text.

"Don't be pressed, C," she told herself while parking. She wanted to see him again—her eyes closed thinking about the warm convulsions he created in her body. But Candace prided herself on recognizing game and she knew better than to like on him too much. "He's a fuckin' kid. Can't get caught up in that."

But she called once more when she was inside, standing naked in front of her bedroom mirror; still no answer. Miss P dropped Emmanuel home close to eleven and after kissing his mother and giving her blow-by-blow details about the bloody brawl between his cousins, he retired quickly and quietly to bed.

At midnight, Candace was restless, wide awake and bored to death. She decided to give Bam a call. He picked up on the third ring.

Though Bam was more attracted to Candace than she was to him, he was easy to talk to and she actually enjoyed their conversations. He never objected much or tried to clutter Candace's world with his own mess. He listened to her vent about Jennifer and huff about her sister's married lover. He chimed in with his comments or questions every so often but nothing more than an, "Oh my," or "Now why she do that?" Candace talked to him until she could barely keep her eyes open. Seconds away from sleep, she plugged the phone into the charger and heard Bam clear his throat.

"Sound like you got a lot on your plate," he said calmly.

"It is a lot right now."

"You goin' let me ease some of that burden off you?"

"What do you mean, Bam?"

"I'm heading to New York this weekend. I got some business to take care of in the city and I was hoping you might join me. Maybe do a little shopping, catch a play if you into that kinda stuff."

"Let me see how the week goes and I'll let you know. Okay, Bam?" she replied sleepily.

"Sounds good. Good night, pretty lady."

"Night, Bam."

CHAPTER 14

When Candace arrived at work the following day, Jennifer was standing outside her office, arms folded across her chest, anxiously tapping her foot.

What the fuck? It's too early for this shit. Candace greeted the receptionist and payroll clerk in the business office and stopped in front of Jennifer who blocked her way.

"What?"

"You know, Candace, we are going to continue to have problems working together if you continue failing to communicate."

Candace rolled her eyes, stepping past Jennifer and unlocking her office door. She wasn't surprised when Jennifer followed her inside.

"Candace, you made a mockery of this building last night," Jennifer continued.

Candace momentarily stood still, then turned and sized up the skinny, long-faced woman in front of her before reaching behind her and closing the office door. "You made a mockery of your damn self, Jennifer."

Jennifer's pupils widened. "Excuse me?"

"You heard me." Candace's neck rolled.

"I don't think I heard you correctly," Jennifer retorted.

Candace shook away her impulsive response to snatch Jennifer up into her small filing closet. *This is the workplace. This is my job. I need this check.* She exhaled deeply. "What, Jennifer? What do you want?"

Jennifer, seemingly unfazed by Candace's question, continued her tirade. "I find it extremely unprofessional not to inform the admissions department of a discharge who fails to leave. I have people lined up to get in this building and when there is a room open, I fill it. I cannot fill a room with someone already in it." Jennifer's voice raised an octave.

Is she fuckin' kidding me? Candace ran her hands through her shoulder-length bob and took another deep breath. She spoke slowly and calmly. "First of all, discharges and notifications are Chrissy's job…"

"Well, aren't you her assistant?" Jennifer interjected.

This bitch is trying to play me. Candace felt heat rising up in her chest, making its way up the back of her neck and causing pressure to form between her temples. She was suddenly so hot she was certain smoke was billowing from her ears.

"Jennifer, get the hell out of my office."

Jennifer gasped. "Excuse me."

Candace's voice skipped a few octaves and before she realized, her hands were on her hips and she was reaching for her office door. "Get the hell out of my office!"

"Excuse me!" Jennifer repeated, clutching her chest as the door swung open in front of her. "I was right; you are unprofessional. Rude, ignorant and unqualified!"

"Bitch, are you seriously standing here in my office calling me names, when you didn't do *your* goddamn job!" Candace was now toe-to-toe with Jennifer waving her finger wildly in the woman's face. "You were supposed to check that room before you brought another person up in here. Don't blame me because of your screw-ups!"

"Excuse me!?" Jennifer screeched, stepping back. "How dare you talk to me like that!"

Candace wanted to pounce. She wanted to slap her or choke her or punch her square between those narrow blue eyes, but before she could even formulate a response, Jennifer was gone, moving with lightning speed in the direction of Denise's office.

Fuck! Candace turned and slammed her office door closed. It wouldn't be long before Denise would be standing in front of her and she'd be going down for losing her cool. *Fuck. I can't believe I let this bitch take me there. It's too goddamn early.* Candace began pacing the floor and as she expected, there was a firm rap on her door a few moments later. Denise entered her office without waiting for an invitation.

"Candace, I need to see you in my office, right now."

Candace's nostrils flared as she nodded. She complied, following Denise out of her office and down the hall. She could see the frozen deer-like expressions on both Allyson's and Danielle's faces. The two girls looked at each other, then back at their supervisor as if they couldn't believe what was happening right in front of them. Candace held her head high.

When she entered Denise's office, a flushed-looking Jennifer sat in one of the chairs in front of Denise's desk, wiping her eyes with a tissue, looking as though she'd been crying.

Candace rolled her eyes. *You've got to be kidding me.*

Denise moved behind her desk and Candace took a defensive position in front of the closed door, crossing her arms over her chest.

"What is going on here?" Denise asked, still standing. She pressed both hands down on the dark mahogany desk and leaned over, staring at the women in front of her.

Silence.

"Don't everybody speak at once," Denise said, jutting her neck out further. Her big green eyes were wide and Candace could tell she meant business.

"Denise," Candace began, "as soon as I walked through the door this morning, Jennifer was standing in front of my office snapping about last night's admission."

"I was not snapping," Jennifer jumped in. "I wanted to know why she didn't alert anyone that the scheduled discharge didn't leave. I simply asked her a question and she got angry and called me out of my name."

The green eyes shot in Candace's direction. "Is this true?"

"Certainly not," Candace replied coolly. "She insulted me, called me 'unprofessional' and 'ignorant,' and I told her to get the heck out of my office."

"Were those your exact words?" Denise asked.

Candace frowned. "No, I said hell. I told her to get the hell out of my office."

"Did you call her a bitch?" Denise asked.

Candace shook her head. "Not at all."

Denise's eyes narrowed. "Candace, Jennifer seems to believe that you called her out of her name. Where would she get that from?"

"I don't know, Denise. Maybe the same place she got that I am Chrissy's assistant and that it was my job to let her know that Mr. Anderson didn't leave."

Denise stepped back. "Mr. Anderson?" She looked at Jennifer who was still dabbing her eyes with tissue. "Two twenty-four? Mr. Anderson?"

Jennifer nodded.

Denise continued, "The same Mr. Anderson who we haven't been able to get rid of for over a year? The Mr. Anderson that falls out in my lobby every time we try to send him to a shelter. That Mr. Anderson? That's the room you were waiting on, Jennifer?"

Again, Jennifer nodded.

"That man is a lunatic." Denise's arms flailed. "Jennifer, how could you not know he wasn't leaving? *I* know he's not leaving. He's the pain in my hide that won't go away. And you scheduled an admission for his room?"

"I received a notice from Social Service that he was leaving yesterday afternoon," Jennifer replied.

"Well, did you verify that he was gone before you approved an admission to come in?"

Jennifer was silent.

"No, she didn't," Candace said with pursed lips. "And she called me three times last night screaming on my answering machine about him. I don't know what Jennifer expects me to do if she doesn't do *her* job, but it's not my fault we didn't have anywhere for the new admit to go. And I don't appreciate her talking to me like she's my boss."

Denise reached for the tall iced coffee on her desk and took a large gulp before finally sitting down. "I don't know what I am going to do with you two. Do I have to separate you like this is kindergarten?"

"No," Candace replied. "Tell her to stay out of my way and everything will be fine."

"Fine? Is it fine to call me out my name, Candace? Even if we disagree professionally, there is no reason for you to disrespect me," Jennifer shouted from the corner of the room.

Candace caught the expletives before they slipped from her lips, swallowing them hard before she spoke, "Jennifer, I show you the same level of respect you show me."

"I have never called you out of your name," Jennifer said, staring at Candace. She then turned to Denise. "And I have never worked in a place where that kind of language is accepted or tolerated."

Candace could see from Denise's expression she felt the pressure behind Jennifer's words. Candace knew she was wrong for calling

Jennifer a bitch, but if it were her word against Jennifer's, they'd have a hell of a time trying to prove she said it.

Denise rubbed her slender chin, tapping her pointer finger against her pursed lips. Candace could tell she was contemplating her next move.

"I need a moment," Denise said after her elongated silence. "Candace, because your coworker has made these accusations against you, I am going to have to investigate, and believe me, I better not find out that you are using foul language in my building, to my team. And Jennifer, you were out of line for your behavior as well. This petty and childish behavior is not the kind I will tolerate in my building, especially from two AIT candidates."

Candace's stomach was in knots.

Denise stood again, walking toward Candace and the door.

"Denise, I...," Jennifer began.

"Jennifer, please," Denise said, raising her hand cutting her short. "I can't right now with you, both of you. Now, back to work and I will proceed with my investigation how I see fit."

Jennifer was on her feet moving out the office behind Candace. Once the door closed behind them, Jennifer sneered at Candace and strode off in silence.

Candace sighed deeply, making her way back to the business office. She checked the clock on the wall. It wasn't even nine a.m. and she was irritated, frustrated and on the verge of losing her job.

Danielle was the first one in her office when Candace sat down.

"Yes?" Candace asked the young brunette while logging on to her computer.

"OOOOHHMMMMIIIGGODDDD! Are you okay?"

"I'm fine," Candace replied.

"Are you in trouble? We thought you was goin' slap her." Danielle's big brown eyes bulged with excitement.

Candace put her head in her hands. "I wanted to, but this is the workplace, Danielle, and we have to behave a certain way. Which is why my tail is on the line."

"Ooh, why?"

"Because of some things I shouldn't have said."

Danielle reduced her voice to a whisper, "'Cause you called her a bitch?"

Candace's heart skipped a beat. *Shit, they'd heard.* She sat up and stared straight into Danielle's big eyes. "Don't repeat that."

"Oh, we won't. Don't worry." Danielle looked behind her at Allyson who was leaning across her desk in an obvious attempt at eavesdropping. Candace glanced at Allyson. Allyson zipped her lips shaking her head vigorously.

Candace's eyes returned to Danielle who hadn't budged from in front of her. "We got you, Candace. I heard Jennifer call you 'rude' and 'ignorant' and 'unqualified' and that's all I know."

"That's all I know, too," Allyson added from across the office.

Candace couldn't help but let out a light chuckle. There was no one in the small business office but Candace, Danielle and Allyson, and they reported to her and they had her back. She smiled.

"Thanks, Danielle."

Danielle winked, bouncing back to her desk. "Sure thing, Miss Lady. Now, can I take off on Friday?"

Candace tossed her Gucci purse on her sage sofa after work and tossed her body down on top of it. She'd kicked her heels off at the door and rubbed her bare feet before propping them up on her small white coffee table. She was seconds from unconsciousness when Emmanuel came bursting through the door.

"What's wrong, Mom?" he asked in a voice that rang loudly in her head.

Candace lifted her hand in an attempt to wave him away, but Emmanuel moved in closer to the couch.

"You okay?" he continued.

"Headache."

"You want me to get you something?"

"Quiet."

Emmanuel sighed. "Well, I'mma go back outside. Cool?"

Candace waved again and she could hear his footsteps creaking back toward the front door. Then a pause and the sound of the footsteps returning.

"Mom?" His voice was a soft whisper. "Did you decide if I could go over Uncle B's yet?"

Candace was silent for a moment, her head tilted upward to the ceiling and her eyes closed. She breathed deeply before parting her lips to respond. "Pack a bag."

CHAPTER 15

"Good morning, sexy."

"Hi," Marci replied, turning over in her bed. She smiled seeing Tommy's name on her caller ID so early in the morning.

"You was sleepin', baby girl?"

"Yes," she cooed into the phone.

"Come have breakfast with me."

"Where are you?"

"I'm in the crib."

Marci sat up slowly, rolling and stretching her shoulders as she rose. "You want to meet me somewhere?"

"Come over here. I'll make you breakfast."

"Oh, hell no! Where the fuck is Donna?"

"She ain't here. You know she went to Atlanta to that weave convention."

"I'm not coming over that crazy bitch house."

"Come on, baby. I miss you. I promise you'll have a real nice time."

"No way, Tommy. You trippin'."

"Aww, babe…"

"Tommy, what I look like creepin' ova my boss' house? That shit ain't cool."

"Marci, this is my house. You come over here because I invited you here. You hear me, baby? Ya' man invited you to his house so he can make breakfast for you."

"Tommy…I don't know…"

"Baby, I want you here," Tommy said forcefully.

Marci shivered, crossing her legs at the warmth rising between them.

She collected the address and in thirty minutes was parking her burgundy Altima on a small side street behind Donna's Mt. Airy home. As Marci walked through the back driveway, she could see Tommy standing outside by a white garage door in a wife beater and blue basketball shorts, his muscles protruding under the tight fit top. He met her with wet kisses, and firm arms grasped around her slim waist before leading her inside. They stepped into a large finished basement complete with a couch and end tables, a huge flat-screen television and game system, a pool table and a washer and dryer.

"You look beautiful today, baby," Tommy said, eyeing her up in her form-fitting and short khaki dress.

Marci struck a pose.

Tommy smiled hard, revealing all of his bright clean teeth. "You look like Kelly Rowland in that *Cater to You* video."

Marci tucked a lock of her eighteen-inch, jet-black Brazilian weave behind her cocoa brown ear and smiled sweetly. "I get that a lot. Kelly reps for the slim chocolate girls. I love her."

Tommy laughed, stepping behind her and rubbing her shoulders while edging her toward the stairs. "I made breakfast for you, baby. I don't want your food to get cold."

Marci marched forward silently entering a spacious eat-in kitchen at the top of the stairs. Tommy, scooting past her, hurriedly pulled out a chair at the table and ushered Marci into the seat. He then served her omelets filled with chopped tomatoes and grilled sausages and served kisses between her bites. He buttered her toast and poured her orange juice and stroked her hair as she sipped.

Marci smiled from the inside out and after chowing down her

meal, she dropped to her knees pushing Tommy back against the sink and began chowing down on him. She sucked happily, the muscles of her jaws working to make him swell. After Tommy's legs began shaking, he lifted Marci off her knees and up to his waist, her legs curling around him. He led her to the end of the long glass table in the middle of the kitchen laying her back down flat against it. He poured syrup in her belly button, spread her legs and purred over her puffy clit. A quick flip and Marci was on all fours on the tabletop poking her backside up into the air. Tommy poured the syrup down her back watching it slide into the split of her butt cheeks. He hungrily licked it out. Marci's body gyrated and jerked uncontrollably, trembling at every titillating touch.

Her body sticky and wet with syrup and her own excitement, Marci held tight to Tommy as he picked her up, carrying her upstairs to the shower. Marci stepped into the big white basin, pulling back her hair and turning on the water.

"You so fuckin' sexy, baby," Tommy said, smiling, staring at her. "I'm gonna get us some washcloths and towels. Okay? I be right back."

Marci nodded and Tommy stepped out of the bathroom and walked down the hall toward the linen closet. He was returning down the hall with towels in hand when the doorbell rang. Marci jumped at the sound, clutching her heart and shutting off the water.

"Who the fuck?" Tommy whispered angrily.

"Who is it?" Marci asked, peeking from out the bathroom door.

"I don't know!" Tommy answered with eyes wide as saucers. The chime sounded again.

"Tommy, it's Aunt Nay," an older woman's voice yelled from the other side of the thick white door. Tommy grabbed Marci out of the tub, pushing the towels into her arms and shoving her into what appeared to be one of the kids' bedrooms.

"Shit," he cried. "Get in here. It's Donna's fuckin' aunt. I'm a get rid of this bitch real quick."

Tommy ran down the stairs adjusting his clothes in the process. The doorbell went off again and Marci nearly jumped out of her skin in the teenage boy's stuffy bedroom. She settled her wet body quietly down on the corner of the bed and could hear Tommy downstairs moving quickly. He was trying to tidy up before opening the door and the woman outside sounded like she was getting impatient.

"Thomas!" Aunt Nay sang, still sounding the bell. "Come on, open this door, boy. It's hot out here."

Tommy finally opened the door after a moment.

"Where them kids at, Tommy? And why the hell you sweating?"

"I was working out," he answered quickly.

"Well, where the kids at?" she asked, referring to Donna's two teenagers from a previous relationship.

"They not here. They went with Tee last night."

"Oh, well, ain't nobody tell me that. Shit, I coulda stayed my black ass home," Aunt Nay said, huffing and fanning herself. "It's hot...and I gots to pee."

Marci heard Tommy begin to interject, but his words were cut short by the sound of creaking stairs. Aunt Nay was coming up the steps with Tommy right behind her. Marci made a mad dash for the closet as Aunt Nay sauntered past the bedroom door heading for the bathroom. Tommy crept into the room. From her crouched position in the closet, Marci could see him searching for her. The closet door was partially cracked and Tommy checked it finding her squatting uncomfortably in the dark cramped space.

"Stay low," he whispered.

Marci crouched further down. She had not finished showering and her body was wet and sticky. Beads of sweat were beginning to run from her forehead and the dirty clothes hamper in the teenage boy's closet was crammed with dingy socks and boxers overflowing to the floor. The loose items of clothing stuck to her moist body.

Marci felt like the woman was in the bathroom forever. "This is some bullshit," she grumbled under her breath. She could hear Tommy downstairs straightening up the kitchen and Aunt Nay finally exiting the bathroom. Tommy must have run to meet her at the bottom of the steps because Marci heard his feet shuffle across the floor and the front door open.

"Aight, Aunt Nay," she heard Tommy say.

"Boy, close that door. You lettin' the air out," the woman snapped back.

Slam! The door shut and Aunt Nay plopped down on the couch. Marci could hear the buttons being pressed on a cell phone and Aunt Nay's voice shouting loud and clear.

"Girl, let me tell you how I done came all the way the hell ova here in this heat and them raggedy kids ain't even here...yeah, girl, I know. Somebody certainly coulda called. It's bein' considrit... that's all."

Marci could tell that the woman was not anxious to go back out into the stifling humidity. She was sweating herself, and after trying to keep still and quiet for more than forty minutes, Marci fell asleep in the closet while Aunt Nay was on the phone. She lifted her eyes, slowly reacquainting herself with her surroundings and noticing how quiet the house was. A second later she was startled by Tommy leaning into the closet.

"That bitch sleep," he whispered.

"What! What the fuck am I supposed to do now?"

"I don't know; let me think," Tommy said, running his hand through his hair and stopping to rub his own tense neck.

"You gotta get her outta here, Tommy. Wake her ass up."

Tommy breathed deeply, puffing out his chest and walking out of the room. Marci heard him jogging down the steps.

"Hey, Aunt Nay. You, you ah need me to make you something to eat?" he asked loudly, apparently startling the woman awake.

"What, boy?" she stammered. "What you want?"

"I was about to cook something while you was sleep. You wanna eat?"

"I wasn't sleep. I was restin' my eyes. 'Sides, I don't eat that shit you been cookin'. I'm 'bout to go anyway." The couch shifted and creaked. "Tell Donna to call me when she get back."

The door slammed and Marci could hear Tommy skipping the stairs.

"What the fuck!" Marci screeched, standing up as he entered the room.

"I am so sorry, baby. I didn't know she was coming over here. She's always in the way. I am so sorry."

Tommy leaned forward to kiss Marci, but she pulled away. He grabbed her by the waist, paralyzing her movement and keeping his groin thrust into her. Marci could not get far and her resistance was momentary. He pressed her back against the wall and her breasts heaved into his chest. Removing her towel, he exposed her bare. sticky, wet body and licked his lips.

"And I still want you here," he said, pulling down his shorts and lifting her body up to his waist. He kissed her lips hungrily, bringing her body down with himself inside her. Marci squealed taking him in as Tommy drove into her with slow, rounding thrusts. She gracefully arched her back against the wall pressing her pussy forward to receive his generous strokes. His hands cupping her behind, Tommy rocked her body, moving into her hard and long. He carried her with him inside the bathroom to the shower, turning the water on over their sultry bodies. He made love to her in the stall, pressing her face against the cool tile before carrying her to his bedroom and laying her on top of the mattress. Marci scanned the room as he lay her down. She caught a glimpse of a photo of Donna on a tall dresser and rolled her eyes, pulling Tommy in closer. He obliged, continuing to slide inside of her, kissing, licking and sucking her all over his bed.

CHAPTER 16

"This house is too damn quiet." Candace huffed, tossing a small load of Emmanuel's clothes into the washer. "The boy's only been gone two days and I miss him already." She closed the lid and flicked the light on her way out of the small utility closet and headed into the living room.

The automatic Air Wick freshener sprayed Candace with a quick mist of Tropical Rain as she walked down the hall causing her to pause and inhale deeply. She stared out into her spacious and tidy living room, smiling at the good job she'd done cleaning up the place.

"Yeah, I miss my son. But thank God I'll be able to keep my house clean for more than a day," Candace said, laughing aloud. Her phone rang in her bedroom behind her as Candace made her way to the kitchen. She busted a U-turn moving quickly to retrieve the device.

Checking the caller ID, she measured the caller worthy of the spare moments she had and picked up with a sultry, "Hello."

"Hello, pretty lady," Bam said with a smile in his voice.

"How's it going, Bam?"

"All is well on my end. How 'bout you, sexy lady?"

"Oh, well. I can't complain. Things are looking up."

"Oh? How so?"

"Well, you know I told you how I had to cuss the white girl out at my job, right?"

"Yeah. How did that turn out?"

"They didn't find out anything during the investigation other than we were arguing, so we both got written up for misconduct."

"You shoulda slapped that girl," Bam said firmly.

Candace burst out laughing. "Bam, you stupid."

"No, baby. I applaud you. You truly are a lady. I know some young girls your age that woulda got to whoopin' ass in the workplace."

Candace laughed again. "You don't know how many times I've thought about attacking that woman. But that's what she'd expect. I know she thinks I'm beneath her, like she's better than me. So, I struggle to keep my cool. But, man, it's hard."

"Yeah, I'm sure, baby."

"I'm mad at myself for even losing it a little this time… I called that chick a bitch. Yeah, I did. Right to her fuckin' face and I wanted to kick her ass, too. But you know, Bam, I'm too cool for that."

This time Bam laughed. "Yes, you are, baby. Crazy, sexy and cool."

"Thank you."

"That's a good mix, makes for good company in a woman."

"Is that so?" Candace asked.

"Yes, and I'm still waiting to hear back from you about enjoying the pleasure of your company, pretty lady, on my trip to New York this weekend."

Candace paused. *Damn, I forgot he asked me to go to New York.* She juggled the notion in her head. "When are you trying to leave?" she asked.

"I'm thinking sometime tomorrow evening. It's only a two-hour drive. We can get there in time to get something to eat, maybe spend a lil' quality time and for me to get some rest 'cause I need to be somewhere early Saturday morning."

"Oh. Okay."

"I've got a nice suite booked at the Radisson in Midtown. Come wit' me, baby. Let Big Daddy show you a good time."

Candace smiled again, trying to figure out what it was she liked about Bam. *Maybe I should go 'head and let this big nigga spoil me. I'mma have to give 'em some, though.* She sighed.

"You're up for a good time. Aren't you, pretty lady?" Bam continued.

"Almost always, Bam."

"Make this one of those always, not an almost."

Candace shrugged. "You know what, Bam. I don't see why not." *It's a Thursday evening. Emmanuel's gone. I ain't heard shit from Chris' ass all week. Shit, I ain't got a damn thing else to do.*

"Great! Let's say I pick you up tomorrow evening sometime around six?"

"Sounds good. How long are we staying? How much should I pack?"

"We'll be back before Sunday seven a.m. service. I got a friend I need to meet up with soon as I get back in town. And, pack light. I told you, baby, let Big Daddy take care of things. I gotchu, okay?"

"Okay. If you say so."

"Good. I look forward to setting my eyes on your beautiful face tomorrow, Miss Candace."

"Good night, Bam."

"Night night."

Candace was glad her Friday was a calm one. Denise was on vacation and Jennifer was out of the building marketing to local hospitals. Candace spent most of her day finishing her billing charges and the rest surfing the web. At close to quitting time, she locked her office door, said good night to her staff and sashayed out of the front building a half hour early.

Let's see, she thought, once she was back at her apartment, flipping through her panty drawer. There were plenty pretty panties to choose from, but she wanted something very subtle for Bam. She pulled a slinky pink thong from her drawer and twirled it around her finger. *A G-string or thong would be too much for him*, she thought, dropping the panties back in the drawer. *Old motha-fucka probably have a heart attack. Maybe some shorts.* Candace reached for a dainty black pair of boy shorts made entirely of lace. She held them up to make sure they were perfect and nodded, knowing Bam would have a hard time catching his breath when he saw how sexy her cheeks looked peeking out the bottom of the panties. A matching black bra was tossed into her small Betsy Johnson travel bag as well as her brush and comb, deodorant and tooth-brush, a sheer nightgown and three dresses.

Candace smiled at her dress selections—a true expression of skilled retail frugality, thousands of dollars' worth of high-end clothes she'd only paid a few hundred bucks for. Her biggest score was the black-and-red BCBG number she'd picked up on ridicu-lous sale at Lord & Taylor one afternoon with Marci. Candace could barely breathe in it, but little sister convinced her she had to have it, especially when the retail tag of $398 had been marked all the way down to $78. There was her black Calvin Klein dress she'd caught on sale at Macy's that she loved; it was wrinkle free and folded easily into her travel bag, and finally, a cute but refined little blue no-name special with soft ruffles around the neckline, cinching silver band around her waist and flowing hem that she'd grabbed from a tiny boutique in Manayunk. Three different looks for whatever the weekend would bring.

Bam arrived in his shiny blue BMW at a quarter to six ready to hit the road for the Big Apple. Candace knew she looked stunning in her all-white attire, her long legs almost completely bare in her tiny white cotton shorts. She slipped on a comfortable pair of silver Guess sandals, silver aviator shades and met Bam outside.

Bam smiled from his car window; looking her over, obviously pleased by the way Candace looked in her short shorts.

"Good, goddamn, girl," he said, mouth hanging open and pulling down his Gucci glasses. "You got enough legs on you, girl, to win a mothafuckin' marathon."

Candace shook her head, pushing her straightened hair behind her ear. Pulling her apartment door closed hard behind her, she picked up her bag and stood for a moment on the sidewalk staring at Bam sitting in the car smiling. He didn't move; he sat grinning at her. Candace looked down at the luggage in her hand, then back over at Bam. Why hadn't he gotten out of the car to get her bag yet?

Bam licked his lips and grinned. "What's wrong, pretty lady? You forgot something?"

"No. But you must have," she responded, hand on hip.

Bam's smile dropped and his eyebrows furrowed. "Why would you say that?"

"You say I'm such a lady. Such a pretty lady, Bam. So then why am I standing on the curb holding my own bag?"

Bam burst out laughing, opening his car door and stepping out onto the sidewalk. "Well, ain't this something?" He chuckled, holding his hand over his heart and walking toward Candace.

She grinned, admiring his tailored slacks, gator sandals and casual button-down blue shirt.

"You callin' me out on my shit, huh? Treat you like a fuckin' lady, huh, Miss Candace? Well, I ain't mad atcha." Bam gently slipped the bag out of her grasp, and carrying the luggage in one hand, extended his free arm, allowing Candace to slip her arm beneath it. She glanced at his Breitling wristwatch glistening in the sunlight.

"Thank you," Candace said, smiling at Bam walking her into the street and opening her car door. She stepped inside, the creamy leather clean and fresh. Bam placed her things in the trunk and climbed in the driver's seat.

He pulled smoothly out into the street heading toward the expressway off Wissahickon Avenue. Candace settled comfortably in the soft spacious seats. She gently stroked the clean leather under her thighs, her eyes scanning over all the amenities in the luxury vehicle. *This is how I need to be riding on the regular.* She crossed her legs, then glanced over at Bam who was watching the road but peeking her way ever so often.

"So, Bam. You're going to show me a good time, huh?"

"Sweetie, I don't have nothing but good times. You'll see with Big Daddy, life is good."

Candace smiled. "Okay, Big Daddy. I'm due for something good."

Bam reached over and patted her thigh. "You've got it, baby."

Candace stared ahead, watching as Bam passed every car to their right, then finally slowed to an even seventy mph. Bam switched on the radio and Gerald Levert came belting out of the speakers. Candace chuckled at the dated tune. After a short while of smooth old school tunes, Candace felt her eyes flutter. She didn't realize she'd fallen asleep until she felt Bam's heavy hand on her thigh again, shaking her softly. Candace awoke to find herself in the heart of New York City nightlife.

"Rise and shine, pretty lady," Bam sang.

Candace sat up wiping the corners of her mouth, her eyes surveying the busy scene around her. Hundreds of people flooded the streets of midtown Manhattan, everyone moving seamlessly through the throngs and chatting to someone beside them or on their cell phones. There had to be a dozen arms waving down the passing cabs. Candace counted at least twenty cabs at the light. Bam's big blue BMW stood out at the intersection like a sore thumb surrounded by a sea of yellow, but no one seemed to notice. The luxury car didn't turn heads in New York like it did in the neighborhood she grew up in.

"We're right here," Bam said, pulling the car up to the front entrance of the Radisson at Forty-eighth and Lexington Avenue. Candace snapped back from her thoughts to see a young uniformed Hispanic kid reaching for her door, staring and smiling. She stepped out with a long stretch, knowing the valet was watching and smiled back politely.

Okay, lil' cutie, she thought, looking the boy up and down. *Damn, he's only gotta be like nineteen, twenty? Oh, Candace...you like robbin' the cradle? Hahaha.*

A second later Bam's arm slid firmly around Candace's waist; she felt his tight squeeze pulling her into his big belly. "Come on, baby. Let's check in so we can go get something to eat," he said into her ear, kissing her cheek.

Oh, boy. Candace laughed to herself, *here we go.*

They entered the two-room luxury suite with a bedroom and a separate sitting room that housed an oak television cabinet, casing a nicely sized flat-screen and two fine quality cocoa brown sofas and matching coffee table. In the second room of the suite was a beautiful king-size bed dressed in crisp white linens positioned squarely in the center of the floor of the master bedroom. Candace surveyed her surroundings. *Nice*, she thought. It wasn't the Plaza, but this place was nothing like the raggedy shack she'd torn up sheets in with Chris.

"There's a terrace?" she asked, not realizing her voice was an excited shout.

Bam smiled. "How else you think Big Daddy do it? Only the best."

Candace smiled, moving past Bam to the far left side of the room and pulling back the thin white curtains covering the tall door leading out to the small landing of their twenty-fourth-floor suite. She unlocked the door quickly and stepped outside. It was beautiful. The traffic from the streets beneath her moving in syncopated rhythm, the stretching buildings surrounding seemed so much more than just slabs of concrete and walls. There was an authenticity to the sights she beheld; it was that something special about New York that made Candace inhale and grin.

"God, I love this city," she said softly to herself. "Damn, it's been like four years since I been out here." Candace shook her head, thinking about her excursions with Prince, when Bam appeared on the small terrace beside her holding two tall champagne glasses. Candace had no idea from where the drinks had come, she hadn't seen Bam open any bottles, but she accepted the glass, sipping coolly on the chilled beverage. *Moscato. Um*, she took another taste.

"Beautiful, isn't it?" Bam asked, stroking her back.

"It is," she replied.

"This your first time in the Big Apple, sexy lady?"

"No, not at all. I used to come a lot when I was younger with my son's dad and I've been on a couple day trips to see a play or shop, but it's been a few years."

"Oh, no," he cooed, frowning and taking her free hand pulling her in close to him. "That's too long. New York is a busy place, a lot to see, too much to do and way too much money to be spent."

Candace, chuckling lightly, asked, "Are you a big shopper in New York?"

"What do you mean?"

"I mean, check you out, Bam." She pulled at the crisp collar of his designer label navy blue shirt. "You can dress and I know you like nice things. It's the reason you like me. So, do you come to New York just to shop?"

"Sometimes." He sipped his glass, pinching Candace's backside and laughing. "Don't worry, baby, I came prepared."

Candace pursed her lips and nodded. "Good."

"Now, go change so we can eat. I'm starving," Bam instructed, releasing his grasp.

Candace slipped into the marble tiled bathroom, retrieving her black favorite from her bag. *I knew you'd be perfect.* She stared at the dress before hanging it up and stripping down to her panties and bra. Though she did not rush, it took Candace no time to change into the tight black piece, strap on her black pumps, smooth her lips over with a bright red hue, swap her accessories and step out of the bathroom in style.

Dinner was delicious. Bam ordered the twelve-ounce Porterhouse and a select bottle of Nicolas Feuillatte Brut Rose champagne that had Candace buzzing by the end of her first glass. Her chicken scallopine was divine and she ate every bit to help absorb the swirling effects of the sparkling wine she consumed so gingerly.

"Are you enjoying the champagne?" Bam asked over his plate.

"I am," she replied, smiling and lifting her glass to him.

By the end of their meal, Bam was buzzing, too, and giggling like a schoolboy on the cab ride back to the hotel. He was snoring by the time Candace made it out of the bathroom.

"Oh, God." She laughed lightly. *This fat mothafucka here already sleep. Hahaha, least I won't be givin' him none tonight. I'm going to bed.* She slipped into her thin black negligee, curling up at the far corner of the king-sized bed, and passed out.

When Candace woke up the next morning, she was alone in the hotel room. There was a note from Bam on the dresser telling her to relax and enjoy breakfast, and he would be back soon. She did just that, after ordering a bottle of champagne from room service to accompany her meal.

"I needed this shit, here," Candace said aloud, plopping back on the big bed and wrapping her bare body in the plush hotel robe. She lay for a moment staring up at the ceiling. "How come I can't treat myself to this kind of shit? I need to be able to live like this on the regular." She sat up and poured herself another glass before heading over to the terrace. Candace opened the door, stepping out over the busy Saturday morning streets of Manhattan.

"I need this shit," she repeated, taking a swig and loosening her robe. Candace held up her glass in cheers and, taking another big sip, moved closer to the waist-high concrete wall protecting her from going over twenty-four floors. Slipping her hand to the knot closing the robe in at her waist, she untied it further, allowing the robe to fall open and expose her bare breasts to whoever could see.

If they lookin' up this high, they need to see something, Candace thought, pulling the white cozy fabric even further apart until her stomach, then waist and finally legs were exposed. She stood quietly for a moment, soaking up the warmth, strength and light from the sun into her almost completely naked body. The robe still adorning her shoulders, Candace sipped again. *Have to make the most of this trip.* She thought of Bam snoring beside her and sighed deeply.

Candace thought of Prince and all the trips they'd taken and the many places he'd promised they would go one day when the streets didn't require so much of his attention.

Her mind created an image of him settled in behind black bars. It was amazing how they used to want the same things in life, but Candace, unlike her son's father, was willing to work both honest and hard for them. Candace squinted her eyes in the bright sunlight, a brightness she wondered if Prince could see or even feel. She missed Prince spoiling her; he'd kept her near to him since she was a teenager and taking care of her was a responsibility he took seriously. Candace always had the best purses and had been to every Red Lobster and snazzy steak house in Philadelphia. But Prince was long gone and she probably wouldn't see him for another four or five years. Candace thought of Bam, she knew she wanted a pocketbook, a big pretty bag.

When Bam returned around ten a.m., Candace was dressed in her classy blue number with silver cinching waist sitting calmly on one of the sofas.

"Good morning, pretty lady," he said, smiling as he entered the room.

Candace smiled back. "Good morning."

"You look nice."

"Thank you. So do you," she replied, admiring his cream linen suit with tan gators. *The big man certainly can dress.*

"Thank you, baby. Did you miss me?"

Candace nodded. She did not ask where he'd been; he did not offer. "I knew you'd be back for me."

"Oh, is that so?"

"Very much so. The day is too beautiful for you to spend it alone."

Bam laughed loud. "Who says I was alone?"

"You weren't with me and that's all that matters," Candace replied coolly.

"You are right about that," Bam agreed, moving in closer to her on the sofa.

"You got some time for me now, big daddy?" she asked, crossing her legs toward him.

Bam licked his lips. "All the time in the world."

"Good, I want to hit up Madison Avenue and do a little shopping."

"Is that what you want?"

Candace licked her lips and said firmly but sweetly, "Yes."

Bam showered while Candace admired her pricy picks of jewelry from Barney's and Chanel. She bit her lip smiling at the $790 price tag on the nude Manolo Blahniks she now owned and the $800 Prada bag she had to add to her collection. She didn't see the price on the diamond-studded tennis bracelet or diamond and pearl-encrusted earrings he had paid for, but she knew they both cost a pretty penny.

Shit! I have to admit, I'm impressed. She traced her nails along the dainty Chanel jewelry box. *A girl could get used to this.* She smiled.

Suddenly, Bam came out of the bathroom, the cozy robe barely covering his rotund belly. Seeing the glassy look in his eyes, Candace's smile fell. Bam moved toward her on the other side of the bedroom, closing her in the space between the bed and the wall. Candace had nowhere to go to move out of his direct advances, unless she crawled across the bed, but he was in front of her face quickly, grinning wide as a Cheshire cat. *Goddam, this nigga want payment on delivery. He is not playing.*

Bam looked down at the bags and boxes on the bed. "You like all those nice things, Big Daddy bought you?"

"I do."

"Yeah? Can you show Big Daddy how much you like 'em?" Bam reached forward touching her cheek gently. Candace began to turn away, but Bam grabbed the hair at the back of her neck and pulled, jerking her head back toward him.

"What the fuck?" Candace yelped.

"Oh, you a tough one, huh, pretty lady? Big Daddy gotchu all alone up here in this nice hotel with all these nice gifts, and I can't play rough witcha?"

"Play rough?" Candace asked, trying to step back and realizing Bam still held her by her hair.

"Play rough." He squeezed.

"Ugh!" Candace shouted. "Stop! That shit hurts."

"Aww, come on, baby. Don't tell me you can't handle Big Daddy, now?" Bam leaned in, pulling Candace toward him and kissing her lips. Candace cringed; his lips were thick but dry and his mustache scratched her face.

She pulled back, putting her hand on Bam's bare chest, noticing his breasts were almost as large as hers. "I can handle it!" she shouted.

"Good. That's what I like to hear."

"Just don't be trying to hurt me." Her voice softened.

Bam loosened his grasp slightly. "Aww, baby. Big Daddy's not trying to hurt you, but he do wanna have some fun witchu." He kissed her again. "Can we have some fun?"

Candace closed her eyes. "We can. Let me slip out of this dress and we can have all the fun you want."

Again, his mouth unwelcomingly met hers before he finally released his grasp, stepping to the side so she could pass. Candace calmly made her way to the bathroom, grabbing the bottle of champagne from the small fridge by the door. She downed nearly half the bottle while slipping out of her dress and taking a warm rag to her girlie to freshen her up. She felt a small buzz immediately, knowing the rest of the intoxication would soon come at the most desirable time—when she was fucking Bam.

Candace stepped in front of Bam, sitting patiently on the bed, in her black lace panty and matching bra, causing him to grin hard and dumb. The champagne surged through her as she swayed her way to him. Bam stood, grabbing at her ravenously, his large hands falling heavy against her skin.

Reaching his hand around the back of her head, he pulled Candace into him, kissing her sloppily. He maintained his hold easing back down onto the bed. She gave in to his aggressive movements and found her knees folding and her face moving toward his lap. Bam pulled open his robe revealing his proud manhood. Candace stared. *Not too bad. Fat, as expected. Could be a lil' longer though, for a man so tall. Wanna call himself Big Daddy? Hahaha.*

The champagne gave her the giggles with Bam thrusting his shaft into her mouth. Candace obliged, moving her mouth over his head. She sucked him in a dizzy blur until Bam pulled her off her knees, then dressed his manhood in a condom from the nightstand. Candace's mouth ran with spit as she stood swaying over top of him undressing. Bam grabbed her tight, pulling her down into his lap.

"Oh, come on now, baby. Come sit on Big Daddy's dick."

"Ooh," she gasped in surprise, settling down on his erection. She pressed her pelvis down hard on Bam, feeling his shaft move up in her, hitting a spot she liked. Bam pumped up and Candace pushed her hips down hard. "Ooh," she moaned. *There it is again.*

Candace began gyrating and rolling her hips at each of Bam's upward thrusts. He grabbed at her waist pulling her breasts into his face, lapping at her nipples swinging by his lips. Candace pushed against his big belly, grinding her waist down and forward on him. She moaned again. *Um, if I keep his dick right here, that shit actually feels kinda good.* "Umm."

"Work that shit on Big Daddy, baby," Bam said, smacking her ass.

Candace moved harder. "Umm."

"You like Big Daddy dick in that pretty young pussy? Big Daddy treat you nice, don't he?"

"Yea," Candace replied through clenched teeth.

"Work that pussy, baby. Ride Big Daddy dick like you want it." Bam pumped as she grinded. "Yeah, I'm all up in this pussy. You like Big Daddy dick in ya pussy, baby?"

"Yea."

"Yea, baby. Work them hips on Big Daddy. I like that. You like that?"

Shut the fuck up.

"You like that?" he repeated after not hearing her response.

"Yea," she stammered, losing concentration and struggling to get back in rhythm.

All of a sudden, Bam flipped her over onto the bed. "Bend over," he commanded.

Candace complied, pressing her face into the pillow and poking her ass up high into the air. Bam slid in and went to work, pounding hard against her. He slammed his meaty dick hard within her walls holding her waist tight in place. Candace reached under herself, between her own legs and began fingering her clit. Bam kept slamming, his thrusts shaking her entire body inside and out. He hit her walls hard and strong and unmercifully until Candace started to yell.

"Oh, fuck. Goddamn, Bam!" She turned, looking back at him. Bam continued slamming. Candace chanted in her head each time her ass hit his waist and his dick jolted up inside her. *Bam! Bam! Bam*, as their flesh met.

"Yea, baby. Big Daddy bouncing that ass!"

"Yes!"

"You like Big Daddy bouncing that ass, baby?"

"Yes!"

"Tell me you like Big Daddy bouncing that ass."

"I like Big Daddy bouncing my ass."

"Yea!"

"Umm," Candace moaned as Bam grabbed a handful of her hair. "Fuck me!"

"Yea, baby. I like that. Big Daddy makin' you feel good, right? Can you make Big Daddy feel good?"

"Yea," Candace answered.

"Yea?"

"Yea," she repeated between the thuds and tremors.

"I want you to do something to make Big Daddy feel real good. Can you do that?"

"Yea."

"Good, baby. Come pee on Big Daddy."

"What?" Candace jerked her head around, staring dead into Bam's eyes. He was serious.

"Come on, baby." *Bam! Bam! Bam!*

Candace moaned loud against her will, struggling to keep a straight face. "You wan…wanna…wanna…what?"

"I want you to piss on me, baby. Please?"

His eyes turned downward, a pleading grin running across his face, still slamming.

"Un unh," she replied, biting her lip.

"You not gonna try it for Big Daddy?" He continued thrusting.

"Un unh."

"Come on, baby." *Bam! Bam! Bam!*

"Huh? Ummm."

Bam spoke, pressing into her. "Come on, baby. I want you to piss on me. Let me feel that warm shit on my chest." Bam pulled out, turned around and sat down beneath Candace's wide-open legs on the floor. Candace stood over him, lowering her woman-hood over his face. He sucked greedily at her clit, interchanging rubs and pats between licks and kisses. Candace felt herself cumming. She clenched her pussy as he twirled and tapped it. Then realizing she did have to pee, she simply went, all over Bam, until the warm yellow-tinted liquid ran down his chest and onto the floor.

"Oh, shit yea, baby," he said, jerking his manhood wildly until he exploded.

Candace stood up straight and stepped back looking at him in his mess. *What the fuck.* She scratched her head while reaching for the wall to help her balance. Bam sat shaking in a puddle of piss and Candace couldn't help but laugh.

"You're into some freak shit, Bam."

"You ain't seen nothing yet."

CHAPTER 17

"I 'on't think I heard you right. You WHAT?!?!"

"Bitch, you heard me. I pissed on that nigga."

Marci fell over laughing, holding her side in hysterics on Candace's couch.

"Shut up, girl." Candace hooted, slapping her own leg, sitting across from her sister. "I ain't know what to do."

"So you pissed on him?" Marci asked, sitting up and wiping away the tears from her eyes.

Candace laughed hard. "You stupid. Girl, yeah. He asked me to."

"What?" Marci asked, giggling. "And ya nasty ass did it. Ill. You nasty."

"Shut up," Candace joked, swatting at her.

Marci dipped back, still holding her side. "Oh, that is too funny. How somebody just ask you to piss on them? Like where does that shit even come from?"

"Mars, don't get me to lying. I don't even know. All I know is he was hitting it from the back hard, too, like, *Bam! Bam! Bam!* I was like, 'Oh shit.'"

"Okay, Big Daddy. That's probably why they call that nigga Bam," Marci chimed in, smiling.

"Right. His old ass was putting in a lil work back there. So I'm like, cool everything is good. Then he start talking all that 'I'm in this pussy shit…Tell Big Daddy you like it.'…blah blah blah, right?"

Marci waved her hand dismissively. "Oh God. Shut up."

"Right. So, I'm tuning him out concentrating on where he's hitting so I can ride this shit out and at least try to get one off. Girl, next thing I know. He like, 'Do something to make Big Daddy feel good.' And this mothafucka asked me to pee on 'em."

Marci toppled over again howling. "Oh, shit, I can't breathe. That is too fuckin' funny. Ohmigod, my stomach hurts."

Candace joined in, tears soon running down her face as well. She could barely get the words out between hearty laughs. "Marci, I swear, I was like, huh? Bahahahaha…. then I was like oh, shit… I really do gotta pee and he was right under me…so…so… I went."

"AHAHAHAHAHA!!!"

"On, his chest and shit! Then he sittin' in the piss jerking off… HAHAHA! I…. I…couldn't…I was stuck…like…what the…?"

"AHAHAHA! Oh my God! That's fuckin' nasty! You a nasty bitch, Candace Reign Brinton."

"Shut cha ass up, Marcine Nichelle Brinton. I know you've done some worse shit than that withcha fresh ass, so don't be talkin' shit."

Marci kept laughing and spoke proudly, "You know I'm into all that freaky shit, but I ain't never had nobody ask me to pee on 'em. I 'ont think I could."

Candace twisted her lips, stood and headed toward her bedroom without saying a word and Marci's head turned, following her sister out of the living room. When Candace returned, she carried her freshly wrapped and bagged souvenirs in her arms.

Marci sat up straight, eyes bulging at the size of the Prada bag Candace sat down in front of her on the coffee table. Beside it she sat her Manolo Blahnik shoe box and two dainty bags from Chanel and Barney's. Candace grinned at Marci's jaw hanging open.

"You don't know if you could what?" Candace asked, pulling the red studded pumps from the box and slipping one on her foot.

Marci shook her head. "Um, tell Big Daddy he can call me Mother

Nature 'cause I'd be dropping some golden showers on that ass, for real. Goddamn, that's a bad shoe!"

Candace burst out laughing. "Tell me about it," she said, catching her breath and waving her arm over her other trinkets. "And this shit ain't too bad either. Take a look."

Marci dug in, pulling the purse from its wrapping. "Oooh," she cooed, running her pink manicured nails over the gold embellishments in the brown leather.

"You like that, huh?" Candace teased.

"Yeah, this is nice. I see why you was pissin' on people."

Candace laughed. "Man, I don't even know what I got myself in to. This nigga's a OG wit' some nice change and some nasty habits."

"Um, ain't that always the case. Them old heads be into something else. Tryna keep they groove, I guess."

"I don't know," Candace said, shrugging. "I know he pulled the shit outta my hair."

Marci scooted over to her sister, reaching for Candace's locks. "Yeah, your roots look like shit."

"Bitch, that's what I got you for."

Marci playfully popped her sister on the top of her head. "Shut up, and come on, sit down so I can get started. Plus, I gotta tell you 'bout me and Tommy."

"Ohmigod, what'd you do?"

"Why I had to do something, Miss Pissy?"

They laughed together until Candace replied, "Because I know you. What'd you do?" She settled on the floor between Marci's legs.

"C, lemme tell you how I went over Tommy's to have breakfast, right...and..."

"Tommy's house?" Candace interjected.

"Yeah, he wanted me to come over 'cause he made breakfast for me."

"At his house? The one he shares with his wife? Your boss?"

Marci nodded. "Yeah. So…"

Candace spun around looking her sister in the face. "Marcine, what the fuck are you doin' at that girl house? Talkin' 'bout I'm nasty. I know you ain't sleep with that man in his wife's house."

"I did," Marci replied, rolling her neck.

"Bitch, you know you wrong."

"How I'm wrong? That's my man's house and he invited me over for breakfast so I went."

"Oh, boy."

"Oh, boy, what? You can piss on old-ass suga daddies, but I can't have breakfast with my man?"

"You grown. You can do whatever the fuck you want. But me pissin' on a single man in a suite he paid for is far different from you fucking a married man in the house him and his wife share."

"You always tryna judge somebody, C."

"I am not. I'm just saying that shit ain't cool. You can't go creepin' in nobody else house," Candace said, staring directly into Marci's eyes.

Marci looked away, shrugging. "Whatever."

Candace sucked her teeth. "Get mad if you want. What if somebody woulda seen y'all or Donna woulda came home early or some shit? You can't be putting ya self in them type situations. Especially not since you work for his fuckin' wife. I mean, come on now, Marci, be for real."

Marci rolled her eyes. "You right."

"I'm just sayin'…"

"I heard you. Turn around so I can get started."

Candace turned back around shaking her head softly. Marci's thin fingers moved swiftly separating the cinnamon strands along Candace's scalp.

Candace's freshly bent curls bounced around by her ears, framing the subtle curves of her face, as she pulled her car into a small space behind Brother's apartment building. She had one hand on her door, almost pushing it open, when two dark blurs flew past her car.

"What the hell?" she said to herself, stepping into the street and looking after the blurs. It was then she realized it was Emmanuel and PJ. Candace squinted, shaking her head, then looked again. *Yup.* It was Emmanuel and PJ, the slimmer of Brother's twin sons, hightailing up the street. Candace looked behind her at the sound of panting and laughed at BJ, the rounder twin, sauntering up beside her, his hand on his side.

"Hey, Aunt C," he panted.

"You all right?" she asked the sweaty preteen.

He nodded, struggling to catch his breath. "Them skinny niggas is fast."

Candace jerked her head back in surprise, looking at the boy who didn't seem to be paying her any mind.

BJ exhaled quickly and began trotting ahead of Candace, moving toward where the boys had stopped up ahead.

Candace could hear them arguing as she approached.

"No! Hell no! I won!" PJ shouted.

"No you didn't," Emmanuel shouted back.

"Yo! Youngin, you can't beat me. I dogged you."

"No, you didn't." Candace heard a chorus of young female voices chime in. "You did not, PJ. E beat you. I seen it."

"Whatever," PJ shouted at the three girls climbing down from the top of the parked cars where they had been watching the foot race. "I won. Y'all blind."

"Ain't nobody blind, PJ. You slow. E whipped you," one young girl, with more bust than Candace thought a girl her age should have, hissed.

"Shut the fuck up, Natalie!" PJ barked.

"Chill," BJ warned, hitting his brother in the shoulder. "E mom here."

All of the children looked up at Candace as she walked slowly toward them.

"Oh, sh…oot," PJ said, correcting himself. "Hey, Aunt C."

"Hey, Mom," Emmanuel said, smiling and running over to Candace. "Did you see that?"

"I don't know what I just saw."

"You just saw me dick PJ," Emmanuel replied, laughing.

"You what PJ?"

"Beat. You just seen me beat PJ."

Candace shook her head. *Aw Lawd.* "I saw it."

"Yeah, I'm fast, Ma." Emmanuel stepped beside her.

Candace laughed. "I know you are. You get them legs from my dad, your grandpop. That's why you long and lean like ya' mama. Ya' daddy people kinda thick. They can't sprint like I used to when I ran track."

"You used to be out, huh?"

"Little boy, I was all that," she said proudly, strolling with her son toward Brother's apartment.

"Uncle B goin' say, I got legs from you, but I got my speed from my daddy when he used to run from the cops."

Candace rolled her eyes. "Don't listen to your uncle, Son. Somethin' is wrong with him."

Emmanuel laughed opening the door for his mother. "Uncle B! My mom here!" he hollered inside. "You stayin' a while, Mom?"

"No, baby. I got work in the morning. I just wanted to check up on you and holla at Brother for a minute." Candace looked to the lawn past Emmanuel at the busty preteen girl and Emmanuel's smart-mouthed cousins. "You need me to stay?" she asked, squinting again.

"I'm good," Emmanuel replied, one foot out the door. "I'mma stay out here. Call me before you leave. Okay, Mom?"

"Okay," Candace answered, kissing her son on the top of his head before watching him disappear back down the lawn. She turned inside the house. "Brother!"

"Yo! Yo, C! In the kitchen!" Brother turned from the stove as Candace entered the small eating space. "What's up, C?"

"Chillin'. What up with you, B?"

"Man, same shit. Tryna keep an eye on my bad-ass kids and yours."

"Yeah? You betta not let ya boys corrupt my son."

"Shit, take his ass home then. I can't make you no promises."

"Ohmigod." Candace threw her hands up.

"What? You see where he at. They asses live outside. I barely see them lil' niggas."

"Yeah. I seen them girls outside, too."

"Yeah, well you know, where there's lil' boys, lil' girls ain't far behind," Brother said, opening the refrigerator and removing a cold beer.

"And the other way around," Candace said matter-of-factly. "That one lil' busty one was all on my son."

"Oh, yeah. I know who you talkin' 'bout, the lil' thick, light-skinned one. Natalie."

"I guess that's her." Candace rolled her eyes.

Brother laughed. "You mad. Leave that lil' girl alone, C. She ain't did nothing to you."

"And she better not be tryna to do nothing with my son, neither."

"They kids."

"And, what's your point? How old were you when you started fuckin'?"

Brother frowned. "Aww, man. How old is E?"

"Ten. 'Bout to be eleven in October."

"Aww, man."

"Exactly. If he's anything like his father, I ought to be scared."

"Yeah, you should be. Me and Prince was smashing at like eleven, twelve."

"I know. And it's always a fast-ass girl ready to be smashed."

Brother shook his head. "You wasn't fast, huh?"

"No, I was not. I was seventeen when I lost my virginity to your brother."

"True, true. I remember that."

"What you mean 'you remember that'?"

"Like I said, I remember that."

"What did Prince tell you?"

"Fuck if I remember all the details from twenty years ago. All's I know is he told me he bust that cherry."

"Shut up, B." She swatted at him playfully. "It wasn't no twenty years, more like twelve or so, and I can't believe he told you that."

"Why not? That's my fuckin' brotha. That nigga tell me everything."

"I guess I shouldn't be surprised. I probably know more about you than I should, thanks to Prince."

Brother sipped his beer. "I don't even wanna know."

Candace shrugged, laughing. "Ya brother send you some money for me?"

"Of course, but what I get for keepin' E?"

"What you need?"

"Cut it the fuck out, C. I'm talkin' shit," Brother replied, reaching in his back pants pocket and counting out a nice knot of twenties before handing them to Candace. "I don't want cha money. Pay ya bills or somethin'."

Candace quickly slipped the bills from his grasp tucking them into her bra. "Thanks. Will do."

Brother nodded. "You straight?"

"I'm good. I'm out. I got work in the morning."

"Ard, C," Brother replied before suddenly digging in his right front pocket and pulling out a small thick bag of greenery. He tossed the weed to her.

She caught it and smiled. "Good lookin', B. See you later." Candace dropped the bag into her purse and exited the small kitchen, then the apartment. She stepped back out into the dimming sun. Emmanuel was still out on the lawn in front of the building with his cousins and the three young girls. Candace approached slowly, listening as best she could.

"Na unh," Natalie, the young busty one, said, snaking her neck. "I could beat him if I wanted. I been running track."

"Beat who?" Emmanuel asked, laughing and jumping back.

"Beat you," she snapped.

"Whateva, Natalie," Emmanuel protested. "I could beat you blind-folded."

"Bet it!" the girl shouted, throwing her hands on her thick little hips hidden under a loose white tee.

Emmanuel was in mid-laugh when he noticed Candace coming down the grass toward him.

"Mom, don't go nowhere. I'm 'bout to beat Natalie. Watch."

"No he not," the young girl said, waving excitedly in Candace's direction. Candace's eyebrows furrowed. *Don't be tryna make nice with me, lil' hoochie. You betta stay the hell away from my son.*

Candace watched as Natalie stepped into the street next to Emmanuel. Candace frowned at the light-skinned girl with strong muscular calves supporting her short thick frame. Before Candace could move closer, another girl shouted, "Go!" and Emmanuel and Natalie took off down the street, Emmanuel moving with long elegant strides, his body lean and designed for speed. Natalie was quick, her firm legs picking up and coming down on the concrete in perfect rhythm.

That damn girl needs a sports bra, Candace thought as they darted past. Candace watched until Emmanuel hit the stop sign at the end of the street and turned around, cheering his victory. Natalie was seconds behind. She hit the sign and frowned slightly as the two trotted together back to the lawn.

Candace smiled as her son approached. "Come here, Man. I got something for you."

Emmanuel stepped close to his mother. "You seen me beat her, Mom?"

"Yup. I seen it. That girl like you?"

"Ew, why you say that?"

"Mothers know."

Emmanuel shrugged. "I don't know, ma."

"Well, here," Candace said, stuffing sixty dollars into his palm. "Call me if you need anything, okay? And please stay out of trouble."

"Yes, ma'am," Emmanuel replied, squeezing Candace's waist.

"Love you, Son."

"Love you, too, Mom."

CHAPTER 18

andace's small apartment was empty when she bounded through the door Tuesday afternoon, rushing for the bathroom.

"I knew I shoulda gone before I left work," she fussed at herself, unzipping her deep teal pants and kicking off her Cole Haan flats. She burst in the bathroom, quickly plopping down on the toilet. She sat still for several minutes. Her home was too quiet, and Candace missed the sound of her son's bouncing steps.

She wondered what Emmanuel was doing at the moment and the image of a young, busty pre-teen came rushing to her mind. Her phone rang in her purse by her feet, chasing away her thoughts.

She jumped, looking at the caller ID and quickly answered. "Hello."

"Hey, baby," Chris said calmly. "What you been up to?"

Candace pulled back on her tongue. *Mothafucka.* She wanted to ask him a thousand questions, but she took a breath and steadied her calm. He wasn't her man and she didn't care at all about him not returning her calls.

"Nothing much, stranger. How are you?" Candace responded.

"Been a little fucked up, but I'm good now. How you?" Chris replied.

"I'm okay."

"You hungry?" he asked.

"Huh?"

"You hungry?"

"A little," Candace responded.

"Well, I'm starving and I'd love to see you. I wanna eat something good, put something on my stomach before I eat you."

"Excuse me."

"You heard me. I want to eat you."

"Oh…"

"Is that a problem?"

"No, no. Not really."

"Good, because I like how you taste."

"I can't tell."

"Why not?"

"I haven't heard from you."

"Just because I been busy doing dumb but necessary shit doesn't mean I haven't thought about the taste of your pretty pussy in my mouth."

"Is that so?"

"Sure is. I'm just trying to see you, babe. I'm hungry as shit and I wanna take you out to get something to eat and spend some time. If you don't want me to eat you, that's cool. But I'mma start begging."

Candace laughed. "Whateva. You don't even seem like the begging type."

"Oh yeah? What type I seem then?"

"The cocky, big-dick young bul type."

Chris's laugh rippled through the phone. "Yeah?"

"Yeah."

"So what that mean?" he asked.

"It means not to play you close."

"What? Come on, don't say that."

"Why not, Chris? It's been like two weeks and I haven't heard a word from you."

"Come on, boo. It's not that deep; the shit I do keeps me up all kinda hours and I just let time slip away from me, but I looked up and realized that I betta not let too much time pass or you might slip away from me."

Charmer. "So whatchu want, Chris?"

"You."

"Is that so?"

"That's so. You still scared to tell me where you live so I can come scoop you?"

Candace laughed. *I'mma have to keep my eye on this one.* She thought for a moment. "Ok, yeah. Come get me. But I can't stay out too late; I have to be to work in the morning."

She gave him the address and Chris was outside shortly, watching Candace descending her front steps in a pair of black tights, a cropped tee and ballet flats. She stood by the curb after locking her door and waited. *Does he open doors? Maybe only when I'm drunk,* she thought, smiling patiently at Chris.

After a moment, Chris's car door opened and he stepped out toward her. "You need some help?" He extended his arm.

"Maybe," she replied, coming close to his side.

Chris smiled, escorting her to the passenger side and slipping her in.

"Such a lady," he teased, plopping down in the driver's seat.

"Always."

"Always, huh?"

"Yup. Plus, somebody's got to teach you youngins how a lady should be treated."

"Right. Right," Chris replied, eyes diverting from the road to Candace and back to the road again. "I guess you the one to do it, huh?"

"Seems fitting."

Chris chuckled. "Fitting, huh? You funny. You definitely a classy lady, though. A freak in the bedroom, but a lady nonetheless."

"Ain't that how y'all like 'em?" she asked, staring at the smooth curvatures of his face.

"I can't speak for nobody else. But I know you're what I like and it's that sexy classy shit about you."

"Yeah?" she questioned coyly.

"Yeah, it makes me want to romance you with all this sweet shit and ball ya dainty ass up at the same time."

Candace shivered, the muscles in her inner thighs contracting. Chris smiled looking at her. She blushed, turning away.

They parked at the Kitchen Bar restaurant in Jenkintown. The sun was setting and the after-work crowd had slowly diminished. They were easily seated and Candace ordered a large Caesar salad with an Apple Martini. Chris ordered the cheese steak wraps with a Heineken.

"Let me get another round," Chris later said to the waiter clearing their plates. "And can you bring me two shots of Pátron, also? Thanks, my man."

Candace turned to Chris, her eyes wide. "Pátron. Who told you I wanted some Pátron?"

"Why not? You be up for work in the morning. Whatchu scared of?"

"'Scared'?" Candace raised one eye, curling her lips. "Calling me 'scared' don't work on me. I'm grown. I just said who told *you* to order Pátron for me."

"I wanted a shot and I wanted you to have one with me. Is that so wrong?" His green eyes begged and shimmered with flecks of grey.

"No," Candace replied, laughing at her own pitiful defeat. She cleared her throat after a moment and asked, "So, what's up with you, Chris?"

"Nothin'. Just wanted to see that pretty face again…and that gorgeous body." He grinned ear to ear.

Candace contained her grin. "It's nice to be thought of."

"Baby girl, you cross my mind more than you know."

"I can't tell." Candace sat back as the waiter placed the drinks and shot glasses in front of them on the table.

"Babe, just because I be caught up in dumb shit don't mean I don't think about you."

Candace sipped her drink. "So, I take it you don't work a nine-to-five."

"Nah, that ain't for me," Chris said seriously, then smiled. "But, I got money. I can take care of you. Treat you nice, wine and dine you. All that good shit."

"Is that so?"

"Very much so."

Candace laughed. "How old are you again?"

"Twenty-one," Chris stated, slightly poking out his chest. "And you're what? Twenty-eight? Right?

Candace nodded.

This time Chris laughed. "Yo, you got girls my age beat."

"Thank you." Candace beamed.

"No doubt. I'm glad you made time for me in your busy schedule."

"Yeah? Well, I told you I would have to pencil you in."

"Pencil me in, huh? That's funny. You goin' make plenty time for me soon enough." Chris downed his shot.

Candace looked at the small tumbler of clear liquid in front of her. She knew her limits with Pátron were low, but she grabbed the glass and threw it back. *Oh, this tequila gets me fucked up quick.* She swallowed hard.

Chris ordered another round.

"Chris, I think you're trying to get me drunk. I told you I have to get up for work in the morning."

"I'm not trying to get you drunk, you grown. But I do want you to loosen up a little. Don't be so scared."

"There you go with that 'scared' shit. What am I 'scared' of, Chris?"

"Me."

"You? You really think so?"

"I know so. Why else wouldn't you let me come in your house?"

"My house?"

"Yeah." Chris looked up as the waiter sat two shot glasses on the table. "First, you told me I can't come to your house 'cause I might be a stalker, but you let me pick you up so I know where you live, now. So, now, I'm thinking you don't want me to come in your crib because you scared of me." Chris tossed back his shot and sipped his Heineken.

Candace raised the small glass to her mouth and swallowed. "Chris, I ain't scared of shit."

Chris laughed and ordered another round.

Candace had more than a buzz strolling back to Chris's car, with him holding her side.

"You goin' let me come back to your place, Candace. Or you still scared of me?" Chris asked.

"I ain't scared of shit!" she responded.

"Say it again," Chris cheered, opening her car door.

"I ain't scared of shit!" Candace repeated.

"Say it again!"

"I ain't scared of shit!" she screamed. She screamed it louder, making their way to her apartment and even louder as they entered her door. And even louder still when Chris bent her over the edge of her couch.

"What you scared of, baby? Huh, tell me what you scared of?"

"I ain't scared of shit," she panted while Chris pounded her from the back. She screamed as his performance exceeded expectation and left her wet and trembling. By the time they made it to her bedroom, Candace was barely standing. Chris laid her down and passed out beside her. Candace felt a slow shuffle under her. She lifted her head and set it gently back down on the pillow. Her eyes fluttered to the clock by her bedside: 3:41. Chris was dressing quickly at the foot of her bed in the dark.

"I can't stay, boo. I got moves I'm supposed to be making right now."

Candace turned over in her sweat-soaked sheets. Chris was out the door before she could rise from the mattress. She collapsed back down and waited for seven a.m.

Her phone rang later that morning while she was dressing, and Candace tripped over her shoes trying to catch the call. Anticipating a voice from Chris, it was Bam.

"Hey, beautiful. Big Daddy misses you. Can I see you this weekend? You wanna go someplace nice?"

"I'm not sure about my schedule, Bam. I'll let you know, okay?"

The second time her phone rang before she walked out the door, Candace didn't run; she knew the ringtone. It was her sister.

"I can't find my man," Marci jumped right in.

"Who, Tommy?"

"Sis, why you think he ain't calling me back. I called twice and sent him two texts. It's been almost twenty-four hours since I talked to my man."

"I don't know, Mars, maybe he's with his wife," Candace responded, sucking her teeth.

"He don't even like that bitch."

"So, what? They still married."

"I can't tell."

"I bet you can't, hoochie."

"What? He ain't no dummy, sis. He only fucks with her because she owns that shop and she got a little money. He don't love her or nothing."

"Even better."

"I can do without your sarcasm, Candace."

"I bet you could do without Donna's husband, too, but you ain't goin' stop fucking him and I ain't goin' start agreeing with it, so let's just leave it at that."

"Leave it at what, Miss-High-and-Mighty? 'Cause you getting some dick now and old head lacing your pockets, you can't support what your little sister's trying to do."

"What are you trying to do?"

"Seduce a future, Candace Reign Brinton."

"Well, Marcine Nichelle Brinton, you can't be counting on somebody else's husband to make your dreams come true."

"He's my man, Candace. We know that and that's all that matters."

"No, Donna don't know that and she still wearing that ring and going home to her husband."

"Whateva, you are no help."

Click.

"You're welcome," Candace said to no one.

Candace tossed the slim phone back into her bag. *I have to get to work and arguing with spoiled-ass Marci ain't goin' to help me get through this day any faster.*

Her cell phone rang in the bottom of her pocketbook as Candace circled the blocks surrounding Temple University searching for a parking space after work.

"Shit," she snapped, turning the steering wheel of her Accord.

"Hey, sexy. Can I see you tonight?" Chris asked, after she'd nearly hit a parked car to retrieve the phone from the bottom of her bag.

"Two nights in a row? To what do I owe the pleasure?"

"You tapped out on me last night. I wasn't done."

Candace laughed. "I was tired and you tried to get me drunk."

"You liked it."

"I did."

"So, can I see you later?"

"Sure."

"Cool," Chris said smoothly. "But, I can't stay long, though. I got some moves to make. But I'm trying to see you, since you be thinkin' I'm avoiding you and shit. Cool?"

"That's fine. Like what time you talking?"

"I don't know. Not late, but I'll be over there, okay?"

"Okay."

Candace counted the seconds in class. Money was interesting, something she'd always enjoyed, but she twitched in her seat anticipating Chris's touch. When she got home, she jumped in the shower, eagerly primping and pampering for her special guest. She stretched her long legs out of the tub and let the water run down her thighs. She massaged her sweet-scented lotion into her brown skin and waited. Candace decided to make a quick dinner. She put some whiting in the oven with a pot of rice and vegetables. She made Chris a healthy plate. Then she waited.

It was nearing eleven and she was growing impatient. *I can't be sitting up here waiting on this boy. I gotta work in the morning.* Candace grabbed her phone. Her first phone call to Chris rang through for several tones, then it sounded as if someone picked up and hung up. Candace's eyes narrowed, staring down at the device in her hand. For a moment, she was unsure of what had just occurred.

Within seconds, the phone rang in her palm. Candace jumped quickly and answered.

"Hey, beautiful," Bam began.

"Hey, Bam," she replied solemnly.

"How's it going, baby? You been too busy for Big Daddy?"

"I've been a little swamped with work and school and all. I haven't had much play time recently."

"Everyone needs to take a break. Don't you agree?"

"I can't argue that." She sighed.

"Are you busy?" he asked.

Candace stood in the middle of her bedroom, her pink and white boy shorts sitting high up her round backside, her nipples pressing through the thin matching top, plates cooling in the kitchen and a candle burning on her bedside table. Candace frowned; she wasn't busy at all. She sat down on the bed, tucking her legs beneath her.

"No," she replied.

"You not hanging out tonight?"

"I'm not much in the mood for hanging out."

"What are you in the mood for, baby girl?"

Candace sighed again.

"Come on. Tell Big Daddy what you want."

Candace bit her tongue. Bam would die if she confessed what she really wanted was Chris's long tongue lapping against her pussy and his thick dick pressing into her walls. Bam would be in shock; he'd probably slam down the phone and never speak to her again.

"Just some peace of mind, Bam," she finally answered.

"I can come over and give you a piece." He laughed.

Candace rolled her eyes. "Not tonight. I have to be up early. I'm about to call it a night now."

"You're no fun, little miss. You need to enjoy life more. All work and no play makes Candace a dull girl."

"I know," Candace groaned.

"You let me know when you ready, Candace."

"Ready for what, Bam?"

"Ready for a real good time, Candace. You not ready, you too tight right now. I'll loosen you up, though, baby girl. Don't even worry about it."

"What are you talking about?"

"Something special I got for you. You'll see soon enough."

Candace huffed. "Good night, Bam."

"Nighty night, baby girl."

Candace fell back against her sheets. She caught herself from drifting off and tried Chris again; this time the call went straight to voicemail. Candace surrendered and fell asleep. Her phone woke her up around one a.m.

"I'm outside," Chris spoke softly.

"And?" her groggy voice replied.

"Can you let me in?" Chris asked.

"No, I'm asleep."

"Come on, babe. Don't do me like that."

Candace groaned, but her desire carried her from her sleep to the front door. Chris followed her in carrying Chinese food.

"You was asleep?" he asked.

"Yeah." Her attitude announced.

He dropped the bag on the countertop beside a plate covered in foil. "You cooked?" he asked, lifting the foil.

"Yeah." More attitude.

"Aww, babe. You mad at me for being so late?"

Candace did not respond, heading into her bedroom. Chris followed, kicking off his Nike Air Maxes at the door. Candace climbed back into her bed and pulled the covers over her shoulder.

"Ma, don't be mad at me. This shit tricky out here. I ain't mean to make you wait for me." He sat down on the bed. "You mad?"

Candace shrugged.

He rubbed her broad shoulders above the covers. "Can I make it up to you?"

Candace sucked her teeth, then suddenly felt Chris slip under the covers and slide down her panties. She attempted to resist, giving in to his soft lips pulling at hers, but she could not refuse the pulsating sensation beating at her womanhood. He buried his face in between her thighs. After several moments of French kissing and sucking at her, Candace came hard. Her body shook and moisture ran lines down Chris's beard when he brought his face above the covers. After an intense session of turning bodies and several orgasms later, Candace was rocked back to sleep. When she awoke the next morning, Chris was gone.

CHAPTER 19

SLAM!

Donna swung open the shop door loud and hard. Everyone inside jumped. Before Lateesh could make her way over to Donna's side, the parlor door swung open again and Tommy burst in.

"What the fuck is your problem?" he yelled.

"You my goddamn problem!" she yelled back.

"Gimme my car keys, Donna!"

"I don't have shit that belong to you. This my shit."

Tommy stepped closer to Donna. Marci stood paralyzed across the room staring at the action unfolding in front of her. Like everyone else, her eyes were focused on the screaming pair. The thudding of her heart resounded like a walking bass line, yet she stood perfectly still.

"Gimme my *fuckin'* keys, Donna!" Tommy's voice boomed.

"Fuck you, Tommy," Donna hollered, standing her ground.

Tommy lifted his leg to move forward, but something seemed as if it caught him in the chest, and he slowly started to look around the room, locking eyes with Marci. He lowered his gaze, taking long slow steps past Donna and opening the door to the cellar.

"Not here, Donna. It's none of dey business."

Donna glanced at the ogling eyes and followed Tommy into the basement. Lateesh was at the door the second it closed with her ear hard-pressed to the wood.

"Nosey bitch," Jerel said to Marci. "Teesh always on Donna dick. Who gives a fuck? Tommy fucks anything walking. It ain't no shock."

"Get the fuck back from the door, Teesh," Jerel yelled. "Nosey bitch."

Lateesh did not move, staying fixed in her position, like a look-out on location. After a moment, Lateesh started to blush and finally retreated back to the other side of the salon. She glared at Jerel who returned the hateful snarl.

"She's a jealous bitch. Don't nobody give a fuck about Donna and Tommy. She goin' take his sorry ass back like she always do, 'cause he goin' give her some good dick, like he prolly doing right now and it ain't goin' be nuffin'," Jerel said.

Marci struggled with the words, "You...you think they fuckin'?"

"Bitch, please. I know they fucking."

"Or he fuckin' her," Quinita chimed in from Marci's left. Laughing, Quinita and Jerel slapped hands behind Marci's back.

"That's one thing that nigga can do real well." Jerel sneered.

"He's blown Donna back out a couple times in that basement," Quinita added.

"Mine too," Jerel whispered to Marci.

Before Marci could turn to face Jerel, the basement door opened and Tommy walked out. He moved quickly and quietly across the shop floor. His eyes never rose to Marci though hers never moved from him. She attempted to penetrate his skin with her stare, but Tommy was out the door with his car keys in hand.

A calm and well-collected Donna emerged from the cellar several moments later. She brushed her brown weave from her eyes and headed over to the receptionist's desk. Her head was high and haughty as she snatched her bag.

"What time is my first appointment?"

"Not 'til two."

"I'll be back then," she stated as she exited, lacking all the grandeur with which she'd entered.

After the boss's departure, Marci turned her attention back to Jerel.

"You fucked Tommy?"

Jerel's candy-painted lips twisted. "Girl, please. Who didn't?"

Marci clutched her stomach; she suddenly felt nauseous. *Son of a bitch!*

Donna cancelled her appointments for the rest of the day but returned at closing to count down the drawer. Lateesh's head turned as soon as Donna came through the door. She trailed behind her, soaking up every word Donna tried to whisper in the back of the nearly empty shop. The shop was clear except for Marci who was finishing her last sew-in.

"That pussy think he slick. I got something for his ass." Donna huffed.

"Girl, you really think he creepin'?"

"I know he up to no good, Teesh. He don't have a job but stay got somewhere to be. Who the fuck he think he foolin'? I know I better be getting some fuckin' jewelry for my birthday. That pussy spent seven hundred at The Jewelry Factory. Seven hundred of my money!"

Marci glanced down at the bracelet on her wrist.

"Donna, no he didn't?" Lateesh asked.

"I am so sick of him. Girl, if it wasn't for that pipe. I'd been cut his ass off."

"You wanna get a divorce?"

Marci's breathing quickened.

"Girl, is you stupid? We don't divorce where I come from. We stick it out. Through hell or high water, that is my husband. Besides, that nigga ain't got no money and we been together since I started my business. He fuck around get half what I got. Hell no. I been at this too long. I be damned if I see another bitch on his arm."

Lateesh cracked up laughing. "I know that's right, Donna."

"That's my husband. And I can't prove he's creeping yet, but I'm going to."

Marci groaned, an invisible weight slipping down onto her, pushing her shoulders into a slump. *Tommy hasn't called me all day. I need this bitch out the picture.*

Marci rolled over in her bed and dialed Tommy's number again; it was the fifteenth time in the last hour. She'd called out sick from work and was home alone in her bedroom in her mother's house stretched out with a migraine and massive cramps. She tossed the phone down, popping another pain pill in her mouth. The excess of Motrin lulled her into a gentle doze. A few hours later, she awoke groggy and began dialing Tommy once more. He finally picked up.

"Aye, baby," he answered.

"Where you been, Tommy? I'm sick and I'm home by myself."

"Uh…I'm a little busy right now. I'mma hit you back when I'm done, okay?"

"But baby, I'm sick."

"Okay, Marci. What you want me to do?"

"Can you bring me some orange juice?"

"You don't have none at home?"

"No. I want orange juice and you."

"I'll be through, K?" *Click.*

Marci frowned at the phone in her hand. She called again but he didn't answer. She felt bad for dismissing her mother's offer of warm soup and ginger ale before she left for work, but Marci had been certain Tommy was coming by to take care of her. She waited an hour for Tommy to arrive with her juice. She called again, and he didn't answer.

Marci was half-conscious a few hours later when she heard her phone ringing combined with a horn outside. Startled, she leaped out of bed, scurrying down the small hall from her bedroom and flung open the front door before turning around to head back to climb under her sheets. Tommy shut the front door behind him and sauntered down the hall, entering Marci's bedroom with a tall jug of orange juice, a brown paper bag and a smile.

"Hey baby, you want me to make you some soup?"

"No," she said, pouting.

"What's the matter, baby girl?"

"You took forever. I could have died."

"Aw, baby." He chuckled.

"It's not funny. I feel like shit."

"I'm sorry. I had some things to do."

"Whateva. Yo, I can't believe you ain't call me after you came in the shop. And I heard you fucked Jerel? When? Why? How you playin', Tommy?"

"That crazy-ass girl. I didn't fuck her. She always lying, her and that nasty Teesh. Donna always got them in the middle of some dumb shit 'cause we stay beefin'. Don't worry 'bout them dumb-ass girls, baby. They just wanna be in somebody business and they wish they was in your shoes." He moved nearer to her on the bed.

"Well, where you been?" Marci questioned from her sheets.

"Just getting some things in order. Why you askin' so many questions today, baby? You really sick, huh?"

Marci frowned, sitting up. "Yes and I don't like all this drama. And you know I hate missing work." Marci huffed. "Even though I hate seeing that bitch every day, I need my income."

"I know you do."

"You lucky we need this money to move into a place of our own," Marci said, coughing.

Tommy snuggled up beside her, rubbing her back. "I know. But, baby, you really are sick. Let me take care of you. Climb back under the covers."

"I hate seeing that bitch every day," Marci repeated, sniffling with the covers wrapped around her shoulders. "She makes me sick, you know. She's so nasty to everybody. And I know she's no good to you. It makes me wanna punch her in the face. I'll never be like that when I get my own."

"I can help you like I helped Donna," Tommy boasted. "How you think she got that prime location for her shop? Because of my connections."

Marci's eyes squinted curiously in his direction. "What do you mean?"

"Donna wasn't shit when she started her business. I got her all the connects; I made the major moves to help her salon pop. Now, she think she the shit and she don't give a fuck 'bout nobody but herself."

"I want my own salon one day," Marci squealed. "Shit, I'm the best damn stylist at Donna's, anyway. We need to make a major move so I can get the fuck outta my mom's refurbished garage."

Tommy looked around at the spacious yet cluttered layout of Marci's bedroom. It was once a large garage attached to the left side of the house, but Marci and her mom renovated the space so Marci could have the huge room and the downstairs bathroom to herself and leave the upstairs to her younger brothers.

"This place is all right," said Tommy.

"It's cool for now. But it's not mine; it's not ours. With your connects, we can get our own, right?"

Tommy nodded.

Marci giggled. "Oh, that'd be perfect. Me and my man. We can own our own business, for your music business and your cars and my vicious hairstyling skills and fashion design skills, we could have a business, like our own brand. We'll host all kinds of parties and shit. It's goin' to be fuckin' poppin'!"

"You excited, huh, baby?"

"Of course. Why shouldn't I be? I love you so much, Tommy. All we need is a shot at doin' us and I know it's gonna be on. What's the problem?"

Smiling, Tommy shrugged. "I don't see any."

Marci's smile slowly slipped from her face. "Then you'll leave her, right?"

"And run away with you?"

Marci nodded. "Who else?" she asked, rolling her neck and crossing her arms over her breasts, letting the covers fall from around her.

Tommy stood and kissed her on the forehead. "Nobody, baby." He kissed her dry eager lips.

Marci's shoulders softened.

"My poor baby sick, huh?"

Marci frowned and batted her eyes.

"It's okay, baby. Get back under the covers so you can rest," Tommy said, standing in front of her.

Marci complied, settling back onto her mattress while Tommy pulled the puffy purple blanket up over her shoulders.

"Oh, baby," Tommy said, suddenly, after standing back up straight. "Where dat bracelet at I gave you?"

"Why?"

"I gotta take it back to the jeweler."

"Why?" she asked, sitting up.

"'Cause, I had grabbed it from a jewelry store my homie works at and he wasn't there the day I went to pick it up, but now he telling me I paid too much for it. Like the Italian bul who own it got over on me. So I'mma bring it back to 'em. So he can get my money right. And I'mma give it right back to you."

Marci's lips curled.

Tommy continued. "It's not about the money, baby. No, it's not like that at all. All I am saying is I wanna make sure this dude didn't gyp me. Feel me, babe?"

"I guess…but…"

"I mean I would want you to go with me, butchu need your rest." He moved toward her dresser.

Marci stared, barely moving, her body stiff from soreness and surprise. Tommy searched for the thin charm bracelet between the clutter on the dresser.

"Where is it, baby, so I can go take care of this real quick and I'mma be right back to take care of you."

"Tommy, I'm not stupid," Marci said through the itch in her throat. "I know you just goin' give it to Donna."

"Why you think that?" he asked, eyes wide as saucers.

"'Cause I'm not dumb. I know she seen the bill."

Tommy sulked. "Baby, I…"

Marci struggled to her feet, meeting Tommy at her dresser. She snatched the bracelet from a drawer in a small jewelry box and threw it into Tommy's face. He caught it at his cheek. "Take the fuckin' bracelet, Tommy."

Before Marci could fall back to the bed, Tommy was out the door.

CHAPTER 20

"Hey, Brother."

"What up, C?"

"How's my boy?"

"He bad as shit!" Brother said, laughing Prince's same deep throaty laugh. "Nah, you know he good. These little niggas running 'round here somewhere. I think they at the pool."

"B, it's Friday night, you can't be letting my boy run wild in these streets."

Brother sucked his teeth. "Streets? C, he somewhere in this fuckin' apartment complex. I told you I got 'em. He a boy, having fun wit' his cousins. Chill, C. He good."

"You ain't no good, B. So that don't make me feel no better."

"Well, I told you to come get his ass then, if you so worried 'bout what we doin' ova here."

Candace bit her tongue. Brother was right. Man was safe and she couldn't deny his lineage, no matter how rough the root.

She was quiet for a moment collecting her thoughts and weighing the option of going to pick up her son or letting them both have an enjoyable summer when Brother's baritone interrupted her thoughts.

"Hello," Brother barked. "What you goin' do? I can't be sitting on this phone all day."

"Tell Emmanuel to call his mother. K?"

"Will do." *Click.*

Candace shook her head while sitting on the edge of her bed half-naked.

"It's Friday night. My job sucks, my son thinks he's grown, my sister is retarded and I really need to get some studying done. But…" She picked up her phone again. "I need a drink."

She dialed Chris's number. No answer, but her phone chimed ten seconds later with a text from him.

Where you at? he asked.

Home…bored…need a stiff one.

LOL Im at Jollies on Broad. Come have a drink wit me.

On my way.

A few minutes later, Candace walked up to Chris at the bar of the bustling establishment on Broad Street. He was chatting with a tall, slim, brown-skinned brother to his left. The guy's red fitted cap was pulled down so low Candace could hardly see his eyes, but she knew from the strong aroma coming from his direction that they were most likely red and slanted.

"Hey, babe," Chris said, turning to greet her.

"Hey."

"This my cousin, Shif." Chris leaned back as Shif leaned forward nodding at Candace.

"What's good, ma?" Shif asked, grinning.

"Chillin'. How you?" Candace replied, taking in his perfect teeth. *Oh, yeah, with them teeth, they gotta be related.*

Shif looked Candace up and down, then patted Chris on the shoulder. "All right, my nigga…Miss Candace. I'm outta here. Be easy, y'all."

"Ard, my nigga." Chris pounded his hand as Shif passed him.

"Night," Candace said to the slim back disappearing through the long bar.

"You just been too busy for me, huh?" Chris asked as Candace turned around and took Shif's seat on his left.

"Why you say that?"

"I don't know. I wish I could see you as much as I dream about you."

"You fulla shit," Candace scoffed, shrugging.

"Damn, why I gotta be all that?"

"Chris, cut it out, okay. I know the game."

"Game?"

"Now you gonna act dumb," she teased.

"Nah, boo. I ain't acting dumb; I'm just not running game on you."

"What you call it then?"

"I don't call it nothing. You the busy professional. I ain't denying I like fucking the shit outta you. I like biting that pretty pussy. Ya fat ass turns me on. Ain't no game, boo. It's real shit."

Candace squirmed in her seat. "Yeah, but, a pretty nigga like you. Come on, Chris, how many bitches you got around the city?"

"What do that matter how many bitches on my dick, C? I'm giving this dick to you."

"Not on the regular." Candace regretted the words the moment they left her mouth.

The prominent muscles of Chris's chin softened. He smiled. "Is that what you want?"

Candace motioned for the barmaid.

"I'm asking you a question, Miss Candace."

"What, Chris?" she replied, looking squarely at the young girl as she placed her drink order.

"Don't get mad wit' me 'cause you want me." His grin widened.

"I didn't say that." She finally turned to look at him.

"What did you say?" he asked.

"I didn't say I wanted you," she replied.

"You didn't say you didn't."

"Cut it the fuck out, Chris. You's a playa and we both know it. You fuck me, I fuck you. I like it like that. Let's keep it like that. Okay?"

"I'm saying, I'm cool with that, if that's what you want. But if you want me on a regular, I'm cool with that, too."

"I bet."

"I'mma ask you again, C. Is that what you want?"

"Is what what I want, Chris?"

Chris leaned into her, staring deep into the soft brown of her skin and the subtle caramel of her eyes that matched the streaks in her hair.

"Do you want me on the regular?"

"Whateva. It's hot in here."

"Aww, come on. Don't do that. You know you miss me. I wanna twist that long pretty body all up. You know that?"

"Actions speak louder than words, Christopher."

"Aww, my whole name." He stepped back, clutching his heart.

Candace playfully pushed her shoulder into him. The muscles of his mouth curled into a seductive grin that moved down her body, reached into her lap and squeezed her panties. Chris leaned into the bar to order some more drinks, getting closer to Candace. But, before he could complete his order, there was a hand on his shoulder. Candace followed the hand to a short, cocoa-brown-skinned girl standing close behind Chris at the bar. The young girl moved forward pushing her big breasts onto his back. She didn't seem to notice Candace.

"Damn, nigga." She bounced her breasts up between the barstools. "Where the fuck you been?"

Candace sneered at the girl's big booty in a poorly made, ill-fitting blue dress and the long red individual braids hanging down the girl's back. Candace rolled her eyes and spun around back to the bar where she could keep from staring but could still hear the conversation.

Chris turned, looking down at the girl and exhaling heavily. "I been tied up, Elsie. Why? What's the deal?"

"Ain't shit," she said. "I ain't seen you, is all. You know you can't just go missing on a bitch like that."

Chris forced a smile, touching her exposed shoulder. "I ain't been missing, El. Just tied up." His eyes journeyed past Elsie to Candace.

Candace sipped her drink and shrugged. *Handle your hoes.*

Elsie spun round following his gaze, obviously seeking out the object of his attention. Her braids slapped Chris in the mouth as she turned to get a clearer view. Elsie looked Candace up and down the length of her long body sitting on the raised barstool. Candace's brown thighs were exposed under a blue-and-white-striped miniskirt, and silver Tory Burch sandals swung loosely from her foot. She crossed her legs deliberately in front of the young girl. Candace knew chicks like her, always in a nigga's face, but wasn't never about shit. She thought Elsie was the type who liked to make a scene and be noticed. Candace sipped her drink again.

Elsie turned back to Chris. "You know her?"

Chris nodded. Candace smirked. *He betta had.*

"What, you been too busy with this bitch to fuckin' call me." Her voice was rising.

Candace propped herself up higher on the barstool. She hadn't come out looking for a fight, but if chick was hunting for a beat down, she could certainly catch one.

"Chill, El. You buggin'."

"I ain't fuckin' buggin'." The scent of alcohol chased the words out of her mouth. "You buggin'. What the fuck! I ride for you and you goin' give me the brush-off 'cause some long-legged bitch. Fuck you, Chris!"

Chris stood up. He was much taller than the young woman whose voice and defensive stand demonstrated she was more than ready to start.

"Chill, El," he warned again. "You drunk."

"I ain't fuckin' drunk. You ain't shit, Chris! How you goin' do me like that?"

"El, come on." He wrapped his arm around her shoulder. "Let's get out of here. You goin' make a scene and you know I ain't into that shit."

"Fuck you, Chris!" The girl pushed back from him and stumbled. Chris grabbed her sharply, snatching her from her close call with the floor. He moved her limp body quickly toward the exit, Elsie jiggling like a rag doll along the way. Chris took her out of the bar. He was gone for more than ten minutes before Candace received a text from him.

DON'T MOVE. I'LL BE RIGHT BACK!

I'M NOT WAITING! she replied.

I WANT YOU! DON'T MOVE!

Candace set the phone down on the bar, noticing a couple beside her. The young girl's smile was wide and her laughter followed each statement the grinning brother across from her made. Candace rolled her eyes, finished her drink and stepped outside for some air.

She looked up and down Broad Street for Chris's car, but it wasn't there. She tried his phone, but no answer. *Oh, come on with the dumb shit. One more drink and I'm out.*

When Candace got back into the bar, two guys had migrated near her stool.

"Excuse me," she spoke to one nearest to her chair.

"No, excuse me, beautiful." He looked her up and down as she slid onto the stool. The brown-skinned brother extended his hand.

Candace shyly accepted.

"How you doin'? I'm Rob."

"Nice to meet you."

"And your name?"

"C."

"That's it? C?"

"That's it."

"You here by yourself, C?" Rob asked.

"For the moment."

Rob gave a pleased grin. Candace smiled back pleasantly, appreciative for the company but not too flirty. He was attractive, coffee-colored skin with slanted eyes and tall, like she liked. But Candace wasn't ready to make any new male friends and there was no telling where Chris was or if he'd be returning.

"Soooo, does that mean you're waiting on somebody?" Rob asked, still smiling.

Candace nodded, crossing her legs and watching his eyes watch her thighs. She raised her hand delicately, signaling the barmaid, and glanced at the silver bracelet shining on her wrist. *Bam. Gotta call him.*

She placed her drink order and was sitting back in her seat when she saw Chris come through the door. She leaned closer to Rob and smiled.

"So, where are you from?" she asked.

"Me, oh, uh…West…"

Chris approached quickly, eyes narrowed. "'Scuse me, brah!" he announced, pushing between Candace and Rob.

Rob began to speak, "Homie, I was just…"

Chris interjected, "Na, she wit' me, dude." He turned his attention to Candace. "Come on!" Chris had her arm and was escorting her outside before she realized what was going on.

"What's up with you, Candace?" he questioned once they made it through the doors and he released his grasp.

"Whatchu mean?"

"Who was dude? That's how you get down? Soon as I step away, you all in another mothafucka face."

"What? Are you serious? You the one with the hype hood rat!"

"Man, fuck that bitch. That's just some chick I used to fuck with."

"Seem like you still fuck with her if you ask me, or *her* for that matter." Candace crossed her arms over her breasts. "She ain't trippin' for no reason, Chris. She your girl or something?"

"You my girl, C."

"Get the fuck outta here with that shit, Chris. I'm not some simple-ass chick."

"And that's exactly why I don't mess with these chickenheads out here like I get down with you."

"Yeah, right. What's that supposed to mean? What's so special about me?" Candace poked out her lips.

Chris rolled his head back in mock disgust. "Are you serious?" He moved up close to her, pinning her to the glass wall. The beat of the music flooded the air and Chris rocked his body to the bass. His breath was warm and moist in her ear. "You're the shit, C." He ran his fingers through her shoulder-length cinnamon bob, tugging it slightly, the way he knew she liked it. "You've got gorgeous fuckin' hair." His hands moved up her back. "A long, sexy-ass body." Down to her waist, his hands journeyed. "A sweet tasty ass." He licked his lips, pressed his mouth to her shoulder and began sucking on her neck. Candace shivered.

"Stop it," she moaned.

"No way." He laughed. "Let's go back to your place."

Chris followed her back to her apartment. He began undressing her as they moved through the front door. She stepped ahead of him toward the bedroom, but Chris grabbed her waist and pulled her back into him so that her round bottom hit him directly in the groin. She could feel his swollen mass against her. She could feel his wet tongue on the back of her neck. Chris swiveled her hips in circular movements against the front of him. He moved his body in syncopated rhythm. His right hand found its way across her raising chest and twirled circles around her erect nipples. Candace's body danced against Chris's in his steady progression toward the bed. Once inside her bedroom, he turned her around to face him and lowered his face to her breasts, his wet mouth smothering her flesh and her body contracting with each suckle.

"I wanna taste you," he said.

Candace sat back onto the bed and began to spread her legs.

"No," Chris began, stepping back from her and sitting down on the floor and stretching his legs out in front of him. "Come here. Turn around and bend over."

Candace didn't understand, though she turned her back to him, anyway.

Chris laughed from under her. "Now, can you touch your toes?"

"What?" Candace asked, peeking behind her.

Chris stretched his arms, reaching up to guide her back. "Yea, baby. I want you to touch your toes and put your pussy right in my face. Can you do that?"

"Yes," she replied, backing up.

"Good. I wanted to try this shit with you the moment I seen you in that gold dress."

Candace laughed feeling his face against her butt. She tilted forward, poking her womanhood out further and stepping her legs on the outside of his legs.

Chris dove in face first, sucking and pulling at her clit. Candace howled with delight.

"Grab your ankles," he instructed between kisses.

Candace leaned forward, stretching and bending her long, toned body and suddenly realizing she was in reach of Chris's lap.

That shit is right there. She reached for his proud manhood, first stroking it with her hand.

She felt Chris pressing his face between her cheeks and licking her up and down. He sucked slowly at her lips, twirling his tongue inside her. He collected her moisture in his mouth, then dragged his sloppy tongue up to her anus, licking feverishly. His strong hands gripped the back of her tight thighs as he arched his body upward pushing his throbbing manhood into her face. Candace moistened her hand with saliva and stroked the wetness up and down his shaft. She felt Chris's moans against her skin. Then she bent her knees a little and her mouth engulfed him. Chris lapped and slurped while Candace sucked and swallowed. Chris was moaning with his legs extended on the floor thrusting his groin up into her mouth, their bodies making a perfect ninety-degree angle. Candace's body began to tremble as he devoured her. Chris pushed himself up further. The more he pressed his full lips into her, the deeper Candace took him into her mouth. Her orgasm erupted over his face. Chris fell back flat on the floor as Candace continued her oral massage.

"Oh my fuckin' God! Baby, that shit feel so good. Come sit on this dick."

Candace stopped sucking and sat down on top of him, with her back to him reverse cowgirl style. She took control, rocking back on her legs and angling her body over his. Chris grabbed her ass, guiding her up and down. She leaned back, then rocked forward and swayed her hips.

Chris moaned. "You ridin' the shit out that dick, baby."

Sweat ran down Candace's body. Chris clutched her waist, pressing his thumbs into the small of her back, and drew her into him. He held her tight as she worked her hips to maneuver the thick muscle inside her. She came again. And again before Chris reached his climax and they both lay breathing heavily on the floor.

When Candace awoke the next morning, Chris was in bed beside her. She slipped out the sheets without waking him. Staring down at the bed, she admired the sprawl of his fair skin stretching off the frame of her mattress.

I'mma fuck his young bul head up. She smiled while making breakfast. She carried a warm plate of pancakes, bacon and eggs to the bedside as Chris was turning over. He sat up and smiled at her.

"Damn, breakfast in bed? What a nigga do to deserve all this?"

Candace grinned standing in front of the bed. "You ain't do nothin' at all."

Chris chewed his bacon. "Yea? Nothin', huh? That ain't what ya shaky-ass legs was sayin'."

"My legs?"

He sipped some orange juice. "Baby, you was 'bout to buckle. That shit was so sexy, ya body shakin' and jerkin' and shit."

Candace playfully slapped his shoulder. "Shut up. You wasn't no better. 'Oh, baby…Ooh, yea, baby, ride this dick. Ooh, baby.'"

"Shit, you was ridin' the shit outta me, girl. Fuck I was 'posed to say? I think you tryna bag me or something? You tryna make me your man, C?"

Candace laughed. "So, if I fuck you and feed you, that makes you my man?"

Chris set the plate down on the bed and stood up directly in front of her with nothing on but blue Polo boxers. He was close enough for her to see the defined lines of his six-pack rise and fall with each calm breath.

"You fuck everybody like you fuck me, C?" he asked, moving nearer to her.

"I ain't fuckin' nobody but you." She took a step back.

"I know that and I wanna keep it that way. That's why you need to be my woman. I'm tryna lock that ass down." He took a step closer.

Candace blushed, backing up into the wall as he continued approaching. "Is that so?"

"That's so, like a mothafucka." He leaned into her mouth. Candace accepted his full wet lips and embraced his strong arms around her waist. She exhaled deeply, letting him overtake her and falling weak to his touch. Chris lifted her off her feet still kissing her hungry lips and carried her back to the bed. He moved the plate to the bedside table with one hand, laying Candace down with the other.

Chris rocked Candace back to sleep. When she woke up, her bedroom was empty, but she heard the television on in her living room. *What the hell?* She climbed out of bed.

"Oh, shit." Her knees buckled when her feet hit the floor. Candace grabbed the bed to keep from falling. "Oh, shit." She laughed again. "My fuckin' knees are weak."

Candace giggled to herself, tracing her hands along the wall as she walked down the hall to her living room. To her astonishment, she found Chris sitting on the couch with his feet up on her coffee table, flipping through the channels.

Chris turned when he saw her. "Hey, baby. Sleep good?"

"I did," she answered, slipping next to him on the sofa.

Chris raised his arm pulling Candace into him. She nestled against his bare chest, propping her feet up beside his.

"Did you sleep?" she asked.

"I barely ever sleep, baby."

"That ain't no good."

"Yea, I usually get a lot done when most people sleep."

Candace shrugged. *I wonder what the hell this boy does. Do I ask?*

Suddenly, Chris's phone rang on the table in front of them. He reached for it and answered. "Yo, man… Nah, ya'll gonna have to get at me when I get back up the end. I gotta spend some time with my missus. She been feeling neglected," Chris said into the phone while rubbing Candace's thigh.

Candace pursed her lips. *He really thinks I'm his woman. Is he serious?*

Chris ended his call and turned back to Candace. "Wanna watch a movie, baby?"

"What, no moves to make? You goin' actually chill in the crib wit' me on this beautiful Saturday?"

"I'm sayin', we can go out if you want, but I'm definitely trying to be witchu whateva we do."

Candace couldn't help but smile. Chris smiled back. Then he kissed her, long sweet and strong. Candace shivered. *This boy kisses me like he loves me. No fuckin' way.*

They watched *Transformers* in the living room before ending back up in Candace's bed. She was upside down, sweating and screaming when her cell phone rang on her nightstand. She didn't move for it. The second time it rang, they were both lying across the bed catching their breath. Candace checked the ID. It was Bam. She placed the phone back on the nightstand and turned back over to see Chris staring hard at her.

"What?" Candace asked at his heated glare.

Chris reached past her and picked up her phone. "Why don't you answer it?"

"What? Boy. Please. I don't ask nothing about your phone. Don't worry about mine."

"Yo, C. Stop playing with me. We come from two different worlds. It's shit I don't deal wit' when I'm with my lady. But I'm not into sharing pussy. So tell your little boyfriends to fall back. 'Cause if you telling me it's mine, then it's all mine."

Candace sucked her teeth.

Chris stood up with her phone in his hand. "I'll break this phone, C. Don't play with me."

Candace jumped up. "I'm not playing. Gimme my fuckin' phone!"

"Tell dude you gotta new man. Make it easy on us both."

"What the fuck are you talking about?"

Chris threw the phone down onto the bed. "I'm out, yo." He reached for his shirt hanging from the foot of the bed.

"Wait! What? Why?" Candace shouted, moving toward him.

"You not hearing me, Candace. I'm feeling you like shit. And you can front all you want, but either that ass is mine or it ain't. I'm not fucking with you if you fucking with somebody else. I don't get down like that."

"Neither do I," Candace snapped back.

"Then what's it goin' be, baby?" he asked, crossing his arms.

Candace moaned to herself at his prominent muscles. *Oh, God, he's so fuckin' gorgeous. But I barely know this kid.*

Candace bit down on her lip, then suddenly pushed Chris back against the wall.

"What the hell?" His eyes lit with curiosity and surprise.

"Lemme ask you something?" she asked, pressing herself into him.

Chris smiled, seeming slightly aroused, his shoulders relaxing and his hands wandering down her body. "Sure," he replied, cupping her behind.

"What do you do, Chris?"

He laughed. "I take care of shit, C." Candace curled her lips and Chris laughed again before pecking her quickly on the mouth. "I like the shit you do for me, Candace. I respect ya hustle even though I don't know shit about what you do. Feel me?"

Candace nodded.

"I'm not all in ya business and I'm not goin' put you all in mine. For your sake, it's better that way."

"So what do you want with me, Chris?"

"You must can't hear today. Let me say it to you like this then… I want you and I wanna keep wanting you, feel me? I don't want you fuckin' nobody but me 'cause I'm feelin' you like crazy right now."

"Is that so?"

He kissed her again, this time longer and deeper, wetter and stronger than the last. "That's so like a mothafucka, baby."

CHAPTER 21

You have a collect call from Gratersford Penitentiary.

Candace tapped the one button on her house phone, settling down at her kitchen table Monday morning before work.

"Hello?"

"Hey, Prince."

"Candy Reign, what's up, love?"

"Nothin', chillin'. 'Bout to go to work. How you been?"

"Stressin' in this mothafuckin' hell hole."

"Stressin'? Why? What's wrong witchu?"

"Nothin'. Nothin', Candy. I be ard. Work good?"

"Work is fuckin' nuts. I'm competing with this snobby-ass white chick for a promotion and this bitch is on my nerves. I have two more weeks of summer classes, then this fall will be my last semester and I finally fuckin' graduate in February…"

"Yeah? You goin' have a degree in what now?"

"Business admin."

"Right, right."

"Yeah, so I'm already registered for my last two courses, 'Laws and Policies' and 'Business Administration.' Then once I get this job I have to sit under an administrator and take my nursing home license exam."

"What?!? My girl, doing big things!"

Candace laughed. *I guess I'm everybody's damn girl.* "Manny's been at B's so I can focus on school and work."

"Yeah?"

"It's been a big help, but he's having more fun than I wanna admit."

Prince chuckled, his voice heavy and deep. "Why you say that?"

"'Cause, Prince, he runnin' round with the twins and this lil' busty-ass hussy…"

"What? Busty hussy." Prince laughed. "Whatchu talkin' 'bout, Candy? The girlies likin' on my boy?"

"Of course. You seen 'im. He fine as hell, Prince."

"Like his daddy."

"Shut the hell up. It ain't funny…lil' big-boobie hoochie all in my son face. I ain't havin' that."

"What the hell you goin' do about it, Candy? Beat up all the pre-teen girls in Philly?"

"If I have to."

Prince laughed harder. "You're fuckin' nuts, girl. You know that? You gotta let that boy be a boy."

"Boys are nasty and girls are worse."

"True, but you can't stop him either way."

"So what you suggest I do, Prince?"

"Talk to him…and make sure he got condoms," Prince said, still laughing.

"What the fuck?!? Hell no! I ain't givin' my ten-year-old son no goddamn condoms. You need to talk to him."

"I will. I'mma call over B's later when I get another chance to call out. It's a lot goin' on in here right now."

"You sure you good, Prince?"

"I'll be all right and I'll talk to E soon as I can, all right?"

"Yea."

"All right, well…I'll call you later, Candy Reign. Love you."

"Love you, too, Prince."

"Mars, you a damn fool. I wouldn'ta given his ass shit." Candace huffed into the cell phone wedged between her cheek and shoulder, unlocking her office door and stepping inside.

Marci wailed on the other end of the phone, "C, I mean I'm cool with it, like, I know chick be all in his shit, and right now buying me trinkets and shit like that is goin' be hard to justify, especially when they get a divorce. We do have to stay low-key, you know? But, damn, he ain't have to lie to me like I ain't know she knew. It's cool, like, all I'm sayin' is be straight up witcha shit, you know?"

"What?" Candace gasped.

"What what?" Marci asked.

"You cool with him taking the bracelet back?" Candace hung her bag behind her door and sat down in front of her computer.

"I'm not sayin' I'm cool with it, but I understand. My man gotta do what he gotta do. And as long as their accounts are still connected, she can see all his business, and I don't want to be the reason why shit gets ugly in the divorce, you know?"

Candace rolled her eyes, turning on her computer screen. "Marci, you trippin'. You really think he took that bracelet back because he was worried about how it would look when they get divorced and not because Donna busted him?"

"I'm sayin' he coulda been straight up with me about her bustin' him. I know that bitch is all up on him right now. She probably know he not in love with her no more and he just tryin' to keep the peace 'til he roll, so it's cool."

Candace started blankly at her screen loading, shaking her head. "You're nuts, Marcine."

"So whatchu sayin, C? You 'on't think I should go to her party?"

"Who party?" Candace asked sharply, her eyes narrowing at the stalled blue screen. She turned off her monitor, then turned it back on again.

"Donna's birthday party. They been talkin' 'bout it in the shop all week."

"Tommy goin' be there?" Candace asked, checking the wires connected to her machine.

"Probably."

"Then no," Candace huffed, tapping the side of her monitor. *What the hell? Why isn't this thing loading?*

"Why you say that?" Marci continued.

"'Cause I don't think it's a good idea to party with your boss while you're fuckin' her husband."

"Damn, Candace. You care more about that bitch than either one of us."

Candace sucked her teeth. "Somebody should."

"Well, I don't and besides, me and Tommy going into business together," Marci blurted out.

"Do his wife know all this?"

"Ohmigod, C. You're fuckin' impossible."

"Whateva. I gotta hit you back anyway. Something's wrong with my computer."

"Bye."

"Bye." Candace hollered out to the receptionist, "Allyson!"

"Yes?"

"Is your computer up?"

"Yea."

"Something's up with mine. Can you get the Help Desk on the line for me, please?"

"Uh…yeah. Sure."

Candace spent forty minutes on the phone with someone from IT before they registered her help ticket and told her they would call her back later.

Great, she thought. *Denise is off, I've got this dumb training with the DON this afternoon and I can't get shit done til then. This is just fuckin' great.*

Nancy Cole, the director of nursing at Wyncote Medical Rehabilitation Center, was nicer than Candace imagined, but she talked way more than Candace liked. Nancy droned on for over an hour about G-tubes and J-tubes, patient charts, doctors' orders and a whole bunch of other things Candace absorbed but had no real interest in. She smiled and nodded as Nancy spoke and jotted notes down in her black-and-white notebook.

Candace rubbed at the back of her neck after Nancy disappeared leaving her behind the nurses' station flipping through charts for up-to-date doctors' orders.

"My head hurts and my back is killing me," Candace moaned, grabbing a small stool from under the nurses' desk and slowly sitting down with the open chart on her lap. Her eyes low, scanning the text, Candace heard a shrill laugh behind her.

"Hello, Candace," Jennifer sneered.

"What do you want?" Candace asked with her back to the woman.

"What an opportune way to put the skills you do have to use."

"Whatever, Jennifer," Candace hissed, finally turning around. "Don't you have something better to do than stand here and get on my damn nerves?"

"Touchy today, aren't we?" Jennifer leaned in, grinning.

Candace's mouth twisted at the cynical expression on Jennifer's face. *Fuck is up with this bitch?*

"Is the job getting to be too much for you?" Jennifer continued.

"Not at all, Jennifer. My system is down this morning, but it's nothing I can't handle."

"Your computer system? Oh my. Did you get it back up yet?"

"No," Candace replied, choosing her words cautiously. "IT is working on it. Did you have any problems logging in this morning?"

"Who me? No," Jennifer replied, faintly touching her left hand to her chest. "I am very careful with my computer. You know, you can't leave your system open and vulnerable for attack."

Candace closed the chart on her lap. "Attack?"

Jennifer smiled. "You know, like the viruses or whatever you call it. They get into your system and ruin everything."

"Oh, okay. I guess so."

"Oh, I know so. You have to be so careful nowadays with these computers, you know."

Candace stared at Jennifer with tightness behind her eyes. "Right."

Jennifer smiled leaving Candace uncomfortable and tense before she turned and walked away.

Fuck is up with this bitch actually trying to be nice? Aww, hell nah. Something ain't right.

"Candace, you have a call on line two. Candace, line two." Allyson's voice boomed over the building's intercom system.

Candace picked up the call at the phone on the nurse's desk.

"This is Candace."

"Hi, Candace. This is Dave from the Help Desk. I'm calling about your computer system."

"Yes. You got it working?'

"Um, yeah. It was pretty bad. Looks like you downloaded something unsafe and your system shut down. I reset all your passwords to your first initial and last name."

Downloaded? What the hell did I download? Candace scratched her head. "Okay. I am not at my desk, but I am going to log on in a minute. I'll call you back if I can't get in."

"Okay, that's fine. But please, Candace, try to refrain from downloading non-work-related materials on company systems. It causes major problems on your end and mine."

What the hell? Candace's lips curled. "Sure, but I don't even…

whatever. I'll call you back if I can't get in, like I said." She placed the phone down on the receiver and scratched her head. *What the fuck did I download?*

Candace quickly typed her name into the password request box and loaded up her computer system when she got back to her desk. *I didn't download anything. What the fuck is dude talking about?*

Candace squirmed in the seat behind her desk as her computer hummed to start and the familiar icons sprang up on her screen.

"Thank God." She sighed loudly. "Emails. Emails. It's like three o'clock in the damn afternoon. I'm sure I missed a shit load of emails." Candace dragged the mouse across the desk, searching for her Microsoft Outlook icon. She clicked once she located it in the bottom-left corner of the screen.

Candace scanned the growing list of emails in front of her. One email in particular, in red high-importance script, stood out to her. It was from Denise. Candace clicked anxiously.

Candace,

As you know, I will be out of the building for the rest of the week at the Director's Conference in Langhorne, but I need to meet with you immediately upon my return. I will be back on Monday. Be prepared to address the email you sent me. Be advised, I am not at all pleased or amused.

Denise

What the fuck? What fuckin' email? I ain't send no goddamn email. What the fuck is she talking about?

Candace hurriedly searched her sent items folder.

"Kate in Corp Fiscal. Shelia Dane, A/R," Candace said aloud, scrolling through the long list. "When the fuck did I send Denise an email? And about what...what the fuck? There's nothing here. I didn't send anything. She's got me confused."

Candace ran her hands around the back of neck, pressing her knuckles into the tight spots. *What the hell is going on? I know I didn't send any emails to Denise. I shut my system down on Friday and rolled the fuck out. It was a slow day, Denise was here, so why would I send her an email if she's right down the hall?... That fuckin' Jennifer just asked me...* Candace felt a swift pain surge through her like a high kick in the chest. She grabbed her heart, her eyes spinning through a turnstile of thoughts. *THAT FUCKIN' JENNIFER...NO WAY... NO FUCKIN' WAY!*

Candace leapt from her seat, charging out into the main office like an angry bull and startling Allyson and Danielle half out of their seats.

"Allyson, you locked up on Friday, right?"

Allyson's eyes grew large at Candace's approach. "I...uh..yes. I...I locked up."

"Did anybody go into my office after I left?"

"After you left?"

"Yes. After I left, Allyson."

"No. No, not that I know of."

"Candace, is everything okay?" Danielle asked from the desk to her right.

Candace looked over to the brown-haired girl and took a slow breath. "No, everything is not all right."

"What's...what's wrong, Candace?" Allyson asked.

"Someone sent Denise an email from my computer."

"Someone?" Danielle repeated.

"Someone," Candace replied, eyeing Danielle up and down, then turning her focus to Allyson. She squinted, looking at the receptionist, before turning back into her office and slamming the door.

What the fuck? I didn't send her a damn email. Shit, I need to tell her that. But what am I supposed to say? "Hey, Denise, I don't know what the hell you're talking about. It wasn't me." Candace sat rapping her fingernails in quick succession atop her desk.

"This is some bullshit." She huffed, checking the time on her cell phone. "Shit, I gotta get out of here. I got class tonight." Candace ran her finger through her hair, looking back at her computer screen. She raised her fingers to the keyboard and began an email to Denise but stopped short in the subject line.

Now what? Can I see the email? How do I ask her that? She began typing.

Denise,
I am not sure what email you are referring to. I would need to see it to be certain I know what you're talking about.

Candace reread her text, stumbling over the words. *That makes me sound like a fuckin' idiot. Like I don't know what's going on. She's gonna think I'm slow.* Candace shook her head, pressing the backspace button until that message box was clear.

"This is some bullshit," Candace repeated, shutting off her computer. "I gotta get the fuck outta here."

"Ohmigod!" Candace hollered, hurrying to her car. "This place is hell! Why do I want to manage a nursing facility again?" She climbed in her black Accord, started the engine and quickly pulled out of the parking lot. "I must be nuts…no, I'm broke. That's it. I need a major pay change and short of robbin' mothafuckas, this is the only way I can see to do it." She massaged the back of her neck with one hand, steering with the other. "My fuckin' head and my back hurts!"

She arrived to class on time but barely able to focus on the lesson and found herself recounting her emails several times while listening to the professor speak.

"Here you go," the young Muslim girl to her left said, rousing Candace from her thoughts and handing her a sheet of paper.

Candace's eyes darted over the assignment page. *Ten-fuckin'-page paper. Due when? Three weeks…Are you fuckin' kidding me?*

She groaned lowly, dropping her head back to her desk. *Fuck my life*. Her head was still down when she felt her phone vibrating in her pocketbook by her feet. She peered over, quietly reading the message from Chris.

Hey baby. How's your day going?

She slid her fingers swiftly across the touch screen. *Fucked Wth??*

Long story

I be over

K

"It's just a bunch a bullshit." Candace huffed, pacing the small space in her kitchen.

Chris looked intriguingly at her, nodding. "That's fucked up, yo," he said coolly. "You really think that chick Jennifer had something to do with your computer crashin'?"

"Chris, lemme tell you something," Candace said, leaning in toward him and resting her hand on her hips. "When you see me in the streets, that's chill-ass Candace; I be on some 'grown woman do what I wanna do' shit. But in the workplace, oh hell nah. I am the elite professional, except for that one time I cussed that bitch out—but other than that I don't download dumb shit at my job;

and I sure as hell don't send outta-pocket emails to my boss. What kinda shit is that?"

Chris's eyebrows raised. "You cursed her out?"

Candace nodded firmly.

Chris chuckled, propping his elbows up on the table and resting his chin on his closed fist, staring intently at Candace. "But how would she get in your shit, though?"

Candace shrugged sitting down across from him. "I dunno. But I know it's too coincidental for her to be talkin' all nice to me and shit about attacks on computers and then *BAM!*" Candace's arms flew up in the air. "My shit jacked up and Denise wants to see me about an email I didn't send."

Chris shook his head, standing and moving toward her. "Be easy, babe. It's goin' be aright. When mothafuckas do dirt, they get dirt. See whatcha boss talking about and just go from there." Chris's hand gently massaged Candace's tense shoulders. "If you the shit like you say you are, your boss knows you ain't about that dumbness. She should hear you out."

"Yeah, but she wasn't sounding too confident in me and my abilities in that email." Candace sighed.

Chris gently lifted her chin. "You goin' be cool, babe. Trust me. Dumb shit like this happens when people try to do better for themselves, but you can't let it get to you. Don't stress; you goin' figure this shit out and keep it fuckin' movin', babe. Okay?"

Candace gave a weak smile, slightly nodding, before Chris leaned in and kissed her softly on the lips.

"Now come, baby," he said, bending down and scooping Candace up out of the chair. "Let's go work out some of that frustration so you'll feel better."

"Oh, yeah," Candace said, draping her arms around his neck. *Oh, my*, she thought, her stomach tingling.

"Oh yeah. I'mma do my best to help you relax."

Candace kissed Chris lightly on the cheek as he carried her into her bedroom.

Candace's stomach turned walking into the building the next morning. She tried not to stare too long at Allyson and Danielle, greeting them quickly before unlocking her office and closing the door behind her. *Maybe one of them had something to do with it? Can't trust nobody.*

Candace plopped down at her desk, flipping on her computer. *I wonder if it's too late to send Denise an email? I could just be like, "Hey, Denise, I'm not sure what you're talking about. Give me a call." Would she think that was too informal? I don't know. She sounded pissed in her email.* Candace shook her head and swallowed hard.

I don't know what to do. Wait...where the hell is Chrissy?

Candace snatched up the phone, hurriedly dialing Chrissy's extension.

"Chrissy, I need to talk to you."

"Well, hello to you, too, darling."

"Oh, shoot. Sorry, Chrissy. Good morning. I need to talk to you."

Chrissy giggled. "Well, you know where I am. Come on up and see me."

"On my way."

Candace felt like she flew to Chrissy's office in seconds, pulling up a chair in front of the chubby-faced woman. She chuckled inwardly taking in Chrissy with her purple eye shadow, pink blush and red lips. *Poor thing could use some lessons at the MAC counter.*

"So what's the trouble, Miss Candace?" Chrissy asked, grinning at her friend.

"Chrissy, somebody's trying to set me up."

"Set you up?"

Candace nodded. "Yes, and I think it's that damn Jennifer."

"Oh my," Chrissy squealed, bright-eyed. "What on earth happened? How is she trying to set you up?"

"Yesterday my computer crashed and then Jennifer—out of nowhere—makes small talk with me about protecting your computer and computers being attacked and all. Then when IT finally gets me in my computer at like three o'clock, they tell me I downloaded something that crashed my system and Denise sends me this email like she's pissed about some email I sent her, but I didn't send her an email and there isn't one on my computer. So what the hell?" Candace huffed, dropping her head.

Chrissy was quiet.

Candace looked up staring at Chrissy's mouth hanging open. She waited for her to say something, but Chrissy was dead silent and stone still, not even blinking. Candace's right eyebrow rose curiously and Chrissy finally twitched, closed her eyes, then opened them again slowly.

"Ohmagosh, I can't even... I mean who in the low?...that there is too many coincidences...ain't no such thang," Chrissy ranted excitedly, swinging her heavy arm in the air.

"That's what I'm sayin', Chrissy. Somethin' ain't right."

"You damn straight it ain't. And you better be getting to the bottom of it quickly, missy, or it's going to be your tail hittin' the fan."

Candace scoffed, shaking her head. "Don't I know it."

Candace was at her desk that afternoon, reviewing charges in client accounts when someone rapped lightly on her office door.

"Come in," Candace said without turning around.

"Candace, these just came for you."

Candace turned to see Danielle standing in her doorway holding an arrangement of beautiful orange and red flowers in a clear vase draped in a gold bow. Candace squinted for a moment, eyeing the bouquet unsure yet smiling.

"For me?" she asked after a moment. Her heart racing, she stood and searched the flowers for a card.

"Who are they from?" Danielle asked, smiling and peering over the envelope as Candace tore it open.

Babe,

Just thinking of you. Don't stress. You can handle this and I got you. Stick with ya boy.

Love,

Chris

"Ooooh look at you, Boss Lady," Danielle sang.

It was then Candace realized she was grinning wide and hard. She fought to contain her smile but couldn't and burst out laughing.

Danielle smiled, still holding the flowers. She smelled them. "They're super pretty. Whoever he is, he got you cheesin'."

"He's a sweet kid." Candace laughed. "So young…but he's got a big…heart." She burst out laughing again.

Danielle chuckled with her as Candace took the flowers. She smelled them, too. They smelled beautiful and fresh and sweet. Candace stood mesmerized by the arrangement. Danielle crept out quietly, closing the door behind her. *I've never gotten flowers at my job before. Okay! Thumbs up, kid.* Candace set the vase at the end of her desk and sat down, still staring at the tall green stems and the brilliant hues of the full foliage. *I like. I like a lot. A lot more than I should.*

She turned her attention back to her computer screen, but every minute or so, she couldn't help but steal a glance at the beautiful bouquet in front of her. And every time she looked, she smiled.

She pulled her phone from her drawer.

Thank u for my flowers. They're beautiful, she texted.

Just like u

☺

And ur welcome. Im glad u liked em.

Am I going to see you tonight?

I dunno babe. Tonight's bad. Got alotta moves to make

☹

Lol don't do that. I wanna c u 2. imma try but if I say I am and I don't u goin be mad

Yup

Lol least u honest

True.

You mad wit me?

Not at all. Thanks again for my flowers.

Ur welcome babe

Candace missed Chris more than she thought she would that night, turning over in her empty bed. She had to admit she liked the way his long limbs wrapped around hers and his juicy lips always tasted so sweet. "Damn kid," she groaned, pulling the covers up over her head. She kept the air on just chilly enough so she could still wrap herself up in a blanket in the summertime. And this night she tugged her puffy green blanket up over her head, wrestling herself back to sleep.

CHAPTER 22

*C*andace awoke the next morning, her head pounding. She sighed deeply while dressing and dragged herself out the door.

This is going to be a long week. It's already Wednesday and I have to wait until Monday to talk to Denise. This is fucked up. I don't even know what there is to talk about because I don't know what the fuckin' email said. I gotta find out what that damn email said...but how?

Candace scratched her head, parking her car in front of her building.

"This is fuckin' bullshit." She huffed, slamming her car door and walking toward the front entrance. "I'm finna get cursed out 'bout an email I've never even seen. How does an email just disappear? I mean, can't IT...." Candace froze. "IT, yes!"

Candace started moving again, this time quicker than before until her legs picked up to a light sprint and she burst through the main lobby, rushing toward her office.

"Hey. Hey, good morning," she shouted to Danielle and Allyson as she passed them, hurriedly unlocking her office door. Once inside, she grabbed the phone on her desk.

"Dave at the Help Desk....He'll be back in at what time? One? Okay, yes, I'd like to leave a message." *I'm going to get to the bottom of this.*

Candace mulled through the mounds of paperwork on her desk, counting down the seconds until one o'clock and a return call from

Dave. By the time her clock read 1:13 she was on the phone dialing the Help Desk again. She finally reached him.

"Hi, Dave. This is Candace at the Wyncote building. I'm calling you because of my system crashing on Monday. Yeah, I'm trying to track down an email that was sent from my computer before it crashed."

"An email? Did you look in your 'sent items' folder?"

"Yes."

"How about the outbox?"

"Yes," Candace huffed.

"Did you look in the deleted files folder?"

"Yes. Yes, I did all of that and the email is not on my computer anymore, but I need to see it. Can you find it?"

Dave paused for a moment before speaking. "Uh, I think so, but I can't do it for you."

"Excuse me?" Candace gasped.

"Due to the nature of your request and the severity of the system failure that just took place on your end, I would have to get an administrator's approval before I could start going into backup and support files."

"What? It came off my computer, but you have to get my boss to say it's okay?"

"Unfortunately, yes."

DAMMIITT!!!!

"I'm sorry, Candace, but there isn't much I can do on this end without an approval."

"But Denise won't be back until Monday and I need this before she gets back."

"I understand, but my hands are tied."

Candace dropped her head back to stop the tears forming in the creases of her eyes from rolling down her face.

Now what? This is my fuckin' job on the line...if Denise really thinks I sent her some inappropriate shit, there goes my chances of being an administrator. That's it. I might as well pack it up. I'm fucked without that email…and it's too late to email her now. Now what?

Candace brushed away the stream of tears running down her cheek. She took a deep breath, pulled her cell phone from her purse and dialed Chris.

"Hey, baby girl."

"Hey," Candace replied dryly, her voice a whimper.

"What's goin' on witchu? Everything aright?"

"No."

"Work still got you stressin'?"

"Yes." Candace wiped the steady tears.

"Aw, babe. Anything I can do to help make you feel better."

"I want you to take me out to dinner," Candace announced.

"Okay. When? Tonight?" Chris asked.

"Yeah."

"Don't you have class tonight?"

"I don't really feel like going. I really want some Red Lobster and some alcohol."

"Fuck that! You goin' ta class. I'll see you after."

"But I'm tired and I really don't wanna go."

"Fuck that, babe. Go to class, call me when you done. I'll take you wherever you wanna go…after class. And we can talk about what's got you so pissed."

Candace groaned. "Fine. See you after class."

"Aright, baby. Talk to you later."

Candace didn't come out of her office much for the rest of the day. She finished her billing charges, shut her computer down, locked her door and headed down North Philadelphia to Temple. She was making a serious effort to pay attention to her professor in class. She craned her neck around the large white man in front of her and raised her hand to get clarification on the paper she hadn't started.

Candace was chatting with the Muslim girl to her left when her phone vibrated in her bag.

"I don't even know where to start," the girl told her as Candace checked her phone.

Whatchu want from red lobster babe. Imma bring it to you.

Candace smiled, typing her response. *Cheddar bay biscuits. New England clam chowder. Seafood Alfredo.*

Damn greedy. LOL

Lol. Shut up and bring me my grub.

Ok, soundin like a fat kid. C u later.

K

Candace slid the phone back into her bag, trying to tuck her smile away as well. But she couldn't and she grinned, thinking of Chris all the way to her apartment. *At least he can put a smile on my face, 'cause every fuckin' thing else is going wrong.*

Candace was sitting across her couch, sipping on a chilled glass of vodka when her doorbell rang. Chris was the only company she expected after class so she stood and quickly let him in.

"Hey, baby," he said, smiling and kissing her on the lips.

"Hey." Candace smiled back, receiving him.

"Yo, I thought you was gonna order a lobster or some shit." He laughed, following her in the apartment.

"Why you say that?" Candace asked, leading him into the kitchen.

"'Cause that's the most expensive thing on the menu. That's how y'all high-siddity, light-skinned, Uptown females do, right? Test a nigga pockets. I ain't no broke dude, though. You coulda ordered whateva."

"First off, balla, I don't even eat lobster. Red Lobster soup and biscuits are the shit. And, secondly, who the hell you callin' light-skinned and high-siddity? Witcha red hair and green eyes. Where the hell did that come from?"

"I know, right?" Chris laughed, shaking his head. "Moms is white, dad's black. I look like her. I ain't never met my pop, bitch-ass nigga."

Candace looked up from the large paper bag she was pulling the food containers from. Chris looked back at her, his face calm and eyes bright. He shrugged.

"So," Candace began, setting the food on the kitchen table. "You got any kids, Chris?"

"A young bul. He's almost one."

"His mom?"

"Is a crazy bitch."

"What's up with y'all?"

Chris shrugged again. "She's young."

"You're young," Candace reminded him.

"Yeah, but I mean, she's young-minded. Like, she don't know what the fuck to do with herself other than sit around and wait for me to pay her bills and shit."

"She don't work?"

"Nah. She says my son keeps her from doing a lot. She said she wanna go to school to be a medical assistant, but she gotta get the money up."

"You helpin'?"

"Of course. That's my seed."

"You betta," Candace said, sitting down at the table and folding her arms over her breasts. "Being a single mom ain't no joke. Even with help from his father, raising my son is hard. So you betta make sure you helping that girl out. She ain't make that baby by herself."

"Damn, boo. You serious, huh?"

"Dead serious. I don't do deadbeat dads."

"Don't worry, babe. I take care of my son."

"Good."

Chris laughed. "I like that you care. But you don't gotta worry about mine's. Just 'cause my dad wasn't shit don't mean I'mma do the same to my son."

Candace smiled. "Respect."

Candace wrapped her hair up, tying the scarf around her tight beehive and setting the brush back down on her dresser. She chuckled lightly, listening to Chris singing in her shower.

"And it kills me….ooohh oohhh oh oh ooooh…."

That boy is special. She smiled walking toward the bathroom door. Suddenly, her house phone rang. Candace scurried quickly over to her nightstand to check the caller ID. *Prince! What the fuck?*

Candace's eyebrows narrowed and jaw tightened, staring down at the phone. *Shit, he know Man ain't here. Why is he calling right now? He never calls me this time of night… Something's wrong.*

Candace clutched the phone in her hand but drew back from answering. *Shit, I gotta answer it. I always answer it. Something's gotta be up for him to be calling me right now.*

Chris sang louder in the background and a heavy knot formed in the bottom of Candace's stomach. She trembled holding the ringing device. *Fuck.*

Candace swallowed hard closing her bedroom door. She slowly answered and accepted the charges.

"Candy?"

"Prince, wha…what's going on?" she stammered.

"What? You busy or something?"

"A little."

Prince was quiet for what seemed like forever.

"Hello?" Candace inquired, biting her bottom lip.

"I'm here," he responded slowly, his voice strained to a quiver. "They tryin' to take a nigga out, Candy."

She cradled the phone in her hand sliding down to the floor by her bed.

"You okay?" she asked, her voice a soft comforting whisper.

"This shit crazy, Candy."

"Why, Prince? What happened?"

"I'mma either die soon or be in this bitch 'til I rot."

"No you not. Don't say that."

"It's the truth. This shit is gettin' real ugly."

"What's going on, Prince? Talk to me."

"Not now." He paused. Candace could hear the tension between his breaths. "I miss y'all, Candy Reign. I miss y'all like shit."

"I know. We miss you, too."

"Man, Candy, I been cool 'til this new guard, man... This shit too crazy right now."

"I can't even imagine."

"I wanna see my son. I wanna see my kids. I gotta get the fuck outta here, man."

"I know, Prince, but...."

"BAAAAAAABBEEEEEE!!! I need a towel!!!" Chris hollered down the hall.

Candace's heart jumped. Prince was quiet. She knew he'd heard. "Prince?"

Click.

Fuck. Candace sank down lower onto the floor, still holding the phone in her hand when Chris emerged from the bathroom naked, dripping water across the floor.

His eyes creased in the bedroom doorway looking down at Candace on the floor beside her bed. "You cool, babe?"

She nodded. "I need a towel."

Candace pointed to a pile of freshly folded towels sitting on top of a hamper in the corner of her room. She stared at Chris moving in front of her, water shining like diamonds on the creases of his stomach. She watched him dry his hard body and make his way over to her dresser. She wanted to be angry with him for letting her son's father hear his voice, but she could not make herself mad with the nude statuesque physique garbed in only a towel in front of her. Chris grabbed the lotion from her dresser and sat down on the end of the bed, rubbing the white almond-scented cream into his legs.

"So almondy." He chuckled and then turned, looking down at Candace. "You cool?"

"I'm good," she replied, placing her hand on his leg. Chris reached for her, helping to lift her up. Candace stood in front of him as Chris pulled her forward onto him lying back on the bed.

"I don't believe you," he replied, raising his lips to meet hers. "But, I bet I can make you feel better."

"Maybe," Candace replied, returning his kisses.

Candace rolled over half-awake in her bed, her arm falling lazily on Chris's bare back. She opened her eyes to the broad span between his shoulder blades. She admired the fair-skinned Adonis lying across her sheets, smiling inwardly at her conquest. Then suddenly, she shook her head. *Oh, hell no. Prince is goin' ta fuckin' snap. I'm never goin' hear the end of this shit.*

She sighed, then held her breath, slipping from beneath her sheets.

What the hell? she thought, standing over her bed and pulling on her bathrobe. *This dude really knocked out. I'm trippin'. I done let my baby dad hear this kid in my house. He spending the night and shit… Get a hold of yourself, Candace.* She scratched her head, her locks a tattered mess, then shrugged her shoulders and made her way to the bathroom.

Candace brushed her hair and her teeth. "Get it together," she said aloud, staring at her reflection in the mirror before washing her face and returning to her bedside.

Chris was still asleep and Candace's head tilted unconsciously gazing over him. She chewed her lip. *So…am I supposed to let him sleep while I go to work?* She stared a while longer. *Nah, he gotta get up.*

Candace quietly climbed under the covers and pressed her body against Chris's long, strong, bare back. She breathed softly against the rise and fall of his breath, then gently kissed the tender skin between his shoulder blades. Chris stirred. Candace kissed again.

Chris turned slowly over to his back, smiling as his eyes met hers. "Good morning, sunshine."

"Good morning," Candace replied, facing him across the pillow.

"You touching on me all early in the morning like you want something," Chris teased, his hand gently stroking her arm beneath the covers.

"Boy, I'm not foolin' with you this morning. I have to go to work."

Chris pulled her body into his. "That's what ya' mouth say."

Candace giggled, pulling away and placing her hands on his chest. "I'm serious." Candace squeezed his flesh under her fingers. *Supple yet firm, not too hard not too soft.*

Chris stared at her with unbelieving eyes, his lips twisted. He laughed. "I wanna believe you…but, it's just that, I wake up hungry in the morning and I want some more of what I ate last night."

Umm. Candace tensed at the sudden moisture between her legs. Chris smiled, staring at her with those softly slanted green eyes. She bit her lip.

Chris leaned forward, gently pressed his teeth into her neck and slightly pulled back on her flesh. Candace gasped. He moistened his full lips with his saliva, moving downward along her skin and kissing sweetly. Candace let out a small hum. He bit again, then kissed, this time working his tongue and sucking her neck. Candace released a deep breath from her surrendering body as Chris slipped his hands around her waist, opening her robe.

"Ummmm...I gotta...I gotta...take a shower...and....ummm... make breakfast...and..."

Chris climbed on top of Candace, turning her to her back and slipping her robe down past her shoulders, still moving his mouth, down her arm and slowly to her elbow.

Whoa, God! What was that? She winced at that strange sensation of having the inside of her elbow kissed.

Chris's lips moved to her anxious nipples, lapping each with his solid tongue, then caressing it between his soft lips in a gentle suckle. He kissed first the right, then the left and then back to the right again before continuing down her tummy. Chris rotated between kisses and bites down the length of Candace's caramel body. Candace's hum grew to a low moan as she clenched her womanly muscles. Chris passed her belly button, first stopping to stick his tongue inside, then down to her abdomen, soft from child-bearing but smooth and strong just the same. Candace did not hide from her nakedness and spread her legs wide as Chris narrowed to the warmth emanating from between them.

His tongue found her eager clit, greeting it with sloppy kisses and gentle sucks. Candace moaned louder. Chris pressed in, devouring her with hungry lips and a giving tongue. Her moans grew accompanied by squirming and her hands fell to the back of Chris's head. She slithered her hips, rolling her pussy along the rhythm of his mouth. Chris slid his hands under her backside, lifting her up.

Oh, God. Candace gave way to the arch in her back, pressing herself into his face.

"Oh, God." The words escaped from her lips as she felt Chris's fingers enter her. "Fuck," she shouted as Chris sucked her swollen clit and massaged his two thick fingers along her insides. He twisted his fingers, then sucked again at her clit. Then he massaged and twisted and sucked at the same time and Candace hollered, "Fuck!!!"

"Ummm," Chris moaned as her body squirmed. He continued the cadence.

"Oh, fuck! Ohhhhh…fffuuuuucccckkk!!! Ummm, ohmigod… ummmm, babe…."

Chris sucked harder, gliding his tongue over the pearl of her proud womanhood. Candace felt her body jerk. *Ohmigod! Oh my fuckin' God…this is un-fuckin'-believable. This shit feels too good. I'mma fuckin' cum.*

Chris kept at it, wrapping one arm tight around Candace's thigh. She screamed, fighting against his strength and the rushing tingle working its way up in her.

"Oh, God. I'mma cum…fuck, baby! You goin' make me cum!" she yelled, twisting her body as best she could.

But she struggled to no avail—Chris had her locked, sucking, kissing, massaging and twirling. Candace wriggled in delight until one swift flick of the tongue caused her body to buck uncontrollably. She wrapped her legs around Chris's head, squeezing him tight as she shuddered and warmth rushed through her from head to feet.

"Ohmigawd!!!" she screamed and screamed again until Chris pulled his saturated face from between her legs.

She trembled, staring up at his bright smile. "I fuckin' hate you," she groaned, struggling to turn over on her side.

Chris stood up wiping his face in his hands. "You love me. You just too scared to say it."

Candace sat up straight. "Don't kid yourself, Chris. I can't fuckin' stand you. I tolerate you because the sex is good."

"Yeah?"

"Yeah," Candace replied, rising to her feet, but her knees buckled and she quickly sat back down on the bed.

"Yeah, right, chief." Chris chuckled, shoving her shoulder, causing Candace to fall back. "You sound tough, but I know you're soft as cotton."

"Soft? This ass, maybe...but that's all that's soft about me." Candace attempted to stand again, this time successfully, and she playfully swatted Chris as she headed back to the bathroom. He moved behind her. Chris washed his face as Candace plopped her naked behind down on the toilet seat.

"What you want for breakfast, babe?" Chris asked, looking up from the basin.

Candace stared at him, confused.

"Don't look at me like that," Chris said, apparently noticing the surprise in her eyes. "Yeah, I cook."

Candace shook her head. "I didn't say anything."

"Good. Don't. Just take a shower and I'll make you something to eat before you go to work."

"You not stayin' here, are you?" Candace asked, unsure of how the words came out.

Chris's brow folded slightly. "Nah. Why? You ready for me to get out?"

"No. I was just asking."

Chris shook his head, washed his hands and headed out of the spacious bathroom.

Candace shrugged stepping into the shower. *Hope I didn't hurt his feelings. I like the kid...but he can't be crashin' here while I go to work.* Candace rubbed the sudsy loofah all over her long body. *He has been such a sweetie during all this bullshit at work.*

Candace took a deep breath after shutting off the water. She quickly patted dry, draped a towel around her body and made her way to her bedroom. She paused for a moment in the hall. *Is that bacon? Is he really in my kitchen cooking bacon?*

Candace applied her lotion, dressing in record time and hurriedly met Chris in the kitchen where he seemed to have found his way around. He smiled in his jeans and T-shirt, handing Candace a heaping plate of bacon and cheese eggs.

"Oh, my," she said, receiving the meal. "This is nice. A girl could get used to this."

Chris chuckled, watching Candace take a seat at the table. "I hope you like."

Candace took a bite. The eggs were delicious and the turkey bacon was cooked to a crisp. "It's good."

"Good. Enjoy. I'mma get dressed so we can both get outta here."

Candace watched Chris saunter into her bedroom. She stood to her feet to get a glass from the cabinet. As she neared the counter, she noticed the cracked eggs shells in the sink with at least three pans, some bowls and what looked like all of her utensils. The milk and cheese sat out on the sticky kitchen counter and an empty bacon package was plopped in the middle of the greasy stovetop. Looking down, she winced at the disarray. *What the hell? Messy mothafucka.*

Chris kissed Candace sweetly outside her car. "I'mma see you later, okay?"

"Yes, when you come back over and clean up my kitchen."

"Aw shit," Chris said, laughing. "I made a mess, huh?"

"Uh, yeah."

"I said I could cook. I ain't say nothing about cleaning."

"Bye, boy," Candace said, climbing in her car and pulling off.

Her shoulders slumped as she neared her workplace. Her body tensed pulling into the parking lot. *God, I don't want to be here. I'd so much rather be home, laid up with Chris. Chris...*Candace smiled. The thought of his morning kisses sent chills through her body. *He's the only good thing I got going right now. My son is too busy with busty hussies to call his mother, my baby's father is probably fuming right now and I'm 'bout to lose my damn job...but Chris...*She smiled again entering her office.

Candace wasn't at her computer more than ten minutes before the phone on her desk rang.

"Hello," she answered calmly.

"Candace, it's Chrissy. What are you doin', darling?"

"Trying not to pull my hair out. Why? What's up?"

"Gotta minute?"

"For you, Chrissy? Always."

"Good. Come see me."

"Okay, I'll be up in a sec." Candace placed the phone back on its base, sitting quietly for a moment behind her desk. *I wonder what the hell is going on?* Candace checked the time on her computer monitor: 8:40. *I might as well go up now before morning meeting.*

Candace closed her door behind her, exiting the Business Office and heading upstairs. Chrissy was flipping through a tall stack of manila folders when Candace finally entered the cluttered box-size room.

"What's up, lady?" Candace asked, stepping into the tight space and finding a seat on a small stool in the corner.

"Sit down. Sit down," Chrissy instructed, fidgeting and closing her door.

"What's up, Chrissy?"

"I've been thinking 'bout what you said, darling. About that email thing with Denise. Now, Candace, you sure you didn't mistakenly write something about her to a friend or something and somehow it got sent to Denise?"

Candace pulled back. "Damn, Chrissy. I thought you knew me better than that by now."

"I do. I do, darling. I want to make sure you're sure."

Candace rolled her eyes. "I'm sure." She sighed deeply, letting her head fall to her chest. "Chrissy, this is serious. What if I lose my job over this?"

"You won't, Miss Candace. Now, you say you didn't send any emails, right?"

"Of course I didn't."

Chrissy settled back in her chair, twisting her fingers together in precocious thought. "You've got to figure out what that email said."

"I know," Candace responded, staring at the folds forming in Chrissy's forehead.

Chrissy stared ahead blankly seemingly tuning Candace out and still kneading her fingers. "And before Denise gets back you need to know who sent it and be able to prove that they sent it."

"I know all of this, Chrissy. What are you getting at?"

"I think you need to talk to your staff," Chrissy replied, sharply turning her eyes toward Candace.

"My staff?" Candace jerked back.

"Yes, your staff." Chrissy leaned in close, reducing her voice to a whisper. "Think about it, darling. You said you locked your office up after you left on Friday and you're certain that you didn't send anything to Denise before you left. And mysteriously your computer crashes? Candace, that don't mean but one thing…"

"Chrissy, if you're about to say you that think somebody hacked into my computer, sent that email to ruin me, then crashed my system to hide the evidence, then you're reading my damn mind."

"Then, darling, I'm telepathic. And I'm thinking that means that email had to come from your computer after you punched out for the day. Who has access to your office other than you?"

"Danielle and Allyson both have keys to my office."

"Both of them?"

Candace nodded.

"Have you talked to them?"

"Yeah," Candace replied with hesitation.

Chrissy pressed in further, close enough for Candace to see the creases in the blue makeup under her eyes. "No, Candace. I mean did you *talk* to them?"

Candace slowly shook her head.

Chrissy's breath hastened as she continued to speak. "You need to get them alone. One by one and interrogate them. Ask them what they know, what you think they know and what you think, they think, you might know."

Candace laughed slightly, watching the jiggling intensity of Chrissy's face.

"You've got to talk to those girls, Candace. My gut is telling me something is up and somebody has to know something."

Candace nodded, processing and subconsciously picturing her and Allyson alone in a police interrogation room. In her mind, she leaned over the table, slamming a heavy hand down on the cold hard steel and causing Allyson to jump out of her seat. Candace shook away the image, standing to her feet.

"Let me know if you need my help with anything, darling. I'd hate to see you go down for something you didn't do," Chrissy said.

Candace shook her head. "Who you tellin'?"

Chrissy chuckled. "Besides, you've got to get to the bottom of this. 'Cause I think I'm just goin' die if I don't find out what the hell was in that email."

Candace nodded, heading toward the door. "Right."

Candace's mind raced while heading back to her office. Throughout her morning calls and bill processing, she wrestled with the words she'd use to get the information she needed from her receptionist and payroll clerk.

This is crazy, she thought. *But I've got to get to the bottom of this. What the hell do I say? I should be stern and direct. Scare them a little… I don't know.*

Candace reached for her phone and texted Chris.

Hey. How bout I have to play detective this afternoon.

She set her phone down, awaiting a reply. After a few moments of silence, she picked it back up to see if her message had gone through. It had.

I hate when he takes long to text me back.

Candace set the phone back down. She decided to call Danielle in first after her lunch. *Okay, I got this*, she coached herself, opening her office door. "Danielle."

"Yes," the young brunette replied, perking up from behind her computer monitor.

As did Allyson who Candace could see her from the corner of her eye.

"I need to see you in my office for a minute," Candace said coolly to Danielle.

Danielle glanced over at Allyson before standing and following Candace into her office.

Candace took her seat. "Shut the door."

Danielle complied, then moved slowly to the front of Candace's desk. "Is everything okay?"

"Sit down, Danielle."

Again, Danielle complied.

"I wanted to talk to you about an incident that occurred on Friday involving my computer."

"Your computer?"

Candace nodded. "Somehow someone gained access to my office and my computer. I am pretty sure I know who this person is, but I am having a hard time figuring out how they got in, when I know I locked my door when I left for the day."

Danielle stared straight ahead into Candace's eyes, her own eyes squinting and a look of confusion spreading across her face.

Candace continued, "Danielle, I know that only you and Allyson have access to my office."

Danielle's eyes widened from a look of confusion to one of concern and she quickly parted her lips to speak, but Candace kept on.

"I checked your time. You punched out after Allyson on Friday, which means you were the last person to leave the office on Friday. You locked up."

Danielle nodded nervously.

"And you mean to tell me you didn't see anything?"

Danielle shook her head, trembling.

"Danielle, I need to know if you let anyone into my office for any reason after I left on Friday."

"No. No way, Candace," Danielle stammered. "I didn't have anything to do with someone getting into your office."

"So, you know who did?"

"No." Danielle shook her head.

"Where are your keys?"

"On my key ring in my desk."

"Are they always in your desk?"

"Most times. Or in my pocketbook. My work keys are on the same ring as my house keys."

Candace nodded. "Have you let anyone borrow your work keys?"

"No."

"Are you sure?"

Danielle nodded quickly. "Positive."

Candace rapped her fingernails atop her desk, staring directly forward at the nervous girl. "Danielle, I know that someone got into my office, and I think that either you, or Allyson had something to do with it."

"Ohmigod, Candace! It wasn't me. I swear," Danielle whined, leaning forward nearly to the edge of her chair.

"Then are you saying it was Allyson?"

"No... I don't know," Danielle stammered. "I mean...I know she left first on Friday, then I clocked out. I locked the front door to the Business Office and left. That's it."

"Do you remember who was still in the building when you left?"

"Umm...yeah. But almost all the department heads were gone."

"Was Jennifer still here?"

Danielle paused, her eyes rolling from side to side seemingly searching her recent memories. She finally looked up at Candace. "Yes."

Candace felt her nostrils flare. She exhaled, then stood. "Okay, Danielle. Thank you."

Danielle stood up quickly. "Is that it?"

"Is there more?"

"No. No. Is that all you need from me? Can I go back to my desk?"

Candace nodded, moving toward the door. When she opened the door, Danielle darted past.

"I'll be right back. I have to go to the bathroom."

Again, Allyson looked up. First in the direction of Danielle's disappearance, then at Candace who stood with arms folded in her doorway.

"I need to see you, too, as soon as she comes back."

"Uh, oh...okay. Um, but, you...you have a call on line two," Allyson stuttered, holding the phone in her hand.

"Who is it?" Candace asked, apparently annoyed.

"The County Assistance Office," Allyson replied timidly.

Candace retreated to her office to pick up the call. Thirty-five minutes later, she hung up the line and opened her door. "Where's Allyson?" Candace asked Danielle after finding the receptionist's desk empty.

"She went to lunch. She should be back in twenty minutes."

Candace rolled her eyes shutting her office door. She checked the time on her phone: 1:25. *That stupid phone call did cut into the girl's lunchtime.* She looked at the time again. *Why the hell hasn't Chris texted me back?*

Candace anxiously tapped the keys on her keyboard entering charges and waiting for Allyson to return. She left her door open so she could see the young girl as soon as she walked back into the Business Office. After a few moments, Candace heard the office door open and Allyson's desk chair creak.

"I think Candace is waiting for you," she heard Danielle say. Candace started to stand up and heard the Business Office door open again followed by nasal laughter.

"Come. Come this way," Candace heard Jennifer say. Candace snapped straight up and turned around to see Jennifer leading two women and an older gentleman toward her. Jennifer smiled as she approached.

"Hey, Candace. How's it going? Do you have minute?"

Candace's entire body tensed. She cautiously spoke, "Um, sure. What's going on?"

Jennifer stepped to the side. "Ms. Cothburne, Mr. Cothburne and Mrs. Gates, this is Candace Brinton. She is our number cruncher, here. She knows everything about all the billing and charges, and she is the girl you need to speak to about Mr. Cothburne's Medicare."

The two women nodded in Candace's direction. Candace smiled, putting on her best business face and extending her hand. "How do you do? Pleased to meet you."

"Now, Candace," Jennifer continued. "Mr. Cothburne and his daughters are interested in admitting Mr. Cothburne to our fine facility. They'd love a tour and a minute of your time to go over some questions."

"A tour?" Candace asked, swallowing hard. She hated giving tours. The procedure itself took over an hour, showcasing all the facility's highlights from the activity room to the dinner menu. Then the families always stopped to ask questions along the way. She had been trained to offer the facility's greatest accommodations and to always remain polite, calm, and patient with everyone along the tour. But Candace wasn't in the mood to remain calm and polite. She wanted to get her claws into Allyson behind closed doors.

"Yes, a tour," Jennifer repeated. "Is that too much to ask right now? I don't mean to bother you; I'd do it myself. It's just that I have to run over to Abington to check on Mrs. Silverman and make sure her readmission paperwork is in order." Jennifer placed her hand on Ms. Cothburne, the youngest daughter's shoulder. "You know, we really do have great working relationships with the hospitals."

"I see," the young woman replied, beaming.

"So, yes, Candace, will you be able to assist Mr. Cothburne and his family?" Jennifer asked, turning her attention back to Candace.

Candace swallowed, quickly stealing a glance in Allyson's direction. *She better not move.* "Sure I can." Candace stepped aside, extending her arm. "Please, come in, have a seat."

By the time Candace finished touring the family and successfully ushered them out of her office, it was just after four. She jerked again, staring at an empty receptionist's desk.

"Where is she?"

Danielle frowned. "She clocked out already. She said she wasn't feeling well."

"Of-fuckin'-course," Candace said to herself, turning back into her office and shutting the door. *Sneaky little bitch.* She grabbed her cell phone. *Chris hasn't texted me back all day. What's up with that?*

Candace was fuming on her way home from work. She felt cheated and angry and disappointed that she didn't get to talk to Allyson. She checked her phone again for a message from Chris before she pulled off. After not seeing one from him, she decided to send another.

Call me

She tossed the phone in the passenger seat and went back to her frustration. *And how dare Jennifer just pull that shit on me like that? She's a slick bitch, too. Slick one and slick two. I bet they asses are in cahoots. Yeah, it's real convenient to have Jennifer just show up with a family out of the clear blue like that. She ain't have to run to Abington. I know Allyson had something to do with my computer getting hacked into now. She's working with that bitch.*

Candace damn near screamed, getting out of her car. She checked her phone again for a return message from Chris, and not finding one, she tossed the phone into her Dior bag. Candace slammed her apartment door and headed over to her kitchen to pour herself a drink, rediscovering the mess left over from breakfast.

"Dammit!" she shouted. "And where the fuck is Chris?"

CHAPTER 23

*C*andace didn't sleep well that night. She tossed and turned, tucking and untucking her comforter between her legs. Her phone remained silent until her morning alarm. She reached for it on her nightstand.

What's up? Call me. She texted Chris before brushing her teeth.

When Candace arrived at work, Danielle was already at her desk.

"Where the hell is she?" Candace asked, glaring over her shades toward Allyson's empty desk.

"She called out sick," Danielle replied, slightly frowning.

"This is some bullshit." Candace huffed slamming her office door. *It's fuckin' Friday and this bitch calls out. Denise will be here on Monday and I don't have shit to say for myself. Fuck!*

Candace picked up her phone. This time she pressed the buttons to dial Chris. His voicemail picked up. Candace clenched her teeth, and struggled not to launch the phone clear across the room. Instead, she took a deep breath and texted her sister.

Sis Im goin thru it. hit me up

Thirteen seconds later, Candace's phone chimed.

At work. Sup?

Stressin work & personal. Call me when u can

K

Candace tossed her phone onto the file cabinet across from her desk and stood up stretching. She took a deep breath raising her arms over her head. She took long slow deep breaths, trying to calm herself. *What the fuck am I going to do?*

Chrissy came to mind and Candace dialed her extension quickly.

"Hey, girl," Candace began.

"Well, hello, darling," Chrissy replied. Candace could tell she was smiling from the rise in her voice.

"You busy?"

"Swamped."

"Oh," Candace responded, slightly disappointed. "I needed somebody to talk to."

"Aw, darling. Now, you've always got me to chat with. But we're goin' have to reserve our chatting for lunchtime 'cause I got boat loads to finish before then. Can it wait and we can take a long lunch?"

"Yeah, that sounds good," Candace replied, rubbing her stomach, which had suddenly started to growl. She realized she hadn't eaten all morning. *Damn, how I forget to eat?*

Candace had plenty of paperwork to focus on until lunch. She pressed her attention to the refunds that needed to be applied and the collection letters that needed to be sent. Before long, Candace looked up and Chrissy was standing in her doorway.

"Ready, darling?"

"Born ready. I'm starving," Candace said, standing. She grabbed her pocketbook from behind her door and followed Chrissy out into the lobby.

"How 'bout we try that deli around the corner; they make great sandwiches. What are you in the mood for?"

Candace shrugged. "I don't even know. But I know I need to eat. Let's just go. I'll figure it out."

Candace strolled alongside Chrissy out the building and to her car. They climbed inside and Chrissy drove to the deli. After parking, Candace stepped out of the pearl Prius, searching her pocketbook.

"Whatcha lookin' for, darling?" Chrissy asked, noticing Candace's frantic search.

"I think I left my damn phone in the office."

"It'll be there when you get back."

Candace huffed. "I guess."

The pair headed into the crowded deli. Chrissy ordered a chicken parmesan sub, and Candace got the grilled salmon salad. She was full and satisfied heading back to the building even though she didn't feel any better about her current situation.

As soon as Candace entered the Business Office, she could hear her cell phone ringing.

"It's been ringing off the hook," Danielle said to Candace as she walked in.

Candace grabbed her phone off the file cabinet. She had eight missed calls and her voicemail icon was lit. Before she could close her door for some privacy, the small device rang again. She answered.

"Ca' I speak to Candace?"

"Who is this?"

"Dis Shif, ma, Chris cousin."

"Yeah," she replied curiously.

"Chris got booked, ma. He fucked up, ma, and he need ya help."

"What?" Candace's heart jumped; a mix between shock, anger and fear.

"He told me to call you, shawty, ya mean? Like you was goin' have some bread or something."

Candace was not sure how to respond. She barely knew Shif, they'd met briefly at the bar, and now he was calling her for help to get his cousin, her young lover, out of jail.

What the fuck? Jail? Oh… un uh. Candace shook her head; she was reeling from the words she'd just heard. *Jail? Money? Didn't this kid know any better? Where was his Get Caught Stash?* She'd been down this road before, but Prince had always been prepared. He taught her how to hide money for rainy days and he always put away a few dollars in case he needed bail.

"Candy Reign, come here!" Candace recalled Prince's voice booming from the end of the long hall in their two-bedroom apartment in Empirian Luxury Towers, a set of ritzy high-rise buildings at the end of Lincoln Drive.

She swayed into the room with a one-year-old Emmanuel on her hip just in time to see Prince jump down off the bed. He extended his arms for his son. Emmanuel leaned forward to his father with a smile.

"Stand on the bed," Prince instructed.

Candace obeyed, kicking off her slippers and stepping up onto the mattress. Slightly bouncing, she asked, "Now what?"

"Try to reach to that piece of drop ceiling."

Candace stretched her arms. Her fingertips graced the panel, but she could not fully reach to push it open.

"Damn, get down." Prince huffed. "I thought ya tall ass woulda been able to reach that."

Emmanuel, again, changed hands and Prince climbed onto the mattress. He popped open the panel and pulled out a black leather satchel.

"What's that?" Candace asked.

"My Gettum Stash."

"Ya what?"

"In case something happen to me in these streets, Candy. I need to know you can get to this and get to me quick."

"*Something like what?*" Candace's lips twisted.

"*What? Something like whatever, girl. Is you crazy? Shit happens every day and I'm not the dumb nigga to say shit don't happen to me. I am the prepared nigga for when shit go down, I'm covered. Feel me?*"

Candace nodded.

"*Now come on, help me find some place to put this that you can get to.*" *Prince laughed*, "*I'll save that stash spot in the ceiling for the change I don't want you to be able to get your little shopping hands on.*"

"*Shut up,*" *she said, laughing and swatting his strong shoulder.*

It wasn't long before Candace was pulling up the board in the back of her closet to get to that leather satchel. Shortly after Emmanuel's second birthday, Brother rang her phone eleven times in the middle of the night. Twenty minutes later, he was pounding on the door. His shirt ripped, his eyes bulged wider than his shoulders and his gun hung in clear view on his hip. He didn't say much. Candace handed him the money, all of it. It was $8,500 when she counted. Prince always added to the bag, never subtracted. Candace thought, he must know he's going to jail for some big shit. *The judge posted bail, it would cost $15,000 to release Prince. He was home the next day.*

Candace released a low mumbling tone, but her thoughts were interrupted by the persistent voice in the receiver.

"Hello! We trying to make this shit happen. I need like 5K, ma," the voice on the other end barked.

She shook for a moment, a quake of infamous familiarity shifted through her. "I gotta call you back."

"Aight, shawty. But I need to know something asap!"

Candace had not held a hustler close to her since Prince, and she'd forgotten about this part of the deal. At least her son's father had his own dollars put away. To get Chris out, she'd have to dip into her personal funds; her bill-paying, gas-buying, grocery-shopping money—not something she was eager to do. This time it was her hard-earned money on the line. She dialed Marci.

"Mars, that's my cushion," she frantically explained to her sister. "My money would be fucked for a minute. Manny's not even here and I know Prince ain't throwin' me no bones. He called the other day. I know he heard Chris here."

"Wow!"

"Wow what? What I'mma do?"

"You are really thinking about doing this shit? *Wow!*"

"What do you mean?"

"This young bul got you wide open. Face it, kid, you in love."

"Who me? Not I." Candace hung up the phone. She grabbed her jacket and headed out the door. She had to get to the bank before it closed; her fingers redialed Shif's number on the way.

"Where you want me to meet you?"

As she drove, Candace could not deny that Chris's presence commanded her heart and there was no way she could leave him stranded. She was more than feeling him. She loved every inter-action they had and she couldn't deny how he made her feel. Now he needed her. Her doubts rang silent, second-guessing questions drowned out by the thudding of her yearning heart. Foot heavy to the pedal, Candace could only think of Chris's eyes, gazing deep into her hers, the way they made her heart skip a beat. The vibration of her pulsating heart caused ripples in her body, rushing down to her vagina and making her panties wet.

By the time Candace reached Delaware Avenue, she was almost certain of the fact that she was in love with Chris, a feeling she hadn't anticipated. That had to be the only cause for actions her logic couldn't justify. What else could be behind why she'd just drained $2,000 out of her checking and $1,340 from her savings?

She'd just gotten paid and wasn't expecting, another paycheck for two weeks. *I can pay my bills and manage until Chris gets back home to tighten up my cushion.*

A black sedan pulled up beside Candace at the designated meeting spot. The tall slim cousin she'd met at the club leaked out of the car. He climbed into the passenger side of Candace's Accord.

"What's the deal, ma?"

"I got a little more than three." She handed him the envelope full of hundreds.

"Good money, good money. I got the end covered. You good, ma. Ya boy should be out by morning. We tryna to get to 'em 'fore they drop dat detainer on 'em. Ya' mean?"

Candace nodded. "What happened?"

"Aw, man. This nigga got caught up in some dumb shit wit' some old niggas and they trying get 'em on a gun charge. He ran from the cops and shit, smacked his car all up. This nigga wildin'. But we gotta get 'em home. Ya' mean?"

"Where is he? You going there now?"

"CFCF. Nah, my peoples goin'. I ain't fuckin' wit' no jails."

"Can I go?'

Shif hesitated. "Nah, you 'on't need to be in dat. Just chill, ma. You did ya part. Sit tight, let me handle my end and wait for ya boy to come home."

Shif stepped out the car quickly. Candace watched the dark sedan disappear.

Candace wanted to be with them when they brought Chris home because she knew she wasn't going to visit him in jail. If she didn't go see her son's father, there was no way in hell she was going to visit Chris, no matter how good the sex.

He'd better come home soon, she thought, maneuvering the winding roads home.

Candace did not sleep well that night. Dark dreams of pressing walls and silken figures grabbing for her through the shadows disrupted her rest. Her sheets were moist and tangled. There was an absence, a deprivation of his voice and seductive tongue. Chris's comings had become as close to predictable as she needed and were desperately desired. Tonight there was no man coming through her door with large hands to touch her and wide shoulders to touch back. There was never more of a need for his presence than when she knew it could not be obtained.

Candace settled at the foot of her bed early Saturday morning. She called Shif, no answer. She figured he was still sleeping. She'd try again later.

The afternoon came and Candace switched off the TV, before flinging the remote across her bed. She pulled the sheets back over her head and closed her eyes, hoping for something even though she wasn't quite sure what. She sighed and turned, flipping the sheets around, then tucking them in between her legs.

"This is crazy," she hummed to herself. "I've called Shif like four times. Why is he not returning my fuckin' calls?"

As if responding to her thoughts, her phone rang—Candace sprang up like a dog in heat, lunging for the device on her night-stand. She didn't even bother to check the ID before she anxiously answered.

"Hello? Hello?" she panted.

"Hey, pretty lady."

Shoulders slumped. "Hey, Bam."

"Awww. You don't sound too happy to hear from Big Daddy. What's the matta, baby? You can tell me."

Candace sucked her teeth before she jumped in. "Work is stressing me out and I'm just so tired. Money is funny. It's a lot right now, Bam, and it's not your problem. I'll be fine. How you?"

"Now, cut that out. You don't sound fine. Why don't you let me take you out; I can relieve some of that stress," Bam said charmingly.

I guess I could use the spoiling and Bam is good for making a girl smile. Ummm, I don't know.

"I don't think I would be good company, Bam," she replied.

"Why you say that? Don't you always have a good time with Big Daddy? Don't I always treat you right?"

Candace had to smile. "Yeah, you do. But when my money ain't right, I get a little agitated and I don't want to take that out on you." *Plus, I'm not in the mood for your pissin' right now, anyway.* "You don't deserve it. I know you like when I'm happy."

"I do. But I also know how to make you happy."

Candace heard Bam smacking on his tongue, a sound he made when he was about to light a cigar.

"How 'bout this," he started. "My trip to Vegas is next weekend. You should come along. I'll make sure you have a good time. Shop a little, drink a little, gamble a lot. Who knows, you could hit big."

"I don't know, Bam," Candace said, sighing. "I'm not up to traveling, right now."

"Okay, baby, whatever you say. Just think about it and when you ready for a ride, give me a call," Bam said nonchalantly.

"Okay." She hung up, still clutching the phone in her hand. She dialed Shif's number. It rang several times before the voicemail picked up.

"The mailbox you are trying to reach is full."

"Goddammit!!" She threw the phone onto the bed.

Candace forced herself to sleep, tossing, turning and keeping her phone within arms' reach. Finally, Sunday afternoon, she sat up in her bed feeling restless and agitated.

"I need to see my son," she said, standing.

Candace called Brother once she got in her car. Manny was outside as expected and Candace drove over to Cheltenham with a thousand things on her mind. She hoped seeing Emmanuel would ease some of her pains.

Emmanuel rushed over to meet her as Candace parked. "Hey, Mom," he said excitedly, opening her car door.

She was right. There was something in his big dark eyes and enormous grin that soothed her soul. *He's probably doing better over here than he would if he was home with me,* she thought, walking beside her son across the grass.

He plopped down on the steps in front of his uncle's apartment. Candace spotted BJ and PJ and the gaggle of girls across the lawn. *That little busty girl over there?* Candace squinted. *Yeah, there she go. Waving. She waving to me?* Candace peered harder at the little brown-skinned girl who appeared to be signaling salutations. Candace rolled her eyes. The girl's arm fell. Candace looked down at Emmanuel who hadn't seemed to notice a thing.

"Man, that girl like you?"

"Mommmmmm," Emmanuel whined.

"What? I can ask."

"You asked already."

"So," Candace snapped, her neck rolling. "I'm your mother. I can ask again and again and again and you betta answer me every time."

"Mommmmmm."

"What?"

Emmanuel shook his head. "Nothin'. I ain't sayin' nothin'."

"You ain't sayin' nothin'? What's that supposed to mean?"

Emmanuel shrugged. "I don't know. Uncle B say it all the time."

Candace shook her head.

"How's work?" Emmanuel asked suddenly.

A knot formed in Candace's stomach. "It's okay."

"You still gettin' that promotion, right?"

Candace cringed. "Of course, baby. I got this thing in the bag."

"Cool. Oh, yeah. I talked to my dad."

Candace dropped her head. *Oh God.* "Yeah? What's up with him?"

"I don't know. He said he had a lot going on and he missed us a lot…oh, and he kept tellin' me to keep an eye on you."

"On me?"

"Yeah, you, Mom," Emmanuel replied, looking her squarely in the face. "What are you up to?"

"Me?" Candace gasped, grabbing her chest.

"Yeah, you, Mom," Emmanuel repeated.

"I ain't up to nothin'," she hissed. "And I'm grown so if I was up to something it would be my business, anyway."

Emmanuel laughed his father's laugh and threw his hands up in surrender. "Mom, I don't want no trouble. I'm just askin' 'cause my dad told me to."

"Yea, well you and your dad need to mind y'all business," she said sharply.

Emmanuel looked up, eyes wide and apparently a little hurt.

Shit, she thought. *I'm snapping on my son for no reason. Calm down, Candace.*

"Sorry, Man," she cooed, patting his head. "It's not you. It's just your nosey daddy."

Emmanuel shrugged. "Whateva. I'm 'bout to go finish playin'." He jumped up. "You staying for a while? Aunt Charlie made hot dogs and baked beans."

"That ain't your damn aunt, and no. I got some things I need to do; plus I gotta go to work in the morning."

"Okay, Mom." Emmanuel leaned over her and kissed Candace on the top of her forehead.

Candace laughed. "Okay, Son." And Emmanuel took off, running through the trimmed grass toward his cousins and the girls.

Candace hit Brother up for a fat dime bag before she hopped in her car and headed home. The weed helped lull her to sleep, but her dark dreams were interrupted in the middle of the night by the steady ringing of her phone.

Candace turned over and groggily answered the blocked ID call. "Yes."

"Who the fuck is this?"

"Hello," Candace stammered, sitting up in her bed.

"Who the fuck is this?" the female voice persisted.

"Bitch, you called me."

"You keep callin' my man."

"Who is your man?"

"Oh, now you dumb, bitch? You know who my fuckin' man is and he don't wanna talk to you, so get off his dick."

"I don't even know who you talkin' about."

"Damn, you fuckin' that many niggas, you can't keep track?"

"Fuck you, bitch," Candace barked. "I don't know who ya man is, but it ain't my fault you can't keep him on a leash."

"You on his top, you trashy bitch."

"Well, he must like how something over here smell, if you up calling me in the middle of the night."

"Fuck you, bitch. Get off my man dick."

The phone clicked, then dead silence. Half groggy and delusional, Candace stared at the device in her hand. She dropped the phone onto her soft sheets as tears fell from her eyes. *This cannot be happening.*

Monday morning Candace had more than butterflies in her stomach as she dressed from work. *Simple bitches calling my phone. Chris's phone is off. So, Shif hoe's calling my phone now. What the fuck?* Candace scratched her head and clutched her stomach. She was nauseous and found herself rushing for the bathroom every time she thought of her pending meeting with Denise.

What the fuck is about to go down? What if this bitch fire me? She started her car. *It's cool. It's cool. We goin' get to the bottom of this, right? At least I can finally see this infamous email. And I'm just goin' tell her it wasn't me. Denise, I ain't send that shit.* Candace pulled into the parking lot. *I'm just goin' to plead my case. How bad could this really be, right? I know I didn't send it and that's all I need to say. It wasn't me.* Candace stepped into the business office. Both Allyson and Danielle were at their desk.

"Good morning," Danielle began.

"Candace, Denise wants to see you in her office," Allyson's tiny voice chirped from her right. Candace felt the temperature of her blood rise.

"Feeling better today, are we?" she asked Allyson.

Allyson nodded weakly.

Candace exhaled. She unlocked her office, set her things inside, then shut the door behind her before heading down the hall to see Denise.

Candace swallowed hard before tapping on her boss's door.

"Come in."

Candace opened the door slowly. "Hey, Denise," she said, stepping inside the large room.

"Candace." Denise stood up. "Good morning."

Candace forced a grin. She could sense the chill in the salutation. "Good morning," she replied.

Denise moved from behind her desk, passed Candace and locked her door. She then quietly moved to the edge of her desk in front of where Candace had taken a seat.

"You know why I wanted to see you this morning, correct?"

Candace nodded.

"Quite frankly, Candace, I am appalled. I honestly cannot believe that something like this would come from you."

"Good," Candace said, slapping her hands on her thighs. "Because I didn't send it."

Denise winced. "What do you mean, you didn't send it?"

"I mean, I didn't send whatever email you got, Denise," Candace said, trying to stress sincerity in her voice.

Denise reached behind her pulling a single sheet of paper from her desk. She handed it to Candace. "You didn't send this to me?"

Candace accepted the paper. She began from the very top and slowly read each word. *What the fuck? Oh, hell no.* Candace's stomach knotted. She wanted to vomit.

"No! No fu…friggin' way did I send this, Denise. Come on!"

"Watch your tone, Candace. See, it's that…" Denise waved her finger in Candace's face. "It's that angry feistiness that makes me think you may be capable of something like this."

"WHAT!?!" Candace jumped to her feet. "No way! No, fuckin' way, Denise."

"See. See what I mean, Candace. Your mouth!" Denise snapped, her eyes large and lit. "Watch your mouth. You've been warned before and I just don't think you get it."

Candace looked back down at the paper in her trembling hand. "But, Denise, I didn't send this. I swear and I'm sorry for cursing now. But, I would never."

"I don't know that, Candace. I believe if pushed, if mad enough, you could say just about anything."

Candace clenched her jaws so tight, her teeth grinded. She searched

Denise's face for some sign of trust, some glimmer of hope that Denise believed her, but there was none.

"And it came from your computer, Candace," Denise continued. "How do you dispute that?"

"I think someone hacked into my computer," Candace stated, struggling to remain calm. *God, that sounds weak.*

Denise cocked her head to one side poking out her lips. "Are you kidding me?"

Candace shook her head. *Shit.*

"So, you're trying to tell me that you think someone broke into your office, hacked into your computer and sent me this email so I would think it came from you?"

"Yes. That's exactly what I'm saying, Denise!"

"That sounds a little far-fetched, don't you think?" Denise eyed Candace up and down, slowly shaking her head. "Candace, I don't know what's harder to believe, the fact that you are capable of sending me an email like this or that someone from my building hacked into your computer and maliciously sent this to me. I mean, really, Candace. What do you expect me to believe?"

"The truth," Candace snapped back.

"I can only believe what can be proven, Candace. And right now, I have proof that an extremely inappropriate and vulgar email was sent from you to me. Like we are girlfriends or something. Candace, I'm not your girlfriend. I'm your boss and you will respect me!"

Candace swallowed and nodded. "Denise, I…"

Denise threw her hand in the air. "Candace, please. As of this moment, you are suspended without pay, pending investigation."

"Suspended?" Candace yelled.

"Yes, Candace. You need to go back home until this thing gets sorted out. You say it wasn't you, fine. Let me find that out for sure. But until then, you cannot be in my building."

Are you fuckin' kidding me? Suspended? No pay? I just gave this boy all my fuckin' money!! WHAT?!?!

Candace was motionless, standing stone still in the middle of Denise's office.

"Candace, did you hear me?" Denise asked.

Candace shook herself back to life. "I…I think so. I'm suspended. I…I can't believe this shi…yeah, I heard you."

Denise stood and walked over to her office door. She unlocked and opened it as Candace turned slowly.

"Candace, I really hope for your sake, that you're telling the truth. But until that is proven, please take your personal effects and go home."

Candace could barely breathe, walking back to her office. She couldn't tell if she was putting one foot in front of the other, but she felt like she was floating along or somehow moving on a conveyor belt like she was in a Spike Lee movie.

She grabbed her pocketbook from behind her door. *This is not happening.* She held back the tears, avoiding the strange stares from Allyson and Danielle.

"Candace, is everything okay?" Danielle asked in a whimper as Candace sulked past her desk.

Candace shook her head, one foot out the door. "No. Everything is fucked."

"Mom," Candace cried into the phone, struggling hard to control the steering wheel. "I just got suspended from work!"

"Ohmigod, baby. Why? What's goin' on? Where are you?"

"Driving to your house. I just left my job." Candace paused choking on her sobs. "And I don't know if I'm ever going back!"

The tears fell in heavy streams, but Candace didn't bother to wipe them away.

"What? Come on here, child," her mother insisted. "Get off the phone driving and get here to your mother. I'm waiting."

Candace could barely see through the puddles in her eyes as she parked on her mother's block. She rushed toward the porch as Karla opened the front door.

"Mom," she cried into her mother's open embrace.

Karla wrapped her arms around Candace and squeezed tightly while leading her inside. She helped Candace down onto the couch, slid a box of tissues in front of her and let her cry. And Candace cried. She balled her eyes out for over an hour, telling her mother all about Jennifer and the malicious email, her sneaky receptionist, Allyson; and Denise sending her home without pay. She left out Chris. *Momma don't need to know everything*, she thought.

"Mommy,…I…I just can't believe all this," she stuttered through choked breaths. "I don't know what to do."

"Well, first things first," Karla began, patting Candace's knee. "You got to calm down and get your head together."

Candace sniffled.

"You can't let folk get the best of you like this. I've never seen you so upset."

"Mom, this is my job we're talking about."

"I understand, baby. But, what don't come out in the wash, surely comes out in the rinse. You say you didn't send it then, that's it! Let your boss do her investigation. You got to believe that the truth is going to come out."

Candace sighed and sprawled out across the couch.

Karla stood up and patted her on the head. "I'm goin' make you something to eat, okay. You need something on your stomach."

Candace nodded and turned her head into the couch pillow. She heard Karla leave the room and before long, she could hear her mother moving pots around in the kitchen.

Maybe she's right. Maybe I shouldn't stress so much. The truth has to come out, right? But...but what do I do until then? I got no fuckin' money. I can't even hit her up without telling her about my dumb ass putting money up for some nigga bail. My mom would flip. Oh, God...fuck my life.

The tears fell again, thinking of her empty bed and empty bank account. At least most her bills were paid, but that left her with no spending money. She'd have to budget every dollar; no manicures, no shopping. She'd given all she had to get Chris out of jail. Candace whimpered.

She cried because it was possible she'd been deceived—that she had let him get too close and he'd stepped off with her heart and her money. She hated to admit that part of her believed he was still locked up, but most of her was unsure and she cried because she was lonely without him. Her whimpers wavered in the air as she clutched the couch pillow.

Candace jumped up suddenly, not having realized she'd fallen asleep. She glanced over at her mother lightly snoring in the chair beside her, then her eyes traveled up to the huge wall clock over her mother's elaborately decorated mantel. *Just enough time to make it to class.* Candace kissed Karla on the forehead before scurrying out the door. She rushed to class, but she could barely concentrate on a word her professor was saying once she arrived.

Her head danced with digits, while the old man spoke—car note, car insurance, rent, cell phone, gas, electric. *If I pay everything that's due, I'm goin' have less than $200 left. Shit. I need groceries and gas. No paycheck coming in to replenish my bank account and no sign of Chris. This is just fuckin' great.*

Candace pulled out her cell phone once she got in her car and dialed Brother. *Maybe he could throw a few dollars my way.*

"Yo, times is hard, C. And, I'm taking care of Man and my own seeds. I can't spare no bread right now."

"What about the money from Prince?" Candace whined into the phone. "I'm in a tight spot, right now, B."

"I feel you 'n all 'dat, C. But, Prince fucked up right now, too. That nigga in solitary confinement..."

"Solitary confinement? For what?"

"I don't even know all that, but I do know I gotta do what I gotta do to hold down his and my own. Feel me?"

"Yeah." Candace sulked.

"I'll toss you what I can when I can, but I'm paying my girl's bills and shit and you know I got five kids."

Candace shook her head, hanging up the phone. *Solitary confinement? What the hell?* She thought of Prince's big ass beating on the other inmates behind bars. She pictured something like the Incredible Hulk slamming people around and pounding on his chest. She felt guilty. Maybe her last conversation with Prince and his hearing Chris in her apartment drove him into wild hysteria. Maybe he was so angry with her he lashed out at the nearest person to him. *Poor prisoners*, Candace thought, driving home. She wanted to cry, but her eyes were too sore for tears.

She decided to try Shif one more time.

"Yo, what the fuck!" she screamed into Shif's answering machine. "Like, you could at least call me and tell me what the fuck is going on. You just took my money and rolled. Is this nigga really even behind bars? I mean what the fuck? You need to call me back and let me know something. It's really not even about the money. I just need to know what's going on with Chris. Is he cool? Yo, what the fuck? I feel like ya'll bullshittin' me! Call me back!"

She dialed her sister next.

"I'm not getting an answer from Shif. Chris phone go right to voicemail. I feel real stupid," Candace stated after Marci picked up.

"You think he got you?"

"I don't even fuckin' know, Marci. Just the thought makes me sick to my stomach."

"That'd be so fuckin' crazy if he not even really locked up."

"Crazy? That ain't even it," Candace snarled, attempting to shake loose the thoughts in her head. What if Chris did burn her for her money and was laid up somewhere with some chick?

"That's some slimy shit. I mean, dude knew you was making money with ya' job and shit, right. You told him you was livin' aright," Marci continued.

"He wouldn't gag me," Candace said, struggling to convince herself and rocking her body slowly from side to side.

"You betta call and find out. What prison you say he at?"

Candace's eyes lifted. "CFCF."

"You know his whole name?"

"Yeah, I know his whole name." Candace sucked her teeth. "What kind of question is that?"

"I 'on't know," Marci said, smacking her gums. "Young bul gotchu all dick dumb, I had to ask."

"Bitch! I know you ain't talkin'. As stuck on stupid as your dumb ass is over married-ass Tommy."

"Whateva. That's my man. Is Chris your man?"

"Fuck no!"

"Whateva, bitch. That's your man. You in love and you ridin'. Now, what's that nigga full name?"

The next day there was no return call from Shif and no sleep. Candace poured herself a glass of vodka and orange juice for breakfast Wednesday morning. Another for lunch.

"Okay, Candace," she coached herself, sitting down on her couch. "You can't just sit here and do nothing." She looked around the empty living room. "Clean up maybe?" But her apartment was immaculate. "I could go get my hair done…fuck, no I can't. No money. Maybe…" Candace sighed. "I can't do shit. But sit here and wait." She stood up. More vodka and orange juice was in order.

Candace dragged her body into her bedroom and collapsed on the bed, wondering why she felt so weary—she hadn't done much in the past three days. *Maybe it's the vodka.*

The phone alarm startled her, causing her to raise her head quickly from the mattress. Candace grabbed the blaring device. *Fuck. I'm late for school.* She tossed on her clothes, still slightly tipsy from her drinking, and scrambled out the door. Rushing, she missed her footing and almost stumbled down her front stairs. Her ankle throbbed as she limped to her car. When she reached the curb, Candace felt her pants pocket for her keys.

"No. No." Her heart pounded. She frantically tapped her pockets again, front, back, then her breast. She ripped open her pocket-book, hurriedly surveying its contents. *Nope, not there.*

"Aww! Come on!" Candace shouted. "You gotta be kiddin' me. My keys?"

Candace's heart sank as she lowered her head, realizing she'd locked her keys in her apartment. Sweat from the gleaming summer sun beat down her face and back. She struggled to hold herself together, dialing her landlord. She knew the management company charged $50 for a let-in. She made the check out to the old Israeli man who showed up twenty minutes later.

"Ohmigod!" Candace fumed as she barreled toward Temple University. She was making good time, catching most of the lights. She jumped onto Broad Street off Allegheny Avenue, ahead of on-coming traffic just as her light turned red. Instantly, lights flashed, and a siren roared behind her.

"No way, no way!" she cried. *Is he really pulling me over?* Candace hesitated and drove another block ahead, inching nearer to her destination. The cop car made a loud walloping sound as it proceeded behind Candace. She slowed, easing over to the side of the road.

"This is fuckin' unbelievable," Candace hollered, slamming her closed fists on the steering wheel. "This cannot be happening to me right now!"

"License and registration."

Candace provided the required documents.

"Ma'am, do you know why I pulled you over?"

"No."

"You turned on red. The sign clearly says 'No turn on red.' You in a rush?"

"Yes, Officer. I'm late for class," Candace spoke calmly, hoping he would change his mind and let her go. "Officer, I really do apologize. I didn't even realize the light was red."

"You wouldn't have at the rate you were going." The officer turned with Candace's information in hand and walked back to his cruiser.

Candace leaned her head back against the seat and pinched her eyes tight, sealing the tears in. *Why? Why me? Why right now? This is un-fuckin'-believable.* The officer returned a few moments later and handed Candace a ticket.

"Slow down, Ma'am, and have a nice day."

"Yeah, right," Candace growled, snatching the ticket from him. She skimmed the text carefully. "Three hundred eighty one-fuckin'-dollars! What!?! For running a red light! Are you fuckin' kiddin' me! What else could go wrong?"

She checked the clock on her dashboard. *Already an hour late for class.* "What the fuck's the point," she grumbled.

Candace shoved the $381 ticket in her visor and took deep steady breaths as she sat motionless on the side of Broad Street. She swallowed hard, reluctant to give back into the tears. She wanted to wail and scream, but she didn't have the strength.

All of a sudden, Candace heard her phone ring. She slowly pulled it out of her bag to check the ID. It was Marci.

"Sis, what's up?" Marci asked.

"Please, you tell me. Did you call? Did you find out if he was locked up?"

"Christopher Foster, right?"

"Yeah."

"You said he was up CFCF, right?"

"Yeah. That's what his cousin Shif told me."

"Um, well, they ain't have a Christopher Foster in their system and no record of one coming in."

"WHAT!?!?!" Candace screeched, feeling a heavy thud in her gut. Suddenly, she heard a slight beep in her ear and quickly pulled the phone back to check the incoming call. It was Shif.

"Marci, this that nigga right now. I'mma call you back," Candace rattled into the phone to her sister before clicking over. She didn't hear Marci's reply. "Yo," she snapped at Shif.

"Yo, Ma. Chill the fuck out blowin' my phone up," Shif snapped back.

"What?!?"

"Yo, you heard me. You doin' too much right now. Fall back."

"What the fuck! I keep callin' you 'cause you're not callin' me back, not saying nothin'. I called up CFCF and they said he wasn't up there. What the fuck is going on with Chris and my fuckin' money!" she screamed.

"Yo, ma. What the fuck are you talkin' 'bout?"

"I'm talkin' about you fuckin' lyin' to me!"

"Yo, I don't know who the fuck you talked to, but that's where the fuck he is. Ain't nobody gotta lie to you about shit, shawty. Ya boy good. They still holding 'em. But we workin' on it. I'll call you when it's something for you to know. But, you got my baby mom trippin'. Stay the fuck off my phone all hype. Aight."

Candace didn't get a word in before she heard the click of an ended call. All of her nerves cringed, throwing the phone down into the empty seat beside her.

"Mothafucka!! How the fuck?!?" Candace punched the steering wheel. "This mothafucka lied to me!"

Unexpectedly, her phone rang again in the seat beside her. She jumped trying to reach for it. This time it was Bam.

"How's it going, pretty lady?"

"When did you say you were going to Vegas?"

CHAPTER 24

andace arrived at the airport tugging her Betsy Johnson printed weekend bag along the ground behind her. Clutching the extended long pink handle, she sashayed her way through the terminal in red strappy stilettos and a white blouse, boasting plenty of cleavage. Her hair was pulled back hair into a loose bun and MAC *Red She Said* donned her full lips.

I can't believe this man wanted me to change my clothes. Candace thought of the comfy baby-tee and flip-flops she'd stripped out of at Bam's request.

"Baby, make sure you wear something sexy for Big Daddy," he'd said when he called, catching her one foot out the door. She kept on her favorite skinny blue jeans and switched out the tee for the blouse and flip-flops for stilettos.

Candace rounded the bend, swaying toward the gate. Bam stood from his seat as she approached.

"My, my, my...girl, you look gooder than lemonade at a picnic."

Candace pushed her glasses back on her head and smiled. "Hi, Bam." She gave him a quick hug and kiss on the cheek.

"Come on, pretty lady. That the only kinda kiss you goin' give Big Daddy?" Bam wrapped his arms around her waist, pulling her in tight and puckering his lips.

Candace winced, quickly leaning in and pecking Bam on the lips. She shook her head at Bam's hard wide smile and she looked him up and down in his coffee-colored linen suit. *Big man can dress.*

She glanced at the shiny bezels on his wristwatch and the huge diamond stud in his ear.

Sad shame he has to pay to keep a bad chick by his side, but his ass goin' pay this weekend. I need to come home with some change and I'm goin' make sure of that, Big Daddy.

Bam grabbed a handful of Candace's behind, boarding the plane.

"You goin' have a good time this weekend, kid. I promise you that," Bam said after they'd snuggled into their first-class seats.

Kid? What the fuck is that? Candace resented the word but opted to let it slide for fear of getting her weekend off to a bad start. *Okay, Bam. I gotchu. I forgot how Big Daddy likes to play this game.*

Candace cleared her throat, batted her eyes and softly asked, "You have plans for us when we get there?"

"Plenty, baby, plenty. We goin' be real busy." Bam patted her thigh, then gave it a firm squeeze. "My frat brother from down Texas owns a chain of barber shops and wanted to have a lil' get-together. Couple of my boys finna meet us there. Play some poker; we gotta couple live bets going on. Some dinners, a show or two, lots of hotel time. And I'm goin' have plenty of time to spend with you, pretty lady. Don't you worry; I'm goin' keep you real close."

Candace smiled sweetly, crossing her legs and patting his hand on her lap.

This is going to be a good trip, Candace. You need this. Fuck Chris. Wherever his ass is at? Figure that shit out when you get back. Maybe Marci made a mistake. I don't know. I don't care. Fuck it. I'm going to Vegas. I'm going to have a good time. I'mma get this fat nigga for some money. She took a deep breath. *It's going to be okay.*

Candace stared out the window during takeoff. *Here we go,* she thought, holding tight to her seat arm. She felt a dip in her stomach as the plane ascended gracefully into the sky. Candace was admiring the fullness of the clouds when she felt Bam cover her with a blanket. She looked over to her right and realized a plush blue blanket was over them both.

Candace felt Bam's hand creeping beneath the covering. He worked his way to her breasts and began massaging them. She took a deep breath. *He starting already.*

Bam loosened her blouse and rolled her nipple between his thumb and pointer finger. Candace winced at Bam's plucking and stroking. He continued until her nipple became as erect as him and pulled Candace's hand onto his lap.

Oh, God. Candace grimaced, gracing the chubby bulge beneath his pressed linen and reluctantly rubbing against it. Bam squirmed in his seat.

"Pull that thang out and put ya hands on it, baby?"

Ohmigod. Nasty ass. Candace exhaled before reaching to unbutton Bam's pants. His erect manhood emerged effortlessly from his boxer briefs and Candace grabbed hold.

Ol' chubby dick. Candace chuckled to herself squeezing him tight.

Bam moaned, letting his large head fall back against his seat. Candace squeezed tighter and began stroking him up and down. After a few moments of heavy breathing, Candace thought she heard a soft snore.

What the hell? She stopped stroking and looked up at Bam to see his eyes closed and his mouth hanging open. He was asleep. Candace sucked her teeth. "Old-ass man."

They landed in Vegas shortly after noon and Candace stood up quickly, eager to stretch her long legs off the plane. Bam grabbed her travel bag and Candace led the way toward the exit. She was only a few feet from the beaming brunette flight attendant at the door when she suddenly and instinctively started to squint. *Goddamn*. She pulled her black Ferragamo sunglasses down over her eyes before stepping off the plane and stopping to look around.

"It's bright and hot as shit out here," she said loudly to no one in particular.

She felt Bam's hands on her waist from behind. "It is the desert, baby girl. Come on." He patted her backside, nudging her forward.

Candace followed the crowd down the stairs and into the massive airport. As she exited the bustling building with Bam by her side, she noticed what seemed like a small fleet of limousines, idling behind the automatic doors. The blazing sunlight slapped Candace in the face as she struggled to see the names some of the drivers held up. Bam must have seen it first, as he quickly and gently tugged her right arm, leading her toward a small tan man with white hair holding a crooked sign that read "Ty Jefferies."

Candace chuckled to herself as the gentleman introduced himself as Mario and opened the door, then secured their luggage. *Damn, I almost forgot Bam had a real name.*

Bam slid into the cool seat beside her and the driver briskly whisked them away toward the MGM Grand in downtown Las Vegas.

Candace fought the urge to ogle out the window as they passed streams of lights and brilliant spectacle-style buildings. It was the brightest place she'd ever seen. The sun seemed to shine brighter here in this populated desert than any place Candace could imagine. It was almost too much sun and Candace kept her dark shades pulled down over her wandering eyes.

Limo service escorted them to the ritzy yet elegant MGM Grand on the Sunset Strip. Candace held her breath climbing out the sleek black car. *Goddamn, it's hot as fuck.*

She entered the spacious gold-trimmed lobby, relaxing her eyes in the less aggressive light. Candace spun around taking in the majesty of it all. *This place is fuckin' gorgeous.* She touched the scalloped gold light fixtures in the hall, stopping behind Bam at the door to their suite.

Bam entered first with Candace stepping into the Signature Suite behind him. The main door led them into the living room of the luxurious multiroom unit. The windows were sparkling clean and wide open, exposing the lines of the city and letting in streams of the glaring sun. Candace moved through the grand room, which to her seemed more like a penthouse apartment, fully equipped with a kitchen, bar and Jacuzzi. She made her way into the massive bedroom. There was an enormous, king-sized pillow-top mattress dressed in clean and perfectly even seven hundred-count linens. Candace bent and traced her fingers along the pillow casings. When she looked up, she noticed a small wooden table in the corner of the room holding a bottle of champagne in a platinum ice chest, a tray of fresh fruit and three elaborately decorated gift bags.

"What's this?" Candace moved toward the table. She tried to read the French label on the champagne bottle, then turned her attention to the bags.

"Just a lil' somethin'-somethin'," Bam replied, grinning and stepping into the room.

Candace began to open the bags slowly. Inside one was a white box. Candace slid the box open and removed a slinky, black Christian Dior dress. In another bag was a small box encasing diamond teardrop earrings. She found lingerie in the last package, two sexy nightgowns: one a white satin top with panties and garter to match and another baby-blue and blush-pink, one-piece lace nightie. *Wow, Big Daddy. We're off to a nice start.* She looked up at Bam and smiled.

"You like how Big Daddy take care of you?"

"Aww, Bam. I love everything." She stood and threw her arms

around his wide shoulders. Bam slid his heavy hands across her waist, pulling her in.

"Yeah?" Bam asked undoing on the buttons on her blouse. "Show Big Daddy how much you love how he take care of you."

Candace swallowed her pride, slipping down to her knees and unzipping Bam's pants.

After a quickie, a shower and a stiff drink, Candace stood on the elevator, adjusting her cleavage in her loose-fitting white top. She pulled down on her tiny pink mini and checked Bam out beside her. He looked clean in freshly creased cream-colored slacks over rust-brown Gucci sandals and a white-and-cream linen shirt with his jewelry shining. They headed down to the lobby to meet up with Bam's friends. At the base of the elaborate elevator, the floor opened up into the grand lobby. Candace moved alongside Bam through the crowded and busy corridor into the house casino. Bam navigated the casino floor in search of his comrades. Candace noticed Bam narrowing in on a small group of about five men standing over a tall table by the back bar. Candace grinned, surprised to see a table of obviously well-to-do brothers laughing and throwing back drinks. Bam grasped her waist, stopping at the edge of the table right in front of the group of men.

Two of the brothers at the table were tall, lean and brown and looked a little alike, though one looked more out of place and sterile than the other. *One of the tall skinny guys is kinda cute.* He was the first to speak.

"Look at this fat mothafucka, here," the cute lanky, brown-skinned brother with the big smile shouted, slapping Bam on the back.

"Roni!" Bam shouted, patting him back.

"Whatitdo, my man?" the other slim brown-skinned one asked, raising his glass and offering a half smile.

"Rich." Bam nodded his way before continuing his greetings across the table. Next to Rich was a short, light-skinned and skinny brother with a wide football-shaped head and to his left was a chubby guy, a little shorter than Bam but just as round.

"Wayne, my boy. I ain't seen you in a minute. Sup my nigga, Conrad," Bam said, smiling and dapping hands to both men.

Candace watched the hand slapping and roaring salutations, waiting for Bam to get to the tall, sexy, bald brother with the muscles and well-trimmed goatee to her far right.

"And, Tone, my man." Bam's voice boomed, reaching for the last of his friends.

Tone, um. Candace bit her lip. *Tone sexy as shit. Lil' salt and pepper on his face all clean, looking distinguished. I like that.*

"Goddamn." Roni, the tall attractive one with the big smile, big eyes, long arms and juicy lips giggled. "We ain't been off the plane ten minutes, this nigga gotta broad."

Bam tugged on Candace, pinching her behind. "Nah, nah, my brother, I brought this here delight with me."

"Say word?" the other tall brother asked.

"All these women round here, you bring one?" Roni teased.

"Hell yeah, he did," roared the shorter chubby friend, Conrad, "You know this mothafucka can't go nowhere without pussy in his pocket. He always bring his toys along."

Pussy in his pocket? What the fuck? Candace shot Bam a look. *Toys?*

"That nigga the only one ain't married," Tone added in a smooth baritone voice.

"So what that mean, Tone? I ain't married," Roni piped up.

"Like hell. You been wit Trina twelve years. Your ass is married," Tone retorted.

"I ain't never said I do."

"You ain't never said you didn't either, nigga," Conrad shot.

The table roared, each man erupting in laughter so much so Candace smiled unknowingly.

"This my special pretty young thing, Miss Candace," Bam said, looking at Candace and holding her arm out on display, after the laughter died down. "I gots to keep her with me."

"I hear that." Roni smacked his chops.

"Yeah, she something special, all right," Wayne, the light-skinned small one, chimed in. "Look at them legs on that stallion."

"He ain't lying, girl," Rich, the other tall brother, chimed in. "You's a work of art."

"So young, too," Tone added.

"Thank you," Candace replied in her softest voice. She looked over the group, her eye catching the broad-shouldered Tone and studying her frame. They locked eyes for a second and Candace held back her smile.

"She ridin' out with us tonight, nigga?" Roni asked Bam, stepping closer to Candace. He reached for her hand, raising it to kiss the back of her palm.

"She sure is," Bam replied, pulling Candace into him by her waist. "And keep your hands off of her."

Roni sucked his teeth. "Aww, nigga, you not sharing?"

The table howled again. *Sharing?* Candace's eyebrows furrowed.

"Fuck no, nigga. She ain't ready."

Candace flinched. *What the fuck is he talking about "ready"?* She shot Bam a sideways glance.

"What we drinking?" Conrad interjected. "I'm trying to have a nice buzz before I hit the tables."

"Fuck a buzz. I need to be fuckin' plastered," Roni added.

"Fuck the drinks," Wayne joined in. "This money burnin' a hole in my pocket. I'll get my own bitch; just let me at the craps table."

"This mothafuckin' startin' already," Rich hissed, shaking his head.

Tone ordered the first round of drinks and the bill went round the table with every man paying his turn until Candace was creeping up on tipsy walking beside Bam back out to the casino floor. The men collected seats at their select tables and Bam positioned Candace behind him at the one end of the craps table. *I have no idea what the hell I'm watching*, she thought, peering over his shoulder.

She was a few minutes into trying to figure things out when she realized that Bam was winning. He squeezed her backside for good luck.

"Aright, baby. You goin' be Big Daddy's lucky charm."

Candace smiled, lifting her eyes, and noticing Wayne at the opposite end of the table with a petite, big-breasted white girl in a gold sequinned dress and flawless blonde extensions, hanging from his arm. The girl giggled at everything Wayne said and rubbed his back as he rolled the dice. Wayne hit just like Bam and the table cheered. The girl jumped up and down, squealing and cheering. Candace clapped for Bam on his rolls and let him palm her ass throughout the night.

When they got back to their room later that night, Bam hit the sheets hard, snoring harder and Candace went down right beside him.

Candace woke up in bed alone the next morning. She opened her eyes to the high white ceiling and squinted at the sunlight bursting through the huge window beside her bed.

"That goddamn sun," she protested, turning over and pulling the covers over her face. She inhaled the soft fragrant sheets and lay quietly for a moment, realizing there were no other sounds in the suite.

Candace sat up straight, turning her head from left to right as she scanned the room. *Where the hell is he?*

Her feet hit the warm tiles of the floor and she stood up stretching in a black nightgown she didn't remember putting on. Candace shrugged and walked toward the bathroom. She ran her fingers along the marble and gold trimming of the bathroom sink before brushing her teeth and combing her hair.

"Bam must have gone to handle some business," she thought aloud, heading back to the bed. "What else is new? Niggas and they business. Fine. I'll enjoy this lavish space all by myself."

Candace plopped down on one side of the king-size bed, staring at the space between where she sat and where the bed ended.

"This bed is huge." She giggled, lying back. "What the fuck—is everything in Vegas enormous?"

Suddenly, she heard the door to the suite open and Bam saunter in breathing heavily.

"Hey, baby girl. You up yet?" he yelled from the other room.

"In here, Bam," she shouted back, sitting up.

Bam entered the bedroom clean-shaven and again dressed to impress.

Candace smiled at him, shaking her head.

"What's that for?" Bam asked, approaching the bed and plopping down beside her.

"Nothing," Candace replied, still smiling as she playfully tugged the collar of his crisp pale-blue oxford shirt. "You always look so handsome, Bam."

"Aww, well, thank you, pretty lady. That means a lot coming from such a beautiful woman such as yourself." Bam patted her leg. "How you feelin' this morning?"

"I'm good. What's in store for the day?"

Bam's mouth curled downward to a frown.

Aww, shit.

"Now, don't get too disappointed now, baby. But I got some things I need to handle today and I'm not going to be able to take you to see a show like I promised."

Candace frowned. "You're going to be busy ALL day?" She realized only after she spoke the words that she might be lonely without his company.

"Rest of the morning and most of the afternoon."

Candace pouted, folding her arms over her breasts.

"Now, be easy on Big Daddy, baby. We're in Vegas. Once-in-a-lifetime opportunities like to come 'round in this town so I got to grab the bull by the horns when I can."

What the fuck is he talking about? Candace curiously raised one brow.

Apparently noticing the distressed look on her face, Bam twisted his lip, then suddenly began smiling. "Now you know, Big Daddy always take care of you, right?"

Candace nodded.

Bam adjusted his big belly to reach his pocket and pulled out his thick leather wallet. Candace could see the overflow of hundreds inside.

He counted off ten hundred-dollar bills and handed them to her. "Go do a lil' shopping on Big Daddy today, baby. Take the limo, go see some sights and buy you something sexy."

Candace graciously accepted the bills but maintained her weak frown. *Aww, but this ain't goin' be enough, Big Daddy. This might last for the afternoon, but I need to take home more than a stack to cover my ass.*

"Thank you, Big Daddy. But that still leaves me to explore the city all on my own."

"I know, baby. But what can I say? Business calls and I am, after all, a businessman," Bam replied, standing to his feet.

"I understand." Candace stood behind him. "I think I'm going to order some room service and relax before I go out sightseeing."

"You can do whatever you like, baby. Order room service, have a masseuse come up to the room and rub you down." Bam playfully reached.

Candace flinched, chuckling and swatting him away. "That sounds nice. I can't think of the last time I had a massage."

"Good. Get you one. They even got a salon downstairs where you can get your nails and feet down. Get whatever you want. Just have 'em charge it to the room."

Nice. Candace smiled. "Okay, cool."

"You goin' be okay?" Bam asked, heading toward the door.

Again, Candace grinned. "I think I'll manage."

After a quick shower, her breakfast of waffles, fruit and champagne arrived. Candace slipped on a backless yellow sundress that gently hugged her waist and flowed loosely to her feet. She called down to the front desk for her limo; she was ready to hit the streets of Vegas solo.

Candace whipped out her camera the moment the sleek black vehicle pulled out onto Las Vegas Boulevard.

"Show me around," she instructed Mario. "I've never been to this city before and I want to see it all."

"All is a lot," he responded.

"You in a rush?" she asked crossly.

"No, ma'am."

"Well, neither am I," Candace replied, pulling out the tourist guide she had picked up in the lobby. "I want to see the Bellagio fountains, Madame Tussauds wax museum. I want to see the Paris hotel and hit downtown for some shopping."

"If shopping is what you want, then Crystals at the City Center is where you want to be."

"Yeah?" Candace leaned forward in her seat.

"Yup," he replied, glancing up at her through the rearview mirror.

"What's going on over there?"

"Real nice, high-end shopping. They've got your Prada and Louis Vuitton, Tiffany and Stern. You name it, they got it."

"Sounds good." Candace sat back in her seat popping the cork on another bottle of champagne. "Take me to the Bellagio first, then Crystals."

After taking Candace to all of her requested destinations, Mario pulled over to a small lot off the strip. Candace hopped out of the limousine and hit the bright strip of designer stores with a mean stroll and peeked into all of the skillfully crafted window displays, each more alluring than the next.

"Ohmigod. I'd go broke living here." Candace walked a few blocks, snapping photos of stores and enormously designed hotels. Half-way down one seemingly endless block, she stopped in front of a small, classy-looking boutique. A purple pair of pumps peered at her through an enormous window and hanging beside them, a long leather and suede color-blocked shoulder bag matching the seductive hues in the heels. They beckoned her inside.

Once through the doors of the cool pastel painted shop, Candace headed right toward the display and checked the tags: the bag, $395 and the shoes, $420.

Shit. Should I get both? I mean, I have the money to cover most of my bills in my hand. Why blow it? I can go home with this cash and start to piece my life back together. But, before Candace could finish her thoughts, she was coaxed into a comfortable chair by a pretty, perky and persistent salesgirl and before she knew it, the stiletto was on her perfectly manicured foot and the comfort of the leather bag massaged her skin. When Candace stood with both shoes on, the salesgirl squealed.

"Ohmigod, they look gorgeous on you."

Candace grinned her agreement.

"I mean, you just can't deny a good shoe when you see it. And they're a perfect fit."

Candace nodded, holding up her dress and examining how the heel accentuated her lean calf muscles.

"And the bag," the girl continued. "Killer. With the shoes, ohmigod."

All right, chick. I know you just want me to buy these damn shoes and this gorgeous bag. Candace clutched the bag in her hand.

"You want me to ring these items up for you?" the sales clerk asked, grinning.

Candace was still for a moment. *Aww. What the hell?* She nodded her confirmation and the clerk hit the total button before Candace could change her mind.

Candace stashed the change from her purchase in her wallet. *Shit, I still have bills to pay. But little over $200 ain't goin' get me far and there's no way I'm returning these shoes, or this bag.* Candace carried her purchases proudly, exiting back out into the blazing sun. *Bam's goin' have to make something happen. The weekend's far from over and I am NOT goin' home broke. No fuckin' way.*

Candace made her way back to the limo and Mario whisked her away to the MGM Grand for a late lunch with Bam. She thanked Mario for his company and stretched her legs out in regal strides, her yellow sundress accenting her curves as she approached Bam and his gawking troop.

"I'm not sharing my goodies," Candace heard Bam say as she

approached. He grasped her tightly when she was within arm's reach. *Fuck's up with this "sharing" shit?*

Sitting in front of the ivory vanity back in their suite, Candace pulled her hair up to examine her profile in the mirror, then let her hair drop back down to her shoulders. She tucked the loose locks behind her ear, stared at her reflection once more and shook her head.

"I guess I should figure out what I'm going to wear before I do my hair," she said, standing from her seat and heading out of the bathroom. She grabbed two dresses on their hangers from the long closet and laid them out across the massive bed. She pursed her lips together, throwing her hands on her bare hips and staring intently at her choices. She had packed her own skimpy red and black BCBG dress with high-waist accents and a plunging neckline that screamed *Only for Vegas*. She fingered the crimson piece on the bed. Beside it was Bam's gift, the body-hugging black Dior dress with an elegant high neckline and cut-out sides giving it a sense of class and seduction.

She picked up the all-black number, draping it over her almost naked body. She pulled her hair back up, then released her grasp, letting her cinnamon locks fall loosely over her face.

Candace smiled at her reflection. *Yes, this is will do for whatever's in store for the night.* She checked the time on her cell phone. *Still nothing from Chris. Fuck him. I've got forty-five minutes to get ready for a penthouse party at Caesars Palace. I'll worry about everything else later.* She cleaned her face and began applying her makeup: a smoky eye, bronzed cheeks and red lips. She pressed her hair into a bone-straight bob before slipping the slim-fitting dress over her long torso. It stopped mid-thigh and Candace flexed her muscles while strapping on her black stilettos.

Candace arrived to the gala event on the nineteenth floor of Caesars Palace with Bam and five other male escorts by her side, plus the skinny white girl with the perfect extensions Wayne had picked up along the way. As soon as they made it through the door of the crowded penthouse, Bam and his crew parted ways. Bam, Tone and Conrad positioned themselves at a large round table and began playing cards. Roni, Rich and Wayne made for the bar. The music was thumping, the crowd was stunning and after a few rounds, Candace was feeling sexy and social. She smiled, heading back toward Bam with his drink in her hand when she noticed a gorgeous, brown-skinned woman gyrating her hips on Bam's lap. Candace chuckled lightly, gently sliding his drink down beside him so not to disturb his personal performance.

Candace grabbed herself a drink and headed to the dance floor. The music moved her as she stepped in line with a cluster of beautiful women and pretty girls. Tipsy and giggling, Candace turned at the pressure she felt on the small of her back. A gorgeous, blue-eyed, dark-haired young woman, almost as tall as her, stepped close to her.

"You are fuckin' gorgeous," the girl of no more than twenty-five whispered into Candace's ear.

"Thanks," Candace yelled back over the music before turning her back to her. But again, Candace felt hands on her waist, this time grasping her bare skin through the cut-out sides in her dress while she danced. Candace spun back around, the long-legged girl did not back down. She stepped closer to Candace, wrapping her hands around her and tracing the top of her behind. *Oh shit.* Candace was paralyzed for a moment.

"I like how you move," the young woman spoke again into her ear.

Candace forced a nervous smile and began rocking to the beat. The woman moved with her in syncopated rhythm. Candace didn't refuse and let the alcohol move the music through her as she swayed to the beat. After a moment of twisting and working her hips into the young woman, Candace closed her eyes biting down on her bottom lip.

Oh, God. I'm wasted. I'm really dancing with this chick. Candace chuckled inwardly. *At least she's sexy.* Suddenly, Candace felt soft moist pressure against her folded mouth. She parted her lips, encouraged by the liquor she consumed, and before she realized it, Candace was swirling tongues with the pretty woman. Her friends seemed to be cheering as Candace opened her eyes. She forced an awkward and uncomfortable smile, taking a step back.

But the woman still didn't let go. She leaned in to Candace and whispered, "No harm, mama. The way you was biting that lip, I couldn't resist. Are you mad with me?"

Candace looked the leggy chick up and down. She had huge blue eyes under a sleek bang with the rest of her dark locks, hanging straight down past her bare shoulders and falling loosely around her overly exposed cleavage. Candace admired her tight, flat tummy in the sheer top she wore over black sequinned shorts. There was no denying how attractive she was and her hands were still around Candace's waist.

Fuck it. Candace leaned back in to the young woman and began kissing her again. The small crowd around them cheered. Candace grabbed another drink from the server walking by, threw it back and kept dancing.

Candace spotted Tone and Roni, laughing and obviously enjoying the show from across the room. She blew a kiss their way. Tone nodded for her to come closer. Candace squeezed the woman's bottom and swayed off in Tone's direction.

"Sit down, beautiful," Tone instructed, patting his lap. Candace turned around, lowering her backside over him when Roni reached up and slapped it. She shook her finger in his face.

"Now, now. This notcha' booty," she teased.

"Whose booty is it?" Tone asked.

"Bam's?" Roni added.

Candace shook her head. "Not at all." She hovered above Tone's lap, squatting and swinging her hips. Tone pulled her down onto him and she began gyrating her body on his crotch.

Beside her, Roni quickly tossed back the drink in his hand and in one swift motion, set it down and snatched Candace onto him. She slid effortlessly and Roni was all smiles. With quick hands, he palmed her breasts and kissed lightly at the back of her neck. After a moment, Tone handed her another drink.

Candace swallowed the strong drink, closed her eyes and worked her hips on Roni's lap until she felt a heavy hand on her shoulder. She opened her eyes to see Bam standing in front of her.

"We need to go. You're wasted," Bam declared, pulling Candace up.

Candace snatched back from his grasp. "I know what I'm doin'."

"Yeah?" Bam laughed. "You think so, huh, pretty girl? Let Big Daddy take you back to the suite."

Candace struggled to stand. She saw a blurry Tone stand also. Bam silently clasped her under her elbows and helped her stagger to the car. She could barely keep her eyes open.

Once on the elevator back at the MGM Grand, Bam slobbered over Candace's neck with his thick tongue and pinched at her breasts through her dress. Candace stumbled and he grabbed her hair forcing her down on her knees. There was no one else on the elevator and Bam pulled out his manhood with his free hand and led her face into his crotch.

"Come on, baby. Suck that dick."

Candace pulled his sweaty meat into her mouth. The scent and taste of him made her gag, but Bam rammed himself in even further. The elevator chimed and he yanked her up off her knees before the doors could slide open. Bam was hanging partly out the front of his pants as they turned down the hall. Candace heard a second elevator chime and glanced behind her in time to see Tone and Roni coming down the hall toward them. Bam drunkenly fought with his pockets to get out the room key. He released his grasp on Candace and she stumbled into Roni who caught her anxiously.

"Whoa. Whoa, baby. You aright?"

Candace nodded. *Goddamn. I'm fucked up. Shit. Get it together, C. This man got his big hands all on you... I wonder if he got a big dick.*

Bam opened the door to their suite and Roni escorted her inside. Tone followed behind.

Once inside, Candace pulled away from Roni and staggered into the bedroom, collapsing on her stomach on the bed and trying to steady the spinning ceiling. Her eyelids felt like tons of bricks as she wrestled to keep them open. Suddenly, she saw Bam's blurry figure enter the room.

"You need to freshen up, baby girl," Bam stated calmly but with a slur, walking over to the bed. He took a seat behind her and Candace sat up. Bam's hand instinctively found its way up her skirt.

"Now, lil' mama," he continued. "I told you Big Daddy would take care of you, right?"

She heard the noises he made and they sounded like words she couldn't make out.

"What do you say to you, me and two of my boys having a little fun tonight? Does that sound nice?" he asked, kissing her neck.

Candace cocked her head quizzically to one side.

"Now, you know I know how to take care of you, right, baby?

My boys wanna know if they can find out just how sweet your candy is. They willin' to pay a thousand each for your precious time. Sound good, right, baby?" He licked her ear while his fingers twirled at the tip of her panties.

Candace was surprisingly aroused.

"We'll take it easy on you, baby. I promise," Bam said in a pleading tone.

The words echoed in Candace's mind and she shook her head for a moment, attempting to regain control of her thought process. *Three of them, fuck me.* The muscles in her womanhood clenched. She thought through the surging liquor. *This is crazy.* She burst out laughing.

"What's so funny, mama?" Bam asked, smiling awkwardly.

"This is Vegas!" Candace shouted with a drunken chuckle.

Bam joined in her laughter.

He's handsome when I'm drunk. But wait... Candace forced on her sternest face. "Two thousand for three of y'all? That don't seem fair," she rationalized.

"You goin' charge *me* for that pussy?" Bam spat, jumping back.

"I'm goin' charge you admission for the show," Candace slurred.

Bam smirked. "You right, pretty mama. Big Daddy always treats you right. I'll make it thirty-five hundred."

I feel like a piece of meat up on the chopper's block. But Candace nodded, accepting the offer and Bam grinned from ear to ear.

"Good. Now, put that white shit on Daddy bought you. Come out when you're ready," Bam instructed, standing and leaving the room.

Candace slipped off her black dress and stood swaying in the mirror and staring at her wavering reflection. There seemed to be three different inflections of her voice speaking to her at one time. *This is crazy. Girl, what the fuck? Oh, God, I'mma be sick. Pull yourself together, girl. What the fuck?* She swayed…*come on, come on. This shit is happening. Ohmigod. I'm…I'm 'bout to fuck three men… For almost four grand. Ohmigod. No, C. Don't. You're better than this. No. Yes, bitch. Is you crazy!?!? You're fuckin' broke. Pull it together, bitch. You need this…get piped all crazy. Take home enough money to cover your ass and keep it fuckin' movin'. No, C. Bitch, this is Vegas!! Ohmigod, I gotta sit down.*

Candace plopped down on the bed. *This is insane. I can't do this. I'm somebody's fuckin' mother. Emmanuel…*She shook her head violently, hoping the thoughts of her son would disappear. *He could never know. No one could ever know. No one will ever know.* She gripped the bed sheets. *What the fuck am I supposed to do? Get this money.*

Candace took a deep breath to steady herself. She didn't recall much about putting on the all-white lingerie set or leaving the bedroom. When she looked up, she was on her knees in front of the couch with Bam's dick in her mouth and Bam's head rolled back drooling.

"That nigga 'sleep," she heard Roni say.

"Sure is," was Tone's reply as he quickly approached Candace from behind, lifted her up and carried her back into the bedroom. He laid her down gently on the bed, slipped the lace white panties off and pushed her legs open wide. Tone pressed his face hungrily into her warmth and Candace groaned loud, rubbing the smooth skin on his bald head. He kissed at her womanhood while he stripped out of his pants and unbuttoned his shirt. Candace rubbed her hands over his wide and defined shoulders.

Tone kissed between her legs one quick time before he settled back to slip on a condom. Without a word, Tone slid inside.

Candace moaned a delighted surprise and Tone pushed himself into a deep spot that made her squirm. He kept his stroke there, strong and steady for a while.

"Oh, God," she hummed, wrapping her long arms around him.

"Nah, nigga. I wanna see." Candace heard the door open with the simultaneous sound of Roni's voice.

Tone kept up his thrusts. Candace closed her eyes enjoying the feel of him inside her. When she looked up, Roni was staring down at her ravenously.

"Oh, shit," was all she could muster as Tone stepped aside and Roni closed in on her. She looked past him to see Tone leaving the room. Candace struggled to focus on the man closing in on top of her. Roni gave her a reassuring smile, all his whites bright and gleaming.

He applied a condom and slipped inside. His stroke was nothing like Tone's, deep and steady. No, Roni's dick was long and thin, like him, and he pounded away at her pussy relentlessly.

After a while, Candace felt numb and a sweat-dripping Roni stopped, sliding off the bed onto the floor.

"Damn, girl. I need a drink. You want one?" Roni pulled up his pants and dragged a limp Candace out into the living room. She spotted Tone on the balcony smoking a cigar. He smiled, giving her the head nod to come here.

I'm coming, she sang in her head, moving toward the balcony as Roni worked the bar.

Bam was still asleep on the couch and Candace moved quietly past him. Tone handed her his cigar once she stepped outside and she drew in deeply. Lightheaded, she leaned into him. His one hand massaged her breasts while the other fondled her behind, working its way beneath her cheeks and stroking her wetness with his fingertips. Candace bit down on her lip as Tone turned her around. Pulling on another condom, he pressed inside of her, leaning Candace against the edge of the balcony overlooking an electric Las Vegas night sky. Again Tone's stroke was strong, pumping along the swollen places inside of her. His humping thrust her forward, but his tight grip pulled her back from over the edge of the balcony.

"Goddamn, nigga. That shit pretty," Roni said from behind her.

Candace inwardly sucked her teeth. *Uh, I don't want him. I like this one better.*

Tone did not stop stroking until he clutched Candace tightly around her waist and shivered his ejaculation into the condom. But before Tone could collect himself, Roni was pulling her away. He bent her back over the balcony and grabbed a handful of her hair.

"Ahhh. Ahhhh, fuck," she screamed as he pushed himself inside of her. She felt his hard hand against her bare behind. He slapped her again, pumping harder. After a moment, he slowed and Candace felt Tone palm her ass. She didn't have to turn to be sure; she knew it was Tone's large hand caressing her instead of Roni's hard smack against her skin.

Tone laughed at Roni wiping his brow and breathing heavily. "You need a break, nigga," Tone teased.

"Fuck...man." Roni gasped. "Pussy too good. Got me breakin' a sweat."

Roni slid out of Candace, pulled off the condom and tossed it over the balcony. Candace, knees wobbling, turned back around. Tone ushered her back into the lounge area and Bam stirred on the couch.

Bam lifted his eyes, smiling at the sight of her. "Come here, baby. You okay?" He patted his knee.

Oh, fuck. Candace swayed in his direction. Bam leaned forward and helped her out, positioning her body on his lap.

"You know what I want baby?" he asked, pinching her nipples.

"What's that, Bam?" she slurred.

"That pussy on me, baby."

"Yeah?"

"Hell, yeah. You done gave my boys a taste of the sweet candy. But that's my suga, and it's my turn."

Candace grinned unconsciously. "You want this pussy, Big Daddy?"

"Quit playin'. Now, come on, put that pussy on Big Daddy." Bam pushed Candace up to her feet and pulled his pants and boxers down to his ankles. He grabbed a condom from the end table and handed it to Candace. "Put it on fa' me."

Candace snatched the condom and quickly dressed Bam's member, then stood back up, folding her arms across her chest.

Roni chuckled from across the room.

"Oh, you feisty tonight. Huh, pretty lady? Come sit on this dick." Bam reached up and yanked Candace onto him.

She spread her legs, pushed back against his big stomach and straddled him. Candace couldn't tell if it was the alcohol or what, but Bam's thick manhood fell right into place. She used all the limber the liquor provided and rode Bam like a bucking cowgirl. Bam clutched her waist for dear life, his mouth hanging open and eyes rolled to the back of his head. He came quick.

"Goddamn, baby. You tryna put that shit on a nigga?" Bam laughed, gently pushing Candace off his lap.

She landed on her butt on the couch to his right. *Tryna? Nigga, please.* "Tryna? Nigga, please." The words jumped out of her mouth.

"Oh, shit!" Roni erupted in laughter. Candace looked up to see him moving toward her. "She talkin' shit now." Roni handed her a drink.

"Yeah, she is. She a fuckin' stallion." Tone chuckled, wiping his brow and adjusting his clothes. He moved over to where Candace was sprawled out on the couch. He pinched her chin and wiped the beads of sweat from her forehead. "Thanks for the fun, babe," he said coolly before turning to leave.

"Don't miss your flight, my nigga!" Roni shouted to him.

"I'll get up with y'all niggas later," Tone replied without turning around.

And with that he was gone. Candace frowned slightly and looked over at Bam who was back asleep. But Roni was wide awake standing in front of her with a cigar in one hand and his dick in the other.

"Come on, baby," he said, releasing himself and taking her by the hand. "Let's go back in the bedroom for a lil' privacy. I been drinking and it's goin' be a minute for I get this nut off. Can you handle that?" He slapped her ass, leading her into the bedroom. Once inside, he climbed on top of her and after at least another half hour of tearing at the sheets, Roni eventually passed out right beside Candace in the bed. She woke up in the middle of the night violently nauseous. She crawled to the bathroom and threw up several times, before blacking out on the bathroom floor.

When Candace came to, she was alone in her hotel room in the bed with a stack of bills and a note on the pillow that read: "Thanks for the fun, hun. You're a gem. Roni left a tip for letting him cuddle."

Bam was nowhere to be found and the empty room left her too much alone with her thoughts. Her stomach turned. Candace climbed out of bed and melted into a hot bubble bath trying to shake away the blurry images of the night. She pressed her fingers into her womanhood and felt the swelling between her legs. She soaked for over an hour.

Her head was spinning when she stood to dry herself and she heard Bam enter the room.

"Hey, pretty girl."

Candace let out a low growl.

Bam chuckled. "How you feel, baby?" he asked, rubbing his hand along her bare back.

Candace simply shook her head.

"You did good last night, baby. Made Big Daddy real proud."

Candace rolled her eyes. She heard Bam order room service and step out of the room. A few seconds later, she heard his heavy footsteps thud back in. "Remember our flight leaves at eleven, baby girl."

Candace groaned but didn't bother to turn around. She buried her head in the pillow and stayed in bed.

Later that morning, Bam reappeared wearing a fresh khaki Kangol and carrying coffee.

"You're such a trooper, my pretty little lady," he said, smiling and lifting her travel bag from out of the closet. Candace was quiet on the plane ride home.

She made it back through her door with an upset stomach, over four thousand dollars in cash, some shoes and a new bag. Yet with all her reward, Candace was sore, humiliated and still without a word from Chris. She cried herself to sleep that night.

CHAPTER 25

"I needed this lil' getaway, sexy," Tommy said, stretching out across the floral sheets on the long bed. He brought his arm down around Marci pulling her into him.

Marci yawned her sleepy eyes awake. "Yeah, I know you did," she cooed, rubbing her hands along his bare chest. "I know what you like, baby. I know you need to get away from that stress." She softly kissed his lips. "I'm here to help you relax, baby. This could be you and me always. Don't you want that?"

"Umm…" Tommy returned her wet kisses. "Hell yeah, I do."

"A lil' bed and breakfast in Rehoboth Beach, right off the water. This is so romantic, babe. I know you love me and I could make you feel good and happy and relaxed like this all the time, if we was together."

"I know you could and I know you will, baby, soon as we get our chance."

Marci giggled, running her hands down the smooth creases of Tommy's stomach until she reached the tip of his boxers and pulled. She pressed her hands down further.

"Whatchu doin'?" he asked, smiling and stretching.

"Lovin' you."

"You crazy, girl. You know that?"

"Crazy about you, baby."

"Yeah?" Tommy asked.

"I love being with you, Tommy," Marci replied, removing her

hand and laying her head on his chest. "I'm always happy when I'm with you. I'm miserable when you're not around and I'm so jealous when I think of you with anybody else, even Donna."

"Jealous? Don't do that jealousy stuff, baby. You not a kid. Kids get jealous. Besides, ain't nothing for you to be jealous of."

Marci pulled her bottom lip in, furrowing her brows and pouting like a scolded child. "I am jealous, Tommy. I want you all to myself. I'm fuckin' tired of sharing. I want to run my own shop and move outta my fuckin' parents' house and I wanna do all that with you. Like, now."

"Ain't nothing wrong with that," Tommy said, smiling and rubbing her back.

"You act like it is," Marci protested.

"No I don't, Marci." Tommy sat up, forcing Marci up as well. "You want a lot and I can give you all that, but you gotta give me time."

"Time? Time to do what?" She crossed her arms over her breasts.

"Time to figure out a plan. Time to get the money up to get you a spot."

Marci sucked her teeth. "Gettin' the money up to get my own shop is goin' to take forever. I don't even know where to start."

"I do."

Marci tilted her head to one side up, looking puzzled at Tommy. "I married the bitch," Tommy said, jutting his neck out.

"Donna?"

"Yes, baby."

"How are you gonna get money *for me* to open a shop from Donna?"

"That's my wife. Business is booming. All I gotta do is convince her she needs to expand. You know, look into opening a new salon. I can get her to let me get my hands on that kinda money if she thinks I am going to invest it in the business."

"But you won't, right? You'll give it to me?" Marci asked, squirming excitedly.

"I'll have to figure out something, some way to get it in your hands."

"So, then you'll divorce her, right?" Marci's eyes sprang open wide as saucers.

"When the time is right, baby. I promise."

Marci straddled him. "Can't you just divorce the bitch now, get half and run away with me?"

"So young and dumb," Tommy responded, patting her thigh. "You watch too much TV, baby. It don't work like that. All Donna money in her business name. The kids ain't mine. I mean, I'd get something if I leave her but not much."

"Well, do she have life insurance?" Marci hissed, throwing her hands in the air. "Can't you just kill the bitch?"

Tommy silently lay back down. Marci stared at him.

After a moment, Tommy sighed from the pillow. "I'm not the beneficiary. I won't get shit if the bitch drop dead in my lap."

"That's fucked up," Marci said, falling forward onto his chest. Tommy wrapped his arms around her. She pushed her lips onto his, kissing him hungrily. Her desire burned like fire through her skin and Tommy held her tight, sealing warmth between the places their flesh met. Marci surrendered in the embrace, settling still for a moment on Tommy's chest, listening to the sound of his heart-beat. She sat up suddenly with tears in her eyes.

"I don't care, baby. Whatever we gotta do, I wanna be with you. I love you, Tommy."

"I love you, too, Marci." Tommy leaned forward, wiping the streams from her face. "Come on, baby. Let's hit the beach. Some sun should make you feel better. I know you in a two-piece will make me feel hella good."

Marci laughed, climbing down from his lap and sashaying into the bathroom while Tommy stood from the bed stretching and yawning.

Marci dug her toes into the sand, sitting in the long white beach chairs behind the small lodging place they'd secured for the weekend. Tommy snoozed in his chair beside her.

She smiled at the soft noises coming from his direction. *I fuckin' love him so much. We're gonna be together, forever. Watch. And then everybody can kiss our asses.* She smiled at Tommy again. *This is what love should be. My and my man. Chillin' on a beach. He look good. I look good. This is how it should be.* Marci took a sip of the vodka-spiked lemonade from the cup holder in her chair. She swallowed the cool libations and smiled. *Watch how good I look tonight. Me and my baby going out for drinks, then a night of crazy lovemaking.* Marci clenched her pelvic muscles, a reflex of her reflections on the night before. *He's not going be able to keep his hands off me. He ain't goin' never wanna go home.*

Later that evening, Marci oiled and lotioned her lean cocoa-brown body before sliding a thin white tube top over her bare breasts. Her nipples gently graced the soft material. *Perfect.* Next, she slid on a skimpy black G-string, pulling a tight white skirt over it and proudly patting her firm behind.

"Damn, girl," Marci said to herself, rubbing more scented body oil across her bare flat tummy. She gently flicked the small stud in her belly button and blew a kiss to her reflection in the mirror before switching off the lights and heading out.

Marci smiled in Tommy's direction as he proudly strolled toward her in a small but crowded tavern they'd located not far from where they were staying. He set two drinks down on the table in front of her before extending his hand to her for a dance. She blushed and giggled as she stood, adjusting her skirt.

Tommy wrapped his hands around her bare back in front of their table and rocked her smoothly to the steady beat.

"Baby, you smell so good," he breathily said in her ear.

"You feel so good, baby," she replied.

"I can't wait to get you outta here and back to our room."

"Me either," Marci laughed, leaning forward and kissing him in the mouth.

"We should finish these drinks." Tommy reached over to the table beside him, grabbing his glass and taking a long hard swallow. Marci followed suit.

"I need to use the ladies room," she said after setting her glass back down.

Tommy stepped aside and Marci switched her hips as she moved for his viewing pleasure. She blew him a quick kiss before pushing open the large brown door at the far end of the bar.

"Goddamn, that man is so fuckin' sexy," Marci said to herself, looking for the cleanest stall. Walking through the long bathroom, Marci glanced up and noticed a tall, older woman with a head full of big poufy curls standing at the sink washing her hands but staring in her direction. Marci looked around, searching for the object of the woman's attention. But there was no one else in the bathroom except them. *Fuck she looking at?*

Marci forced a fake grin the woman's way.

"Hello," the woman said, staring Marci up and down with a scrutinizing eye.

"Hello," Marci replied sarcastically.

"That's a very pretty skirt you have on." The woman's voice lacked the kindness to make the compliment sincere.

"Thanks," Marci said dryly before entering a stall. *Fuck is her problem? Old jealous bitch.*

When Marci flushed and exited the stall, the woman was still at the sink, this time touching up her lip-gloss and reworking the pins in her big, curly weave.

"Sheesh," she huffed. "This heat is killing my weave." The curly-haired woman laughed, glancing at Marci wash her hands.

Marci fake grinned again.

"Does the humidity by the water bother your hair at all, girl? I mean, your hair is so nice. I'm jealous."

Marci giggled, relaxing just a little. "No, I don't sweat a lot so I really don't have a lot of problems with my hair. Plus, I'm a stylist so I know what I'm doing."

"A stylist? Really? In Rehoboth?" Curly turned from the sink facing Marci and staring her straight in the eyes.

"No. I'm from Philly."

"Oh. What salon?"

"Are you from Philly?" Marci asked.

"Originally. But I live out Jersey. I'm just out here vacationing with the husband, you know?"

"Right." Marci nodded.

"So what salon did you say you work at?"

"Just a small shop off Sixty-ninth Street."

"Oh. I don't know that area well."

Marci shrugged.

"I'm out here for a little vacation with my husband," she continued. "Who are you here with? Your husband?"

"Yeah. I am," Marci said, blushing.

"Oh, okay," Curly said, picking up her purse from the sink basin. "Well, you young lovers enjoy your evening. And keep that hair fly, girl. I love it."

"Thanks," Marci said, watching Curly collect her things and walk out the door.

Marci reapplied the shimmer to her lips before washing her hands and returning to the table where Tommy sat staring at his phone.

"You ready to go, babe?" he asked, looking up as she approached.

"Yeah. We can go."

But before Tommy could stand, a young waitress scurried over carrying a tray with two full drinks. She set them on the table in front of them.

"We didn't order these," Tommy insisted, pushing away the glasses.

"The woman at the end of the bar did," the waitress answered, nodding in the direction from which she came. "She said it was for the young couple in love."

Tommy's eyes narrowed, scanning the bar. Marci saw her first, the woman from the bathroom. She smiled their way. Marci smiled back, raising her glass.

"Who the fuck is she?" Tommy asked, his eyes low and face tight.

"I met her in the bathroom. She was nice." Marci sipped her drink.

"Why the fuck does she keep looking this way and how the hell does she know we're a couple in love? What did you say to her?"

"I didn't say much. She did all the talkin'. Asked me about my hair and whatnot," Marci answered, shrugging her shoulders. "Then she asked me if I was here with my husband."

Tommy craned his head, reducing his voice to a whisper and stared sharply in Marci's direction. "And what did you say?"

"I said, yeah."

"Why the fuck would you do that?" Tommy asked with fire behind his gaze but his voice still low.

"I...I don't know." Marci swallowed hard. "Because she asked and what was I supposed to say. No, I'm here with my married lover."

"You shouldn't have said shit." Tommy stood to his feet. "Come on. Let's go. Now."

"But my drink…"

"Fuck them drinks." Tommy stared back in the woman's direction. Again she waved. "I think I know that bitch. We need to leave. Now!"

CHAPTER 26

Candace returned from Las Vegas early Monday morning. She collapsed on her bed and then rested most of the day, not bothering to unpack. She skipped class that evening, deciding instead to soak in a hot bath until her skin wrinkled and she felt the grime of her sins begin to slip away. *I'll work on my paper later*, she thought, submerging in the tub.

Dressed in her bathrobe, Candace sat on the edge of her bed and uncurled the knot of twenties and hundreds from her carryon bag. She counted out the amount she needed to pay her bills and tucked the rest securely in the back of her panty drawer. A warm glass of vodka carried Candace back to bed that evening.

Tuesday morning she was actually feeling a little better and decided to run to the bank before getting her nails done. She hit the supermarket and picked up her weekly essentials, then she sat down at her kitchen table and paid all her bills.

Later that evening, Candace was home putting away the last of her things from her trip, smoking a blunt and listening to Sade in her oversized night shirt when she heard a knock on the door.

Who the hell? Candace inched toward the door. She peeked through the peephole, but the view was blocked. "Who is it?" she yelled aggressively.

"Open the door."

Candace instantly recognized the voice.

"Mothafucka!" she screeched, yanking open the door.

Chris stood smiling in the threshold. "Hey, babe. You miss me?"

"Fuck you!" Candace screamed, punching him in the chest. "Where the fuck have you been? And where the fuck is my money?"

Chris's smile fell. "Well, hello to you too."

"Fuck you," Candace repeated. "You's a lyin' son of a bitch!"

"Damn. Why I gotta be all that?" Chris asked, stepping forward.

Candace shoved him back. "Don't come the fuck in here. You're a liar. And I want my fuckin' money!"

"What money? What the fuck are you talking about? Damn, can I come in?"

"NO! Fuck you. I want the money I put up to get your black ass outta jail. 'Cause you wasn't even fuckin' in jail. You fuckin' liar!"

"What!?! Yes the fuck I was locked up. Where the hell else you think I been?"

"How the fuck should I know? But I know you wasn't up CFCF. My sister called and wasn't no Christopher Foster there."

"Fuck, babe. 'Cause my legal name ain't Foster."

"What?!?!" Candace felt her heart lurch in her chest. "What the fuck is it, then?"

"My name is Christopher Dillion Jackson. Jackson's from my bitch-ass pop, but I hate that fuckin' name. So, I never use it."

Candace's eyes bulged out of their sockets. "Ohmigod!!! I am that kind of girl…" She stumbled back from the door.

"What kind of girl?" Chris asked, quickly stepping inside and closing the door.

Candace sat down on the edge of her couch reeling. "The kind of girl that don't know the last name of the nigga she fuckin'."

"Cut that shit out, babe. It's not like that."

"What the fuck is it like then, Chris? Or is that even your real first name?"

"Cut it out, C," Chris said, calmly stepping toward her.

"Why the fuck did you lie to me? And where the fuck is my money?"

"WHAT FUCKIN' MONEY!?!?! What are you talkin' about?" Chris screamed, throwing his hands in the air.

Candace jerked back, catching herself for a moment, then jumping to her feet.

"The fuckin' money I put up to bail your black ass outta jail!"

"Didn't nobody put no fuckin' money up for me! Why the fuck you think I been sittin' in that bitch! Hell, I woulda been home if I'da got bail."

"WHAT!?!?!" Candace's heart was racing as she struggled to catch her breath.

Chris grabbed her heaving shoulders. "Babe…"

"Get the fuck off me!" She shoved him back. "I gave your fuckin' cousin over three thousand dollars to get you out!"

"What!?!? Who…Shif?!?!"

Candace spoke slowly, concentrating on each word to be sure Chris didn't miss a beat. "Your cousin Shif. He called me and told me you got locked and you needed like five grand…"

"Get the fuck outta here!"

"No," Candace continued. "I gave that nigga thirty-two hundred!"

"WHAT!?!?!" Chris shouted, wide-eyed. "That's why that pussy been duckin' me! You gotta be fuckin' kiddin' me!"

Candace snaked her neck. "Do I look like I'm fuckin' kiddin'? I gave that nigga my money! Where the fuck is my money, Chris?"

Chris took a deep breath. "Babe, no bullshit, I swear to God, I didn't know you put up shit. Shif ain't did shit for me. I been tryna get a hold of this nigga since I got released. This pussy M.I.A."

"What!?!?"

Chris shook his head, his nostrils flaring. "I told him to call you. I did. When I got booked, I got hold of 'em at his mom crib and told him to get your number out my phone. I did, 'cause I only needed two stacks real quick and I knew I could get it back to you asap."

Candace folded her arms over her breasts.

"Babe, when I talked to that nigga, he said you was like, 'Nah, you ain't have it.' I didn't know nothing about your money 'til just now."

"Where the fuck is your cousin?"

"Babe, don't worry. I'm on this nigga head. Trust me, I'mma getcha bread back. I promise you that."

"You are not for real. This is not for real." Candace paced the floor, massaging her temples. "So, your fuckin' cousin burnt me for three grand?!?"

"Fuck that! I'm not accepting that," Chris said, quickly rushing to her side. "Babe, I'm sorry this shit went down, but I'mma get on this nigga. I promise that. I'mma get your money back, babe."

Candace pulled away from his grasp, turning and heading toward the kitchen. She could hear Chris following close behind.

"Babe, you hear me?"

"Fuck you, Chris," she mumbled.

"What?" Chris approached her quickly.

"I said, fuck yo…" But before she could turn around, he was up on her, pushing her face down onto the kitchen table and hoisting her nightshirt up her back.

What the fuck? Candace almost went down hard but caught herself with one hand, extending the other out behind her to push Chris back.

"Get off me!" she protested. But Chris snatched her arm back behind her and Candace's face hit the table. His fingers spread, clasping around the front of her neck.

"Chris, stop!" she screamed, feeling sudden warmth between her legs.

"You always talking that tough shit," he yelled, struggling with his pants. "All that fuck me shit! That's what you want? You wanna fuck me!" Chris grunted, tugging at her panties.

Candace wondered if he could feel how wet they were as he pulled them down her legs. "Get off me!" she yelled, bucking back against him and feeling the stiffness of his manhood rising against her behind. He pulled down his pants.

"No. No the fuck I'm not getting off you. You wanna fuck me, baby? Huh? Cuz I wanna fuck you! I been thinkin' 'bout my pussy forever!" He rammed himself inside of her.

Candace screamed, the forceful pleasure erupting from her inside out.

Oh, God. No. No. No. He's not supposed to feel this good. His lyin' ass don't deserve no pussy. Oh, God. Her walls contracted around Chris and her orgasm came almost instantaneously.

"Fuuuuucckkkk!!!" she wailed, pushing back, but Chris did not retreat. He pushed further into her, lifting his body up high and hard against her resistance.

Ohmigod. Candace trembled. *No. No. No. I can't. He can't...No.*

Deep inside, Chris executed several quick hard pumps and Candace could feel the length of him in the bottom of her stomach. She clenched her muscles, squirming over his. Chris pulled her body close to him so her back arched against his chest and he squatted beneath her thighs, almost sitting her up on his lap. He remained relentless in his thrusting.

Candace screamed out again. "Oh, God! Stop!"

Chris slid her down, breathing heavily.

Candace saw her chance and pushed off of him, making a beeline for the living room. But Chris caught her by the swing of her loose cinnamon ponytail.

"Where you goin'?" he asked, clutching her hair. Candace stumbled, coming down on her knees and began crawling in rapid stretches across the floor. Chris came down quickly behind her, grabbing her by the waist and flipping her over onto her back with a loud grunt.

Candace spun around to see his handsome face. "Mothafucka!" She slapped him. Chris slapped her back. Candace winced and slapped him again. Chris smiled.

"Mothafucka!!" she screamed, charged and angry. Candace lunged forward with all her might, pushing her upper body against Chris, thrusting him over, and landing on top of him. "Lyin' son of a bitch!" she screamed, grabbing for his throat, but Chris was faster, quickly clasping the bottom of her shirt and snatching it forcefully over her head.

"Sonofabitch!" she screamed, covering her bare breasts.

"Why you so mad, baby? Huh? Just tell me you miss me." Chris pursed his lips, making kissy faces and grabbing her waist.

"Fuck you!" she yelled, trying to push off him to stand.

But, Chris grabbed her arms, yanking her back down and pulling her arms together behind her back. He bounced Candace up and down on his lap, shaking her side to side like a rag doll. Chris leaned forward and licked her breasts. Candace shivered but pulled back. *No. No. No.*

Chris clasped her wrists tightly, skillfully securing them together in one of his huge hands and freeing up his other. Candace struggled to control the movement of her body against his strength. But, Chris grabbed tight to her waist and pulled her bouncing bosom into his face and hurriedly sucked one breast into his mouth.

Fuck no. Candace winched at the gentle tingle. "Stop," she spoke much more lightly than before, yet still tugging away from his touch. She trembled at the wet suckle and subtle laps of his tongue. Chris pursed his lips, drawing out her erect nipple with a kiss. Candace's body instinctively twisted as she clenched the pussy muscles pressed against his lap.

Chris released her wrists, moving with quick calculation and still sucking at her breasts, he raised his backside off the floor with Candace on top of him. Candace pressed her newly freed hands against his chest and hurriedly tried to stand. Chris clutched her waist, easing her back down on top of his anxiously erect manhood.

"Fuck," Candace yelped in pain. Still, she could not fight the sensation of him slipping inside of her and she widened her legs to straddle him.

"You rode for me. Now ride this dick." Chris pumped up into her. "This your dick, baby. You hear me?"

Candace's knees dug into the floor as she wrestled to fight her own enjoyment. She stared down into his penetrating green eyes. Chris stared back, a slick grin lifting his top lip. Candace wanted to run, she wanted to hate him, but the pleasure was undeniable and before long Candace was giving her body into his deep strokes. Grinding her waist up and down against his lap, she pulled up on her toes and bounced against his thrusts. *Oh, goddamn.*

Chris cupped her under her backside, keeping her elevated so he could watch his shiny wet skin slide in and out of her. "This my pussy, C? This shit belongs to me?" he asked, squeezing her cheeks.

Candace was silent, pulling her bottom lip into her mouth. *No. No, fuckin' way. He don't own shit!*

Chris pumped harder into her. Candace groaned at the pressure filling her inside. She was not his; she did not want to be. *But, God, he feels so good.*

"Is this my shit, C?" he asked again, slowing his strokes and pulling Candace down onto his lap.

Candace let no words escape her mouth. She looked away.

Chris chuckled lightly, then suddenly flipped her over onto her back with little effort and spread her legs wide. Holding her thighs open and apart with his hands, he dove face-first into her lap, sucking and spitting all over her swollen clit.

Candace let loose the groan that had been growing in her belly, her legs flailing madly in the air. Chris grunted a sound of pleasure at her response, which seemed to encourage more sliding of his long fingers in her wet opening. The twirl of his fingertips, combined with the titillating pressure of his tongue and fat lips on her fat lips, threw Candace's body into convulsions. *No. No. No. No.*

"Yes! Yes! Yes!" She bucked her womanhood against his face as her eruption ran over him, soaking his beard until it was soggy and shiny when he came up for air.

Chris stopped only to ease himself on top of her and enter her again. He lifted her legs, bringing her knees together in the air and pressing them back toward her face and asked again, "Whose the fuck is it?"

Candace trembled, peering up at his face between her ankles. He pressed in deep until she screamed, "Your pussy, baby! It's your fuckin' pussy!" She spat the words out quickly and was instantly angry with herself.

She screamed and thrust Chris off her, making a mad dash for the bathroom, but he was right on her heels. He burst in before Candace could close the door, grabbing her by her hair from behind. Chris shoved her face against the mirror, lifting her right leg up onto the sink and digging back into her. Candace begged for mercy. "Oh, God. Please. Stooooppp!!!"

"Fuck, no. Why you runnin' from me?"

"'Cause…yoooouuuuu…ain't…shit….," she stammered. She could feel Chris's sweat dripping down onto her back as he clutched her waist, pounding deeper and harder. Candace screamed and her knees buckled.

Chris caught her under her stomach, never sliding out. "You okay, baby?" he asked, softly kissing the back of her neck.

"Noooooo. Get off me," she hissed. "You fulla… shit and I doooon't want you here."

"You don't want me?" Chris asked, pumping slightly.

"Fuck no! Stop!"

"Why should I stop?" He pushed far into her. He filled her up and Candace froze, fighting every burning urge to move on his dick.

"Because you're trying to fuck me stupid, Chris! And I'm not the fuck dumb!" she said through clenched jaw.

Chris slowly backed out of her and Candace hurriedly spun around to see the hurt look on his face.

"Not at all, baby," he said, wiping the sweat from her brow. "I'm just trying to prove how much I care for you."

"By lying to me, then fucking me like you love me?"

"I do love you," he said, staring her squarely in the face.

Candace jumped back at his words. Chris looked at her with serious focused eyes.

"I don't wanna just fuck you," Chris spoke finally. "You'll see." He grabbed her arm and pulled her into his chest. He kissed Candace in her mouth until she kissed back. "I wanna give you all I got, Candace. I promise you that. But right now, a nigga just got outta jail and your pussy is all I been thinking about."

Candace sighed her defeat giving Chris a slight smile.

With that, Chris reached to his left and turned on the shower. He removed the remainder of his clothes quickly, before ushering her into the tub. He stepped in behind her, carefully lowering himself to his knees.

"What are you doing?" Candace looked down at him strangely as the shower water flooded over her scalp, trickled across her face and down her body.

Kneeling in front of her, Chris tapped her left foot. "Step up," he instructed, catching Candace's foot and setting it up on the side of the tub. Then he tapped the other foot and led it up to the small concave dip in the shower wall. Candace's long body rose above the tub so high her head overlooked the shower curtain rod.

Chris scooted beneath her spread legs, reaching his arms around her thighs and bringing her pussy right down on top of his face.

"Ohmigod." Candace quivered at the sensation of his mouth. She held on tightly to the shower curtain rod, the flow of the water and the flick of Chris's tongue overtaking her senses. "Ohmigod, baby." She reached for the back of his head.

Chris's face was soaked from her juices and the water cascading down onto him. He moaned.

Candace's knees wobbled, trembling as the orgasms surged through her body.

"Damn, baby. You taste so good." Chris stood to his feet, grabbing Candace's wet body and lifting her out of the tub. Candace wrapped her limbs around him, kissing his full wet lips as he carried her into the bedroom.

When Candace woke up, it was almost one a.m. and Chris was sitting at the foot of her bed smoking a blunt. He passed it to her as she sat up.

"Hey, babe," he said, smiling.

"Hey," she replied, sitting up and receiving the L.

"You sleep good?"

"Yeah. I think." Candace yawned. "I don't even remember falling asleep."

"You tapped out," Chris said, laughing. "Went down like Frazier."

Candace laughed, shaking her head. "No, I didn't."

"Yeah, you did."

Candace yawned, looking at Chris sitting comfortably on her bed. "So, what's your plans?"

"You know that jail shit and this shit with Shif got me fucked up, babe, and I need to get back on my feet."

"Yeah, I bet. You owe me some money."

"I know I do, baby. I got you. I promise you that. I'm on that nigga ass, believe that! But I need a small favor."

Candace's lips curled. "What now?"

"I need to hold your car."

"What? Why? What happened to your car?"

"I totaled it running from the cops."

"Are you gonna tell me why the fuck you got locked up?"

"I'll fill you in on all the specifics later, babe. But I need to make a run real quick. I gotta check up on some things and see if I can't get my hands on my fuckin' cousin. Okay?"

Candace huffed.

"Look," Chris scooted closer to her on the bed, "I know you held me down while I was booked, babe, and I appreciate it. Don't think I don't. But I really just need to go check on some money. I can't do this broke shit, baby."

"I feel you. You definitely need to get back on your feet."

"Yeah?" Chris said seriously.

"Hell, yeah. What good are you to me broke?" Candace laughed, standing and grabbing her keys from the dresser.

"That's how you feel?" he asked, his grin wide and bright, his teeth clean and perfectly aligned.

"Just be safe," Candace said, tossing Chris the keys before climbing back under her covers.

"Gotchu." Chris was out the door before her eyes closed.

Chris was back by daybreak. Candace was sitting at her kitchen table balancing her checkbook when he walked through the door. She slid the ledger into her purse, standing to greet him.

"Well, good morning."

"Good morning," Chris replied. "You miss me?"

"Maybe. How was your night? Productive?"

"You could say that. I got some good things working for me."

"Did you find your cousin?" Candace asked, nearing the sink.

"Not yet," Chris said, walking up behind her. "But I'mma need your help with something, though."

"Something like what?" Candace asked, the pitch in her voice raising.

"Do you think you could front me like another stack? I'mma make it move quick, trust me."

"What, Chris? No, fuck no. I'm already out three grand fuckin' wit' you."

"I gotchu, baby. I told you. But, I don't have too many choices right now. I can either throw some guns in some niggas' faces or I can flip some shit real quick. My man got a real hot block on smash down North. I promise to get your bread back to you asap."

"Chris?" she whined.

"What, babe? This block doin' the pussy. If you let me get my hands on like a stack, I can bring you back fifteen to two in two days. That's at least five on top of what you giving me. Until I find Shif, I gotta do something, babe."

Candace was silent. *Do you know what the fuck I had to do to get this money?* Chris stepped closer to her, rubbing his hand along her back.

"Babe, I know you been holding me down, I love that shit. I love that you love me, even though you don't wanna say it."

Candace rolled her eyes. She didn't want to believe he loved her, let alone confess her love for him. Chris started to kiss her passionately—wide, wet, open-mouth kisses. He engulfed her. Chris brought her body closer. Within minutes, she was beneath the covers locked in sweet sweaty embraces.

While Chris slept, Candace crept over to her dresser, retrieving the money left over from Vegas buried far in the upper-right corner of her panty drawer. She counted out a thousand.

When Chris turned over in her bed, there was a plate of bacon and eggs on the nightstand beside a tall glass of orange juice and ten one-hundred-dollar bills.

"Thanks, baby." He stood and kissed her.

"Just do the right thing with it," she said, rubbing his bare chest.

Chris stood to leave after dressing quickly, lacing his Nikes and shoving the bills in his pockets. He paused for a moment as he headed out. "Babe," he started.

Candace was a few steps behind walking him to the door. She raised her head. "Hmm?"

"So...you just got this kinda cash just lyin' 'round ya crib?"

Candace swallowed hard, composing the expression of her face.

"Don't be askin' me questions," she responded, playfully placing her hands on her hips, rolling her neck and poking out her lips.

Chris chuckled. "You funny. Butchu right. I ain't goin' ask you nothin' 'bout ya bread."

"Thank you," Candace said firmly.

"Cool. I'm not goin' be all day. I promise. The sooner I leave, the sooner I get back here and spend time with you. Do some studying and let me get outta here, babe. Cool?"

"Cool. Just be careful," she warned.

"I will, baby." Chris kissed her again, walking out the door.

Candace was in the kitchen frying chicken later that evening when her phone rang.

"Hey, baby. What you doin'?"

"Cooking."

"What you cooking?"

"Some chicken."

"Yum. Sounds good."

"Yup. What time you be back?" Candace asked, leaning against the refrigerator. "What time you be back?" Candace asked again after she'd eaten without him. "What time you be back?" she asked a third time long after the streetlights on her block had come on.

"Soon as I finish up out here, babe, I'm coming straight to you."

"All right. Just come on," Candace insisted.

"I coming, babe."

Candace called Chris again after a few more hours passed.

"Where are you?" Candace asked, the irritation apparent in her voice.

"On my way to you, babe. Soon as I'm done."

"Well, what time is that goin' be, Chris?"

"Babe, please. Give me some time to take care of a few things and I will be there."

It was four a.m. when Candace awoke and Chris was still not back. She dialed his number again. This time Chris didn't answer. Candace waited and tried him back several minutes later. Again, no answer. The sun rose on Thursday and Candace was still home alone with no pickup or return call from Chris.

"Chris, really? I need you to call me back ASAP! Like, where are you?" she screamed into his answering machine. "Chris! I swear to God you need to call me! Now!"

An hour later, her phone rang. She answered angrily, "Where the fuck are you?"

"I'm outside, coming in now."

Candace ran to the door, yanking it open and snatching the keys out of Chris's hand.

"What the fuck? I been blowing you up. Where the fuck you been and why you ain't answer my calls?"

Chris pulled off his Phillies fitted cap, tossing it onto the sofa. Candace noticed his fresh cut and change of clothes. "Ma, I told you I had a lot to do."

"So you couldn't pick up the phone?"

"No, not every time you call I can't," he responded sternly.

"What?" Candace asked in shock. "If you can't pick up when I call, then you don't need to drive my car."

"Babe," Chris said, placing his hands on her shoulders. "It's been a long fuckin' day. I been on the move for hours. Can a nigga take a nap and I promise you we can talk about this shit as soon as I get up. I'll take you out to breakfast and everything. Will you still have an attitude with me then?"

Candace crossed her arms over her breasts. "Probably."

"Please, lemme just close my eyes a little," Chris begged.

Candace was cross, but Chris massaged his strong fingers into her tense shoulders and began leading her into the bedroom. He kicked off his shoes, stripped to his boxers and climbed into her bed. Candace stood watching him with her lips tight. She didn't say a word.

Chris responded to her silence. "I just been going through a lot, baby. I been out hand-to-hand grindin' it. Don't be mad at me. Give me a minute to recoup and I promise you can have my undivided."

"I don't want your undivided, Chris."

Chris sat up. "Well, what do you want?"

"I don't know, Chris," Candace said sincerely, sitting beside him on the bed. "What do you want from *me?*"

"I just want to sleep, baby. Can I crash for a minute? I'm so tired."

Candace sucked her teeth. "I guess so, but don't get too comfortable."

Chris was asleep before she finished her sentence.

Chris slept only a few hours before finally coming out into the living room where Candace was lying across the couch watching *Law & Order*. She studied him as he sat down beside her, easing off her slippers and rubbing her feet. Her head rolled back and she bit down on her bottom lip, closing her eyes.

"You hungry?" he asked, looking up her leg.

"Yeah."

"Come on, let's go to the diner. I want some waffles."

"Sure," Candace replied, standing. She dressed quickly in blue cotton shorts and a white-and-blue-striped tee and met Chris at the door. They drove down Germantown Avenue to the Trolley Car Diner for breakfast.

"I'm so tired," Chris said, stretching outside the car in the parking lot.

"I bet."

"It's a lot goin' on right now. But I can handle it, you know. I'm tryna get my hands on this bread so I can take care of my lady." Chris slapped her butt.

"Ya lady, huh?"

"Yeah, you my lady. What, I'm not your man?"

"Nope," Candace replied, smiling and strolling beside him.

Chris stopped walking. "So, what am I then?"

"My friend."

"Oh, so you fuck all your friends raw dog and let them stay at ya crib and push ya wheel?"

"Hell, no," Candace snapped.

"So then, I gots to be much more than a friend."

"I guess so." Candace shrugged.

"You guess so, huh? Wow! Well, maybe we should leave." Chris started to walk back toward the car.

"What?" Candace was surprised but couldn't make out whether he was joking or not. She stood still for a moment, until Chris got close enough to the car she could see her lights flicker as he unlocked the doors. Moving quickly, Candace followed in his direction.

"What are you doing?" she yelled once she was in earshot.

"I'm leaving."

"Why?"

"I told you, C. I don't play games with this. If you my girl, say you my girl. Don't spit that friend shit to me."

"Are you kiddin' me? You don't know if that's really what you want." She stepped into his face.

"So what you thought I was just spending all my time with you 'cause I like how ya ass sit up in them shorts?"

"I don't know what you want, Chris."

"Yeah, you do. You know exactly what I want."

"You tryna be my man, Chris?"

"You know that!"

"You never asked."

"I been askin'!" Chris huffed. "What, you want an official request?"

"If you want an official title?"

Chris looked Candace up and down. "You trying to be my lady, C?" he asked.

"Nah, that ain't it."

"What! What you want from me? Some ole sappy shit, huh?"

"Yup. And why not, nigga? You in my crib every day."

"And you suck my dick every day."

"And you eat this pussy every day."

"Yup, I tears it up." He smiled. "And that's all the more reason for you to know that you my girl."

Candace rolled her eyes. "I don't belong to anyone."

"Yeah right. C, will you be my lady?"

The question rolled out of his mouth quickly and without pause. Candace smiled. "Sure. Why not?" She shrugged playfully.

Chris grabbed her and pulled him into her. He kissed her with full sloppy wet lips, slipping his tongue inside her anxious mouth. He rubbed his hands along the curve of her backside, giving it a final hard slap before releasing her.

"Come on. Let's go get some waffles. I'm hungry," he said, entangling his fingers in hers and leading Candace back toward the diner.

CHAPTER 27

Thursday morning Marci strolled casually into D's Designs with her head high and back sore from Tommy's passionate bites. Flipping her long, dark weave over her shoulder, she pranced proudly toward her station.

"Damn, girl. Them couple days off did you good, huh?" Jerel asked, swinging her curling irons in front of her.

Marci giggled. "Girl, if you only knew."

"Um huh," Quinita chimed in. "You look...relaxed."

Marci, Quinita and Jerel erupted in laughter.

"All I'mma say is, me and my boo had a real nice looooong weekend," Marci hooted, craning her neck.

"I bet." said Jerel, smiling.

Marci looked around the salon, noticing there were only a few clients.

"It's dead in here today," she said, checking her phone for the time. "Donna not here yet?"

"No. I guess she comin' late 'cause Cherise said she cancelled all her appointments for the morning," Quinita answered, tidying up her station.

Fat bitch. Marci shoved her pocketbook under her counter. *Always a day late and a dollar short. Don't even know how to run a business. That's why I'm fucking your husband. Nananana...*

Marci turned to organize her station just as Lateesh stepped through the salon door silent and grinning, staring in her direction.

Marci's top lip curled. *Bitch.* She rolled her eyes.

Lateesh snarled.

"Fuck is her problem?" Marci grumbled to Jerel.

"Whoever knows?" Jerel replied with a shrug, still primping away at the hair in front of her.

Just as Marci parted her lips to speak, the salon door burst open and Donna stormed inside. Marci's eyes folded curiously as Donna quickly rushed in her direction. Before Marci could say a word, or move out of the way, Donna was on her. A closed fist smashed into her mouth. Marci stumbled backward, toppling her chair, and Donna jumped at her.

"You stupid bitch! You fucking my husband!" Donna screamed.

"Ohmigod," Jerel hollered and shoved the woman out of her chair.

"Yeah!" Lateesha jumped up and down. "Whip that lil' disrespectful bitch ass!"

"What the fuck?" Quinita stepped back.

Marci stumbled back hollering in pain but quickly gained her composure and rushed at Donna with fists flying. Donna landed another wallop of a punch and sent Marci reeling backward again. Donna moved in, pounding on Marci's face like a jackhammer. Suddenly, Jerel leapt in wrestling Donna back.

Marci struggled to stand, spitting the blood from her lips. She cocked back and shot a huge wad of red mucus and saliva in Donna's face.

"AAHHHHHH!!!!" Donna roared, wiping the red spatter from her cheek. "Fuckin' whore!" Donna lunged again, shoving Jerel to the side and grabbing Marci by the top of her hair and hurling her to the floor.

"Get the fuck off me, you fat nasty bitch!" Marci wriggled to free herself from Donna's grasp and grab hold to her own weave.

"Fuck you, Donna. Yeah, I been fuckin' Tommy and he 'bout to leave your dumb ass, too. Now. How you like that?"

"How you like that?" Donna replied, jerking Marci's head to one side and grabbing a pair of scissors from her station.

Marci watched as her eighteen-inch dark Brazilian weave fell to the floor "OHMIFUCKINGOD!!!!" Marci wailed, seeing the gleaming shears in Donna's hand.

Clip. Another smooth chunk of hair hit the floor. Marci screamed and leapt up, punching Donna in the mouth. Donna didn't budge.

"Get off me!" she cried. But Donna clutched her hair tighter.

"Oh, man. Let her go, Donna," Quinita begged from a few feet away.

Marci could see Jerel close behind Donna with one hand over her mouth.

"Get this bitch off me!" Marci screamed. But, no one moved a muscle except for Lateesh who pursed her lips, shaking her head.

"You just a disrespectful little hoe, huh? Bouncing around this fucking shop like you run this mothafucka and you got the audacity to come at my fuckin' HUSBAND!"

Whap! Another punch to the face. Marci's head jerked back and she began sliding down against the wall.

"Bitch, is you crazy?" Donna continued, yanking her back up to her feet by what was left of her hair.

Marci wailed at Donna, scratching and clawing at her arms and face. "Get off me, you stupid fat bitch!"

Jerel rushed in again, struggling, but successfully pulling Donna back.

"Fuck you, Donna." Marci screeched once she received her freedom. "Tommy's my man now. That's MY dick and it's damn good, too. Ask him. He loves me and he loves being face-first in the pussy. Bustin' raw in my shit and everything!"

Marci's words seemed to enrage Donna even further and she swelled almost twice her size and effortlessly tossed Jerel off her again. Donna grabbed the tattered ball of hair on top of Marci's head and starting dragging her toward the door—Marci kicking and screaming along the way. Lateesh hurriedly opened the door in front of them and Donna tossed Marci on her ass out onto Sixty-ninth Street.

"Stay the fuck out, bitch!" Donna slammed the door.

"Ohmigod!" Marci jumped up quickly, scurrying to compose herself. "No the fuck…" She was marching back toward the salon door when it suddenly opened and her purse flew out, slapping her in the face and spilling all of her personal effects out onto the street. Marci, scrambling to catch her makeup from rolling down the steep hill, caught a glimpse of herself in a store window and screamed again.

"Fuckin' bitch!" She quickly collected her things and took off running up the street to her car. After turning onto the small side block where she usually parked, Marci noticed her Altima sitting low. "Nooooo….Nooooo."

She squatted beside her vehicle, inspecting the damage—all four tires had been split wide open. "MOTHAFUCKA!!!!"

Marci wanted to go back and fight. She wanted to attack Donna and rip her hair out, but her shoulders slumped and her rapid breathing gave way to tears. Despairingly, she climbed inside her car screaming and crying. She tried Tommy, but there was no answer.

She was in her car for almost a half hour before she decided to call her sister.

"Slow down. Slow down… What the hell… And you're where?" Candace asked again after Marci had taken a deep breath and repeated herself. "I'm just coming from getting something to eat. I'll be there in fifteen. Stay put," Candace instructed.

As expected, Candace pulled alongside Marci in fifteen minutes.

"Always on point," Marci said, hopping out of her car and into her sister's.

"What? What the fuck?" Candace cringed, looking at Marci's busted lip and tattered hair.

"I wanna go back in there, C! I owe that big bitch a beat down. You comin' with me, right?"

"Fuck no, Marcine! I came to get your ass, not fight the bitch whose husband you fuckin'."

"Damn, so you just goin' let your little sister catch one like that? What kinda big sister are you?"

"The kind that told you to leave that married mothafucka alone."

Marci sucked her teeth. "Whateva. I thought you was goin' come up here and help me fuck her up."

"I am helping you. I'm taking your black ass home so you can get cleaned up."

"Fuck no, Candace! I just can't let her get away with this shit!" Marci pulled at what was left of her weave. "Look at my fuckin' hair! That crazy bitch tried to kill me."

"Well, what do you want to do then?" Candace said, staring into her sister's wild eyes.

"Go 'round back," Marci instructed.

Candace complied, turning her car into a small lot used by some of the business owners along the long strip of stores on Sixty-ninth Street.

Marci spotted Donna's Escalade. She opened Candace's glove box, popped the trunk and jumped out of the car. Candace could see Marci gripping the tire iron and running toward a big green SUV. Marci ran behind the shop, peering over her shoulder as she ducked between the few cars parked out back. With four quick hate-filled thrusts, she busted out the back and side windows.

"Fuck," she gasped, hopping back into the car with Candace. "Fuckin' truck's too big. I couldn't get on top to get at the front window."

Candace burst out laughing hysterically and pulled off into traffic.

"What? What's so funny?"

Candace shook her head. "You need serious help, Marcine."

Marci chuckled lightly through her pain and over her tears. "I don't need no help. I'm good. I just need to talk to Tommy, is all, and we can get this shit over with."

"Over with? Whatchu mean?" Candace asked, stealing a glance to her right.

"That shit between them is over. I know it is, now. He ain't got no choice but to make a move, now. You feel me? Now, we can be together for real. No more hiding."

Candace threw her hands up. "Ohimigod, girl! You're fuckin' nuts! Have you even talked to him?"

"I called him like eight times. And he ain't call me back yet. It's going right to voicemail."

"Maybe Donna whipped his ass, too." Candace chuckled.

"Shut the fuck up, Candace. This shit is serious. I'mma kill that bitch. I can't believe her big ass jumped on me like that. I should press fuckin' charges."

"Are you serious?"

"Damn right, I'm serious. That fat bitch assaulted me."

"You're fucking her husband. I'da whooped your ass, too."

Marci sucked her teeth, folding her arms across her breasts.

"You know you were wrong," Candace continued.

"Well, if I was so wrong, why you cool wit' me bustin' out her windows, then?"

"Right or wrong, you're still my sister. And nobody gets to fuck with you but me." She squeezed Marci's knee.

Marci winced in pain. "I can't even believe this," she whined, pulling at her hair.

"Believe it, sweety. That's what happens when you mess with married men."

"I know you ain't talkin' 'Miss What-Happens-in-Vegas-stays-in-Vegas.'"

"Whateva." Candace's stomach knotted.

Marci laughed. "Still won't tell me shit. Huh? You musta been a real slut. Let me find out Miss Prissy was cutting up."

Candace tugged on her sister's tattered weave. "We ain't goin' talk about nothin' getting cut, okay?"

"Get off me. I know you was all kinds of naughty, so don't be judging me," Marci hissed.

"My lips are sealed," Candace responded coolly.

"I betcha legs wasn't."

They both burst out laughing.

"Shut the hell up. That's why you gotcha ass whooped."

"Whateva, C. I know I need to talk to Tommy ASAP. And he still not answering his phone."

"Give it a minute. You'll talk to him," Candace said, keeping her eyes on the road.

Marci pouted her lips, looking down at the phone in her hand. She tried Tommy again. Still no answer. "I can't believe this shit."

"You want me to take you to the hospital or something?" Candace asked suddenly.

"No, I'm good. I just need to get some ice for my face and my hand. I can't fuckin' believe that fat bitch jumped on me."

"I can. I woulda jumped on you, too. But what you need to be trying to figure out how she knew you was screwing her man."

"I don't know. I don't even care. Why is he not calling me back?" Marci shook the phone.

"You want me to take you home?" Candace asked.

"Fuck no! Just take me to your house. I need to clean up and figure out how to get my fucking car."

"Um… you sure? Ain't ya mom at work?" Candace stammered. "I can just take you home so you can clean up and take it easy for a minute."

"Damn bitch," Marci yelled, flailing her arms wildly in the air. "I just had a bitch jump on my fuckin' forehead and I can't come over your fuckin' house. What the fuck is that all about?"

"No, Marci… I just…um…"

"What? You hidin' a nigga or something?"

Candace kept her eyes on the road, silently dodging Marci's swollen-lipped inquisition.

"You are!" Marci screamed, then grabbed her face in pain and screamed again, "Bitch, you are! Who? Chris?"

Candace nodded.

"Ohmigod! Where the fuck did he come from? Was he really locked up? Ohmigod! You wasn't goin' tell me? What, he stayin' with you now?"

"Yeah, he was locked up. How 'bout his fuckin' cousin never put the money up for his bail…"

"What!?!" Marci jumped back. "That's crazy!"

"Yeah. So, he just crashing for a minute, trying to get back on his feet and get my money back."

"Wow. So that's your man now?"

"No."

"Whateva." Marci twisted her wrists in the air. "Man still at his uncle's?"

"Yup."

"That's why you cuttin' the fuck up. Your mommy responsibilities been put on freeze for the summer and you don't know how to act. First ,Vegas, then live-in dick. Do Chris know you went to Vegas?"

"No and don't say nothing," Candace snapped.

"Ooohh, you must've really been a whore."

"Shut up. He just don't need to know about my trip. You know, 'what happens in Vegas...'"

"Stays in Vegas," they sang together.

Candace forced a grin as she pulled onto her narrow block and parked in front of her door. She opened the door for Marci before glancing down at her phone and noticing her voicemail icon lit.

I don't remember having a missed call, she thought, bringing the phone to her ear and closing the door behind her. Candace watched Marci give a quick wave to Chris who was on the couch and disappear down the hall to the bathroom. Candace blew Chris a kiss as he stood from the couch to greet her. Simultaneously, Chrissy's voice came in loud and clear in her ear.

Chrissy?!?! She stopped in her tracks.

"Well, hello, darling. I'd sure appreciate it if you give me a call as soon as you can. I've got quite a bit to tell you. (giggle) Girl, I got my hands on that little Allyson and the child sang like a canary. Wait 'til you hear what else! But I ain't sharing it with an answering machine. So, call me back, darling. You're gonna flip!"

"Ohmigod!" Candace almost dropped her phone, rushing to her bedroom, leaving Chris standing in the hall. As she pushed her door open, Candace's phone rang in her hand. It was her job.

"Hello," Candace answered, stepping into her room.

"Hello, Candace. It's Denise."

"Hi, Denise."

"Hi, Candace. Um, well, I'm calling you because we've concluded the investigation concerning the email sent from your computer and I'd like for you to come in to the office first thing in the morning."

"Tomorrow morning?"

"Yes, Candace. And, first, please let me say that I apologize for not believing you."

Candace's heart leapt.

"It seems that you were right about someone misusing your computer," Denise continued. "Are you available to come in to-morrow to discuss this matter in person?"

"Yes. Yes, I am," Candace said, grinning.

"Good. I'll see you, say, nine a.m.?"

"Yes. Nine, it is."

"Good. See you then." *Click*.

Candace balanced herself in her bedroom doorway, collecting her thoughts. Slowly, she approached the bathroom and pushed it open to find Marci clipping and trimming her once long, luxurious mane into a sharp-edged bob.

"I think I just got my fuckin' job back," Candace announced.

"Well, at least one of us got good news." Marci dabbed her swollen eye with a wet rag.

"I need to call Chrissy," Candace said, ignoring her sister's self-pitying remark.

Candace headed back to her room and dialed the number to the building.

"Good afternoon. Wyncote Rehabilitation Center. How may I direct your call?"

"Danielle? It's Candace. I got a missed call from Chrissy. Can you put me through to her?"

"Ohmigoodness, Candace." Danielle's voice was a squeaky excited whisper. "It's crazy in here. Chrissy had Allyson cornered in the breakroom because she found out Allyson helped set you up and

Denise fired Jennifer and Allyson." The words rushed together in one breath.

"What?!?!?" Candace gasped. "Where's Chrissy?"

"Hold on, I'll page her."

"Ohmigod," Candace squealed while on hold. She stretched her neck. Marci had come out of the bathroom and Candace could hear her and Chris talking in the living room.

"This is Chrissy," the familiar Southern twang pronounced.

"Chrissy, it's me, Candace. What the hell's going on?"

"I was hoping this would be you, darling."

"Chrissy, what the hell is going on?" Candace repeated.

"You should answer your phone when I call you, Miss Candace," Chrissy said with a slight giggle. "I can't talk to you right now 'cause I got a family waiting on me to give a tour, seeing as how we no longer have an admissions coordinator."

"What the fuck?" Candace hollered.

"Everything all right, babe?" Chris called from down the hall. Candace paid him no mind, focusing all her attention on her conversation over the phone.

"You heard what I said, darling." Chrissy laughed. "Now, I'mma have to call you back—and Candace, just know, I got ya back, girl."

Candace's heart skipped two beats. She hurriedly rushed back into the living room to Marci and Chris in mid-conversation.

"Damn, all your tires busted?" Chris asked, sitting down on one edge of the couch.

"Yeah," Marci replied from the other edge.

"You goin' have to get that shit towed."

Marci sucked teeth. "Then what?"

"I can get you some used tires. Like twenty-five a pop. You lookin' at a bean fifty for the tow from Sixty-ninth Street."

Candace jumped in. "I got my fuckin' job back!"

"Yeah, babe?" Chris smiled, walking over to her.

"Fuckin' unreal! Denise wants to see me tomorrow. Turns out Allyson had something to do with this whole thing, and her and Jennifer got fired."

"DAMN!!!" Marci howled. "That's crazy. How they find that out?"

"I 'on't know. Something to do with Chrissy!" Candace squealed. "Yo, that's my girl! Danielle said she had that girl hemmed up in the breakroom."

"Now that's gangsta." Chris chuckled.

"Good, I'm glad you got your job back, 'cause I don't have any money to get my car towed right now. Plus, I can't afford new tires."

Candace's jaw dropped.

"Can I borrow two hundred fifty?" Marci asked, tilting her head and batting her eyes at Candace.

"You spoiled little bitch. You betta be trying to get some fuckin' money from Tommy. This shit is his fault."

"He ain't been calling me back," Marci whined. "I keep trying him. You think he's okay?"

"No. I think Donna beat the shit outta him, too."

Chris laughed. "This Donna must be a boss bitch. She tearing y'all up like that."

"She ain't shit," Marci protested. "Just a fat bitter bitch, mad 'cause her man is leaving her for me."

Candace rolled her eyes. "Whateva. Just tell that nigga, Tommy, I want my money back." Candace retreated into her room while Marci iced her eye and Chris resumed his position in front of the television. When Candace returned, she brought back the money for her sister. Candace looked down at Chris on the couch. "You can handle this for her, right?"

Chris stood up. "If you need me to, I got it."

Chris disappeared into the bedroom and made a few calls. They were to meet the tow truck by her car in an hour. Later, Marci's ride was on its way to the shop and had new tires by two p.m.

Marci was silent as Candace drove her to pick up her car.

"You all right over there, Mars?" Candace asked, peeking at her.

"Just thinking," Marci replied, her head low.

"About?"

Marci was again silent, looking down at her phone.

Candace shook her head. She knew her sister all too well. She sighed deeply before she spoke. "It'll be all right, Mars. I promise," Candace said sweetly. "You'll talk to him."

"When, C? I need to talk to him, now. I gotta see him."

"Don't go over that girl's house, Marcine," Candace warned.

Marci sucked her teeth. "I just need to talk to him."

"About what? Damn! Didn't you just get your ass whooped by his wife. What the fuck else you want?"

"I want love, Candace! Damn! Everybody want the same thing. I just wanna be in love. And I love Tommy! Damn!"

Candace was silent, staring intently at the road. After a moment, she cleared her throat.

"Fuck love!" She slammed her fist on the steering wheel. "Love gotchu lookin' stupid, all beat the fuck up! Chasin' somebody else's husband around. What the fuck is love? What? A feeling? Your horny-ass emotions you can't control. Love gotchu trippin'. Shit. You want love so fuckin' bad? Wait for your own shit! Then when you got a dude that's all about you and you can be all about him like your psycho ass wanna be, then you can be in love. But until then, stop trippin' off a nigga that don't belong to you."

Marci folded her arms like a scolded child, staring quietly out the window.

Candace pulled over into a small tire garage on Haverford Avenue. They spotted Marci's Altima sitting up pretty with four new wheels.

Marci smiled hopping out of the car. She stopped after a step, turning around and squatting at the window of Candace's car. "I know whatchu sayin', C. I do want my own."

Candace smiled at her little sister. "Good. Now leave that married man alone."

"I am, C. Thanks again." Marci nodded, standing and walking toward the mechanic shop. She waited until Candace had pulled off before adding, "But I gotta figure out what the fuck is going on with Tommy first."

Marci paid the young mechanic and climbed in her car. Patting the steering column, she smirked. *Glad to have you back, baby*. Marci knew precisely where she wanted her faithful vehicle to take her. She started it up and headed toward Mt. Airy in search of some answers.

When Marci spotted Tommy's blue Charger, she parked her car around the corner, marched right up to the front door and started banging. Marci leapt back at the sight of Tommy's face when he swung the door open. His lip was split right down the middle and there was a protruding lump with black and purple discoloration on his forehead.

Marci let out a sick wail. "Baby, what happened to you?"

Tommy took one look at Marci and reeled at her busted lip and swollen eye. "What the fuck are you doin' here?"

"What?" Marci felt the thick knot of tears rising up her chest. "What do you mean 'what am I doing here'? I came here to see you, Tommy. And show you this." She pointed to her puffy face. "Your fuckin' wife attacked me and you wanna know what I'm doin' here? What the fuck do you think I'm doing here? What happened, Tommy? What did you say to her?"

"Baby, I am so sorry," he replied, reluctantly stepping aside and letting her inside.

Marci moved in close to him and began examining his face. She softly stroked his cheek. "What the fuck happened to you?"

Tommy moved Marci's hand from his face. "I came in the house and she was waitin' for me with a fuckin' bat. Broke my phone and everything. That's it, you know. I can't take this shit!" Tommy threw his hands up.

Marci's eyes brightened. "Divorce her. You finally see she ain't no good for you. We can be together. Fuck her."

Tommy grabbed Marci by the shoulders. "I can't do nothin' right now—is you crazy? She got me by the balls. There's a lot involved here."

"Like what, Tommy? She beat the shit outta you and me. You don't love her. You love me, right?"

Tommy dropped his head. "Yeah, baby, but..."

"But what, Tommy?" Marci's head cocked to the side.

"I...I...I..."

"You what, Tommy?" Marci propped her hands up on her hips, standing directly in front of him. "You love me, don't you?"

"Yes, baby," he said, looking up at her but keeping his head low.

"You wanna be with me. Don't you?"

"Yes."

"So what the fuck's the problem? The cat's outta the bag now!"

"I can't leave now, 'cause I got a lotta other shit ridin' on Donna. And you know, she's my wife."

Marci felt a punch in the gut. She looked around her for a second as if somehow Donna has mysteriously entered the room and landed a solid blow to her stomach.

"What? What are you saying?" The tears poured down her battered face.

Tommy hung his head lower. "I'm sayin' that now is not the right time for us."

"What?!?!" Marci choked through her sobs. "What the fuck was all that talk then, Tommy, huh? About you loving me and wanting to be with me? That shit was all fuckin' talk!?!"

"Marci, keep your voice down," Tommy warned, reaching for her.

Marci snatched back. "Why would you lie to me? Why would you pretend like you love me?"

"I do love you," Tommy said with a heavy sigh. "It's just that I can't do the shit you need me to do right now. And it's causing me problems at home."

"What?!?! At home? I thought we were trying to build a home, Tommy? You and me?"

"We were, baby. We still can. But, not right now. I can't."

"But, Tommy…," Marci whined.

Tommy quickly peered out the curtain, then turned back to a sniveling Marci. "Listen, Marci. I can't get caught up in this with you right now. I'm putting a lot of other shit on the line that I can't fuck up. I do love you, baby. I truly do. But I gotta take care of some shit before we can run away together." He paused, checking the curtain again. "I think you should go. I don't know when Donna's gonna be back and I don't want no more drama." Tommy moved closer toward the door.

"Are you fuckin' serious?" Marci's voice snapped out of a whimper into downright outrage. "Are you trying to put me out?"

"Marci, baby, it's not like that…we got kids and…"

"It's not like that? It's not like that? What the fuck is it like then, Tommy? Ya' wife can punch me in the face, slash my fuckin' tires, I can suck ya' dick, but I can't be in your house!" Her voice continued to rise. "You wasn't worried about them fuckin' kids when you was eating my ass out on the kitchen table!"

"Marci, please keep ya voice down. My neighbors." Tommy stepped toward her.

"I don't give a fuck!" Marci pushed Tommy back. Tommy extended his arm to touch her shoulder, but Marci dipped and swung on him. "Fuck you, Tommy! I thought you loved me!"

Tommy attempted to catch her wailing fists, but one slipped through and she landed a jab right on his chin. Tommy froze. His eyes narrowed and his face turned beet red. Marci stared nervously at him.

Suddenly, Tommy grabbed Marci by the neck, hoisting her up on the tips of her toes. "Yo, now you buggin'! Don't put ya fuckin' hands on me, girl! Get the fuck outta my house!"

Marci clawed her nails into his wrists as Tommy opened the door with one hand. Marci's head was spinning as her feet stumbled over the threshold. Tommy pushed her backward, tossing her out onto the steps. Marci fell hard on her hands and scraped her knees.

"MOTHAFUCKA!!!" Marci started screaming madly. TOMMY, I FUCKIN' HATE YOU! YOU AIN'T SHIT!" She jumped from the ground and started kicking the front door.

Tommy hollered from inside, "You crazy-ass bitch! I'mma call the police!"

Marci kicked harder and screamed louder. "AHHHH!!! AAAH-HHHH!!! I HATE CHU!!!" she wailed, bringing her fists down against the door.

"Get the fuck away from my door!"

Marci ran toward the front of the house, collecting rocks from the gravel path as she went. She stood out on the front lawn, screaming and tossing the rocks at the front windows of the house.

"Fuck you, Tommy! You sneaky son of a bitch! And that's why Donna whooped your ass, too!!!"

The small stones did little damage, so Marci threw them down and took her show to the street. As she rushed toward Tommy's Charger yelling and screaming, Marci noticed a few of the neighbors opening their doors.

"I better make this quick since I guess your neighbors 'bout to call the police!" Marci shouted, climbing onto the hood of Tommy's car and jumping up and down like a mad ape. Her feet landed flat and heavy against the blue aluminum, bending it inward with each thud.

"TOMAS EVANS IS AN ASS-EATING BASTARD!" she screamed. Marci jumped and stomped until she was almost out of breath. She slipped down off the car, reserving some wind to make her escape. Marci rounded the corner of Donna's block gasping but with a grin on her sore wet face.

CHAPTER 28

"Oooh, God. Girl, calm down," Candace coached herself as she parked in the front lot of Wyncote Rehabilitation Center. Her stomach fluttered and her hands trembled as she switched off the engine. Taking several deep breaths, she began reapplying her lip-gloss.

"Here we go," she said, pushing the door handle and stepping out of her car, then coolly striding toward the front entrance. She stepped inside the building and headed straight to the Business Office.

Danielle jumped from her desk when Candace came through the door. "Candace! Ohmigod. I'm so happy to see you." Danielle's smile was wide, nearly filling her whole face.

Candace smiled in return. "I'm glad to see you, too."

"It's been crazy in here. First, don't nobody know anything about billing. You've got that. People were in here asking about charges and co-pays and didn't nobody know how to do what. Then, outta nowhere, Chrissy catches Allyson in the breakroom and all hell breaks loose."

Candace leaned over Danielle's desk listening intently. "What? What did you see?"

"I saw Chrissy rush into Denise's office, dragging Allyson by the arm and they were in there for like an hour. Then Denise paged Jennifer and man…oh, man…"

"What!?!?! What happened?"

"All I know is that there was a whole lot of screaming. Jennifer stormed out and Allyson came out—bawling her eyes out—and started cleaning out her desk. She didn't say a word."

Candace let loose a thick heavy laugh. Feeling a weight rise off her shoulders, she smiled. She chuckled just as Denise entered the Business Office.

"Good morning, Candace," Denise said, a pleasant look on her face. "Glad to see you in such a good mood."

"Yes, Denise. There's lot to smile about."

"I see. Well, good. Please come in my office. We need to talk."

Candace stepped quickly. "Certainly."

Candace composed herself and pulled up a chair in front of Denise's desk. Denise walked behind her dark oak workstation and slid into her leather desk chair.

"Candace," Denise began, folding her hands together in front of her. "I'm not certain what you have heard concerning the," Denise paused and gestured with two fingers on each of her raised hands, "let's just say 'excitement' in this building this week, but there is a lot concerning you that I would like to justly clarify."

"Okay," Candace responded, nodding slightly. *Yes, let's clarify all this shit.*

"First, Candace. You were absolutely right about someone hacking into your computer and maliciously sending me that email."

Candace's eyes widened. She wanted to jump up and down and yell, 'Bitch, I told you so.' But she coolly controlled her outburst even though her heart was pounding in rapid successions in her chest.

"I apologize for not believing you, Candace. You have always been a trusted employee and I wavered in my confidence in you. For that, I am truly sorry. But, given the history between you and the guilty party, I had reason to have concern…"

"Guilty party?" Candace jumped in.

Denise nodded. "Yes. Jennifer."

Candace laughed, shaking her head. "I knew it."

"Along with Allyson," Denise continued.

"That I didn't know, and honestly don't understand," Candace stated.

"Well, according to Allyson, Jennifer pretty much blackmailed her to get access to your office. She was scared and made a dumb decision. She didn't have any malice toward you, but I believe Jennifer had her convinced she was going to get her fired."

"Wow," Candace gasped. "Jennifer really? I can't even believe she would do all that just to get to me."

"She saw you as competition."

"Oh my God, I see. And was willing to do anything to get me out of the way."

"Right, Candace. And that is what concerned me at the end of all of this."

Candace stared straight ahead at Denise.

"I mean, ethically," Denise continued, "it's as if Jennifer's moral structure completely crumbled. I could not believe she sunk to such lows just for a promotion. It has me wondering what else she is capable of. I can't have that. It's despicable and people like that can never be trusted."

Candace nodded.

"Again, Candace, I am sorry that I did not trust you. The content of that email...I just couldn't imagine someone coming up with something like that."

"Me either," Candace confessed. "I know that I've let Jennifer get to me in the past, but never would I violate any relationship that you and I have, for her sake."

"I understand, Candace. And I appreciate that and I can appreciate how cool you have remained during this situation, and all of your encounters with Jennifer." Denise laughed. "Even though I know you called her a bitch."

Candace sat up straight. "Denise, I..."

Denise stood, her lips twisted slightly. "She is a bitch. A sneaky conniving brown-nosing little bitch who is going to get what she rightly deserves with the company's pending criminal investigation."

"Whoa!" was all Candace could speak without cursing. "There are criminal charges against Jennifer?"

"Potentially. Computer hacking, email fraud...they're all criminal offenses"

"What about blackmail?" Candace offered, hoping her desire for Jennifer to end up underneath a prison wasn't too obvious. "Is blackmail a criminal offense?"

Denise laughed. "I believe so, if Allyson pursues it."

"Oh, okay." Candace nodded, with a little shrug. "I was just curious."

Denise laughed again. "I see. Well, Candace, as I said, I am so sorry all of this has happened, but I would love to have you back first thing Monday morning, with back pay for your days off, of course. We need you."

Candace smiled. "I'd love to be back."

"Good," Denise said, walking from behind her desk. "And as far as that last seat in the Administrator in Training Program, it's yours."

"Yes!" Candace jumped up and grabbed Denise in a huge hug. Denise smiled genuinely, returning the squeeze.

"Congrats, Candace," Denise said, stepping back, but still smiling. "You are a hardworking young woman and I am confident you will do well."

"Thank you, Denise."

"You're welcome," Denise replied, opening her office door. "Have you talked to Chrissy yet?"

Candace stepped into the doorway. "No, not yet."

"She's upstairs. You should go see here. I'm sure she's got more to fill you in on."

"I'm sure." Candace giggled.

"She's a good friend, Candace. She really had your back through all of this. If it weren't for Chrissy, Allyson wouldn't have come forward."

"Really?" Candace paused for a moment, then cocked her head and looked at her boss sideways. "Denise, what *did* Jennifer have on Allyson? And how did Chrissy find out?"

Denise laughed. "Why not let Chrissy tell you. She deserves that."

Candace chuckled again, stepping out the office door. "Okay."

"Good. See you Monday morning, Candace."

"You got it, Denise. Thanks."

Candace exited Denise's office and all but sprinted around the corner to the elevator. After three quick jabs to the up button, she turned to the stairway, hopping the steps two at a time. She burst into Chrissy's office breathless but grinning.

"Hey, doll!" she shouted.

"Well, hello, darling!" Chrissy smiled hard, exposing all of her white teeth behind her orange lipstick.

"Chrissy, I could kiss you." Candace threw her arms around Chrissy's broad shoulders.

"Kisses are nice but I take cash." Chrissy giggled.

Candace laughed as she sat down across from her. "I bet you would. But I wouldn't even know how much to give you, girl."

"Darling, you don't owe me a thing." Chrissy waved her hand dismissively. "I knew you were innocent and the truth would surely come out. I just helped it along."

"Is that so, huh?" She slapped her hands on her thighs to keep her legs from shaking. "Well, tell me what happened. I'm dying over here."

"Hmm, where should I begin?" Chrissy leaned back in her chair.

"Let's see. I was going down to the breakroom yesterday to warm up my baked lasagna and I see Allyson over there in the corner on her phone. And I say to myself, let me go talk to her since Candace never got the chance and see if she knows how somebody got into your office. As I start walking toward her, I hear her say your name and then something about being so sorry…"

"'Sorry'? Sorry for what?" Candace interjected.

"I don't know, but that's what I was going to find out," Chrissy continued. "So then she turns around and sees me and hurries up off the phone. So, I spoke to her real pleasant-like and made nice conversation. Then I asked her if she knew anything about what happened to you. Of course she played dumb at first, but then I told her that I knew someone had to have access to your office and that I found it so convenient how she so suddenly became sick the day you wanted to talk to her about it and that I was now increasingly curious as to what she was so sorry for." Chrissy shook her head matter-of-factly from side to side, then slapped her knee. "Well, darling, don't you know, the poor little thing's eyes got big as dinner plates. She started lookin' all frantic and nervous and tried to stand up to leave. I slammed my hand right down on that table and I went on to say how it was a sad shame that someone like you who had been so good to her and such a good boss could be in jeopardy of losing her job. She started to get a little teary-eyed and I knew I had her. I told her I knew how Jennifer had always had it out for you and when it all came out, Jennifer was going down big-time and, darling—that child sang like a canary. She spit it all out—told me Jennifer had caught her smoking marijuana in the back of the building with one of the guys from housekeeping and was threatening to tell Denise. She gave Jennifer the keys to get into your office, but Allyson didn't know what that sneaky lil' hussy was up to. Jennifer had the poor dumb girl believing she was going to get a big promotion and take Allyson with her when she got a building of her own."

Candace's mouth dropped. "Are you serious?"

Chrissy nodded. "Yes, darling. It was a mess. So I haul-tailed it to Denise's office with Allyson on my arm and made her confess everything. Denise was pissed. Then she called in Jennifer and, my, oh my, that woman hollered."

"Jennifer?" Candace's brow spiked.

"No. Denise. Jennifer tried to holler. She tried to say something, but Denise wasn't for it and she let her have it. Called the woman trash, said her actions were reprehensible." Chrissy coolly folded her hands together and rested them behind her head. "She fired them both on the spot. Told them to get the hell out of her office and outta her damn building."

"Get outta here!" Candace slapped her leg again.

"Darling, it was too good to miss. I called you right away, but you were too busy having fun on your little vacation to take my calls."

"I guess you could call it a vacation," Candace said, laughing. "I get paid for my week off and I did take a quick trip to Vegas."

"Now see, look at how God works. You thought you lost your job and you got it back plus paid time off."

"Yup and I got the last spot in the AIT program, too."

"Get out!" Chrissy shouted, leaping from her seat. "That's freakin' fantastic, darling!"

"I know, right? It's just a lot. Like, wow, Jennifer really tried to take me out."

"She sure did, darling. But I told you, I've got your back and I know you're too good for that."

"Thanks, Chrissy." Candace smiled, rising from her seat. "But I tell you what, though..."

"What's that?" Chrissy looked up.

Candace proudly placed her hands on her hips. "I must be one bad bitch if someone is willing to risk their job and criminal charges just to knock me out of the running for a job."

Chrissy stood. "Yes, you are, darling. Yes, you are certainly one bad bitch."

As Candace left the building, she couldn't help smiling. She rushed toward her car. She called her mom as she slid behind her steering wheel.

"Yes, Mom. On the spot. Right? I can't believe it. Yes, Mom. Yes…yes, Mom. I know. Okay. Yes, Mom." Candace looked at her phone and laughed. "Yes, Mom. I love you, too."

Next call was to Chris.

"Hey, babe," he answered.

"You still at the crib?"

"Yeah, but I'm 'bout to leave. Why? What's up?"

"No, no. Stay there. I'm on my way."

"Okay. How'd everything go?"

"I said I'm on my way," Candace responded, playfully.

"Okay. I'm here. Bring your ass."

Candace hurried through the door to catch Chris sitting on the edge of her bed tying his Jordans. She rushed toward him, wrestling him back onto the mattress.

"Hey," she said, pouncing on him and sitting herself up on his lap.

Chris laughed, lying back and grasping her waist. "Hey, you. You must have good news."

"Yeah."

Candace spilled it all sitting on top of him. She told Chris about her trusted confidante, Chrissy's detective work, which resulted in the uncovering of Allyson being blackmailed by Jennifer for getting high at the workplace and Denise screaming on Jennifer and Allyson before firing them both.

Candace's head snaked as she accentuated each syllable. "And she threw that bitch out...on...her...ass!" Candace jumped up and did a quick two-step. "Man, I wanted to do a damn tap dance around that building."

Chris's bright eyes gleamed, a huge smile swept over his face. "That's what's up, babe. I'm happy for you. You must really like your job."

"Yup, and I got the promotion I was up for," Candace boasted, her head high. "This AIT program is going to put me right where I need to be."

"That's what's up, babe," Chris said, his smile never slipping. "So, when we start celebrating?"

A sly grin crept across Candace's face as she moved toward him and placed her hands on his lap. She unfastened his belt, creeping downward. His manhood was fully exposed and in her hand by the time she reached her knees.

"I thought we could start now," she said, before wrapping her lips around him.

Chris moaned and reached for her hair, giving it a firm pull and exciting Candace to deep-throat him. She sucked and kissed until he grew firm, then took him as deep as she could without gagging.

"Aww fuck, babe," Chris huffed, stroking her locks. "You do that shit, babe. You like sucking my dick?"

"Um huh," Candace replied, her mouth full. She continued her oral massage until Chris squirmed and he snatched her back by her hair.

"Un unh," he said, shaking his head. "You trying to make me cum. Nah, we can't have that. Come here. Let me taste that pussy."

Candace was naked in seconds and Chris spread her limbs across her neatly made bed sheets.

After a lazy afternoon of lovemaking and ordering in, Candace was still naked hanging off the side of her bed when Chris walked back into the bedroom in his boxers and handed her a glass of something clear. Candace accepted, sitting up and sipping, thinking it was water, but she jumped back at the shockingly bitter taste of vodka.

"I figured you could use a shot of something after that performance you put on," Chris said, laughing at her twisted lips.

Candace threw back the shot. "No, you're the one who stole the show. My ass is goin' be sore for days."

"What a nice lil' ass it is, too," Chris said, slapping her bare backside. "I hate to say goodbye to it, but I got some shit I need to handle tonight, babe. I'mma need to use your car, though."

"How late you gonna be?"

"I don't know," Chris replied, shrugging and sitting down beside her on the bed. He was quiet for a moment, then looked over at Candace, staring deeply in her eyes. "You sick of me yet?"

"Huh?" Candace asked, her eyebrows tilting inward.

"You sick of me all up in your space and driving your car and shit? I mean, it's cool. I understand. Don't no broad want a leech-ass nigga."

"What?" Candace replied with a light laugh. "Not at all. You're not a leech. And, it's been a long time since I've had someone to come home to. I like you being here." She paused, then added, "But I don't like you being in the streets so much."

"Now, don't start that trying to change me shit, C. This is who I am." Chris's back straightened as he stared down at her.

Candace pulled her covers over her bare breasts and spoke matter-of-factly, "I didn't say anything about trying to change you. I just said I didn't like it. Just because I acknowledge it's what you do, don't mean I'm comfortable with it."

"You would be if I was on my square." His eyes softened as the words left his lips.

"What do you mean?"

"I'm not a broke nigga, C. I get to a dollar quick. I'm just fucked up at the moment," Chris explained, his hands moving emphatically in front of him.

"I know." She placed her hand on his lap.

"Look, I appreciate you havin' my back right now." Chris turned his body toward hers. "You's a boss bitch for real. But I gotta get this paper right, like, right now. I need bread, my son need shit and I gotta get ya money back to you. And I gotta do it quick else I ain't goin' be no good to nobody. Not even you." He gripped the front of his boxers. "This dick alone ain't goin' keep you happy forever."

Forever? Candace smiled at the word.

"I know," she spoke after a moment. "I want you on your feet. I told you before, you're no good to me broke, but I don't mean that so you can go out here and kill ya' damn self tryna do for me or impress me. I got me." She looked at him intently. "I been had me."

"But I *wanna* have you. I wanna be able to keep you in the nice shit you like, them Prada bags you be rocking, ya' fly glasses and shit. I'm trying to be the nigga that pay for your hair to get done and help you out when you need. I don't like not having money. It makes me feel sick to my stomach. Where I'm from, ain't nothing worse than a broke-ass nigga."

Candace scooted over beside him. "And you're not that dude, Chris. I'm not goin' stop you from getting your money. But I am goin' warn you to be careful running the streets so much. It's nothing out there for you, for real."

"Oh, you preaching to me, now," he teased.

"Shut the fuck up." Candace shoved him lightly.

Chris stood up, kissing her passionately in the mouth. "I be back, babe. Okay?"

"Okay."

Candace was home alone early in the morning when she woke up from her sleep with dry lips. She was on her way out of the kitchen with a glass of water when Chris came through the front door. They startled each other.

"Rough night?" he asked, looking at Candace in her too-big T-shirt, scratching at her wild hair.

"I should ask you the same," she teased.

"Busy, but that's how I like it." Chris tossed a small bag onto the couch and moved to embrace her. She slipped effortlessly into his arms and they made their way back into the bedroom.

Candace awoke again, later that same Saturday morning with her son on her mind.

"What, you don't miss your mother?" she asked a groggy Emmanuel after dialing Brother's number. She heard the scuffle of his uncle waking him up and handing him the phone.

"Cut it out, ma." He yawned.

Candace could hear him groaning as he stretched on the other line. Imagining his gangly brown limbs, she felt a warmth near her heart. "I'm serious. You don't even call me no more. If I was dead up in the hospital, you wouldn't even know it."

"Yes, I would. Uncle B would tell me."

"Oh." Candace clutched her heart. "Is that so?"

"Ma, I'm just teasin'. You know I miss you, but I am having fun this summer. Isn't that what you wanted?"

"Of course."

"You miss me, Mom?" Emmanuel asked, sincerity seeping through his tone.

"Of course, son. Do you even have to ask? You know this house too quiet and clean without you."

Manny chuckled.

"You be good, Emmanuel. You hear me?" she said softly as she turned over in her bed.

"Yes, Mom."

"Let me know if you want me to come get you or if you need anything, okay?"

"Maaa," he whined, once again the independent and confident ten-year-old. "I'm cool."

Candace shook her head, being all too certain that he was.

CHAPTER 29

"That boy." Candace laughed and swung her feet over the bed onto the floor, then she stood up and stretched. When she glanced back down at Chris, still entangled in her bed sheets, a smile forced its way to her face. *And this boy.* Her lips raised softly, as she internally sang... *All in my bed. All in my head. What am I going to do with him?*

Candace walked toward her bedroom door, but turned when she heard Chris roll over and groan.

"Where you going?" His face never moved from the pillow.

"Bathroom."

Chris looked at her through squinted green eyes, then shook his head and patted the empty space on the bed next to him.

Candace smiled. "Nope, gotta brush my teeth."

He frowned, shook his head again and patted the mattress even harder.

Giggling, Candace shook her head no.

"Don't make me get up," Chris warned, pushing back the mint-colored covers.

"Get up." Candace threw her head back as she put her hands on her hips. "I ain't scared."

"I don't want you to be scared." Chris sat up slowly. "Being scared ain't goin' help you. I want you on your A game."

Candace burst out laughing. "My 'A game,' huh? Whateva, boy. I'm going to brush my teeth."

"No you not. You goin' bring your ass back to this bed like I said." Chris scooted forward slightly resting on the edge of the bed.

Candace took a step back, silently mouthing the word "No."

"Okay." Chris placed his feet on the floor. "I see how you want it."

Candace took another step back, waving her left pointer finger in the air, as if to mock him. Chris curled his lips and nodded, then slowly and silently lowered his head. Candace watched him and cautiously took another step back. She stared at the sandy-brown waves on the top of Chris's head while he looked down at the floor. Candace quickly glanced behind her, checking for the door. In a millisecond, she glanced back at Chris and he was rushing toward her.

"AHHHH!" Candace screeched, and took off running down the hall.

Chris chased her into the living room where Candace darted around the couch. They circled it three times before Chris finally stopped to take a good look at her.

"Why you gotta make this hard?" he asked, rocking behind the sofa.

"Why you messin' wit' me?" She bounced on her feet from side to side, trying to contain her laughter. "I just wanna go to the bathroom."

"I told you bring your ass back in that bed." Chris pointed down the hall. "Didn't I?"

"You ain't my damn daddy." Candace snaked her neck.

"Oh, I ain't ya' daddy, now, huh? I was your daddy last night when I was bussin' that ass."

"So! Whatchu' sayin'?" Candace dared him with lips twisted.

"Getcha ass back in that bed!"

Candace laughed hard but tried to keep her face stern. "I'm not."

"No?"

"Nope." She stuck out her tongue.

Chris's light eyes opened wide. "For real?"

Candace stuck out her tongue again, this time, adding a quick flip of her middle finger.

His mouth sprang open in surprise, but Chris remained silent.

"I told you, I'm not scared of you, Chris," Candace said, rolling her eyes. She barely blinked before Chris lunged forward, the top of his long body stretching over the back of the couch. Candace tried to scream and run and jump out of the way, but Chris caught her right arm and snatched her forward. Candace tried to pull back, but Chris held her tight and Candace was laughing too hard to resist the pull of his fingers pressing in right above her elbow.

Chris held onto her arm as he rounded the couch getting closer.

"Owww!!" she cooed, giving him a playful frown. "You're hurtin' me."

Chris's lips curled, looking at her with disbelief. "You in pain now, huh?" He shoved her down onto the couch cushions. "I thought you was so tough?"

Candace landed with a thud and a playful pout. "I am tough."

"But you bitchin' already." Chris leaned in.

"I ain't bitchin'."

"No? 'Ohh, you hurtin' me,'" he teased in a falsetto. "What do you call that?"

Candace squinted her eyes, biting down on her bottom lip. Suddenly and forcefully, she jumped up and hurled herself forward with her arms extended in front of her, slamming Chris dead center in his chest and sending him reeling backward over the coffee table. She bolted for the bedroom before Chris even hit the floor.

"Ohh shit!" she heard him holler as she slammed her door behind her. "That's how we playin', now?" Within seconds, her doorknob rattled. "And you goin' lock the door?" Chris banged.

"Who is it?" Candace sang out.

"The nigga that's goin' whip your ass. That's who," Chris sang back.

"I don't think so," she teased in a high-pitched voice.

Chris pounded harder.

"Nobody's home!" Candace yelled, stepping away from the trembling doorframe.

"I'mma break this mothafucka down if you don't open it."

"You ain't goin' break shit!"

"Don't test me, C. I'mma kick a hole in this mothafuckin' door. I promise you that!"

"I dare you."

BOOM!

Candace felt her room shake as Chris's foot slammed against the door. Her heart jumped and her eyes popped open wide.

"What the fuck!" she yelled. "Stop! Stop! Stop! Don't kick my fuckin' door! Are you retarded?"

"Then open this mothafucka then!"

"I ain't openin' shit! And you bet not kick my shit, neither!"

"What?!?!?" Candace could hear Chris's bare feet shuffling across the floor. He pounded his fist against the door again. "Open up, C."

"Nope."

"Okay." Chris let out a slight chuckle and then it sounded as if he moved away from the door.

Candace strained to hear, but there was silence in the hall for a few moments. She crept closer to the door as she listened to the sound of Chris's feet shifting along. *Is he mad? Ohmigod, is he really leaving?* After a few quick seconds, she could tell he was coming back her way but wondered what he was doing. Candace's eyebrows furrowed as she stared at the still and quiet door. Then suddenly the knob turned, twisted, and seemed to jiggle slightly and after a few seconds, there was a quick click and Chris pushed the door wide open. He stood in the doorway in nothing but his boxers, holding a butter knife and a paper clip.

"What the fuck?" Candace gasped. "Did you just jimmy my lock?"

"Fuck all that." Chris threw the tools to the floor. "What's that big shit you was talking, Miss Bitchin'?" He took a step. "Don't kick my shit!" Another step. "Am I fuckin' retarded?" Another step.

Candace froze in the middle of her bedroom floor. She trembled and tried to move, but it was too late. Chris pounced, tackling her onto the bed.

Laughing, Candace landed with Chris on top of her. He grabbed her hands and quickly hoisted them up over her head. This time, Candace didn't fight back, allowing herself to be swept up in Chris's passionate touch. He pressed his mouth into her before moving upward, his tongue swelling in her ear as he nibbled tenderly on her ear lobe. Candace moaned as Chris kissed and licked his way down her body, peeling off her nightshirt and panties along the way.

Once completely naked, he turned her onto her stomach and pressed his strong fingers into her back. Candace moaned as he massaged her tense muscles. She felt her body contract, then release at the pressure of his touch. His steady hands worked her over, digging deep into her shoulder blades and down to the subtle arch in her back. Candace rested one side of her face on her pillow and closed her eyes. Chris's hands grasped her behind and she felt him spread her cheeks apart. His thumb pressed into her warm places, giving her just a quick stroke before moving down to her thighs.

Candace sighed. She wanted more and instinctively arched her back a little, poking out her behind.

"You like that, huh?" Chris laughed softly. "Pokin' that thing out for me." He brought his hands back up to her anxious ass and opened her cheeks once more.

Candace moaned as his fingers slipped inside of her. Suddenly, she felt a hard slap.

"Sit up on your knees," Chris instructed. "Poke that pussy all the way out for me."

Candace obeyed, hopping up onto her knees. He pushed her legs apart, keeping his thumb gyrating on her swollen womanhood. Candace felt her excitement spilling onto him.

Chris moaned. "That shit so pretty, baby."

Before Candace could reply, she felt a sudden rush of tingling warmth come over her. "Ooooohhh God," she screamed as Chris pressed his face into her from behind. "Fuck!"

He sucked and licked.

Candace grabbed for the pillows in front of her. She tucked them under her chest and buried her face down, trying her hardest not to scream. Her body jerked and gyrated uncontrollably until Chris pulled away. She raised her head, gasping for air and trying to collect her thoughts when suddenly she felt Chris's hand on her waist and his manhood plowing full force inside of her.

"Fuck me!" she wailed. "Oh, God!"

Chris dug deep in search of buried treasure, lifting up her ass cheeks to make room for his steady thrusts. He pounded until Candace found her face pressed against the headboard. She couldn't push back or resist, so she braced herself to receive all he gave. And Chris gave until his body slowed and, clenching her ass tight, he let out a deep heavy groan.

"Goooooodddddaaaaaammmmmn, babe!" His body twitched behind her.

Candace dropped to her stomach, still struggling to catch her breath. Chris fell to her side, sweating and smiling. They lay naked and breathless for a few quiet moments until Candace finally collected herself and spoke.

"I can't stand you." She playfully mugged him.

Chris grabbed her arm and pulled her into him. He kissed her, his mouth still moist from her juices. Candace kissed back, then rested her head in his chest.

Candace didn't realize she'd fallen asleep until she woke up, naked wrapped in Chris's arms. She kissed his firm bicep. He pulled her tighter. She closed her eyes and nodded back off.

They spent most of the day Saturday wrestling and making love until the sun went down and Chris sat up in the bed beside her.

"Babe, I got a couple things I need to take care of tonight. And I need to take your car; is that cool?"

Candace lifted her head slightly. "Can you bring me back some ice cream?"

Chris stood up laughing. "Ice cream? What kind, greedy butt?"

"Butter pecan," Candace replied, turning back over in her tangled sheets. "I like the kind from the Chinese store on Germantown Avenue."

"I gotchu, baby. I be back. Okay?"

"Uh huh," Candace moaned half-conscious.

The sun came up Sunday morning and Candace rolled over to an empty bed. She lay there for a moment staring up at her ceiling and the streaks of light coming through her sheer curtains. She reached for her phone to check the time: 5:43. *It's so early.* She thought of Chris. *But so late. Where is he?*

Just as Candace's fingers slid over the screen to find the number, she heard her front door open, and a moment later Chris stepped into her bedroom.

She couldn't tell if it was the comfort of knowing he was safe or the rusty hue of his hair and skin or maybe it was the way the sun flickered off the green in his eyes, but Candace realized at the moment that he was probably the most handsome man she had ever seen—and she couldn't think of a time where she had been more pleased to see a man walk into a room.

"Good morning, beautiful," he whispered, kicking off his sneakers and moving toward the bed.

"Good morning, handsome." She trembled beneath the sheets.

Chris stripped out of his jeans, pulled his T-shirt over his head and climbed into bed beside her. He wrapped his arms around her and Candace unconsciously exhaled.

There was something about the way he held her. Something about the feel of his flesh against hers, and his breath rising and falling to the same rhythm that seemed to lull Candace back into soft slumber.

She opened her eyes some time later to the sun still peeling through her curtains and an empty bed. She checked her phone once more: 9:14.

Candace slipped from under her covers, draped on her robe and headed to the bathroom. As she stepped out of her room, she could hear the television on in the living room. She continued her course, brushing her hair and her teeth before making her way down the hall to find Chris on the couch eating a bowl of Emmanuel's Fruity Pebbles cereal.

She stepped behind him, placing her hand on his exposed shoulder beneath his wife beater. Chris squeezed her hand. She leaned forward and kissed the top of his head.

"You hungry?" she asked, walking around to the front of the couch.

"A little, but I was goin' wait for you to see if you wanted to go out to eat."

Candace shrugged. "I don't really feel like it. I can make us a nice breakfast."

Chris looked up at Candace settling onto the cushion beside him. "Yeah? Like what?"

"Pancakes and bacon?"

He frowned. "Nah."

"Okay. How about some sausage and home fries?"

"Ummm, sounds good, but nah. I'm not big on home fries."

"Okay. What about some fish and grits?"

"Cheese in the grits?"

Candace stood up smiling. "Is there any other way?"

She stepped into the kitchen and opened her freezer, pulled out a bag of whiting and set a small pot of water on the stove to boil. After a moment, she looked up to see Chris staring intently at the news.

"How was your night?" she asked, seasoning the flour for the fish.

"Um, so-so." He turned to face her and then stood. "My morning's looking better, though."

"Yeah?"

"Yeah." Chris strolled into the kitchen. He walked up behind Candace as she faced the sink, measuring her grits, and began kissing the back of her neck.

Candace bit down on her bottom lip.

"You in here, early Sunday morning, makin' a nigga some fish and grits, C. That's love." Chris pressed into her slim five-eleven frame.

"You think so?" Candace turned to face him. Chest to chest, she stood her ground against the six-five, cream-colored, green-eyed, tattooed Adonis.

"I know so," Chris stated plainly.

"You think I love you, Christopher?"

"I know you love me, Candace." His cool breath swept across her face.

She shuddered at the sound of her name rolling off his lips.

"Tell me you don't." Chris's eyes peered deep into hers.

"Huh?" Candace felt her heart start to race.

"Tell me you don't love me, Candace." Chris's hands found the perfect curve of her waist, settling there affirmatively.

"I didn't say I didn't," Candace replied.

"Then tell me you do." Chris's face was soft but serious.

"Tell you what, Chris?" She knew what he was asking—something she was afraid to confess.

"Tell me you love me."

"Do you love me?" Candace inquired.

"Yes," Chris answered, without taking a breath.

"Tell me," she insisted.

"Candace, I love you. I'm in love with you."

Candace's heart skipped ten thousand beats and she smiled despite herself.

"Your turn," Chris persisted.

"I…I love you, Chris." Candace laughed as she felt tears swelling in her eyes. "I really do love you. I am thankful for you and I didn't realize how much I needed you in my life until you were all the way in it. And I can't imagine it without you."

Ohmigod, I said it. Now what? What am I going to tell Emmanuel?

Chris leaned in, pushing Candace against the sink and kissed her. He kissed her long and deep until Candace couldn't feel or see or hear anything but him.

CHAPTER 30

Chris laced his sneakers at the foot of Candace's bed while she sat behind him, thumbing through the pages of a thick textbook and scribbling into a notebook on her lap. "You goin' be out late?" She looked up from her notes. The sun had set and her sheer curtains waved gently in the cool summer night breeze.

"Nah, not too late. I got a couple things to check on, but I shouldn't be long."

"Okay. 'Cause you know I start back to work tomorrow and I can't be late."

Chris stood and turned to face her. "I wouldn't do that to you, babe. I know ya' work is important. I be back before you even miss me."

"I miss you already," Candace said, smiling seductively.

"That's what I'm talkin' 'bout." Chris leaned over the bed and kissed her passionately. "I'll be back soon, babe. I promise."

She smiled to herself as the door closed behind him. *Now, to this damn paper.*

Candace sat up in her bed in the middle of the night. She checked her phone: 2:08. She dialed Chris. He picked up on the second ring.

"Yeah, babe?"

"Where you at?" she spoke groggily into the receiver.

"Handlin' something, babe. What's up?"

"I'm up." Candace sensed the tension in his tone and replied with her own. "What time you comin' home…in?"

"Soon as I'm done here, babe. But I gotta go, okay? I'll be *home* soon."

Candace laughed and her shoulders relaxed. "Okay, just remember I gotta be to work in the morning."

"I know, baby. I'll be there. Love you."

Candace paused but only for a moment. "Love you, too."

Smiling, she slid back under the covers, knowing he would be beside her in the morning when she woke for work.

Candace turned over at the sound of her seven a.m. alarm.

She jumped up when she realized she was alone in her bedroom. She reached for her phone. No missed calls. No messages. She listened for a moment for any noise from down the hall. She jumped up and headed to her empty living room, then back down to her room. *What the fuck?* She hastily pulled up Chris's icon on her phone and dialed. He didn't answer.

"What the fuck?" she repeated aloud, her heart thudding in her chest. "Where the fuck is he?"

She dialed again. Again, no answer. Candace took several deep breaths before walking slowly into the bathroom.

"It's okay, Candace. Calm down. He'll be here any second. He knows what today is. He wouldn't do that to you."

Candace reassured herself as she brushed her hair. *It's okay*, she thought as she pulled her T-shirt over her head. She stepped back into her bedroom in only navy boy shorts and stared at her reflection in the tall mirror on her dresser. *But what if he's hurt?*

She dialed Chris again. Again, the phone rang with no answer. *FUCK!*

Candace stormed into the living room, snatched the remote off the coffee table and flipped straight to the news, a habit she'd acquired from years of dealing with her son's father.

"If I don't make it home to you, best believe the reason why goin' be on the news." Candace recalled Prince telling her so many times before.

She watched intently as the slim white man recapped all of the weekend events in the city of Philadelphia. Three murders on Saturday, a house fire in Logan early Sunday morning, and a shooting outside the SugarHouse Casino last night. She didn't know what she was listening for exactly, but she didn't think she'd heard it yet. So she turned the volume up loud and headed back to her room, breathing slowly as she dressed. *It's okay. It's okay.*

Candace paced the floor, her impatience growing as the minutes passed. *Where the fuck is he? How am I supposed to get to work? Are you fuckin' kidding me? Oh my God, my car. It's okay. It's okay.*

She fastened her floral A-line skirt. "Okay. Okay. So, I'm just goin' have to catch a cab to work."

She buttoned her softly accentuating lilac blouse. "It's okay he's just handling business, right?" She sat down on the bed, then clenched her fist. *I know that pussy bet not be out with some other bitch in my shit.*

"Oh, fuck. Come on, Chris. Answer the phone!" She dialed him again. She was furious and scared and even more frustrated that all she could do was scream obscenities into his voicemail. "Yo, babe! What the fuck! Where are you? You know I need to get to work."

"Like, come on with the dumb shit, Chris. I got shit to do. I don't know where the fuck you are or what you're doing, but you need to come on."

"Babe, I really pray that you are okay and not hurt or locked up or anything like that. I really, really do. Please call me and let me know what the fuck is going on."

"This is some bullshit, Chris! Like, I don't know what type shit you on, but you're fuckin' with my money!"

She kept dialing and redialing, but as 7:30 approached, Candace knew if she didn't hear back from Chris soon, she'd have to call a cab. *I can't risk it.* She picked up the phone less than five minutes later and dialed the number to the Germantown Cab. They could have someone there in forty to forty-five minutes. She had to be to work by 8:30. That gave her just enough time to make it to her first day back to work on time.

Candace's stomach was in knots. She made herself a bagel, only for fear of passing out, and kept her finger on her phone all the while, dialing Chris—yet, still, no response. She flipped to a different station as the news replayed in the living room. A different announcer repeated the same stories, three murders on Saturday, a fire in Logan and more on last night's shooting robbery of twenty-four year-old Anthony Benatucci Jr., son of renowned Philadelphia mobster, Big Tony Benatucci, outside the SugarHouse Casino on Delaware Avenue. Candace looked up at the picture of the slim attractive Caucasian male sporting a sleek clean-cut and a thick platinum chain over a crisp striped button-up. Candace noticed his smile as the announcer went on to say that the young Benatucci had apparently won an undisclosed amount while gambling at the SugarHouse and was believed to have been followed by an armed gunman who attacked Benatucci, breaking his nose before robbing him and shooting him in the leg.

Damn.

The announcer went on to link the handsome young victim's father, Big Tony Benatucci, to the heavy mob scene in Philadelphia. He described him as a local gangster connected to several ongoing federal investigations. He concluded the snippet by adding that the suspect did get away and there were no witnesses at this time.

Candace stared at the screen, her brows pinching together. *No way...he...*she was rattled from her thoughts by the sound of her phone ringing in her hand. She yanked it up close to her eyes and quickly answered the unrecognized number. It was the cab driver calling to let her know he was outside. "Okay, I'll be right down."

Fuck. Just then Candace realized she'd have to use her spare house key since Chris had her key ring. She slipped the single key out of her jewelry box and into the bold color-blocked bag she'd purchased in Vegas, then checked the time: 8:10. Candace hurried to the door in her purple pumps.

"Come on, Chris." She dialed again, pulling her door closed behind her.

No answer. Candace held back the tears; she dabbed her face with a tissue so not to mess up her makeup. But, she wept in the cab, ferociously dialing Chris's number. Still, Candace managed to steady herself as she entered the Business Office.

"Come on, C. Put your game face on," she said, turning the office doorknob. "You can get through this."

Surprisingly, her first day back to work was better than even she expected, given her rough start and the sudden worry-filled condition of her life.

Danielle seemed genuinely happy to have her boss back. She smiled all day and rushed to Candace's side, doing whatever Candace required in order to help her catch up on her work. She proudly showed Candace how well she'd maintained, what she could, in the office while Candace was out.

Denise was glad to have her back, as well, and treated Candace and Chrissy to lunch. Candace's day was busy, but fun, and she was glad to be working again. Still, her mind was elsewhere. She kept checking her phone for Chris's call. She tried to reach him after her Medicare meeting and again after her sign-in with the

Douglass family. She called again between her marketing calls and before she gave a walk-in tour. By quitting time, Candace had exhausted her thoughts of all tragic possibilities and her body felt the depletion. She called a cab to take her back home.

Candace pushed through the front door of her apartment that afternoon with slumped shoulders. She headed straight to the kitchen and pulled out a bottle of Cîroc. *I need a shot.* She threw back a small amount, then refilled her glass and tossed back another. She pulled out her phone and dialed Chris. Again, no answer. Another shot.

"This is some bullshit!" she screamed and hurled the delicate glass across the room. The small goblet shattered against the wall. "Fuuuuuuck!!!"

Candace stormed into her bedroom. "I can't believe this shit! I gotta be the dumbest bitch on earth."

Candace surveyed her room, looking for any glimpse that Chris may have been there, but there was none. Everything was as she'd left it and Candace began to cry while standing in the middle of her bedroom floor. Her breathing was hard and choked up by heavy sobs. She staggered to the side of her bed and sat down.

She didn't know what to do or who to call. Not her mom or Marci. Maybe Brother, but what would she say? Some young bul stole her car and her heart.

She fell face-first into her pillows. *Where the fuck is Prince when I need him? In jail, behind bars. Because he's a fuckin' criminal. Just like Chris's no-good ass. What the fuck is wrong with me?* She cried some more. Heavy tears soaked her pale pillowcase causing her makeup to run through.

Candace slowly pushed herself up from the bed and took a deep breath before she stood. She shuddered at her ghastly reflection in her dresser mirror. She was a wreck: red face and puffy eyes with black stuff running down her cheeks. She sighed and dragged herself into the bathroom.

At the sink, Candace splashed cold water on her face. She wiped off her mascara with a makeup remover cloth. When she went to throw the stained cloth away, she noticed Chris's washcloth in the trash. *I didn't put that there.* She picked it up. It was damp. Candace turned the orange rag over in her hand and screamed when she saw blood on the other side.

"What the fuck!?!" She threw the rag back down into the trash. *Ohmigod, he's hurt. He could be somewhere dying. Ohmigod! What the fuck should I do?*

Candace's heart pounded so loudly in her chest, it almost drowned out the sound of her own thoughts. She sat down on the toilet, breathing slowly and staring at the bloody rag in her bathroom trash can.

What if that's not his blood?

There was no answer she could conjure. But Candace knew if that was the case, that rag had to go. She jumped up, swinging open the cabinet beneath the sink and pulled out her long yellow cleaning gloves and a bottle of bleach. She put the gloves on, then carefully removed the rag from the trash again. She placed it in the sink and dowsed it with bleach until the red and orange faded into a pale pink. Then she wrung out the excess moisture down the drain. Next Candace grabbed her hair scissors from the small cubby on the space saver behind her toilet. She snipped away at the rag, cutting it into thin strips, which she, one by one, flushed down the toilet. When she was done, Candace poured more bleach down the sink and over her gloves. She peeled them off and tossed them into the trash. She pulled the liner from the can and hurried to the small dumpster in the back of her apartment building. It was Monday; she knew the trash trucks would be down her block by seven a.m. the next morning. She tossed the bag in, then rushed back inside, grabbed her scissors from the bathroom, and headed into the kitchen. She turned the flame on high under a small pot of water and threw her scissors in the pot.

Next, she scrubbed her bathroom clean. She wiped down everything—the tub, the sink, the tiles and wall—with a bucket of hot water and disinfectant and bleach. Her head spun at the smell of the concoction, but she sank her bare hands into the water, regretting throwing away her gloves, and kept cleaning until everything in the blue and white room sparkled. Candace wiped the sweat from her brow with her forearm and opened the window in her bedroom. She stood there for a moment, feeling the dizzying effects of the chemicals and the vodka. She swayed unconsciously, feeling too nauseous to stand still. Her stomach hurled and Candace bolted for the bathroom. She stumbled and made it in time for most of her vomit to make it into the toilet. But some hit the side of the bowl and splattered alongside the tub and onto the floor. Candace was on her knees and the sickening scent of the toxic fumes caused her to hurl again. Slowly, she pulled her sweaty face up from the bowl and began crawling clumsily across the floor. Coughing harshly, she collapsed at the foot of her bedroom door.

"Oh, God," she cried, rolling over onto her back. "What the fuck is going on? I… I…I gotta pull myself together." She closed her eyes and inhaled deeply. *Get up, Candace.* She lay still for a moment. *Get up, Candace.*

She coached herself once more when she heard her phone ring in her room. She scurried to her feet, darted toward her bed and snatched the phone off the sheets before a third chime and looked at the name on the screen. Brother. *It's Emmanuel. Fuck! I can't. I can't talk to my son right now, like this. I'll have to call him back.*

Candace sat down on her bed, wiping her mouth with the back

of her hand. *Oh, God, my son. What can I say to him?* She looked at her reflection again in the dresser mirror across from her bed. She looked worse than before, her eyes swollen and red, her face pale and her hair a mangled mess. *Emmanuel could never see me like this. What the fuck am I doing?* She shook her head, then stood up slowly. She headed for the kitchen and poured herself a glass of cool water, then sat down at the table.

"Chris, where are you?" she whispered.

Night fell with Candace still pacing the floor and calling Chris. She'd made several calls to the local police precinct to see if a Christopher Jackson had been picked up. She even tried a few hospitals, Einstein, Temple and Jefferson. However, no one had any information for her. After recleaning her bathroom and sweeping up the shards of glass in her living room, Candace poured herself another shot of Cîroc and fell weeping to the side of her bed. She didn't know she'd fallen asleep until the ringing of her phone woke her up. Through blurred vision, she reached in the darkness to find the device.

"Yes," she answered, without lifting her head.

"Babe! Babe! Where are you?"

Candace sprang up. "What! Chris?!? Where am I? Where the fuck are you?" The relief of hearing his voice settled some of the nausea in her stomach but did not quench the fire burning in her heart.

"I'm coming to you now."

"What!" Candace swung her feet off the bed. "Where the fuck have you been? I been fuckin' callin' and callin'! You got my fuckin' car! How you goin' do me like that!"

"I'm on my way, C. Calm down."

"'Calm down'!?! You don't give a fuck about how I make a living and how I get by. All you fucking do is take take take! You so fuckin' inconsiderate! Did you even think about how I was goin' get to work?"

"I needed to handle something really big, baby. I promise you won't be mad when you see what I got."

"What you got?" Candace scoffed, "What you better fuckin' have is my fuckin' car, Chris, before I call the cops!"

"The 'cops'? Baby, chill. I had to make a power move, baby. Please, babe, calm down. I'm coming to you now. I'll explain everything."

Candace was quiet for a moment until the image of the bloody rag flashed before her eyes. "What the fuck type shit you into, Chris? Why was there a bloody washcloth in my bathroom? What the fuck did you do?"

"Fuck!" Chris snapped. "I forgot about that shit…"

"Was that your blood, Chris?'

"No, baby. I got into a fight wit' some dude. I think I broke his nose and his shit leaked all over me. I'm sorry, baby. I meant to take it with me. I'mma get rid of it."

"I did, already."

"What?"

"I already got rid of it."

"You did?"

"I just fuckin' told you I did!"

Chris laughed. "Good girl."

"Good girl, my ass. Bring me my fuckin' car!"

"I'm on my way, babe. I promise. I got some good news for you, C. Ya boy is on. I promise I made a move to make you proud."

"What? What the fuck are you talking about?"

"I know you mad, baby. But I had to get low for a minute. Just be ready for me, baby, please. I'm coming your way. I be there in less than ten. Okay?"

"Just hurry up!" Candace threw down the phone.

She jumped from her bed and threw on a pair of tights and some sneakers.

"I'mma wait for his ass outside," she huffed, rushing toward the door. She hurried outside to the curb, looking up and down the dark street.

Headlights moved slowly down the block from her left. She squinted in the bright light until the black Envoy crept past her. Both white passengers in their early thirties looked her way. Candace ignored their stares and looked down at the time on her phone: 1:42. *Fuck y'all lookin' for this time of night? Damn junkies. Out here in the middle of night, searchin' for a hit.* She sucked her teeth as the car sped on and she kept peering hard down the end of her block waiting for Chris to turn the corner.

"He's goin' give me my keys, now. Right fuckin' now!"

A few moments passed as Candace paced anxiously outside her apartment. Again bright lights turned the corner onto her block. Her heart jumped into her throat but dropped back down to her chest once she realized it was the same black SUV.

Ohmigod. What, are y'all lost? This is Chestnut Hill, dickheads. You can get you something good a few blocks down in Germantown. The SUV passed her again. *Fuckin' morons.*

Candace watched its taillights disappeared with a right turn at the end of her block. She rolled her eyes and as she turned her attention back to her left to the other end of the street, the familiar front lights of her faithful Accord approached.

"Ohmigod!" Candace yelled, as Chris pulled to a stop right in front of her. The passenger side door swung open. Candace peered in to see Chris grinning proudly.

"Hello, gorgeous," he sang. "Get in."

"Gimme my fuckin' keys!" Candace bent into the open door with her hand extended.

"Come on, take a ride with me, baby." Chris's smile didn't fade. "We can celebrate."

"Celebrate what, Chris?" Candace's lips folded, but her arm stayed out in front of her. "I don't wanna celebrate shit. All I want is my fuckin' keys."

"Babe..."

"Or you can park my shit and come get your clothes the fuck up out my house!"

Chris frowned. "Aww, come on, baby. You don't mean that."

"Like hell I don't. Where the fuck have you been? You know what...it don't even matter. Just give me my shit!"

Chris's head dipped low inside the car as he spoke to her. "Come on, babe, calm down. I only been at the casino."

"The casino!?!" she hollered.

"Yeah, babe. I came up big."

Something flashed in her brain. "What? What the fuck are you talkin' 'bout?"

Chris's lips parted to respond, but his eyes quickly diverted to the rearview mirror and the dim headlights that had just turned the corner behind them.

Candace looked up. "Really? This better not been them same white dudes. This the third time they been down this block."

"White boys?" Chris's neck jerked back, his eyes squinted into the glaring lights that now sat motionless at the top of the block. "Candace, get in the car."

She looked back down at Chris. "No, Chris! Give me my fuckin' keys!"

"That's them dudes from the SugarHouse," Chris said to himself, then turned his eyes back to Candace. "Candace, get the fuck in the car!"

"Chris, what the fu..." But before she could finish her words, Chris lunged his long body out of the open door and grabbed her.

"GET THE FUCK IN THE CAR!!!"

She could see the fear searing through his beautiful green eyes and then she heard it: POW! POW! POW! Three gunshots rang out in the quiet Chestnut Hill night. The Envoy's tires ripped against the concrete almost setting sparks in the air. Chris snatched Candace into the passenger seat. Candace came down face-first, hitting her head against the armrest. The heavy door swung shut behind her as Chris took off with maximum momentum.

He accelerated up the small street, almost taking out the traffic light at the corner as he made a sharp left turn. The SUV followed, maneuvering the tight turn at equal speed. Chris took a hard left on McCallum Street and headed toward Lincoln Drive. Clean through stop signs, the black Accord cut through the smooth dark night like a sharp blade to warm butter. Chris was sweating. Candace was screaming.

"What the fuck is going on?" she begged.

"Chill, C. I got it! Just hold on and be quiet!"

POW! POW! Shots popped behind her.

"Ohmigod!" she screamed, ducking down in her seat.

More slugs exploded from the vehicle behind them. Chris steadied the wheel with one hand and plunged his free hand under the car seat. He snatched back a small black gun. Chris swung a hard turn off Greene Street, then reached his arm out the window and fired back.

Pop! Pop! Pop!

Candace screamed again. "What the fuck is going on, Chris?"

"Get the fuck down!" Chris commanded, using the gun-wielding arm to push her down into the seat.

She could feel the heat from the recently fired weapon on her temple. Candace kept screaming. "Ohmigod! Chris please, stop!"

"Chill, C!" He handled the turns harshly, jumping across both lanes of the narrow throughway.

"Ohmigod, Chris! I'm goin' be sick." Candace clutched the seat.

The back window shattered. She squealed and Chris ducked his head. He turned his weapon behind him again and released four more shots into the night. Suddenly, Chris lurched forward. Candace watched the strain on his face and saw blood burst out of his right shoulder.

"AHHH! FUCK!" he wailed.

Candace jumped back in her seat. She screamed hysterically, her body trembling. Chris dropped the gun and gripped the wheel with both hands. Blood seeped from his arm. Candace felt the acceleration jerk her back as Chris floored it. She looked over at him, his face reeling beams of sweat, his shirt soaking mercilessly with blood.

"Chris!" she shrieked, reaching for him.

He pushed her off as he hurled through the light at Wissahickon Avenue. "Sit back, baby!"

I'm going to die, she thought as the streets seemed to melt away in front of her. *My son.*

Pow! Pow! Pow! Three more shots tore through the car and opened wide holes in Chris's back and arm. He lost control, throwing them seventy miles per hour into the third turn on Lincoln Drive. The car slammed into the divider, ping-ponged across to the guardrail and flipped over on its top. Candace's body rattled like a bobble-head doll as the car skidded on its roof to a stop at the edge of a rusted railing, stopping them from flipping over into the shallow water at Forbidden Drive.

Candace could feel herself slamming against the inside of the vehicle.

Bang. Bang. Bang.

Too many thuds to the head and she was out cold.

CHAPTER 31

"You okay, baby?" Candace's mother asked, shutting Candace's apartment door behind her. "Oh, it smells like bleach in here."

Candace shook her head and slowly moved toward the sofa.

"Mom, you need me to get you anything?" Emmanuel asked, rushing toward his mother's side.

Candace sat down. "No. I'm okay. Really." She looked up into her mother's and sister's concerned faces.

After a moment, Karla spoke, "Well, how 'bout I take Manny home with me and let you get some rest. Okay? How's that sound? I think that's best."

Candace's eyes moved to Emmanuel, standing directly in front of her. His full dark lashes bristled as he stared at her with daring eyes.

"What do you think?" she asked him.

"I think I need to stay here," he replied promptly.

Marci chuckled, Karla huffed and Candace smiled.

"Well, you heard the man," Marci said from behind the sofa.

Karla twisted her lips. "Candace, really, you need your rest," she insisted.

"I can help her," Emmanuel persisted proudly. "I need to take care of my mom."

Candace's smile spread.

Her mother carried on, "I know how you feel, baby." Karla moved toward her grandson and placed her hand on his shoulder.

Emmanuel turned to face her. "But your mother really does need to rest. She's been through a lot. Just give her some time to recover." She looked down at her daughter and gave a slight grin. "I promise, ya' momma wants you here, bad as you wanna be here, but I know what's best. You got to let her rest."

Emmanuel frowned, turning back to his mother. Candace reached for his hand, the sudden movement causing her to wince in pain. She frowned back at him and shook her head.

"She's right," Marci chirped. "I'm here. I'll take care of her."

Emmanuel kept his pleading eyes on Candace.

"Mom-mom is right, son," she spoke slowly.

Emmanuel's lips curled straight up and his shoulders drooped. "Mommmmmm?"

"I know, baby. But, I'm a mess right now. Give me a minute. I just want to sleep."

He sighed deeply. Then spoke sternly, "Okay. But I'm not staying long."

Candace laughed and winced again.

"Go get some stuff," his grandmother said, smacking Emmanuel on the behind.

He grunted, marching off toward his room.

"I'll help him," Marci said, stepping behind him, leaving Candace and her mother alone in the living room.

Karla sat down beside Candace on the couch and crossed her arms over her chest.

"Candace, I thought you was done with all this foolishness when Prince went to jail. What the hell are you doing, girl? You know you coulda been killed!"

Candace sighed cautiously through fractured ribs. "Mom, I didn't know…"

"Candace, I mean, what the hell?" Karla continued. "You got

me thinkin' you chasing after this dream job and you runnin' 'round here with another dumb dope boy. Don't you already have a baby by a damn criminal? Girl, what else you want? To be laid up dead somewhere with nobody but me and Marci to raise your son. Or better yet, how 'bout his Uncle Brother. You want his father's people to raise Man?"

Candace felt a tight pinch in her chest. Her mother was right and she had no defense.

"Mom, I…"

"You what, Candace?" Her mother exhaled deeply.

Candace felt the tears swelling in her eyes. "Mom, I don't even know…I just, I just got caught up…"

Just then, Emmanuel and Marci stepped out into the hall.

Her mother softly stroked her hair. "It doesn't matter now, baby. All that matters is you're alive." She kissed Candace's forehead.

After she kissed her mother and her son goodbye, Candace clutched Marci's hand tightly as she hoisted her up off the couch.

"How you feelin', boo?" Marci asked, easing Candace down the hall and into her room.

"Like shit." Candace sat down on the edge of the bed.

"Yeah." Marci stood in front of her, shaking her head.

"I'm so…so…so confused." Candace stared off blankly. "I feel like I don't even know what just happened."

"A lot just happened." Marci sat down next to her sister.

Candace dropped her head, shaking it from side to side. She felt a knot rise up in her chest and the tears beginning to form in her eyes. "And, Chris…"

Marci sighed.

Candace glanced over at her and noticed the moisture swelling in Marci's eyes. "He's dead, Marci…I mean, like, fuckin' dead."

The tears ran down Marci's face. "Yeah, C. It's crazy." She placed her hand on her sister's lap.

"I can't believe this shit, Marcine."

Marci rubbed and squeezed her sister's thigh.

"He was just here, just making love to me all crazy, Marci. Telling me he loved me. I told that boy, I loved him…and he died, Marci." Candace's neck snapped back in anger.

"I know, C. I knew you loved him."

"Yeah, I did! Like, Ohmifuckingod. I really just want to pick up the phone and call him." Candace pounded on the bed. "How? How did he become so important to me so fast? Did I really just fall in love and then he fuckin' dies? Marci, what kinda shit is that?"

"I don't know, C. It's unbelievable. I…I don't even know what there is to say." They were silent for a moment, Marci's hand still on her sister's leg. "Do you even know why they were chasing y'all?"

Candace groaned as she reflected on the dark deadly night. "I think he robbed that kid down at the casino, Marcine."

"What?" Marci gasped.

"Yeah. You heard about that robbery down at the SugarHouse? Where that mob kid got shot?"

"No, fuckin' way!" Marci's eyes sprang wide. "Don't tell me Chris is the one that…"

"I think so." Candace hung her head. "And so do the detectives that came to see me at the hospital."

"Oh, shit!"

"I know." Candace grimaced. "I don't fuckin' understand. I mean, I knew he ran the streets, but I didn't know he was in to that."

"A stick-up boy? Goddamn." Marci's eyes were round and shiny as glazed donuts.

"I'm so stuck," Candace huffed.

"I can't believe that shit. He shot dude…and what? Them mafia people came for him?"

"I guess so. It was two white dudes in a black SUV. They circled my block twice while I was outside waiting for him because he had disappeared with my car."

"What the fuck?"

Candace shook her head.

"Ohmigod. That shit is so serious, C. You better thank God you only got a collapsed lung and slight fractures in your ribs and arm." Marci caught her sister's eyes and said in a serious tone. "You know real gangstas don't give a fuck. They'da killed you, too, just because."

Candace could only nod her agreement.

"Damn that's crazy, Chris," Marci continued. "I really liked him for you."

Candace stared over at her. "Why you say that?"

Marci smiled. "He made you happy, girl. Had you walkin' on cloud nine."

Candace's lips lifted gracefully. Then, gradually they fell to a frown. "But, he's gone now."

Marci's lips drooped as well. "I know…It's going to be okay, though. You're going to be okay."

Candace nodded slowly. She took a deep breath. "I know. But, it's just so much to process. And this shit hurts, you know? My body hurts. My head hurts. My heart hurts. Shit, my fuckin' car is hurt."

"Your car is gone, baby."

"I know…fuck!" Candace eased back onto the bed.

"What are you going to do? What about your job? You know they sent flowers to the hospital?"

Candace sighed shaking her head. "Mommy called the insurance people already and they said my car is covered. She told 'em Chris was driving my car without my consent and knowledge."

"Damn, she told the police Chris stole your car?"

"Pretty much."

"Wow." Marci shook her head. "Smart thinking, Mom."

Candace looked blankly ahead. "I guess." She shrugged. "Denise left me a message, just saying to get well soon and hurry back. It's…it's still just too much…" Candace rocked slightly. "But, I can get through this, right?"

"Right. You're strong, sis. You can get through anything," Marci assured her. "I know I'm through dating married men."

Candace peered over at her.

"I'm too old and too cute for that dumb shit. I want something that's all mine. You know what I mean?" Marci asked.

Candace huffed slightly shaking her head. "Umm huh."

"I'm serious, C. I'm done with that."

Candace closed her eyes. "I hear you."

Marci sucked her teeth and stood up before lifting the rest of her sister's legs completely onto the mattress. "Come on. Lay down," she instructed.

Candace inched up to her pillows and dropped her head. Marci stepped out of the room and quickly returned with a glass of water and some pain pills. Candace sat up and took the medicine and after a long hard swallow, she looked at Marci. "I want to find out when the funeral is."

"Okay. You want me to go with you?"

"I don't know if I should go, but I just want to know where it is. Maybe we can just drive by and find out where the burial site is or something."

"If that's what you want." Marci stepped out of the room once more as Candace eased back down into the pillows and drifted off to sleep.

Marci was on her phone walking into her bedroom, when Candace opened her eyes.

"Yeah, okay. Thanks." Marci ended the call and looked at Candace. "Hey. You okay? Need anything."

"Some water." Candace sat up.

Marci darted off and came right back with a tall, cool refreshing glass and handed it to her.

Candace took long gulps. "Thank you," she said, after passing the glass back to her sister.

Marci sat down on the bed. "How are you feeling?"

Candace shrugged. "I still don't know."

"Well," Marci began, "The funeral is at Mount Calvary on Forty-third and Elm… tomorrow."

"Tomorrow?"

"Tomorrow. At ten a.m."

Candace huffed a deep breath out of her nose.

"Do you want to go?" Marci asked.

Candace thought for a moment. She was still brooding when she heard Marci clear her throat. She looked up, catching her sister's curiously squinted eyes.

"Candace?" Marci inquired.

"Yeah?" she replied pensively.

"Do you know how much Chris robbed that kid for?"

The muscles in Candace's face tensed. "No. Why?"

"I'm just sayin', them mafia boys got dough. If he was out gambling, he mighta came up big."

"So whatchu sayin'?"

"Did the police say they found anything on Chris?"

"No. They didn't say."

"Did Chris come back here?"

"I don't know what the fuck he did," Candace snapped. "All I know is he had my car. I came home from work and there was a bloody rag in my bathroom."

"Ohmigod. Ewww."

"I got rid of that shit."

"I know that's right."

"But I don't know anything else. I never got a chance to ask him anything. That's all I told the police when they asked me at the hospital. As soon as he pulled up, they started shooting. That's all I know."

"Oh, man. Wow." Marci scratched her head. "Well, did you check your house?"

"Check my house? For what?"

"Bitch, anything!" Marci jumped up and marched toward the dresser. "He left that rag here. That means he came here after he robbed dude."

Candace watched Marci snatch open one dresser drawer and tear threw it, then another. "Marci, what are you doing?"

Marci turned back and looked at Candace with huge unbelieving eyes. "Looking for the money, dummy. What do you think I'm doing, stealing your panties?"

Candace shuffled to the edge of her bed, watching Marci rummage through her drawers.

"Did he keep clothes here?" Marci asked, bending at the last drawer.

"Some," Candace replied. "He's got a couple pair of jeans in the top of my closet."

Marci made a mad dash for the closed white door on the same side of the wall as the bedroom door. She yanked it open and reached up to the top of the closet where several pair of jeans were neatly folded. She snatched them all down and they hit the floor with a heavy thud. A heavy enough thud to catch Candace's full attention.

Candace stood up, breathing slowly and curiously inched her way toward the closet and her sister sifting through the pile of jeans on the floor.

Marci overturned a few pair before a small but thick black satchel plopped out. Marci's eyes sprang open.

"What the fuck is that?" Candace asked.

"I don't know." Marci picked the bag up off the ground. "But we sure as hell 'bout to find out." She unzipped the bag and looked inside. Her jaw dropped. "Holy shit!"

Candace moved in closer as quickly as she could. "What? What is it?"

Marci tilted the open bag her way so Candace could get a good look at the thick wads of bills stuffed inside the small satchel.

"Holy shit!" Candace repeated. She snatched the bag out of her sister's hand. "How much do you think it is?"

"Hell if I know. Count that shit!"

Candace and Marci dumped the money out on the bed. There were four thick knots, which after counting turned out to be ten-thousand dollars each.

"Forty fuckin' grand!" Marci shouted, rubbing hundreds over her bosom. "Are you kidding me?"

Candace stared down at the blood money on her bed. She didn't know quite how to feel. She couldn't find joy in the surprise loot. There was guilt embedded in her emotion, knowing that the man she loved, and who loved her back, had lost his life for forty thousand dollars. It didn't seem worth it and she would have gladly traded it all to have Chris walk back through her bedroom door and hold her one more time. She cried, staring down at the crisp bills.

"Dammit, Chris," she sobbed. "For what? For this? Goddamn you, Christopher. You stupid son of a bitch!"

Candace fell to the bed as Marci curled her fingers around the bills. Candace stared at the money for a long time. There was so much she wanted to do, so many things she could name that she needed. But, the thought of her shopping and splurging did not provide her any comfort for the tragedy of Chris's death, for a life cut so short, for a child without a father. She was still for a long time before it came to her. Candace knew what she needed to do.

Candace looked over at her sister. "Marcine, I wanna give that baby some money."

Marci's eyes narrowed as she shot Candace a distasteful stare. "What baby?"

"Chris's son."

"Chris had a son?!? Really? You never mentioned that to me."

"He barely did. But, I have a son and this shit is hard and my kid's father is in jail. This kid's dad is dead."

Marci hung her head. "How much you wanna give him?"

"Ten."

"Ten thousand dollars?" Marci hollered, clutching the bills in her hand tight.

Candace quietly yet affirmatively nodded.

CHAPTER 32

andace stood naked in front of her bedroom window overlooking the cobblestone walkway in the front of her apartment. She peered through the sheer gold curtains, patting the itch under her leopard-print head scarf. She pulled her hand down from her head and traced the short scar under her right breast. It had only been three weeks since the fatal accident that had ended Chris's life, but her body and her heart seemed to be healing well.

She yawned before snatching her pink robe off the edge of the bed and covering her bare body. Candace was merely a foot in the hall when she heard the toilet flush. Emmanuel stepped out a second later, fully dressed in black shorts, a white polo shirt and a pair of clean Pumas.

"Good morning, Mom," he said, smiling and walking past her toward his room.

"You're up pretty early," Candace responded, her eyes following him down the hall.

Emmanuel stopped at the foot of his bedroom door. "You said our flight leaves at ten, right?"

"Yeah. It does but…" Candace's words were cut short by the sound of her house phone ringing.

Emmanuel took off running toward the kitchen. "I'll get it!" he screamed, nearly clearing the counter as he reached over it to grab the phone.

Candace watched him curiously.

Emmanuel's eyes sparked with excitement. Then he pulled the phone away from his ear and pressed a button on the receiver.

Prince! Candace's heart jumped in her chest. She felt like it had been so long, too long almost, since she'd heard his voice. Was he okay? Where had he been? Did he know about what she'd just gone through? Candace didn't know and couldn't wait to ask.

"Hey, Dad!" Emmanuel sang.

However, Candace knew her questions would have to wait until Emmanuel was through and she watched him wedge the phone between his shoulder and his ear, disappearing into the living room.

"I need to talk to him when you're done," she hollered, heading back to her room to get dressed.

"He said he need to talk to you, too!" Emmanuel shouted back.

Aww shit. Candace dressed quickly, slipping a simple pink sundress over her bronzed statuesque body. She checked her luggage one more time before she zipped the last bag and dragged it out into the hall. She looked up at Emmanuel walking toward her with the phone still at his ear.

"She right here…I know…I told her…Uh huh. Yes, sir…I love you, too, Dad." He handed Candace the phone.

She took a deep breath and a long hard swallow, bringing the phone up to her face. "Hello."

"What's up witchu, shawty?" Prince's voice came through like fine wine.

Candace shook her head as she walked back into her room. "Everything."

"That's what they say. I got some of the scoop from B."

"Yeah?" Candace asked.

"Yeah," Prince replied. "But I wanna know how you feelin' after all this. So tell a nigga, what's really good with you, Candy Reign?"

Candace sat down on the bed, racking her brain. She didn't know where to begin.

Prince cleared his throat. "I'm listening."

Candace opened her mouth and the tears poured. "Prince, I been shot at. In a high-speed chase. The guy I was with was killed…"

"This the nigga that was at ya crib, last time I talked to you?"

"Yeah," she replied honestly and a bit ashamed.

"Go 'head," Prince instructed with no judgment in his tone.

"I almost lost my job 'cause the white bitch, Jennifer, tried to set me up." Candace paused and scratched her head. "Let's see, what else. Oh yeah, my car was totaled and I had to apply for an extension to finish this semester at Temple so I can graduate on time, and we're moving into a new place so the mob won't come after me and Man…"

"That's a dead issue, baby girl." Prince's voice was calm. "You ain't gotta move."

Candace's eyes folded in curiously. "Huh?"

"Ain't nobody coming to ya crib after you and my son," he said confidently.

Instinctively, Candace's shoulders softened. There was no need to inquire further. She was silent for a brief moment, and then a subtle crease rose in her cheeks as she looked across the room to her suitcase in the hall. "You know what, Prince? I'mma be okay, though."

"Yeah?"

"Yeah," Candace said, turning to her golden reflection in the mirror. "It's been a hard summer, but I've made it through."

"What about the job?" Prince asked.

"What do you mean?"

"That promotion shit you was tellin' me 'bout? What's up with that?"

"Oh," Candace squealed. "I got it! Once my competition got fired, it was all on me."

"That's what's up! When you start?"

"I start training under another administrator when me and Man get back from Florida, and sit for my licensing exam in October."

"Oh, yeah. Florida, huh? You doin' more than all right. What the money like?"

"Nice."

"Yeah. What's nice, Candy?"

"Sixty eight, my first two years. Year three we looking at nothing less than eighty."

"Get the fuck outta here!" Prince cheered.

Candace beamed. "Yup."

"I'm proud of you, baby girl. Keep doin' your thing."

"Yeah."

"And leave them knucklehead-ass youngins alone, anyway. You too old for that shit."

"I am not old!" Candace snapped.

'I ain't say you was old. I said you *too old*. There's a difference."

"You right," Candace said, laughing. "But where the fuck *you* been, Prince?"

"Fuck you mean, where I been? I been here, shit. Where I'm goin'?"

Candace shook her head. "I mean we haven't heard from you in a minute."

"My son heard from me."

The words hit Candace hard. "So what that mean? You wasn't fuckin' wit' me?"

"Cut that shit out, Candy Reign. You know I'mma always fuck witchu, but you out here fuckin' wit these otha niggas and I ain't really tryna hear all that when I call. Feel me?"

Candace sucked her teeth. "You the one wanted me to go out

and get some dick. You told me I was too uptight about my money and my ass."

"Yeah, I told you to buss a nut. Not fall the fuck in love wit' these nut-ass niggas."

"How you know I was in love?"

"I know you."

Candace exhaled deeply. She was quiet, searching for the right words to say.

Prince found his own, "I miss you, though."

Candace's breathing softened and her full lips lifted slightly as she replied, "I miss you, too."

"You should come see me and bring my son."

"Our son."

"Whateva. Just bring him and your sexy ass up here so I can get my hands on you."

Candace thought for a minute. "Maybe."

"Nah, don't gimme that 'maybe' shit. Tell me you goin' come see me, soon."

"I don't know, Prince. I might."

"Might, huh? Okay, well. I might try not to bite the shit outta you when I see you."

"See. See. That's it right there. That's why I ain't comin'. I ain't fuckin' with you."

Prince laughed a deep heavy laugh. "Yeah right. Who else you goin' fuck wit' like me?"

Candace shook her head from side to side as if he could see. "Not a soul."

"That's right. You goin' always…"

You have one minute remaining, a sterile computer voice announced.

Candace's shoulders fell.

"I want you to take care of yourself out there, baby girl," Prince continued, though seeming to deviate from his original thought. "You and Man gotta hold each other down 'til I get out this joint."

"They goin' set you free one of these days, Prince?"

"Fuckin' right or I'mma bust out this bitch. Either way, I'll be home to reclaim my throne."

The seconds depleted on their conversation and again the operator chimed in, *You have thirty seconds remaining.*

"I love you, Prince." Candace confessed.

"Always, Candy Reign," Prince reassured her. "Take care of yourself and *our* boy until I get home."

"Will do."

ABOUT THE AUTHOR

Sharai Robbin is the mother of two young daughters, a long-time member of the famous Eveningstar Writer's Group, editor at Oshun Publishing, owner of Good Ground Literary Services, LLC and Editor-in-Chief of *BlackCityTV* online magazine.

Born and raised in Philadelphia, her love of literature began after reading Nikki Giovanni's poem, "Ego-Tripping," when she was eight years old; and she wrote her first novel while attending Girls' High School. She later attended Temple University, graduating with a dual degree in Communications and English and is presently pursing a Master's degree in English at Arcadia University.

Robbin's love of Philadelphia shines through in her writing, as she beautifully blends the lines between street life and working class through her own real-life experiences.